Praise for *The Art Forger*

"If *Bridget Jones's Diary* and *The Da Vinci Code* had a love child, this would be it."
                                                                                    —*Elle*

"[A] highly entertaining literary thriller about fine art and foolish choices."
                                                                                    —*Parade*

"Classy and pleasurably suspenseful . . . An entrancingly visual, historically rich, deliciously witty, sensuous, and smart tale of authenticity versus fakery in which Shapiro artfully turns a clever caper into a provocative meditation on what we value most."   —*Booklist*

"Warning: Don't dig into this book if you have something to do . . . An addictive thriller."   —*Redbook*

"An engaging tale about art, cupidity, and a Faustian bargain . . . Shapiro convincingly depicts the rarefied art world that lionizes a chosen few and ignores the talented, scrabbling outsiders on the fringe. Shapiro is adept, too, at showing the white-hot heat of an artist engaged in creating a painting. She knows art history, painting techniques, and how forgers have managed through the centuries to dupe buyers into paying for fakes . . . Inventive and entertaining."
          —*The Boston Globe* (a *Boston Globe* Best Crime Book of 2012)

"Readers seeking an engaging novel about artists and art scandals will find *The Art Forger* rewarding for its skillful balance of brisk plotting, significant emotional depth and a multi-layered narration rich with a sense of moral consequence."   —*The Washington Post*

"[Shapiro] has such interesting things to say about authenticity—in both art and love—that her novel becomes not just emotionally involving but addictive."   —*Entertainment Weekly*

"By mixing art, history and complex characters, *The Art Forger* produces a thrilling canvas." —Rona Brinlee of The BookMark on NPR.org

"Blazingly good. Shapiro drops you where you've never been before, into the whole, cracklingly alive world of art galleries, art forgeries, and the unexpected recesses of the human heart, where what we do for what we love can have terrifying consequences. As original as a real Degas, it's also as unforgettable."
—Caroline Leavitt, author of *Pictures of You*

"[A] taut but philosophical suspense novel . . . Shapiro weaves both threads of her narrative seamlessly for a surprise twist . . . Few thrillers carry this much heft so lightly." —*Wilmington Star-News*

"Shapiro hits the jackpot . . . *The Art Forger* is smart, sexy, and spellbinding. With a twisting plot, irresistible characters, and a spunky, memorable heroine, Shapiro's latest novel will appeal to fiction lovers and mystery devotees alike . . . This book's a recipe for fun." —Redbookmag.com

"This well-researched work combines real elements . . . with the understanding that the art world is as fragile and precarious as the art itself, particularly for young hopefuls. A highly recommended debut that would be great for book discussion groups." —*Library Journal*

"A cleverly plotted art-world thriller/romance . . . This is convincingly researched, engaging storytelling. Intelligent entertainment."
—*Kirkus Reviews*

"[A] nimble mystery . . . Shapiro's brisk narrative takes the reader through Boston's art world, the logistics of forgery and the perils of attribution."
—*The New York Times Book Review*

"I loved this book! From the moment I started reading I was absorbed in the story and I could not put it down!" —*BookBrowse*

"A story that is thrilling and also has genuine emotion."

—*Devourer of Books*

"A page-turning mystery . . . The author has done her research. At times you can almost smell the turpentine as she explores the world of the reproduction copyist . . . [A] satisfying tale."   —*The Florida Times-Union*

"Vivid and entertaining, illuminating the mysterious and rarified art world and how human nature—particularly a desire to protect one's reputation— can overwhelm logic, professionalism and even morality."

—*Concord (NH) Monitor*

"Informative, sexy and exciting, with key plot twists that are genuinely unexpected."   —*BookPage*

"*The Art Forger* is one hell of a novel."   —*January Magazine*

"You won't be able to put down B. A. Shapiro's *The Art Forger* . . . What a treat when a novel is pure, delicious fun."   —*Hudson Valley News*

"An engaging and successful literary thriller . . . Shapiro layers her novel with intrigue, mystery, history, and motivations to tell a memorable story."   —*Beth Fish Reads*

"Shapiro deftly takes on the role of magician, dazzling us with ingenious sleights of hand and a narrative juggling act. Watching her bring all the pieces together makes for an exciting and very pleasurable read. If you love art, a mystery, and a tale of unrequited love, this tale is for you."

—*Shelf Awareness*

"Clever and fascinating."   —*Publishers Weekly*

THE ART FORGER

Also by B. A. Shapiro

The Muralist

The ART FORGER

A NOVEL BY

B. A. SHAPIRO

ALGONQUIN
BOOKS OF
CHAPEL HILL
2013

Published by
ALGONQUIN BOOKS OF CHAPEL HILL
Post Office Box 2225
Chapel Hill, North Carolina 27515-2225

a division of
Workman Publishing
225 Varick Street
New York, New York 10014

First paperback edition, Algonquin Books of Chapel Hill, May 2013.
Originally published by Algonquin Books of Chapel Hill in 2012.
Printed in the United States of America.
Published in Canada by HarperCollins*Canada* Ltd.
Design by Anne Winslow.

This is a work of fiction. While, as in all fiction, the literary perceptions
and insights are based on experience, all names, characters, places, and incidents
either are products of the author's imagination or are used fictitiously.

Library of Congress Cataloging-in-Publication Data
Shapiro, Barbara A.
The art forger : a novel / by B. A. Shapiro.—1st ed.
p. cm.
ISBN 978-1-61620-132-6 (HC)
1. Gardner, Isabella Stewart, 1840–1924—Fiction. 2. Degas,
Edgar, 1834–1917—Fiction. 3. Art—Forgeries—Fiction.
4. Art forgers—Fiction. I. Title.
PS3569.H3385A78 2012
813'.54—dc23   2012009037

ISBN 978-1-61620-316-0 (PB)

20 19 18 17 16 15 14 13

To Dan, who never gave up

A painting is above all a product
of the artist's imagination;
it must never be a copy.

—EDGAR DEGAS

GARDNER HEIST 21st ANNIVERSARY

Largest Art Theft in History Remains Unsolved

Boston, MA—In the early morning hours of March 18, 1990, two men dressed as police officers bound and gagged two guards at the Isabella Stewart Gardner Museum and stole thirteen works of art worth today over $500 million.

The cache included priceless masterpieces such as Rembrandt's "Storm on the Sea of Galilee," Vermeer's "The Concert" and Degas' "After the Bath." Despite thousands of hours of police work, a lapsed statute of limitations and a $5 million reward, the artwork has not been recovered.

Over the last two decades, the FBI investigated known art thieves and suspects connected to organized crime, international terrorism and the Catholic Church. Agents followed leads across the United States, Europe and Asia. Suspects included the son of a police officer, the Irish Republican Army, Whitey Bulger and the Boston mob, an antiques dealer, a Scotland Yard informant and a New York City auction house employee. No arrests have been made.

The Gardner Museum asks that anyone who has any information on the whereabouts of the lost artworks contact the Boston office of the FBI.

Boston Globe
March 17, 2011

One

I step back and scrutinize the paintings. There are eleven, although I have hundreds, maybe thousands. My plan is to show him only pieces from my window series. Or not. I pull my cell from my pocket, check the time. I can still change my mind. I remove *Tower,* a highly realistic painting of reflections off the glass Hancock building, and replace it with *Sidewalk,* an abstraction of Commonwealth Avenue through a parlor-level bay window. Then I switch them back.

I've been working on the window series for over two years, rummaging around the city with my sketchbook and Nikon. Church windows, reflective windows, Boston's ubiquitous bays. Large, small, old, broken, wood- and metal-framed. Windows from the outside in and the inside out. I especially like windows on late winter afternoons before anyone inside notices the darkening sky and snaps the blinds shut.

I hang *Sidewalk* next to *Tower.* Now there are a dozen, a nice round number. But is it right? Too many and he'll be overwhelmed. Too few and he'll miss my breadth, both in content and style. It's so difficult to choose. One of the many reasons studio visits make me so nervous.

And what's up with this visit anyway? I'm a pariah in the art world, dubbed "the Great Pretender." Have been for almost three years. And suddenly Aiden Markel, the owner of the world-renowned Markel G, is on his way to my loft. Aiden Markel, who just a few months ago barely acknowledged my presence when I stopped by the gallery to see a new installation. And now he's suddenly all friendly, complimentary, asking to see my latest work, leaving his tony Newbury Street gallery to slum it in SOWA in order to appreciate my paintings, as he said, "in situ."

I glance across the room at the two paintings sitting on easels. *Woman Leaving Her Bath,* a nude climbing out of a tub and attended to by a clothed maid, was painted by Edgar Degas in the late nineteenth century; this version was painted by Claire Roth in the early twenty-first. The other painting is only half-finished: Camille Pissarro's *The Vegetable Garden with Trees in Blossom, Spring, Pontoise* à la Roth. Reproductions.com pays me to paint them, then sells the paintings online as "perfect replicas" whose "provenance only an art historian could discern" for ten times my price. These are my latest work.

I turn back to my windows, pace, narrow my eyes, pace some more. They'll just have to do. I throw a worn Mexican blanket over the rumpled mattress in the corner then gather the dirty dishes scattered around the studio and dump them in the sink. I consider washing them, decide not to. If Aiden Markel wants in situ, I'll give him in situ. But I do fill a bowl with cashews and pull out a bottle of white wine—never red at a studio visit—and a couple of glasses.

I wander to the front of the studio and look out the row of windows onto Harrison Avenue. The same view as *Loft.* I spend a lot of time in this spot, pretending to work through my latest project, but mostly daydreaming, spying, procrastinating. It's four stories up, and each of the six windows in front of me stretches from two feet above the floor to two feet below the fifteen-foot ceiling.

This building was once a factory—handkerchiefs, some old-timer told me. But the old-timers aren't known for their veracity, so it could have been hats or suspenders or maybe not even a factory at all. Now it's a warren of artists' studios, some, as in my case, live-in studios. Illegal, of course, but cheap.

According to media hype, SOWA—South of Washington—is the new trendy district in the south end of Boston's South End; the north was the new trendy area about ten years ago. But to me, and to anyone who spends any time here, it's barely on the cusp. Warehouses, projects, a famous homeless shelter, and abandoned basketball courts form the base of a neighborhood erratically pockmarked with expensive restaurants, art galleries, and pristine residential buildings protected by security. The roar of I-93 is so constant it sounds like silence. I wouldn't want to live anywhere else.

Below, Aiden Markel turns the corner from East Berkeley with his lanky, graceful stride. Even from half a block away, I can see he's wearing perfectly tailored pants—most likely linen—and what's probably a $500 shirt. It's eighty-five degrees on a late summer afternoon, and the guy looks as if he stepped out of his Back Bay condo on a cool September morning. He pulls out his cell, glances at my building, and touches the screen. My phone rings.

THERE'S NO ELEVATOR and no air-conditioning in the hallways and stairwells. As we hit the fourth floor, Markel's breathing is steady and his clothes are bandbox. Clearly, the man spends time in the gym. Not to mention that he hasn't stopped talking since I let him in the door. No one would guess we've barely spoken to each other in three years.

"I was around the corner from here just the other day," Markel says, continuing his running monologue of small talk. "Dedham and Harrison. Looked at Pat Hirsi's newest project. You know him, right?"

I shake my head no.

"He's working with cobblestones. Very ingenious."

I pull open the wide steel door with two hands.

Markel steps over the threshold, takes a deep breath, and closes his eyes. "Nothing like the smell of an artist at work." He keeps his eyes closed, which isn't exactly what I want him to do; he's supposed to be here to look at my paintings, fall in love with them, and set me up with a one-woman show at Markel G. Right. Like that's going to happen. Although, what is going to happen or why he's here is beyond me.

"How about a glass of wine?" I ask.

He finally opens his eyes and gives me a slow, warm smile. "Will you be joining me?"

I can't help but smile back. He's not classically handsome, his features are too large for that, but there's something in the way he carries himself, the wide deep-set eyes, the dimple in his chin, that tugs at me. Charisma, I guess. That and our shared history.

"Sure." I grab a pile of canvases I somehow forgot were on my beaten up couch and lean them against an even more beaten up coffee table. Sometimes I think I'm a living parody of myself: the starving artist sleeping on a mattress in her studio to save on rent. Yet, there it is.

Markel doesn't move. He stares at me for a long moment then shifts his gaze over my shoulder, a wistful look on his face. I know he's thinking about Isaac. I probably should just say something, but I don't know what to say. That I'm sorry? That I'm still upset? That I lost a friend, too?

I pour wine into two juice glasses as he settles into the couch. Not an easy feat as it's lumpy and too deep for comfort. I should get a new one, or at least a new secondhand one, but the landlord just raised my rent, and I'm pretty much broke.

I sit in the rocking chair across from him and lean forward. "I heard your Jocelyn Gamp show went fabulously well."

He takes a sip of his wine. "It was her molten pieces. She sold everything she had. Plus three commissions. Amazing lady. Amazing artist. The Met's requested a studio visit."

I like how he doesn't take any of the credit. "She sold" rather than "I sold" or even "we sold." Extremely rare among the runamok egos of most dealers and gallery owners.

"Not often a Boston show gets covered in the *New York Times,*" I suck up.

"Yes, it was quite the coup," he admits. "I'm glad to see that you're still following the goings-on in the art world even though we haven't exactly been following yours."

I look up sharply. What the hell does that mean? But I see that his eyes hold compassion, maybe even a little guilt.

"Isaac's *Orange Nude* sold last week," he says.

Ah. As everyone knows, I was the model for *Orange Nude.* Even though it's an abstraction, there's no denying my long, unmanageable red hair or the paleness of my skin or my brown eyes. If I hadn't thrown it out the door when we broke up, I'd probably be living in a condo in Back Bay instead of renting in an industrial building in SOWA. But then again, I'm not the Back Bay type. "Don't tell me how much you got for it."

"I'll spare you the pain. But the sale started me thinking about you, about the raw deal you got."

I struggle to keep the surprise off my face. In the last three years, no one outside of a few art buddies and my mother—who never really understood what it all meant—has looked at the situation from my point of view.

"So I decided to come down and see what you've been up to," he continues. "Maybe I can help."

My heart leaps at the offer, and I jump up. "I pulled out a few from my latest series." I wave at the paintings. "Obviously, windows."

Markel walks toward the pieces. "Windows," he repeats, and he takes in the whole dozen from a distance, then approaches each individually.

"It's urban windows, Boston windows. Hopper-esque thematically, but more multidimensional. Not just the public face of loneliness, but who we are in many dimensions. Unseen from the inside. Or unknowingly seen. On display from outside, posturing or forgetting. Separations. Reflections, refractions."

"Light," he murmurs. "Wonderful light."

"That, too. Without light nothing can be seen. And with it, still so much is unobserved." Studio visits make me talk like a pompous art critic.

"Your light is amazing. The subtle values. Almost Vermeer-like." He points to *Loft*. "I'm struck by the difference in value in the light from the far left window through to the right ones." He steps closer. "Each slightly different, and yet each such a luminous part of the whole."

I'm also pleased with that particular play, but Vermeer, the master of light . . .

"How many glazings are you doing?"

I'm reluctant to admit the truth. Not only are very few artists using classical oil techniques these days, but those who are aren't nearly as compulsive as I am about layering. I shrug. "Eight? Nine?" Which is actually low for me.

"It's reminiscent of the light falling on the black-and-white tile floor in *The Concert*." He walks closer to *Loft*. "The light bouncing off the building here. It's almost as if it's caressing the diamonds of the chain-link."

He steps back, examines the paintings closely, just as I had earlier. "I love how you're playing with classical style and contemporary subjects, with abstraction. But it's the realistic pieces that grab me." He waves dismissively at *Sidewalk*. "The abstracts aren't nearly as strong."

"Not too OTC?" I ask. OTC is "over the couch" in artist-speak, a derogatory term for paintings purchased by buyers who want their artwork to match their décor.

Markel laughs. "Not even close. I've been trying to tell people for years that realism isn't dead. That nothing can touch a great talent in classical oil."

A rush of warmth fills my body and races up to my face. It's been a long time since anyone said anything like that about me.

"I have lots more," I say, heading over to the three-tiered shelving I built to house my art books and canvases, although now it's all canvases and my books are in semiorganized piles on the floor. The shelves are a mess, of course. But a mess I know intimately.

I begin pulling paintings before he says he wants to see them. I grab the stepladder. I need it so I can reach the highest shelf, which is where I store most of my more realistic paintings. The ones I figured no one would be interested in.

"These some of your reproductions?" Markel calls from the other side of the room.

I look over my shoulder. "Yeah. I don't usually have any completed ones here. But the truck's tied up all week, so the Degas isn't getting picked up till Friday."

"Reproductions.com. Got to love the name. Saw the article

in the *Globe* last month. Nice exposure for you." He hesitates. "I guess?"

"Not exactly the kind I'm looking for." Just what I need: publicity for pretending to paint someone else's masterpiece. "I tried to get out of the interview, but Repro wouldn't stand for it."

"Are they doing as well as their hype?"

"Probably better," I say, although I'm not really listening and not at all interested in Repro. I'm too focused on pulling my best paintings, but not too many. Light. Interesting value is what he wants, deep and translucent. I grab one. Not strong enough. Then another.

"Now this is OTC," he says, pointing to the Pissarro, which although incomplete is obviously filled with trees covered in masses of white blossoms.

I laugh. "For the pretentious."

"But poor," he adds.

I lumber down with three canvases under my arm. "Not all that poor. Those things go for thousands of dollars. Tens of thousands for the bigger ones. Unfortunately, I only get a fraction of that."

I quickly remove my more abstract paintings from the wall. Replace them with the ones I've chosen. I turn to him, but he's staring at the fake Degas.

"You're damn good at this."

"It beats waitressing."

His eyes don't leave my rendering. "I'll say."

"Degas' later work isn't all that hard to copy. Not like his early oils. They're a real bitch," I say, trying to be polite when every part of me wants to grab Markel and pull him to the other side of the studio. "What with all those layers. Painting and waiting. Painting and waiting. Could take months, maybe years."

"And Reproductions.com has you do that?"

"No. Never. A piece like that would have to sell for hundreds of thousands of dollars." I come to stand by him. "Degas is my specialty, his oils in particular. I'm actually certified—whatever that means—by Repro, after I took the requisite classes." I wave to the piles of books in the corner. "I'm working on a book proposal about him. His relationship with other artists, dealers, collectors of his day. Cross-germination. That kind of stuff. But I'm not working on it as hard as I should be."

Markel's eyes remain glued to the Degas reproduction. "This seems like a better use of your time. Do they appreciate you?"

"Sometimes I get a bonus when people order a Degas with the stipulation that I'm the artist," I shrug. "Although you can hardly call a person who copies a masterpiece an artist."

He doesn't contradict me, and I gesture him back to my real work. He steals a last glance at *Woman Leaving Her Bath* before he follows.

We stand in silence, staring at my windows. I force myself to remain silent, to allow the work to speak for itself.

After two minutes that feel like twenty, Markel touches my arm. "Let's sit down."

We walk over to the couch and sit on opposite ends. He finishes off his wine and pours himself another. I decline his offer of a refill, wanting the wine, but fearing I'm too jittery to hold onto it.

Markel clears his throat, takes another sip. "Claire, I've just been given the opportunity of a lifetime. A chance to do good, real good for lots of people. And I hope you'll feel the same way about the one I'm about to give you." He pauses. "Although I suppose yours is really more like making a deal with the devil."

I have absolutely no idea what he's talking about, but I catch the word "opportunity." "And you're the devil?"

He shakes his head vigorously. "The devil's the one who gave me this opportunity. Although I've no idea who he is. He's levels away from me."

"Like Dante?"

Although I meant it as a joke, he ponders the question, a professor attempting to answer a precocious student. "No. I guess that's wrong. Pawns are the better analogy. But clever pawns. Who can capture the queen. Either way, I'm mixing my metaphors."

"I've got no problem with the devil. I'm one of those people who thinks heaven would be boring. But being a pawn has never suited me."

This time he does laugh, but I can tell it's forced. "Then we'll stick with the devil."

Enough of this. "Okay," I say. "What are we talking about here?"

He locks his eyes on mine. "Something not quite on the up-and-up."

I don't break the stare. "I thought you said it was an opportunity to do good?"

"The end is good. It's just the means that are a bit iffy."

"Illegal?"

"There's illegal and there's illegal."

"And which one is this?"

Markel looks across the room at the Degas and Pissarro.

And now it all makes sense. "Oh" is all I can say.

He takes a sip of wine, relaxes into the lumpy couch. The most uncomfortable part of this conversation is clearly over for him.

I cross my arms over my chest. "I can't believe that after everything that's happened, you, of all people, would even consider asking me to forge a painting."

"How much does Reproductions.com pay you?"

"They pay me to copy, not to forge."

"So you said a fraction. A few thousand a picture? A little more?"

Often it's less, but I nod.

"I'll pay you $50,000. Plus expenses, of course. A third up front, a third on completion to my satisfaction, and the final third on authentication."

"Is this because of what happened with Isaac?"

"It's despite what happened with Isaac."

I'm stupefied by this answer, and it must have showed on my face, because he says, "You're the best for the project."

"Out of all the thousands of artists you know?"

Again, he looks across the room at the Degas reproduction. "You're the only one I'd trust with it."

"How do you know I won't talk?"

"It's not your style," he says, which is true. People who have been on the wrong side of rumor know when to keep their mouths shut.

"What about turning you in? I could always go to the police."

"Not when you understand what's at stake," he says.

"So tell me."

"I meant what I said about your paintings, Claire. You have a unique talent. You always did. Just because you've been blackballed doesn't mean you can't paint." He pauses. "I'd also like to give you a one-woman show at the gallery."

I barely conceal a gasp.

"In six, nine months," he says. "After you've finished this project. Do you think you could have twenty paintings ready by then? Of the realistic highly glazed?"

I turn away to hide my longing. My own show at Markel G. An impossible dream.

"I'm pretty sure I can get the same *Times* reporter who covered Jocelyn Gamp to cover you," he says.

The *New York Times*. Sales. Commissions. Studio visits from the Met. My heart actually hurts.

"Claire, please look at me." When I do, he says, "I'll protect you. Like I said, I'm levels away from anyone with any knowledge, and you'll be a level away from me."

"What's the part where we get to do something good?"

"I'll tell you all the details when you're on board."

"There's no way I can agree to something this mysterious."

Markel stands. "Just give it some thought." He touches my shoulder. "I'll check in with you next week."

"You really are the devil, aren't you?"

"If you believe in the devil."

Which, of course, I don't.

Two

When Markel leaves, I flop down on the couch and stare at the pipes and vents chasing each other across the ceiling, trying to process the strangest studio visit ever. Markel G. My own show. The sweet possibility of reclaiming all that's been lost, everything I've ever wanted. But a forger? A pretender? The absolute last thing I want to be.

You're damn good at this.

I climb out of the couch, walk over to the front windows, and stare down on Harrison Avenue. I look over the chain-linked parking lot to the elevated highway in the distance, then to my window paintings lined up along the walls.

You have a unique talent. You always did.

Damn him. Damn him and his compliments and his offers and his strings.

I grab my backpack and head to Jake's, the bar where everyone knows my name. Unfortunately, not only does everyone know my name, they also know about Markel's visit.

There's illegal and there's illegal.

When I reach the bar, I square my shoulders and push open the door. Jake's is clearly and proudly old neighborhood, nothing like the ritzy places drifting south from Back Bay. Here, there are no blue martinis, and the tables are scarred from years of use, not purposely distressed to look chic. There's no valet because the clientele walk from their tiny apartments or studios. A neon BUDWEISER sign hangs in the narrow window to scare the hip away.

Most of my buds are already here; it's six, after all, the drinking hour. To be followed by the eating hour—hot dogs, burgers, and BLTs comprise the menu—followed by another drinking hour. Or hours. Right arms shoot straight into the air as each person catches sight of me. Our gang sign.

Mike points to the open bar stool next to him. "Here" is all he says as he turns back to his conversation with Small. Small's name is Small because she's very small, maybe five feet, and that's generous. She says she named herself Small to confront the issue head-on and because her real name is so ethnic it labeled her. Mike's only half a foot taller than she is, but far too unsure of himself—not to mention he's a man—for that kind of piercing self-deprecation.

I slip onto the stool. Maureen, owner and bartender, opens a bottle of Sam Adams and puts it down in front of me. She knows I don't want a glass.

Rik, buff, handsome, and with kangaroo eyelashes every woman I know covets, leans from behind to give me a kiss. "Do tell," he demands. Rik's the one graduate-school friend who stuck by me after the "Cullion Affair" slithered its way into the MFA Museum School as well as the art scenes in Boston and New York. I love him for it.

I return the kiss. "And hello to you, too."

"I want to hear every last delicious detail." Rik always wants to hear every last delicious detail.

"Well, he seemed to like some of my stuff, especially the paintings where I applied . . ." I lower my voice in imitation of Markel's tenor, "'. . . classical realism to contemporary subject matter.' He said he'd give me a call, but I'm thinking he was blowing me off."

"Did the great man tell you why he suddenly decided to grace you with his oh-so-fabulous presence?"

"Just what he said before. That he wanted to see what I was up to."

"Nothing about Sir Isaac Cullion?" When I don't answer, Rik adds, "Not even one teeny-tiny single solitary word?"

I've known Rik long enough to know that if I don't give him something, he won't let go until he's got the truth. I heave a dramatic sigh. "He did tell me he sold Isaac's *Orange Nude*. That it made him think of me."

Small turns toward us, and Mike puts a hand on my shoulder. Maureen leans her elbows on the bar. Danielle and Alice, who are on the other side of Rik, stop talking. Everyone looks at me expectantly. There are few secrets among us, especially not career ones—and these are probably the only people who actually believe Isaac lied.

"Didn't go well?" Mike asks. We sometimes call Mike "the church lady" in joking salute to his keen sense of right and wrong. He'd be horrified at Markel's offer. And even more horrified that I didn't refuse outright.

"I'm guessing not, although I wasn't expecting much." A lie everyone recognizes. They've all said roughly the same thing after a career disappointment. It's how we survive.

"A shot of tequila for my friend here," Mike says to Maureen. Aside from Rik, who isn't really an artist anymore, Mike's the only one of us who can afford actual drinks. He's a lawyer by day, painter by night.

I knock back the shot as soon as it's in front of me. The warmth spreads down my throat and into my empty stomach. A dangerous thing if Maureen decides to comp me a second shot, which, under the circumstances, she probably will.

"Any idea how much Markel got for it?" Small asks.

I know she's talking about *Orange Nude*. "I told him not to tell me."

"More to the point: Does anyone know if Cullion actually painted it?" Danielle's voice is thick with sarcasm.

There's dead silence in the bar; I stare into my empty shot glass. Although she doesn't mean to, and would never purposely hurt anyone, Danielle often steps over the line she doesn't see. It's like her tact sensor is missing.

"Claire knows," Rik jumps in. "She was there. And she wasn't wearing any clothes."

I throw him a grateful glance and hold up my hands. "Present and nude as charged. I can attest to its authenticity."

"Never should've given it back to the old fraud," Rik says to me. "You didn't even—" He stops, frowns, and we all follow his gaze. "Well, well, well," he says sourly, "if it isn't the fabulous Crystal Mack, our own local artist at work. Slumming it tonight?"

"Oh, darlin'," Crystal says as she slides onto the stool next to Rik. "Don't be silly." She kisses him on both cheeks. "Talking about the *Orange Nude* sale?" She looks at me and winks. "I heard mid–six figures." She's overdressed, as usual. Something clingy and expensive in that trendy green that makes me look seasick. Unfortunately, it looks just fine on her. Blondes can wear any color they want.

"Probably out of testimony to the beauty of the model." Rik throws his arm around my shoulders. "Rather than the skill of the artist."

"That," Crystal smiles at me sweetly, "or the power of scandal." Crystal, too, often steps over the line—but her eyes are wide open.

Maureen puts a second shot in front of me.

We turn away from Crystal and break into smaller conversations. Crystal orders a double scotch straight up and begins an animated discussion with Maureen, pretending that the bartender isn't the only one willing to talk to her. Not that Crystal cares. Her purpose in coming here is to make herself feel better by making us feel worse. It works every time. The good news is that no one will ask any more questions about Markel with her around. The last thing anyone wants to do is give Crystal more ammunition.

By nine, Rik and I are the only ones left standing. Everyone else has gone home, and although we know we should, too, we linger at the far end of the bar. The two tequila shots have worked their magic on me: I'm all loose and stretchy, comfortably buzzed.

"I've still got options," I say.

Even though we haven't mentioned Markel in over an hour, Rik knows exactly what I'm talking about. "You've got lots of options, Claire Bear. Lots more than you even know."

"Markel told me that just because I'd been blackballed, that didn't mean I couldn't paint."

Rik's eyes widen. "Oh, honey, he actually said that to you? What an asshole."

"No, no," I say quickly. "He didn't mean it like that."

"Well, then how the hell did he mean it?"

"I think it was a compliment."

"Some compliment," Rik mutters.

"So," I say, "I made it to the final round of the *ArtWorld* Trans contest. And I haven't been rejected from the Cambridgeport Show yet."

"What's the Trans thing?" Rik isn't a studio artist anymore, so he isn't up on the latest contests and juried shows. He landed a job in the curatorial department at the Isabella Stewart Gardner

Museum right out of graduate school—which was an amazing coup—and has happily worked his way up to assistant curator in four years. He claims he doesn't miss the "drudgery, backstabbing, and poverty of being an artiste." Sometimes I believe him, sometimes I don't.

"The submission's got to reflect whatever you think Trans means," I explain. "Transpire, transplant, transcendent, transfusion, transmutation, transgendered."

"Sweet," Rik says, and I can tell he's running through the paintings stacked in his closet to see if any would work. He blinks his eyes to stop the parade. "What'd you submit?"

I shrug as if I don't really care. "A few from my window series. Transparent, transition, transpose, translucent. I figured if every painting had a bunch of Trans, it might give me an edge."

"Sounds like a plan."

"I heard next year it's going to be Counter, so I thought I'd submit some of my repros as counterfeit."

"Funny," Rik says, in a way that clearly indicates he doesn't think so. "So how's that going anyway?"

"Markel liked them."

Rik homes right in. "What interest could Aiden Markel possibly have in repros?"

"I don't know, Rik. I can't read the man's mind. They were there, I guess."

Rik holds his hands up. "Sor-ry. Didn't mean to step on any toes."

"No, no," I say. "It's me who's sorry. Sorry."

"It's okay." Rik grins. "We all know you can't handle your liquor."

He insists on walking me home. It's only a few blocks out of his way, so I acquiesce. Men got to do what they got to do. Even though I'm no fool about living in the city. I know the rules. Walk in the middle of the street or at least at the far edge of the sidewalk, be aware and tuned into surroundings, no white ear buds (steal my iPod), no texting (I'm distracted), no playing with apps (steal my iPhone). But above all, never, never, never look like you're lost.

We step out of Jake's into the thick summer air and head down the sidewalk, past the back alley of ChiRom, the Asian-Dominican fusion restaurant that's presently all the rage. A couple of men in grungy clothes are sitting, actually listing, against the Dumpster, passing a bottle of whiskey, and laughing uproariously. A well-dressed couple approaches us, glances into the alley, and crosses the street.

"Do you think Markel's visit could've had something to do with Isaac?" Rik asks.

"Isaac's dead." I'm surprised by the sharpness of my tone.

Rik stops and turns to me. "Hey," he says softly. "You okay?"

"Why does everyone think it has to be about Isaac?" I snap. "Is it beyond belief that he might just be interested in my work?"

Three

THREE YEARS EARLIER

"Give it up, Claire," Isaac said. "I'm done."

"You're not done. You're just indulging yourself."

"Perhaps."

Isaac and I were lying on the bed in his studio. But we weren't naked, and there had been no sex, which wasn't my idea. When I came in and found him sprawled out in the middle of the afternoon, I'd used all my womanly wiles to get him out of his slump—literally and figuratively. I'd succeeded at neither. He insisted on wallowing. This, unfortunately, was nothing new.

I guessed he was bipolar, but who could be sure when he refused to see a doctor? I wasn't about to intervene. Health nagging was a wife's responsibility, not a girlfriend's. But when it came to totally screwing up his career, I had to take a stand.

I pushed myself to a sitting position, and Isaac put his head in my lap. I twisted a curl of his dark hair. He looked up at me with those amazing blue eyes and touched his finger to the end of my nose, then to my mouth. I kissed it and placed his hand over my heart. "Isaac," I said, "you're a royal pain in the ass."

"But I have many other fine qualities?" he asked, in his deep chocolaty voice. A teasing smile lit up his face, and, as much as I wished it didn't, it lit me, too.

There was everything wrong with this relationship: I'd been his student, he was forty-four to my twenty-eight, he was prone to bouts of depression interspersed with brilliant bursts of artistic production and irresistible magnetism. Even the separated-for-three-years marriage with a pending, but not yet executed, divorce was an old cliché. But it was new to me.

"Don't try and charm me when I'm pissed at you," I said. "I'm not going to let you do this. It's the Museum of Modern Art, you idiot."

"And that's all it is, Claire. An art museum. We're not curing cancer here." He took his hand from my breast and wrapped his arm around my waist.

"You're so full of shit."

"That, too."

"You can still do it, you know," I said. "You've got two weeks."

"Twelve days, but who's counting?"

"It's not like you've got to wait for glazes to dry. You could do three wet-over-wets in that time if you put your mind to it."

"You could do three wet-over-wets," Isaac said. "It's a matter of drive."

"So where'd your drive go?"

"High gas prices?"

I punched his arm. "That doesn't even make any sense."

"See? I'm not up to it."

"Karen Sinsheimer thinks you're up to it." Sinsheimer was the senior curator of painting and sculpture at MoMA. She was the one who'd noticed Isaac's work at Markel G and commissioned a painting for her show *Survey of Recent Painting and Sculpture*.

Such a stick-up-the-ass name for a show highlighting the best emerging talent.

"Karen Sinsheimer saw paintings I did a year ago."

"And your point?"

"No point." He leaned over, grabbed a detective novel from the end table, and opened it. He smiled up at me guilelessly. "There's a bunch more over there." He gestured to a shelf filled with shiny new books. "I wish you'd give one a try. Then we could read together and talk about it."

I didn't bother to respond—he was well aware I wasn't partial to mysteries—so I sat there fuming while he turned the pages. I knew I should leave, but I wasn't willing to give up so easily. Not only was I madly in love with the guy, but I recognized, as did many others, that he was a great talent. As in a major artist of our time. And if he didn't take himself in hand, he was going to lose the biggest opportunity of his career.

This MoMA gig was no little thing. Sinsheimer had gone around the world and commissioned work from artists who had broken out in the past decade. Although the museum hadn't released an official list, word on the street had it that roughly fifty painters and sculptors were included. Which meant that Isaac had been chosen as one of the top twenty-five rising painters in the world.

"Isaac," I finally said, trying to sound stern. "Let's brainstorm."

"We don't have to, I already know who did it."

I snatched the book from his hands and pushed him off my lap. "The MoMA piece is going to be part of your time series, yes?"

"That was the plan."

"But it's not anymore?"

"As you well know, nothing I've tried has worked."

"Why?"

He shrugged. "It all sucks."

"Why?"

"Don't do this, Claire. It's boring. Mind-numbing, actually."

"Just answer the question: Why does it suck?"

He crossed his arms over his chest.

I couldn't help it: My eyes filled with tears. "Oh, Saac."

"Okay, okay," he said, sitting up. "Why do they suck? Why do they suck?" He looked off into the distance. "I guess they suck because they're too dark."

"Color or theme?"

"Both."

"So let's come up with some ideas that are light."

"It's a dark topic."

"Not necessarily."

"Time is the devourer of all things," he intoned, his voice deep and ponderous. "As it passes, people die, buildings fall, civilizations disappear."

"How about a more upbeat interpretation? Birth? The rejuvenation of spring?"

"Iron rusts. Silver tarnishes. Copper turns green."

"So don't do a time painting," I said. "Do something else."

"Time to time. Time and place." He threw his arms open wide. "Time to live, time to die, time to cast away stones."

It was difficult to keep a straight face. "Time to paint?"

Isaac wrapped me in his arms. "My girl," he said.

"How about time as the fourth dimension?" I asked lazily, as he outlined my ear with his tongue.

"Sounds interesting," he murmured, working his way down my neck.

I pushed him away. "Does it? Interesting how? What do you see?"

Isaac groaned. "Claire . . ."

"Work with me here." I jumped up and went over to an empty easel. "Got a clean canvas?"

"No."

"Don't be ridiculous."

"I don't feel like painting today."

I walked to the oversized drawer under a wall of shelving—Isaac's studio, unlike mine, had been designed by an architect and built by a master carpenter—and pulled out the largest canvas. It had been sized and was ready to accept paint, so I put it on the easel. "What color do you see?"

"Claire . . ."

"Time as the fourth dimension," I said. "A running river, the future ahead, the past behind, yet all existing simultaneously. What color for the underpainting?" I grabbed a can of turpentine and began poking around his paint tubes. "Raw umber? Sienna?"

Isaac shook his head.

"I see movement," I continued. "Thick paint flowing, always flowing, over and under itself, forward and back. Wet-on-wet. Scraping through the layers of paint to reveal what's underneath, scraping through the layers of time. All there, but above and beneath each other, some seen, some almost seen, some overwhelmed and hidden by another layer of time."

Isaac came over to the easel and took the turpentine out of my hands. "It's a charming idea, but it's not going to happen. You've got the will, but I don't."

"Let's start it together," I begged. "Let's just do the underpainting. See where it goes, how it affects you. Maybe once you get into it, it'll take off."

Isaac kissed me on the forehead. "I don't have the will to fight you either."

So I began to paint, using Isaac's brushes, Isaac's oils, Isaac's series, and Isaac's style. He would correct me now and then. Show me how to use his impasto technique to put down thick swatches of paint with the entire brush. How to use wide, powerful strokes, how to get my whole body behind it. How to apply wet color on top of wet color and then scrape through the top layers to bare the ones beneath.

In many ways, it was the opposite of what I did, how I painted, but I loved the freedom of it, of working with Isaac. Of being Isaac. We did this together almost every day for over a week, me painting and Isaac mostly reading or napping, occasionally giving me an instruction.

"What would you think, Saac," I asked one afternoon, "if we added in painting style as another level of time?"

He shrugged.

"You know, like going from the classical wet-over-dry to the contemporary wet-over-wet? Maybe some representational flowing into abstraction?" I waved my brush at the canvas. "Like here, through the layers of the artistic time?"

Again he shrugged.

So I diluted his paint with turpentine and proceeded to apply a series of thin layers of paint, zapping the moisture between each application with the hair dryer I kept in his bathroom. In the end, the lower right quadrant was covered with crescents of highly glazed, representational, and abstracted hourglasses floating through time.

When the painting was finished, Isaac squinted at the crescents and grumbled that they looked more like me than like him. Then he signed his name and took another nap.

Four

It comes as no surprise to me when I have trouble sleeping that night. Especially after my nightmare about being chased through Markel G by people wearing menacing, feathered Mardi Gras masks. As I raced into the back room, wondering when the gallery had moved to New Orleans and searching for an exit I couldn't find, I noticed that although all the paintings on the walls were mine, there was someone else's name on all the little white cards. Which scared me way more than the masked marauders.

At about three a.m., I give up on the tossing and get up. I make a pot of coffee and wander over to my computer to play some solitaire and check my e-mail. A subject line jumps out of my inbox: "*ArtWorld* Trans Contest Winners." My heart pounds and my stomach clutches. Shit. I want this bad. Need this bad. My hand hesitates over the keyboard. I click and shut my eyes.

When I can bring myself to open them, I scan down the screen for my name. No Roth. I page down to see if there are any more lists. No more lists. The familiar sick feeling twists my insides. I don't know whether I didn't win because of Isaac or because my submissions weren't any good. And I don't know which is worse.

ArtWorld is to the arts what the *New Yorker* is to literature, and their judges are luminaries in the field. Luminaries who have been blackballing me—as Markel so aptly put it—since Isaac died.

I page up to see who won. "Shit," I say out loud and throw my cell phone at the couch. It misses and breaks into two pieces on the floor, as it always does when I throw it. That's how it broke into two pieces in the first place.

But I don't care. This is almost worse than losing. The winner is Crystal Mack. Crystal, who sold three OTC paintings at the *Local Artists at Work* show at Markel G to a bunch of rich suburbanites who wouldn't know a print from an original oil. Crystal, that no-talent phony in her trendy new clothes, sucking up to all her trendy new friends at the Oak Room. Crystal, who is going to elevate insufferable into a completely new realm. I delete the e-mail then remove it from my trash bin to make sure I never see it again.

Fuck her and her derivative pastels.

I think of Markel's offer and imagine Crystal's face as I tell her about my one-woman show at Markel G: disbelief, followed by anger, followed by raw, overpowering jealousy. Even in her deluded imagination, she has to see herself as years away from her own show. It would be sweet. Tequila shots would be flowing at Jake's. Probably for a month.

What if I did do it? What if it all worked out, and Markel and I did something good? What if I did get my own show? All of my windows, standing proud on the walls of the real Markel G. Me standing proud in the middle of them. All the little white cards with *my* name writ large. Lots of red dots denoting sales. No feathers.

Although I'm a professional copier and have studied and mastered the techniques needed to create the illusion of authenticity, aside from a single Repro class, I'm no expert on actual forgery, about the ways to mislead experts, about how it all works. I hesitate, then Google "how art forgers make money."

The first article is titled, "Art Forgers Cash in by 'Russifying' Cheap Works." Forgeries of Shishkin and Malevich are big, as is transforming mediocre nineteenth-century European landscapes into Russian paintings. Exactly why or how the latter is done isn't explained, but evidently the gullible nouveau-riche types can't get enough of it.

There's a post on the story about a dealer named Gianfranco Becchina who, in 1985, convinced the J. Paul Getty Museum to pay him almost $10 million for a forged Greek statue he claimed was from the sixth century BCE. The Getty hired antiquities experts, geologists, lawyers, and authenticators who used every high-tech technique, from electron microprobe to mass spectrometry, to verify Becchina's claim. Everyone was fooled, and the museum purchased the fake.

And then there's John Myatt, who pulled off what is considered the greatest art con of the twentieth century by painting and selling over two hundred "undiscovered" works by well-known dead artists. But the con isn't the best part. It turns out that after a short stint in jail, Myatt established a successful business selling his forgeries as forgeries at between one thousand and ten thousand dollars a pop. In 2005, he had a one-man show at the Air Gallery in London, appropriately called *Genuine Fakes*, which had people lined up for blocks.

Probably the most brilliant of the bunch was Han van Meegeren, a frustrated Dutch painter who spent six years in the 1930s formulating the chemical and technical processes needed to create a forgery that would hoodwink the dealers and critics who refused to recognize his genius. He used toaster parts to create an oven to bake his canvases and was a stunning success. He made a fortune until one of his "Vermeers" was found among postwar Nazi loot, and he had to prove he'd forged it to avoid charges of treason for selling a Dutch national treasure to the enemy.

My favorite, though, is the story of Ely Sakhai, a minor New York gallery owner who made over $3 million buying up middle-market paintings—minor works by major artists that sell in the five-figure range—and hiring artists to forge them. He then turned around and sold both paintings as the original to double his profit. The fakes, along with the actual certificates of authenticity, went to Japanese collectors; the real ones were sold through New York auction houses. He got away with this for years until, in May 2000, the unsuspecting owner of a phony Gauguin decided to sell his version through Sotheby's at the same time Ely consigned the original to Christie's. Poor, clever Ely Sakhai. Caught with nowhere to hide. And he had such a good thing going.

But the most important thing I learn is something I already knew but had somehow overlooked. There's no crime in copying a painting—obviously, as this is how I make the money I dutifully report to the IRS every April—the criminal part doesn't come until a copy is put up for sale as the original. Ergo, the seller, not the painter, is the crook.

ON ITS MAPS and brochures, Boston's MBTA calls the Silver Line a "line" so that riders will equate it with the city's Red, Green, Blue, and Orange Lines, all of which are subways. While the name is obviously just a marketing ploy, it's incredibly annoying to anyone who takes the Silver Line. That's because the Silver Line is a bus. A bus primarily serving poor, minority areas.

Rik's ex-boyfriend Dan is an urban planner, and he says in the transportation field it's officially called BRT: bus rapid transit. As I sit on this BRT, headed for Beverly Arms, stopped in traffic and sweating as the hot summer sun burns through my window, I'm not fooled either. It's a bus and rapid it ain't.

Beverly Arms, like the Silver Line, is a misnomer at best, a spiteful cruelty at worst. The name makes me think of my great-aunt Beverly, whose huge bosom I loved to snuggle in when I was a little girl. Unfortunately, this Beverly is a juvenile detention facility for boys who have committed a crime for which, had they been adults, they'd be in a state prison. Someday, most of them will be.

I've been teaching art classes there on and off, usually once a week, for almost five years. It started in grad school as part of a community service requirement, and after graduation I stayed on. The kids like the class—and me—because it gets them out of afternoon chores. I'm a sucker for being liked.

Beverly Arms has all the style and warmth of a Soviet-era gulag: blocks of colorless concrete interrupted by identical rows of tiny, sealed windows. The good news is that the windows don't have bars. The bad is that the wire mesh shrouding them is so thick that barely any light seeps inside. Bars would be better.

When I finally get there, I'm run through my paces, akin to an airport security check on a Middle Eastern man with a suspicious visa. When that part's over, I have to answer a series of questions that the guard already knows the answers to, as he's grilled me at least a hundred times before and is holding my driver's license in his hand. I used to try to joke with him about this, but it failed miserably, so now I wait for each question and give him the answers he already knows in a patient monotone. Sometimes it's hard to keep a straight face.

"Claire Roth."

"173 Harrison Avenue, Boston, Massachusetts."

"Art teacher."

"Arthur Marcus, Director, Art DYS."

"Green East."

He checks his notes and glares at me as if I, too, have committed a crime. "GE 107," he barks. That's the room I always use. Maybe the kids would do better if someone in this place actually had a sense of humor.

I wend my way through the serpentine corridors, contending with a countless number of thick, heavy doors. Press the button, look up and smile at the camera, wait and hope that whoever's running central unit today isn't a jerk. In the past, I've waited up to ten minutes to be buzzed in, and I can only imagine the satisfaction at central as they watched me shifting from foot to foot.

I found out the hard way that they can both see and hear you. One afternoon, when I first started coming here, I made the mistake of muttering something under my breath about the asshole who wouldn't open the door. Not very smart. Turns out the asshole is the great and powerful Oz behind the Beverly Arms curtain, and she never forgets a slight. I hope she's not in charge today. The buzzer sounds, and, relieved, I pass through the door, which slams and echoes behind me. I'm stopped in twenty steps by yet another door.

As I head into the last leg of my trip to GE 107, I would be happy to be accompanied by the great and powerful Oz. I walk through the isolation unit, my eyes forward, and try to block out the screams of the angry boys being held in the cells lining the hallway. Some are detoxing, and others are "beefing" with each other through the cracks at the bottoms of their doors, continuing the fights from the streets that got them on this hallway in the first place.

Everything in here is painted that sick pea-green always associated with institutions. Does blue cost any more than green? Or how about a cheery yellow? When I first started doing this, I thought maybe the walls were green because it was the green block.

But no. Turns out the entire place is the color of decomposing vegetables. That's what gave me the mural idea: Maybe losing some
of the green would help the kids. I'm told the recidivism rate is at
73 percent. There's not much to lose.

The deal on the mural is that each kid has to draw something
from the outside that he misses using charcoal on newsprint; pens
and pencils aren't allowed because they have sharp points that can
be used as weapons. When the drawings are finished, we're going
to project them on the wall of the dayroom, trace them, then paint
them. Good-bye rotting veggies.

I don't tell the boys what to draw or make any judgments about
its value. I don't even give them pointers on technique unless they
request it. My theory is that the boys—"youths," as they're always
referred to in here—have lots of art inside them and that my job
is to give them materials and let it rip. Xavier is drawing one hundred cans of beer, and Reggie is doing a remarkably good sketch of
a needle and a dime bag of heroin. All I ask is that they work during class and remain true to themselves. The kids have no problem
with the latter. They're burning to express their own private truths.

The boys are led into the room by a social worker I haven't seen
before. Burnout is common, and it's easy to see why. There are only
ten boys today, down from thirteen last time. One is new. Four
missing. I don't ask where they are, as I don't ask what they've done
to get themselves in here. I don't want to know.

I say hi to Jonathan, Xavier, Sean, Johan, Christopher, Reggie,
Brian, Christian, and Andres. Most of them respond appropriately. The new social worker, Kimberly Deeny, introduces herself
and Manuel, a tough-looking, pumped fireplug of a kid who refuses to look me in the eye. I'm guessing he's about twelve. With
a swagger, Manuel takes a piece of charcoal and the blank sheet
of newsprint Kimberly offers, then waits, his face set to cover his

anxiety, for everyone to take their seats. Woe be to the new guy who sits where he shouldn't.

Kimberly, who has no idea which drawing belongs to whom, hands them to me to distribute. She's pretty and young, with a wild mane of reddish-brown hair pulled back into a staid bun; it escapes in tendrils around her face, an unfortunately sexy look. Her baggy clothes do as good a job at covering up her cute little body as the bun does her hair. The boys check her out and elbow each other in the side. Way too pretty and way too young for this job. I wonder if she'll be here when I come back next week.

Everyone but Manuel and Xavier start to work. I spend a few minutes explaining the assignment to Manuel and then squat next to Xavier. He's well over six feet, lean but muscular. Although he must be a star on the basketball court, he has such a sweet face and demeanor that it's difficult to imagine him trying to beat anyone or, for that matter, doing anything that would put him in here. Clearly, looks are deceiving. Because of his height, Xavier appears to be at least eighteen, but I've got him pegged at fourteen or fifteen. A very tender age to be missing a hundred cans of beer.

"What gives, X?" I ask.

He shrugs.

I examine his drawing. The cans themselves look as if they were drawn by a small child, but the labels are quite intricate. He's got the Budweiser script down.

"Looks like you're almost there. How many more you need?"

"Too many."

"You don't have to do a hundred if you don't want. That was just one idea."

Xavier shrugs again.

"It's not the number?"

He looks down at the drawing, shakes his head.

Squatting is starting to hurt my quads, but sometimes you've just got to say nothing and wait. When this doesn't work, I touch his arm, which I'm not supposed to do.

He looks up.

"What?" I ask.

"It's the silver."

"Silver?"

He jabs his finger at the cans. "Bud's silver. Those are the ones I miss, and you said it's got to be true. And there's only gonna be red, blue, and yellow."

He's got a point. The budget is extremely tight, but Al, of Al's Art Supply, offered a discount if I took only primary colors. Something about overstock. I figured I could mix the three and get all the colors we needed, but Xavier is right: There's not going to be any silver. These kids always surprise.

Once again, I think of Markel's offer. If I took it, I wouldn't have to stick to the state's stingy, line-item allocation—art classes for juvenile offenders not being an easy sell. I'd have money, $50,000 worth of money. I'd have the means to augment the government's narrow-minded tightfistedness. Or maybe I'm just looking for an excuse to strike back at an art world I believe has wronged me. Claire Roth, a twenty-first-century Han van Meegeren. Hopefully, Markel doesn't know any Nazis.

I stand. "No problem, X. I'll figure out a way to get you your silver."

He looks at me blankly, clearly not used to getting what he needs.

So many good uses for ill-begotten gains.

Five

I climb the four flights to my studio thinking about Xavier's paint, Crystal's astonished face, and my paintings hanging at Markel G. I think about doing good—whatever good might be—and how there's no crime in copying a painting. Markel's a local celebrity, and if anything unscrupulous had ever been linked with his name, I, and the entire city of Boston, would be aware. Even Isaac, who tended to see the worst in everyone, trusted him.

I call Markel. "How good is good?" I ask without preamble.

He chuckles. "It's something I'm sure you've wished you could make happen."

"Like world peace?"

"Maybe not quite so grandiose, but in a smaller way, yes."

"Could you be any more vague?"

"Probably not."

There's nothing to be said to this, so I ask, "Tell me again how many people we'd be helping?"

When he says hundreds of thousands, perhaps millions, I figure he's running a bit hyperbolic. "Really?"

He laughs. "I know it sounds nuts, but yes, really."

I hesitate.

"It's your call, Claire," he reminds me. "I can get someone else if I have to . . ."

Someone else? "Okay," I tell him. "I'm in."

A few days later, a wooden shipping crate is delivered. It's huge, at least six foot by six foot. It's thick, too, as if it could hold half a dozen canvases, although I'm guessing there are only two, at most four, inside.

If there are three or four, it's likely Markel wants me to create a pastiche, an "undiscovered" painting the forger compiles based on past works of a well-known artist, like John Myatt did. But if there are only two, it's Ely Sakhai's paradigm I'll be following, and one of the paintings will be an original by an established artist—or a minor work by someone more famous—and the other canvas will be the same age as the original. After I strip the paint off the second one, I'll paint my copy onto it so the forgery is on a canvas and frame authentic to the artist's era and carbon dating won't give us away.

I'm dying to know whose work is in the crate, but Markel said not to open it, that he would be here within the hour. He made me promise. But what's a promise among thieves?

I check the crate on all sides, notice there's a rip in the tape at the top left corner. I climb the stepladder, stick my finger in and pull. I manage to make a hole an inch round and press my eye to the opening. Of course, I see nothing. I grab a hammer and a crowbar, hesitate, then use the back end of the hammer to jab the tape again. There's not much give left—the whole crate is held together by nails—but I dig in and double the size of the hole. Now I see bubble wrap.

I hardly ever get to base my Repro paintings on originals, as most of the real McCoys are in Paris or London, and Repro sure isn't sending me across the Atlantic. Once, I was doing a Botticelli for them—*Tragedy of Lucretia*—which is owned by the Gardner Museum, so I got to work from that original. Unfortunately, the Gardner is incredibly stodgy, allowing only pencil drawing and no cameras. Still, the repro came out better for it.

The idea of a high-quality piece of artwork in my studio both electrifies and terrifies me. If I were a betting woman, I'd wager Markel is playing the Ely Sakhai game, and the painting is a lesser work I'm to forge so he can sell it to some unsuspecting collector as the original. Seems an odd thing for Markel to be involved in. He's way too rich and philanthropic, not to mention supportive of struggling artists, for his motive to be greed. But as I've no idea what the "good" is, I'm in no position to judge.

In truth, aside from the interactions I had with Markel as Isaac's dealer—some extremely taxing, to say the least—as well as the usual rumor mill and media hype, I know very little about Aiden Markel. A decade ago, in his midtwenties, he was an art wunderkind, bursting onto the Boston scene, making it big, and staying here, rather than taking off to New York or Paris. He represents many renowned national and international artists, which has pulled Boston from the art backwaters and into the light. Although he's only six or seven years older than I am, he's so accomplished, it might as well be decades.

I drop the hammer, grab the crowbar, and contemplate the crate. I climb back up the stepladder, stick the crowbar in the hole, and give it a good yank. The crate lets out an almost human shriek and starts to come apart. I do it again, get a bit more leverage, and the space between the two pieces of wood widens. But I see that I'm going to have to remove most of the nails first, so I switch back to the hammer.

As I methodically work through the nails, I think about the money Markel's bringing with him. Almost $17,000. This is more money than I've ever had at any one time. I owe about twenty-five grand on my student loans, and a chunk will go toward that. Then I'll pay the landlord the last two months' rent and cover the tab I've been running at Al's Art Supply. Al and the landlord have been really good about it, but witty, self-deprecating stories will only get a girl so far. Plus, I'm running low on pigments and mediums, not to mention brushes, and there's no way Al will front me any of that if I don't pay up.

I look around the studio. A real bed, instead of a mattress. A couch a person could sit on without slipping a disc. A computer that doesn't take twenty minutes to boot up. A cell phone that isn't in two pieces. The list is endless.

The phone rings, and I see it's Markel. I go down and let him in. This time, he's not at all chatty. When we walk into the studio, he immediately notices I've started in on the crate but doesn't seem surprised.

"So you couldn't wait," he says, without the slightest touch of irritation.

I shrug. "Haven't gotten very far."

"So I see."

This visit, I offer no wine or nuts. We stand in front of the towering crate for a long moment, not speaking. Finally Markel says, "We should talk."

I point to the rocking chair and take a seat on the couch. I fold my hands in my lap and wait.

He pulls an envelope from inside his jacket and places it on the table between us. It's quite thick. "I hope you don't mind," he says, as if he's discussing the weather, "but most of it's in cash."

Seventeen thousand dollars. I feel lightheaded. "Of course not, no problem," I say, in what I hope is a casual tone, although I can hear that it's not.

He puts his feet flat on the floor and leans toward me. "I don't want you to think I'm patronizing you, but we need to go over how you'll handle the money."

I do think he's patronizing me. "I'm quite capable of handling the money."

"Based on what you told me about your pay scale," he says, as if I haven't spoken, "I've written you a check for eight thousand dollars on the Markel G account. This is official payment for your services, which you will deposit in your regular business account and report to the IRS. Just in case anything goes wrong, this will prove we had a standard reproduction agreement and will put you at arm's length from anything else I'm involved in. The rest is cash."

I glance at the envelope and then look quickly away. Nine thousand dollars in cash.

"You'll have to set up a couple of accounts in different banks," he continues. "Don't deposit more than a few thousand in each so as not to raise suspicion. There's two thousand in fifties you should just keep. But don't spend them in the places where people know you. Use them at the supermarket or the mall."

"Is all this really necessary?" I'm not much of a money person, having never had any, and my palms are beginning to sweat.

"It's my job to make sure there are no mistakes." He counts out the next directions on his fingers. "No major purchases, no expensive vacations, and no undisciplined gestures like an extravagant gift for your mother or treating everyone at your favorite bar to a drink."

"I'm not a child," I say, feeling patronized again. "I understand what we're doing here."

"No." He stands up. "I don't think you do."

I stand, too. "Maybe it's time you enlightened me."

He walks over to the crate and grabs the crowbar. "You keep on with the nails, I'll work with this."

I shoot one last glance at the envelope sitting on the table, then join him. With more than a few grunts and a good deal of sweat, we manage to wrestle the paintings from their enclosure. As I guessed, there are only two. But both are encased in so many layers of bubble wrap that, to my disappointment, they're hidden in plain view. The canvases are unframed and of identical size, large, but not as large as I expected, probably four foot by five foot. I wonder which is the valuable one.

"This isn't going to be like your Reproductions.com gig."

"I'm guessing you chose me for this project because you know I know that."

For a moment he looks taken aback, then he visibly relaxes. "Sorry," he says. "Sorry for being such an asshole, but this whole adventure is out of my league."

"So why are you doing it?"

"You'll see." He flashes me a mischievous smile. "Got scissors?"

He cuts the tape, and I pull back the bubble wrap. Within minutes, the painting is standing naked and revealed. I immediately recognize the artist, if not the specific work.

"Meissonier," I say. It makes sense. Ernest Meissonier was a second- or third-tier late-nineteenth-century painter. His specialty was military subjects rendered with meticulous realism. He painted in oil in the classical style and, if I remember correctly, considered himself the second coming of Rembrandt, even though no one else did. But what about Meissonier's painting could make a million people happy?

"They say," Markel tells me, "that Degas claimed that everything Meissonier painted looked like metal except the armor."

I laugh and step closer to inspect the painting. "There are tons of layers here. An unimpeachable forgery is going to take a long time," I say. "Are you sure it's worth the effort?"

"No," Markel says. "It wouldn't be."

I stare at him. "This is the one that's going to be painted over?"

"Removed, actually."

Obviously, I know there can be no painting under the one I'm to create, as this would be easily detectable with a simple X-ray. But still, to destroy a Meissonier . . .

"It's a very minor work, despite its size, and there are some, ah, questions of provenance."

Any interest I had in Meissonier immediately evaporates, and I turn to the other, still bubble-wrapped canvas. "Who?"

Markel looks positively impish. "Don't you want to wait and be surprised?"

"No."

Markel laughs. "No delayed gratification here."

"Never my strong suit."

Markel hesitates.

"Who?"

"Degas, of course."

I can hardly breathe. I cut my teeth on Degas as a kid in museum drawing classes. And now, here's one of his original works, touched by the great man himself, right in my very own studio, only a couple of feet away. And if Markel chose me as the forger, it's got to be one of Degas' oils.

My heart races. I'm going to have the incredible good fortune of living with a work by Degas, touching it, breathing it in, studying its every last detail, ferreting out the master's secrets. It's a great gift. Perhaps the greatest. One that will inform my painting forever. Sweet. Incredibly sweet. Now I really can't breathe.

Markel begins to carefully cut the tape holding the bubble wrap together. There are many more layers of wrap on this one.

I stand speechless, mesmerized, unable to move to help him,

unable even to think. *Degas, Degas, Degas* is the only refrain my brain can dole out.

He works painstakingly, much more slowly than when he unwrapped the Meissonier.

It's nudes. I think three, maybe four. Part of Degas' bathers series. A time when, in contrast to most of his contemporaries, he focused on the moments of ordinary life. A flash of blue, green, coral. Even under a full layer of bubble wrap, the brilliance of Degas' colors surge. Which painting is it? He was so prolific during this period. But my brain freezes. I can't think of a single one.

As Markel strips away the final layer and the painting is uncovered, I'm momentarily confused. My first thought is that it's not a real Degas. That it can't be. Then I gasp. Not only is this a real Degas, it's a Degas I've seen before. Many times.

"No," I cry, and it sounds like a moan.

I should have guessed from the size of the canvas. This is no ordinary Degas. It's one of his great masterworks. *After the Bath,* the last of five he gave the same name, but by far the most famous.

And that's the least of it. This painting was torn from the walls of the Isabella Stewart Gardner Museum, the only one taken intact, still within its frame. But it and all the other works stolen that rainy night by a couple of bumbling thieves have never been recovered.

In front of me stands one of the most valuable paintings stolen in the greatest unsolved art theft in history.

From the pen of

ISABELLA STEWART GARDNER

June 10, 1886
Paris, France

My dearest Amelia,

I cannot tell you how distressed I am that we missed you and
your bridegroom. And by only two days! The waters between London
and Paris were so treacherous that the ships did not sail, and your
Uncle Jack and I were forced to spend two damp and miserable
nights in a horrid guesthouse in Brighton. I trust your trip home
went better.

We were so looking forward to seeing you in your honeymoon
finery, beautiful and blushing on Sumner's arm. I console myself
that we will return to Boston soon, and that I may be received at the
apartments of Mr. and Mrs. Sumner T. Prescott Jr. immediately upon
our arrival. If only your dear departed parents and your sweet brother
Joe could do the same.

London was almost as foggy and dreary as Brighton, and all
the parties were dreadfully dull. But now that we are in Paris, this

city of such wondrous beauty and light, all is well in the world. It is marvelous to be once again surrounded by people of wit and gaiety.

We have been to plays and soirees, and this past week we ventured into one of the new café-concerts, and oh, what a splendid spectacle. We were entertained by dancers in costumes so tight and shiny they might have been dancing in their own painted skin! Your uncle, as you might guess, was a bit put off, but I loved every minute, as I do so love the French!

And then there was last night! Oh, last night! Last night, your Uncle Jack and I dined at the home of our dear friend Mr. Henry James. (Do you remember meeting him at Green Hill on his long ago trip to America? Likely not, as you were so young, but he was charmed by you and your boisterous brothers.) To my great pleasure, Henry had included James Whistler and John Sargent in his invitation, both of whom I know you remember well. Then, just one week ago, Henry informed me that Edgar Degas would also be joining us.

While I am very familiar with Degas' work, I have never had the privilege of meeting the great man. (It is my opinion that his layering and luminosity rival many of the old masters, particularly *Portrait of René de Gas* and *The Young Spartans*.) I am determined to return from this trip with at least the promise, if not the purchase, of three major pictures at a reasonable price, and so the addition of Mr. Degas to the table was most welcome.

I have heard that Mr. Degas has an appreciation not only for a woman's shoulders and neck (which given my plain face are my best features to put forward) but also for her clothes. I immediately visited the salon of Charles Frederick Worth, who dressed both the Princess

Pauline de Metternich and the Empress Eugénie. To my amazement, in only one week, he designed a magnificent silk gown that flows smoothly over my hips and chastely over my bosom but leaves my shoulders bare. It reveals in a way that is not too revealing, and your Uncle Jack was pleased.

Although, as far as I am aware, Mr. Degas' name has never been linked romantically to another's, I was confident that, as the only woman at table, I would be able to pull the ropes and handle the ribbons sufficiently well to secure his attentions. I admit to only you, my dear niece, that both Mr. Whistler and Mr. Sargent have been quite easy prey in the past.

We, of course, discussed art and literature, particularly how much Henry dislikes Trollope's *Framley Parsonage* and the rumor that George Eliot is a woman! The wines and punch made us gay, and to listen to James Whistler and Edgar (yes, he instructed me to call him Edgar!) in friendly dispute over Parisian versus Venetian light was a great joy and a unique privilege.

Then Edgar began to discuss his connection, both in art and in friendship, with those who call themselves "Impressionists." I am so certain that a man of his talent should not waste it on such indulgences that I asked him why he would throw clumps of wet pigment on a canvas instead of wielding his fine eye and brush toward the delicate glazing he does so well? I wondered if Vermeer or Rembrandt would do such a thing, and I told him I thought not, and that neither should he.

Rather than being angry, as a lesser man might have been, Edgar began to laugh so loud and so hard that we all had to join in. He touched his wine glass to mine and said, "Touché, Mrs. Gardner. Touché." (I had instructed him earlier in the evening to call me Isabella, but he seemed unable to do so.) I, of course, was charmed. Do I flatter myself in the thought that perhaps I'll be able to help Edgar Degas see the error of his ways? Perhaps this is too scandalous an idea. Nonetheless, I shall try.

And then, to make this magical evening even more magical, Edgar and I discovered our mutual love of horses and horseracing, and he invited all of us at table to sit in his private box on opening day at Longchamps! This I shall not miss.

Though I was unable to get a guarantee from any of the three artists to part with a picture or accept a commission at a price I could afford, each of them (privately, of course) did promise to consider such a thing. Mr. Degas insisted that we visit his studio. Which, of course, we shall do.

When we rose to take our leave, Edgar raised my hand to his lips and told me it had been years since he had "spent such a charming evening with such a charming dinner partner."

So, my dear girl, I must end here. Please write of all the adventures of your grand tour and all the details of your homemaking. Please don't choose all your linens and draperies, as I would so love to assist in the decoration of your home and boudoir.

I am your loving,
Aunt Belle

Seven

I stare at *After the Bath* as if my eyes are tethered to the canvas. As a child, I sat on the floor of the Short Gallery in the Isabella Stewart Gardner Museum, pencil in hand, struggling to draw this very painting. The slope of a back, the shadow of a towel fold, the extension of an arm. *After the Bath.* I am awed. I am thrilled. I am horrified.

"I, it," I sputter at Markel. "I can't have this here. You've got to take it back." Even as I say the words, part of me is screaming: *No, leave it, please leave it right where it is.* "It's way too valuable, priceless. Not to mention stolen. I can't take responsibility for—"

"Of course you can have it here," Markel says. "It's the perfect place. If anyone sees it, they'll figure it's one of your reproductions." His calculation is as impressive as it is appalling.

I can't take my eyes from the brushwork, the depth of the values, the saturation of the colors. How did Degas do it: rabbit-skin glue in his sizing? yellow ochre in his underpainting? egg temper in his medium? But these are only technical questions. The genius of this painting is much more than technique—and quite impossible to replicate. How could Markel ever think I would be able to create a credible forgery of this magnificent beast?

"Don't worry, I'm going to give it back," he says.

"But you just brought it." I'm having trouble thinking clearly with the canvas so close to me.

"Back to the Gardner Museum."

"Now?"

Markel's eyes twinkle. "Later. After you've worked your magic. That's the doing-good part. I sell your copy and give the original back to the museum."

"If you sell it as the original, it's a forgery not a copy."

"Call it whatever you want. The important point is that a Degas masterpiece is returned to both the Gardner and the world. A pretty good thing, don't you think?"

I speak as if coming out of a drug-induced fog. "But some innocent collector is going to be out millions."

"Not so innocent. Remember, whoever buys it believes he's buying a stolen masterpiece."

"Like that guy? What's-his-name?" My mind refuses to work. "You know, that dealer in New York who had duplicates of paintings forged then sold both as the original? Starts with E . . . Ely Sakhai."

"Claire," Markel says. "You're not listening. Not even to yourself. Yes, Ely Sakhai did forge paintings and sell them both as originals. But that's not what we're going to do. We're going to *give* the original back to its rightful owner. It's a completely different thing."

"Then the buyer will find out about it," I protest. "He'll go to the police."

Again the twinkle. "And what will he tell them? That his stolen masterpiece turned out to be a fake? And anyway, he'll have no idea who sold him the painting. I know how to protect myself."

I need him to slow down. His fast answers are coming too fast.

Yet my questions won't stop either. "What about the sellers? Won't they be pissed?"

"They get their money, what do they care?" Markel shrugs.

Then I realize what's really bothering me. "The other paintings. The other ones stolen from the Gardner. You know where they are."

He looks me straight in the eye. "I have no idea."

I hold his gaze. "You know where you got this one."

"Actually, I don't."

"But—"

"I was contacted by someone who asked if I had a high-end client who might be interested in a 'significant' piece of art. I said that, of course, it depended on the piece, but yes, I probably did. To make a long story short, I had a number of conversations with a number of people, who used what I can only assume were false names—which is exactly how I intend to handle the sale from my end. And finally, one told me what they wanted to sell.

"At first I said no, that I had no interest. But then I started to think about returning it to the Gardner and came up with this plan. I called them back and said I thought I had just the right person."

"You can't be serious."

"Think about it," Markel says, warming to the subject. "*After the Bath,* back in its rightful place in the Gardner Museum. Millions of people are thrilled. The seller gets his money, and the collector gets what he believes is a Degas, at least until he finds out the truth in the press, and then it will be too late. You and I get to feel really good about ourselves. Not to mention, your own work gets the exposure it deserves."

"It can't be that simple."

"The alternative is that some other broker sells it to some crook who most likely keeps the painting underground, moving it through the black market as collateral for weapons or drugs. Not taking care of it. Never to be seen. This will save *After the Bath* from that fate."

I don't really understand what he's talking about, and I'm not sure it makes sense. "Why don't you just give it back to the Gardner now? Why do you need the rest of it?"

"I have to cover my back. And my expenses."

"You need money?"

"Don't be naive, Claire. It doesn't suit you."

"But the gallery? All your artwork?" I'm honestly puzzled.

Markel hesitates, then says, "The last few years have been tough. Business is way down, as is the value of art. And those alimony payments never change."

"But you could collect the reward."

"Not if it's returned anonymously. And I can't get my name or the gallery involved. Even if there's no chance of prosecution."

Markel has clearly thought this through, and I can't find any glaring holes in his logic. Which might be the problem. There's something too pat, too convenient, about the explanation. But I figure that's the least of my difficulties.

I turn back to the painting. It's a depiction of three nudes toweling themselves dry, not an unusual subject for Degas in the later part of his career, but it's rendered in his early classical style, dense layers of vibrant color set on top of one another, expressing the inexpressible with a luminosity that indeed makes Meissonier's work look like dull metal. I want to touch it so badly that I have to clench my fists to keep my arms by my sides.

"This is the opportunity of a lifetime for you in many ways," Markel says. "Not to mention the adrenaline rush of the century. You strike me as the adventurous type. Why not give it a shot?"

"For the obvious reasons," I mumble.

"They don't seem all that obvious to me."

I shake my head.

"Claire?"

Finally, I whisper, "I'm not good enough."

Markel's laugh bellows out of him and bounces around the studio. "I misunderstood your reluctance. I thought it was some kind of misplaced morality."

I jut my chin forward. "Well, it's that, too."

He winks and says, "Let me know what you need." Then he walks across the room and closes the door behind him.

THE ROOM IS dark, and I'm lying on my mattress. I've been up most of the night. I feel *After the Bath* like a human presence: massive, breathing, haunting, yet also comforting. As if Degas himself is with me, risen from the dead. His genius, his brushstrokes, his heart.

I think about the Gardner Museum, about the frames that hang empty on the walls of the Blue Room, the Dutch Room, and the Short Gallery. The frames hold nothing where the stolen artwork used to be, marking the loss, waiting stoically for the return of their raison d'être. I've been to the museum many times since the robbery, and I always stop in front of these frames to ponder the fate of their missing centers.

Much has been written about the Gardner heist, but very little is known. Or, more correctly, those who know aren't talking. A $5 million reward, no questions asked, no chance of prosecution for the return of the thirteen works, and nary a nibble. The statute of limitations has run out, and still no one's come forward with even a reasonable rumor. In this global Internet village we live in, it doesn't seem possible, yet there it is. I climb out of bed, flick on the light, and stand in front of the painting.

It's such a magnificent being. So alive, yet more like the sensation of life, rather than how life actually is. Color and emotion pulse from the canvas. Once again, tears fill my eyes, and this time I let them run down my cheeks. I should return it to the Gardner right now. It isn't fair to keep such a masterpiece hidden away.

But I don't want to give it back. I want to live with it, spend time with it, paint it. I know I shouldn't, but I reach out and tenderly run my finger over the hand of the bather on the right. She's seated, one leg raised as she towels her ankle dry. I decide her name is Françoise. The other two are Jacqueline and Simone.

Eight

The exterior of the Isabella Stewart Gardner Museum is underwhelming, to say the least. The façade is plain, almost unbroken by windows or decoration, an unwelcoming fortress. The first time I saw it—I must have been about seven—I cried when my mother told me this was the museum she had been raving about. But when I went inside, my tears quickly dried.

The museum is essentially an ornate Venetian palace turned in on itself, a seven-year-old girl's delight. Instead of canals, a magical four-story central courtyard faces the interior walls. A greenhouse of sorts. The roof is glass and the floor is a sensuous garden filled with freestanding columns, whimsical twelfth-century lion stylobates, and all manner of statuary. A Roman mosaic sits at the center, surrounded by an ever-changing installation of flowers and shrubs. A pair of towering palm trees reach up to the sunlight, climbing beyond the third floor.

All four walls, which rise at least sixty feet, are cut by tiers of stone-fronted arches, notched doorways and windows, marble balustrades, and exposed stairways overflowing with flowers and greenery. The rooms at the perimeter of this courtyard form the bulk of the museum. Isabella Gardner built this monument to live in, to house her art collection, and to leave to the public upon her death.

Although I'm here to meet Rik for lunch, I climb the stairs to the second floor and walk through the Early Italian Room and the Raphael Room and into the Short Gallery. I need to see *Bath*'s empty frame. The gallery is only about ten feet wide and has to be just about the worst place to hang a painting as large as *After the Bath*. But Isabella, who was eccentric, to say the least, personally determined the placement of each of her 2,500 pieces of art and then decreed in her will that nothing was to be changed, removed, or added. Ever.

It is this conceit that created the hodgepodge that is the Gardner. In contrast to the openness and brilliance of the courtyard, the shadowy galleries are filled with mismatched groupings of furniture, fine art, and random trinkets. Priceless paintings are hung over doorways, and 3,000-year-old sculptures are hidden in corners.

Poor lighting and cramped spaces render this clutter even more claustrophobic, and there's barely a piece of artwork that's shown to its best advantage. But since 1924, the year Isabella died, the museum has stayed as its mistress wished, as charming and capricious as she was herself. Only the thieves were able to best the old girl.

I walk up to the empty frame, the hollow enclosure where *After the Bath* once lived, and I'm overwhelmed by shame. I press myself into a corner, try to make myself small, hoping no one will notice me, recognize my culpability. And nobody does. As I relax and pull to a stand, to both my surprise and consternation, a surge of adrenaline nearly knocks me over. I am suddenly jubilant. I have *After the Bath*. It's in my very own studio, where I sleep and paint. Degas' masterpiece, to look at whenever I want. To smell, to even touch, that most forbidden act within museum walls. And, I remind myself, I'll be partially responsible for its return home.

I watch the people filing past, looking sadly at the vacant spot, wondering as I've always wondered. I have an overpowering urge to tell them, to shout to the world that it's mine, all mine. I turn abruptly and leave the room, calming as I wend my way to the small café hidden behind the tiny bookstore on the first floor.

Rik and I kiss, hug, exchange pleasantries and a bit of gossip, order our food, and then I ask him a few questions about the robbery.

"Why this sudden interest in the heist?" he asks.

I shrug. "I've always been interested. Isn't everyone?"

Rik takes a bite of his burger. "Guess the rumor that Whitey Bulger had them with him in Argentina was as false as all the rest."

"Couldn't he have had them there anyway? Before he was arrested? Maybe they're still there now."

"Nah. I never believed Whitey or any of the Boston mob were involved. If it was organized crime, they'd have sold most of the cache pretty fast, and at least a few would've surfaced by now."

"Then who did it?"

"I'm thinking some European. The robbery involved planning, disguises, and deception. That's how art thieves work in Europe."

"Not here?"

"Hardly ever."

"You think the paintings are in Europe?"

"After all these years, they could be anywhere," Rik says. "Although lots of people assume they have to be hidden away in some greedy collector's attic, my guess is that they're being used as collateral for weapons and drug running. Sometimes terrorist groups swap stolen paintings for their imprisoned comrades."

Markel alluded to this, too. "No James Bond and Dr. No?"

"This works out better for the thieves. It's tough to sell the paintings outright because everyone knows they're stolen, so they use them on the black market. Say, for example, that you want to buy a load of cocaine for $1 million, which you know you can turn into $4 million in a week. You don't have $1 million, but you do have a Rembrandt worth at least $30 million. So you offer a moneyman the painting as collateral for the mil and another million when the deal's done. If the deal falls through, moneyman's got something worth much more than he gave you, and if it works, he gets double his investment and returns the painting to you. Ergo, you end up with $2 million tax-free and a $30 million painting to run through the same scheme when the next opportunity comes around."

"Great for the thieves, lousy for the paintings."

"You've got that right," Rik says. "It's awful what happens to them. They get stashed in places that are too wet or too hot or too cold. They're cut from their frames. Ripped. Destroyed." He presses a hand to his stomach. "I get sick just talking about it."

I, too, am nauseated by the image, the ravaging, the waste. "Blood paintings."

"Like blood diamonds?" Rik laughs without humor. "But instead of slave labor, it's art that's exploited, sometimes massacred."

This is a fate I refuse to imagine for *Bath*.

When I leave the museum, I rush home to be with *Bath*. It feels as if I'm hurrying to meet a new lover: the excitement, the desire, the seemingly endless drenching of serotonin. I whip the sheet off the canvas, and there she is. Alive and intact. Even more beautiful than I remember. I've set her on a large easel and pulled up a folding chair so I can sit in front of her, drink her in.

Every time I look, I see something new. Now I notice how much green there is. The blues and the oranges are so vibrant, the women's skin so pale and luminescent, that I was distracted. Green fills the entire painting, gently stretching out behind all the sharper colors, but very much there.

Then I'm struck by the women's faces, all in profile, yet each her own. Most of Degas' bathers are either painted from behind, have an arm thrown over their faces, or are loosely sketched, but these women are clearly individuals. Françoise, with reddish hair and a sharp nose, sits to the right, her leg outstretched; Jacqueline, at the center, tall and powerful, looks over her shoulder at the raised knee Françoise is toweling; Simone, introverted, her features too small for her round face, dries her hair crouched at Jacqueline's feet.

There's been an argument going on for decades among art historians with too much time on their hands: Was Degas really an Impressionist? Those who say no point out that Degas didn't paint outdoors, plein air, as did most of the Impressionists, and that he didn't boldly splash thick pigments on canvas to capture the moment in front of him. Instead, he did multitudes of sketches and detailed drawings and then worked on the piece slowly in his studio.

But to me, the argument is just semantics, an exercise in mental masturbation. True, Degas painted neither plein air nor spontaneously, but he had his own way of bringing his impressions into the heart of the viewer: his focus on the movement of racehorses and ballet dancers, his depiction of the ordinary milliner or washer woman or bather, caught in a complete lack of self-consciousness.

I turn from *Bath* and squat before the piles of books flanking the north wall. I have a couple of Degas piles: biographies and criticism; books of his drawings, prints, and paintings; diaries and collections of his letters; notebooks of scribbled lecture notes. I also have two books devoted to only his preliminary sketches. Not to mention all the library books, many overdue, on his contemporaries that I've been using for my book proposal.

I pull out his sketchbooks and bring them back to the chair. I open the first one and flip through the bather sketches. Degas often used the same models in a number of different paintings. I'm searching for Simone, Jacqueline, and Françoise.

I find a couple of Simone and turn back to the painting for a closer look at Jacqueline. Again, the power of *Bath* assaults me. Although I'm sure I can master the technical aspects needed to avoid detection—stripping the old Meissonier canvas down to the sizing, mixing the correct nineteenth-century paints and mediums, using the proper period brushes—I have no idea how I'll master reproducing the commanding gestalt of Degas' masterwork. But *Bath* reaches out to me, touches my heart, and I know I have to try.

I'M WORKING DILIGENTLY on the Pissarro for Repro, but all I want to do is go through the Degas sketches and find my three French ladies, maybe even a compositional drawing for the whole painting. I make a deal with myself: one more hour on the Pissarro and then I can take a quick break with the books. Whatever else I've decided to do, Repro pays the rent. It also, as Markel so accurately pointed out, gives me a cover.

I'm just settling back into the Pissarro when Markel shows up with a very expensive-looking bottle of champagne and a pair of crystal flutes. Obviously, he remembers the juice glasses from his first visit. We toast to our arrangement and the Gardner regaining its treasure. I pull the sheet from *Bath*.

He takes a small step backward as the force of the painting hits him. It's clear he feels the same way about her as I do. I motion him into the folding chair and pull the rocking chair over for myself. We sit in silence, sipping our champagne and looking at her.

"Like two old folks watching a sunset," he says.

"Sometimes I cry when I look at it."

A pause, then, "Me, too."

"I was at the Gardner yesterday," I tell him.

"Looking at the empty frame?"

I nod my head but don't take my eyes from the painting.

"Didn't feel as guilty as you thought you were going to, did you?"

I whip around. "Why do you say that?"

"It's true, isn't it?"

"Of course not," I say with conviction. "I did feel guilty. I even thought about bringing it back."

"But you didn't."

I shrug.

Markel's laugh is warm and rich, without a touch of condescension. "You've fallen in love with her."

"Is it that obvious?"

He touches his flute to mine, and our eyes lock. "Takes one to know one."

"The faces are so specific, so individual, not like most of his nudes."

Markel looks at the two books of sketches on the floor in front of him. "Find any of them?"

"I just started looking, and although there are hardly any faces in the sketches, I think I've found a few of Simone."

"Simone?"

"Françoise, Jacqueline, and Simone," I say pointing to each in turn. "Hard to be in love with someone whose name you don't know."

Nine

Markel and Karen Sinsheimer, a senior curator at the Museum of Modern Art, stood in front of *4D,* which rested on an easel in Isaac's studio. Isaac and I hung back.

Tall and sleek, wearing an outfit that probably cost more than my monthly rent, Karen moved closer to the painting. She took a few photos with her phone, typed in a few notes. The slick, white-blond hair against her youthful face and the taut, lean body came together to create the message she clearly worked hard to send: the no-nonsense, powerful New York professional woman.

No one said anything. We just stared at the canvas. Wine and nuts sat untouched on the coffee table. Isaac shifted from foot to foot. I tried to look only marginally interested, as if *4D* were just another one of Isaac's paintings, this studio visit no more important than any other.

This was the first time anyone beside the two of us had seen *4D.* Karen was here to decide whether it would be accepted for the MoMA show, and by doing so, give the painting its authenticity. Markel was there in his role as Isaac's dealer, but his opinion mattered to us almost as much as Karen's. Markel knew Isaac's work better than anyone. If he was fooled, we were home free.

I wished we'd put out water. I needed some but didn't want to move. Isaac and I had been fitful and edgy before they showed up. We knew what we had done, what we were doing, and we didn't know how it was going to turn out. I glanced over at Karen, who was taking a photograph of my hourglasses, and at Markel, who was also inspecting them, and thought I might faint. I assumed Isaac was in a similar state.

I had tried to get him to talk about how he felt. But, of course, in true Isaac fashion, he evaded, joked around, then evaded some more. Maybe he didn't want to talk or maybe he didn't know how he felt.

For me, it was simple. I had painted *4D* as a gift, to help him when he needed help, to get him through a bad patch. As far as I was concerned, *4D* was a bridge I helped build to carry him to his next piece. And I wanted more than anything for Karen and Markel to buy into the painting, for it to hang in the show, and for Isaac to move on and do the kind of work only he could do.

Karen turned and held out her hand to Isaac. "Congratulations, Isaac. It's wonderful. Better than wonderful. Better than any of your previous work that I've seen. We'll take it."

I hadn't realized I was holding my breath until I heard it come out in a long hiss. I threw my arms around Isaac and squeezed long and hard. He barely responded. Shock. Shock and relief. I stepped away, grinning.

"Great. Fabulous." Markel pummeled Isaac on the back. "I agree. It could be your best." I knew that this wasn't just "agent speak." Markel truly agreed.

"Thanks," Isaac said stiffly, almost trancelike. "Thanks both of you." Then he looked over at me. "And a tremendous thanks to you."

While the three of them clustered around the painting, I went to the freezer and pulled out the bottle of champagne I'd hidden behind the ice cream. "Champagne, anyone?" I called.

Markel came over and took it from me. "May I do the honors?" I scrounged around the cabinets for wine glasses and handed them to Markel. "Let the festivities begin."

When we finished off the champagne and moved on to wine, Isaac began to loosen up. In fact, he became positively loquacious.

"Yes, it was really eye opening to work with time in a completely different way. The series has always been about time as linear, flat, a speck of our experience. But this opened it all up, pulled it out in all directions, gave it depth." He shook his head as if to clear it. "I can't even remember when I came up with the idea." Then his eyes lit on mine, and he grinned. "It was Claire." He raised his glass to me. "Let's drink to my brilliant, talented, beautiful Claire."

We all toasted, and then he leaned over and kissed me. "Who's a great talent in her own right. It won't be many more years, Karen, before you're showing her work."

"I'd love to see some," Karen said.

"You'll be sorry you said that," I warned. "I have your number." Maybe there was such a thing as karma, as Small was always insisting. Maybe this was my payback for helping Isaac.

"Please do call. Send some slides. I should be in Boston again in a month or so, and if I like what I see, I'll pop over for a studio visit." Karen Sinsheimer was nothing if not politic, and I understood it might mean little. But it also might mean much.

"Oh, you'll want to make a visit," Markel said. "Claire's work is different from Isaac's." He waved at *4D*. "In some ways, night and day from this. But she's got a sure eye and an even surer brush. The quality of her colors is quite remarkable."

"Amen to that." Isaac gave my shoulders a squeeze, then turned to Karen and resumed his musings. "You know, *4D*'s got me thinking about a series within a series, time in many dimensions. First dots, then lines, then our world, then across space, black holes. Who knows where it might take me."

"That sounds like it could be interesting," Karen said.

But Isaac knew as well as the rest of us that "interesting" was a euphemism for boring. "Or maybe I'll just stick with the fourth dimension for a while," he amended. "Time as a river, always flowing, always there." He threw some cashews into his mouth. "Upstream to the future, downstream to the past. All of it, along with the present, existing simultaneously. You just have to float high enough above it, perhaps in the fifth dimension, to see what it really is. To see where to step in. And where to step out."

"Now that sounds very cool," Karen said with real enthusiasm. "Keep talking."

Isaac leaned back in his chair, hooked his hands behind his neck, and looked at the ceiling. "I see movement. Thick paint flowing, always flowing, over and under itself, forward and back. Wet-on-wet. Scraping through the layers of paint to reveal what's underneath, scraping through the layers of time. All there, but above and beneath each other, some seen, some almost seen, some overwhelmed and hidden by another layer of time."

I tried to catch his eye as he spoke my words, claimed my ideas, but he was fixated on the ceiling.

"Now that concept's got legs." Karen waved at *4D*. "And *4D* is a great beginning, your starting point for the real exploration of—"

"Who we are," Isaac interrupted. "Where we stand in relation to the cosmos. How it all might fit together."

"Let me know when you've got something to show. But think

about including more of this." Karen pointed to the crescents. "I just love the layering of meanings. The play with painting styles across time."

"Already on it," Isaac assured her.

She checked her watch, stood, and placed her glass on the table. "Well, this was a delightful afternoon. I thoroughly enjoyed myself." She turned to Markel. "I've got to catch the next shuttle, but if you want to take a cab with me out to the airport we can talk. Start to make the arrangements."

Markel was, of course, amenable. We all shook hands and congratulated each other; there were hugs and kisses and lots of laughing. As she walked out the door, Karen reminded me to call. I promised her I would.

When they were gone, Isaac drew me into a deep hug. "I'll never be able to thank you enough," he whispered into my ear.

"Hey, Karen Sinsheimer's willing to take a look at my stuff. That's thanks enough in my book."

He buried his head in my hair. "Never, never, ever be able to repay you."

"I'm not looking for repayment, Saac. Just for you to move forward." But the praise for *4D* reverberated in my ears.

Better than any of your previous work that I've seen, Karen had said.

It could be your best, Markel had echoed.

Ten

I do as Markel suggests and open three accounts at three differ-ent banks: two savings and a money market. I also buy a couple certificates of deposit, on the advice of the woman setting up one of the accounts, and put the check in my checking/debit card account at yet another bank; I have no separate business account as Markel had assumed. I write one check to the landlord, drop one in the mail to pay down my student loan, and head for Al's Art Supply with a blank one because I can't remember how much I owe. All of this feels really, really good. I'm thinking how great it's going to be to have a working camera on my phone.

Al's is on Shawmut Avenue, not far from my studio, and it's everything one would expect from an urban "little box" art store: a cramped, tiny footprint chock full of overstuffed racks, shelves, and row upon row of narrow paint drawers—all wrapped in the delicious aroma of turpentine, paint, and dust. A writer friend once told me that when she walks into a library anywhere in the world, the smell makes her feel instantly at home. That's what Al's does for me.

What is unexpected is Al. The first few times I came in, I thought Al was a clerk, that the real Al, the owner, who I pictured as an elderly, grizzly type, was off checking inventory in the back room. Even when she told me her name was Al, it took me a while to make the connection. Al as in Alvina. On the outside, she's a chic, handsome woman, and on the inside, she's a mother hen.

"Beautiful Claire!" she cries as I walk in the door. She steps from around her high counter and gives me a hug. "I figured you'd be in this week. That you must be getting short on supplies." She stands back. "I think you've lost weight. Are you forgetting to eat again? Do you want to blow away in the wind?" She sighs. "Of course, on you it looks fabulous."

"And on you it doesn't?"

Al's deep-coppery skin, extraordinary cheekbones, and willowy grace bring to mind those Kenyan runners who always win the Boston Marathon, although she claims to be the scion of American slaves. She has close-cropped hair and at least a half-dozen piercings in each ear, from which hang all manner of wondrous earrings.

After I settle up my account, I head toward the back of the store to pick up a few things I need to begin working on *Bath*. I'm nowhere near ready to start in on the actual painting, but as I study and prepare, I can be stripping the Meissonier, which, depending on the condition of the canvas, could take anywhere from a few days to a few weeks.

I grab some acetone for solvent and rectified petroleum for restrainer as well as a bunch of packages of cotton wool; Meissonier's painting is large, and I'm going to need to change cloths frequently to keep the canvas clean. I add a bottle of hydrogen peroxide and some blotting paper, figuring the old sizing will be yellowed and need bleaching. Who would have ever thought that Ellen Bonanno's authenticity obsession would come in so handy? During her Repro classes, we all rolled our eyes when she made us strip a canvas, knowing there was no way Repro would ever spring for such an expensive process.

When I actually start painting my version of *Bath,* I'm going to need everything from brushes to paint to varnish, but I haven't figured out exactly what kinds Degas used, so these will have to wait for a later trip. But I do pick up plenty of silver paint for Xavier before I head home.

When I get back to the studio, instead of starting to strip the Meissonier, I sit down in the chair in front of *Bath.* I lift the two books of Degas' sketches from their pile on the floor and begin to browse through them. But even as I switch from casual surfing to close examination, I don't see what I'm looking for. It's very weird. I've found a number of sketches of *Bath*'s Simone and Jacqueline, but I can't find any of Françoise. Degas was obsessive about his drawings, renowned for doing twenty or thirty studies for a single painting. So where are the studies for Françoise?

Of course, they must exist somewhere, or at least have existed at one time. Neither of my books claims to include every sketch Degas ever made, but one is called, *Edgar Degas: Sketches and Drawings, 1875–1900,* which is when Degas did his bather series. Degas is also well known for using the same models, even the same sketches, in multiple paintings. And while he would change the composition of each work, the same model, often in quite similar poses, would show up from one painting to the next. This constancy gives his series paintings an extraordinary cohesiveness.

I find what appear to be a few compositional drawings for *Bath,* but while Simone and Jacqueline are identical to the women in the painting in front of me, Françoise is not. In the sketch, Not-Françoise has a different body, and she's standing rather than sitting, creating an asymmetrical composition, which is how the vast majority of Degas' paintings are balanced. I wish the sketch had more than just a few lines for a face.

Could there be a sixth *After the Bath*? It's not unheard of to discover an original painting stuffed in someone's attic hundreds of years after it was painted. Or, more likely, Degas may have planned to do a sixth but never did. I focus on finding more differences between the two women. In the painting in front of me, Françoise is sturdy and coarse-looking, as are almost all of Degas' bathers, but his sketches of Not-Françoise depict a smaller and more delicate woman with a tiny waist. Although I can't be sure as the face is only roughed in, the model in the sketches doesn't appear to be as pretty as the model in the painting, so it's possible Degas just replaced her with someone more attractive. But then, where are the sketches for the final Françoise?

I study his drawings, study *Bath,* do it again. I go to my Degas book piles and find more of his bathers, all of whom are hefty, not a single waist among them. And as before, there are quite a few drawings and paintings of Simone and Jacqueline but no sign of Françoise.

Boston's Museum of Fine Arts couldn't be more different from the Gardner. From its grand entrances flanked by Corinthian columns to its ultramodern additions, there's an overwhelming sense of brightness, openness, awe. Towering ceilings and wide sweeping spaces filled with both artificial and natural light flatter the artworks and allow the visitor to experience them to their fullest. There's no clutter, lots of comfortable benches, and you're allowed to use pens. Cameras even.

The MFA owns over seventy Degas paintings, drawings, prints, and sculptures. About a dozen works are oil on canvas, but only five of these are on display when I go over. The rest are on loan or in storage.

My favorite of the five is *At the Races in the Countryside.* It's a portrait of a young husband and wife sitting in a carriage with their infant and wet nurse under a luminous blue sky, which takes up the entire top half of the painting. A few tiny horses and tents are scattered in the far background, giving the image both depth and a cheerful attitude. Although considered part of his horseracing series, there's barely any racing imagery in the painting. Degas was a well-known jokester, and I'm sure he was goofing on someone when he gave it its title.

In contrast to the airy, bucolic feel of *Races,* the other four paintings—two portraits of Degas' father, one of his sister and brother-in-law, and one of an aunt with her daughters—are all darkly painted with rich, emotional undertones of sadness and separateness. While he never married and rumor has it that he had few dates, either male or female, Degas was supposedly a very faithful and loving member of his large, extended family. Yet, looking at the grimness of these portraits, one has to wonder.

But I'm not here to enjoy the paintings or to psychoanalyze Degas. I'm here to study Degas' composition, his brushstrokes and painting techniques, his use of line, shadow, light, and movement. Although I have the original at home, my painting will be better if I immerse myself in as much Degas as I can.

Three of the paintings are hung in the Impressionist Gallery, one in the Nineteenth-Century European Gallery, and the last in the rotunda connecting to Old Masters. The galleries are adjacent, and I walk from one painting to the next, then back around again, and then again. I want to get a sense of the five as a whole, as the work of a single master, before I start studying their details.

As always, when I'm surrounded by Degas' work, I'm filled with admiration for the man, with an overwhelming joy at being in this moment, in the presence of such greatness. A visual orgasm. I once heard an interview with a musician who said he didn't get art museums, that they left him cold. He claimed he was too auditory and museums didn't make any noise. I'd rather be dead than feel like that.

I'm touched by Degas' artful use of asymmetry to catch the viewer off guard, to bring her in, then to reveal so much. In *Edmondo and Thérèse Morbilli,* his solemn brother-in-law dominates the image while Degas' sister is smaller, slighter, sadder. Yet the way she touches her husband's shoulder, the way she leans into him, shows that she's not saddened by him, but along with him. In *Duchesa di Montejasi,* his homely aunt is alone in the right two-thirds of the painting, while her two daughters are pushed closely together—whispering? sharing confidences their mother has no part of?—in a narrow slice at the left.

His work is astounding. The way he creates light from within and without, faces glowing with life where there is only canvas and paint. The way he captures movement with the tilt of a head or the hem of a dress drifting off the edge of the canvas. His use of dark and light values to create texture, depth, and shadow. How he seizes an unselfconscious moment of everyday life, like the mother and wet nurse in *Races* pressed together as they proudly gaze at the infant, then sends it galloping away.

I settle in with the paintings, taking notes on Degas' brushstrokes, the thickness of his paints, his juxtapositions, his signatures, his well-drawn lines, and the saturation of his colors. Anything I can find that will help me better understand *Bath.* I pull my trusty Nikon from my backpack and shoot a dozen photographs of each of the five paintings: from across the room, from medium distance, from as close as I can get without setting off an alarm.

Actually, I do set off an alarm, but only once. A guard gives me an annoyed, reprimanding look, and I hold up my hands. "Sorry," I mouth. This does nothing to appease her, and she begins to follow me through the galleries, daring me to put my foot across the line again.

My camera's got a powerful macro setting, and the close-ups of Degas' brushstrokes are almost works of art in and of themselves. Unfortunately, one of the characteristics of his earlier classical painting style is a lack of visible brushstrokes, but not even Degas can hide every stroke.

I take a few steps forward, as close to *Edmondo and Thérèse* as I can get without tripping the alarm. The guard stands right behind me. I lean even closer to the painting, making sure to keep my feet behind the red line, and snap a photo.

Isn't there someone in here more worthy of stalking than me? A kid with greasy fingers? A purse snatcher? A dangerous criminal plotting a robbery? Then it occurs to me that the guard is probably doing her job a hell of a lot better than I'm giving her credit for. In all likelihood, I *am* the most dangerous criminal in the building.

Eleven

As soon as I get home from the MFA, I whip the sheet off *Bath,* wanting to see it immediately after studying the others. As my eyes fall on the painting, though, my stomach clenches. It takes my mind a moment to catch up with my body, and I realize I'm feeling dread.

I drop to the chair in front of her. What the hell am I dreading? I remember my very first reaction to *Bath*: *This is not a real Degas.* But that's ridiculous. There's no way this painting is a forgery. Or is there? I think about John Myatt and Han van Meegeren and Ely Sakhai. It's not as if it hasn't been done before. And then there's the missing Françoise sketches.

I stare at *Bath,* then close my eyes and envision the five Degas I just studied. I lean close and examine the paint. It's fractured with craquelure, as it should be. Over decades, liquids evaporate and paint shrinks, while humidity and temperature changes cause the wooden stretchers to expand and contract. These phenomena cause tiny webs of cracks to form. And this looks to me to be roughly a hundred years worth of cracks, which is about right.

I turn the painting over and study the back of the canvas. It appears to have been made in the late nineteenth century. There are signs of oxidation along the edge of the stretchers that hold the linen taut, and in places, the fibers have become brittle and slightly rotten. Generally, any oil-on-canvas work over two hundred years old has to be transferred to new stretchers because of this type of deterioration. My guess is *Bath*'s got another seventy-five or so years to go. Again, just about right.

The stretchers themselves are soft in places from decay. The tacks are rusty, as are the small leather squares that have protected the canvas from this rust for all those years. And there's quite a bit of dust between the stretchers and canvas. I pull out the Meissonier and turn it over. It looks very similar.

Although oil paint dries enough in a couple of weeks to take another layer of glazing, it can be fifty to seventy-five years before all the liquid has evaporated and the surface is completely dry and hard. In Ellen Bonanno's fanatical Repro classes, she showed us a test to ascertain if a painting is younger than fifty. I grab a piece of cotton wool and soak it in alcohol. I can't believe I'm doing this.

I approach *Bath,* still turned to its back side. I find a spot where paint has leaked over and hold the alcohol swab just above the surface: if the paint is new, the alcohol fumes will cause it to soften, to desaponify. I position the swab about a half inch from the canvas, hold my breath. The paint remains unchanged. I press a finger to the spot. Hard as a rock.

I hesitate, then tap the swab directly on the paint. I look at the cotton wool. Completely clean. I do the same with the Meissonier. Same results. I return the painting to the easel and once again take my seat in front of it. It passed all my tests: craquelure, oxidation, soft stretchers, brittle linen fibers, rusted nails, dust, and now the alcohol test. It appears to be the real thing.

But, as I've learned from my research, a painting can be stripped down to its sizing, a glue mixture brushed directly onto the bare canvas, which roughens the canvas and keeps the layers of paint from detaching themselves. When the old paint is removed, the fractures created over time remain. And when the forger applies new paint over this fissured sizing, the bumpy skeleton necessary to create the craquelure is retained. Tacks can be rusted by spending a couple of weeks in water. Old wood to make stretchers isn't difficult to come by. Lavender oil can be substituted for linseed oil, which will allow the paint to harden in about twenty years. Or high-tech ovens based on van Meegeren's techniques can set it in hours.

There's no doubt that *Bath* is a marvelous work, rich and true. The idea that even the most expert of forgers could have produced it is hard to believe. Markel didn't notice anything wrong with it, and he has a much finer eye than I do. Although, as I know all too well, people see what they expect to see. Including the so-called experts.

I decide it doesn't hurt to play devil's advocate. What if, for argument's sake, some incredibly talented forger did produce the *Bath* sitting in front of me? Someone like John Myatt or Han van Meegeren? Thousands of forged paintings have been purchased for millions of dollars and hung on museum walls. Many of them still are. Couldn't something like that have happened here?

Or maybe *Bath* is a high-quality contemporary forgery. Unlikely, if it's been hanging in the Gardner Museum for over a hundred years. On the other hand, what if the original was stolen at some earlier time and this one hung in its place? But someone would have noticed the change—curators, historians, guards, patrons.

It could be a forgery made after the painting was stolen in the heist. Someone could be doing to Markel what Markel is doing to his unscrupulous collector. But I have to assume that Markel had the smarts and the resources to determine its authenticity before he agreed to broker it.

That leaves a nineteenth-century forgery. But Degas was alive when Isabella Gardner purchased the painting, and she most likely bought it directly from him. According to the little I know of her, she was a woman who would not have been easily fooled. Nor would her dealer, Bernard Berenson, considered in his day to be America's leading expert on European painters.

So, again, the only possible conclusion is that the painting in front of me is a real Degas, painted by the master in the 1890s, sold to Isabella Stewart Gardner soon after it was finished. *Bath* met the standards of every analysis I did and countered every point against authenticity I could come up with.

Relieved, I cover it with the sheet and head over to Jake's.

AT THE BAR, I order a shot of tequila. Despite all my tests, arguments, and counterarguments, there's something itching at the back of my brain, unpleasantly so, and I want to stop scratching at it.

Maureen raises an eyebrow as she pulls out the bottle. "Bad day?"

I shrug. "Same old."

Mike, Rik, and Small look at me sympathetically.

"I've got some news that'll make you feel even worse," Danielle says.

All five of us roll our eyes.

But Danielle doesn't get it. "It's fucking Crystal Mack again."

"No," Small moans.

"The Danforth." Danielle.

"Christ. She's going to be insufferable." Rik.

"How does the Danforth even know about her?" Mike.

"I'm guessing *ArtWorld*," I say. "They just had that big contest.

Trans. Remember? One of the Danforth curators was a judge. Also the Whitney."

"I wouldn't mind so much if she were any good." Small.

"How long before she's down here?" Danielle looks at her watch. "An hour? Maybe half that. Wouldn't want to let too much time go by without using us to shine herself up."

Rik throws his arm around me. "Nothing for you, Bear?"

"The Whitney owns three Cullions," I say, trying not to sound bitter and probably not succeeding.

Mike turns to Rik. "Let's hear the rest on that trip to Paris."

"You didn't tell me you were going to Paris," I cry, with mock annoyance, more than happy to piggyback on Mike's thoughtful change of subject. "What's up with that?"

"Just found out, but it's for work, not pleasure. I started to tell Mike and Small. We're doing an exhibit on Belle's acquisitions from her travels to Europe. My boss took Italy. Sheryl's going to London, and I got stuck with Paris." He grins.

Danielle holds her thumb and forefinger a quarter of an inch apart. "Can you hear my teeny, tiny violin weeping?"

"Didn't you tell me Isabella Gardner was a Venice freak?" I ask.

"Paris was her second favorite."

"That stuff about her walking lions down Tremont Street?" Small asks. "And about wearing a GO RED SOX hat to the symphony. Are those true?"

Rik crosses his arms over his chest. "It's really annoying that that's the extent of what most people know about Belle. She was the first great American art collector, man or woman, and she's remembered because of a couple of lion cubs and a headband."

We all laugh at his pomposity. He gives us the finger, along with a wink.

"So, how'd she get to be the first great American collector?" I jump in before the conversation can turn. "Man or woman."

Rik scowls at me. "She studied and had a great eye. And, of course, she had Bernard Berenson."

"Not to mention tons of money," Danielle says.

"And what about all those forgeries that were all over the place back then?" I ask. "Before they had all these high-tech ways of figuring it out?"

"I heard Michelangelo used to borrow paintings from his friends," Small pipes in, "copy them, then return the copies and keep the originals for himself."

"Well, that would have worked out great for his friends," Mike says. "They'd own a Michelangelo."

"They may not have had all the technology we have now," Rik says, irritated that we're not taking his Belle seriously enough. "But they still had plenty of smart and talented experts. Art historians, critics, dealers, authenticators. They got it right most of the time."

"Must've been what happened at MoMA. All those smart and talented Isaac Cullion experts," Danielle says.

Twelve

THREE YEARS EARLIER

I didn't go to the MoMA opening. I had an exam the next morning. Initially, I was so bummed to miss the opening that Isaac tried to get me out of the test, but when he couldn't, I found I didn't mind all that much. I wanted to be with Isaac, share in his moment of glory, hobnob with the rich and famous. But I wasn't sure I wanted to listen to everyone raving about *4D*, about Isaac's great talent. Of course, it would be quite the rush to see one of my paintings in MoMA. And it wouldn't be.

So I stayed home and studied. But I had trouble concentrating. I kept picturing what Isaac must be doing at every moment. Here he was, pacing the empty gallery, scoping out everyone else's work. Waiting. Then the crowds. From silence to pandemonium. The beautiful people strutting. The critics clucking. Then the congratulations, the glad-handing, the cooing, the fussing, the sucking up. And, if all went as Markel expected, Isaac being feted as the new of-the-moment man.

Isaac called a bit after midnight, and I could hear the drinks he'd had. "The museum arranged for a fabulous suite. Views of the park. Full minibar." The rattle of ice. "I'm exhausted, but I had to talk to you."

"Was it wonderful? How'd it go?"

"Only thing that could've made it better was you. Oh, babe, I thought about you all evening. Wanted to share it with you. A victory for both of us."

"This is your time, Saac. I'll get mine soon enough."

"Very soon. Very, very soon. Breakfast with Karen tomorrow. We'll talk."

I was filled with a warm rush of gratification. This was the type of relationship I'd always dreamed of. Mutual respect. Mutual support. Great love. "Tell me about the show. Any indication on the reviews? Any noise on a sale?"

He mumbled something I didn't understand, followed by, "—meeting with the committee next week."

"Committee? What committee?"

"Acquisitions."

"At MoMA?"

"Karen said there's interest in buying it."

I was stunned. "MoMA wants to buy *4D*?"

"For their permanent collection."

"Isaac, that's wonderful, astonishing. It's—"

"Don't want to talk about it. Jinx it."

I was well aware of Isaac's many superstitions and laughed. "Okay, okay, we'll wait until it happens."

"Wouldn't even have a chance of happening without you."

ONE OF MY paintings was hanging in the Museum of Modern Art. In New York City. Part of the permanent collection.

The pinnacle of any artist's career, a peak few live to see. And here I was: twenty-eight, alive, and bursting with work, full of hope for my future.

I admit, sometimes it was tough to watch Isaac get all the acclaim. But mostly, I was just so thrilled for him, thrilled with his improving mood, thrilled with our plans for our life together, that it didn't really matter. And he'd managed to get Karen Sinsheimer to promise to review my slides the day they arrived. As I'd told him, it was his moment, and I was willing to wait for mine.

It was all so mindboggling. Dizzying actually. *4D* was a hit. A huge hit. It had somehow touched a nerve—and not just in the art world, in the general public as well—and was streaking toward iconic. Like Andy Warhol's soup cans. Or maybe it was just the Internet. Viral marketing and all that.

Whatever the cause, Isaac Cullion and *4D* were linked, and they were stars. He was on the *Today Show,* and *4D* was on the cover of *ArtWorld*. We joked that *4D* had almost achieved refrigerator-magnet status. A week later, MoMA started selling them in their gift shop.

Then Isaac began to believe his own press. The more he talked about *4D* and the new paintings he was "working" on that it had inspired, the more he seemed to buy into his own lies. Only I knew he wasn't working on any new paintings. He was as blocked as he'd been before *4D*. Maybe more so.

Isaac was fragile at best, unstable at worst, and the situation was sending him to the wrong end of his continuum. But now, for the first time, I saw his temper. He snapped brushes in two and threw canvases at the walls. He stayed locked up in his studio for days, refusing to speak to anyone, including me, screaming at any poor soul brave enough to knock on his door.

And then we started to fight. First over little things, then over bigger ones, but never over *4D*—the elephant that was driving him crazy and driving us apart. I loved him and wanted to help him. I alone understood his situation, knew the depths of his lies, appreciated what playing the imposter does to your psyche. Because, of course, I was living the mirror image. Not that Isaac ever acknowledged this. And not that I ever brought it up.

It wasn't his fault. Any more than it was mine. We'd never thought about what would happen if *4D* became a phenomenon. And why would we? It was a one-in-a-million shot. So I decided that if I was patient, if I waited long enough, he would make peace with it. And maybe I would, too.

Instead, one day, he showed up at my studio in tears. He told me I was his soul mate, that he loved me more than he loved himself, more than life itself. Then he told me he was breaking up with me. Going back to Martha.

"You need someone younger, happier, healthier," he said.

"That's ridiculous," I said, figuring that one of his sulks was in control. "I don't want someone younger. Not even happier and healthier, although that does have its appeal." I reached over to hug him. "I want you. Just as you are."

He jumped from the couch. "You deserve a man who'll appreciate you, love you the way you should be loved."

"You just told me you loved me more than life itself." I was trying for levity, but there was something about the look in his eye, the slump in his shoulders, that told me this wasn't an ordinary Isaac mood swing.

He took a few steps away from me. "I can't, I won't, be the one to stop you from finding true happiness."

And then I understood what was happening. "Bullshit," I yelled, standing and coming toward him. "That's a load of grandiose crap."

"No, no. I'm hurting you," he said, backing even farther away. "Every day. And I don't want—"

"This isn't about hurting me," I snapped, furious at his purposeful self-deception, his cowardice, his excuses. "This is about what hurts you. It hurts you every time you look at me because you know that I know the truth."

Isaac stood silently, his head bowed, as I gathered up everything he'd ever given me, including *Orange Nude,* and threw it into the hallway. "Get out and take your shit with you, you asshole," I ordered.

And he did.

Thirteen

As I walk home from Jake's, I consider all the times the experts have been wrong: the earth is flat, women's brains are inferior to men's, a black man will never be elected president of the United States. The list is endless. It's almost as if, in time, everything we're convinced is true will be proven false. Like *Bath*? Could the experts have just gotten it wrong? I think about Danielle's comment about MoMA. Of course they could have.

Maybe someone else painted *Bath* and Degas claimed it as his own, which seems hard to believe of such a talented artist. Although, this was actually pretty common during the seventeenth and eighteenth centuries, when students copied the master's work, and sometimes to make money, the master signed them. But the practice had largely died out by Degas' time. But then, there's Isaac Cullion.

When I get home, I once again review all the evidence, which overwhelmingly supports authenticity, but this doesn't quiet the uncertainty in my gut. This is a gut that's gotten me into trouble in the past. Like how I knew in my gut I was meant to live in Paris and then lasted barely three months. Like how I knew in my gut Isaac Cullion would never do anything to hurt me.

I stand and turn my back to *Bath,* then I whip around, trying to catch a precognitive impression. I do it in the other direction. I turn off the lights, turn them up again. I stare without blinking for as long as I can. I hang off the back of the couch to view it upside down.

I sit down in the chair and look some more. Mentally, I circle the Impressionist and European Galleries at the MFA, through the rotunda, and back again. Degas' paintings whirl in my mind's eye. I feel their psychological power, the commanding draw of their asymmetry, the light pulsing from both within and without. I pull out the notes I took when I was there, read them again.

I close my eyes. I see the well-defined shadows of the umbrella in *At the Races* falling on the mother and nanny, expressing the joy of high noon on a sunny, summer day. I feel the guilty pleasure of watching, as if through a keyhole, the family dynamics in *Duchesa di Montejasi with Her Daughters.* I step into the depth created by the foreshortened figures and the blocked-out furniture receding off the canvas in *Edmondo.*

I open my eyes and stare at the painting in front of me. At Simone and Jacqueline and especially at Françoise. The symmetry bothers me. Françoise's stiffness bothers me, as do the unremarkable shadows around her. As does the lack of interaction between the three women.

I remove the SD card from the camera and plug it into my computer. A couple of clicks of the mouse, and a few of the photographs I shot at the MFA drop into the tray. It's clear that only the close-ups are going to be of any use. I print a few more brushstroke photos and sit down to compare them, but the individual brushstrokes in both *Bath* and the photographs are barely discernible.

A painter's brushstrokes are as unique as a person's handwriting, and this fact has been used to determine genuine versus fake for centuries. It seems that it's the same with writers: Once an author has developed a style—use of language, sentence structure, a favorite verb or adjective—it remains amazingly constant over time. I reprint the photos with a tighter focus.

I rummage through a few drawers, find my jewelers' magnifying loupe, and put it to my eye. Yes, at this magnification, some of the brushstrokes are visible, but not all that many. If I were dealing with almost any of Degas' later paintings, or those of his buddies Manet, Pissarro, or Cassatt, there would be plenty to see, as these artists often put down broad, thick strokes of paint. But when ten or twenty layers of glazing are applied, the effect is one of smoothness and translucence. And that's what I have here.

I sift through the photographs until I find one where the strokes are close in size to those in *Bath*. I hold it up against the painting, move it around, look for similarities and differences. There's not much to compare.

Then I notice that in the center of the image a few brushstrokes are visible. I cut the photo in half and press the edge against a spot in the lower left-hand corner of *Bath* where Jacqueline's upper arm also contains visible brushstrokes. I put the jewelers' loupe to my eye and shift back and forth between the photo and the painting. Although I'd need two paintings side-by-side to be certain, the two do appear to be the work of the same man. Still, I'm not satisfied.

THE NEXT DAY, the bus—that wonderful Silver Line— gets stuck in traffic, and I'm late for juvy. This is really bad, as the boys, youths, will be kept in their cells until I arrive, which will not make them happy. When I finally get there, Kimberly, the way-too-pretty social worker, brings them all into GE 107.

GE 107 is in the basement. The ceiling is low, and huge steam pipes hug it, hissing dampness. Anyone over five-foot-seven, which is a good percentage of the boys, has to be on constant guard to avoid being scalded by the hot metal; at least one forehead is stamped with a red burn at the end of every class. There aren't any windows, often not enough chairs, and both of the tables are wobbly. Still, the kids have an amazing ability to block out their surroundings and surrender to their inner artist. I suppose blocking out their surroundings is something most of them have been doing since day one.

"We've been waiting for you," Reggie whines. "It's been, like, an hour." I'm fifteen minutes late.

Johan turns to Kimberly. "Does that mean we get an extra hour to paint?"

Kimberly claps her hands. "Okay, Ms. Roth's going to pass out the paints and brushes." She points to the three guards standing in the corners of the room. "We're triple-staffed today." It's unnecessary for her to explain why.

I look over at a table holding brushes and about thirty small cans of paint. I can't see what colors they are. "Did the silver paint clear screening?"

"We really need for you to be here on time," Kimberly says in a low voice. "The youths get edgy when there are unexpected changes." She looks over at the guards. "As you can imagine, that isn't a good thing."

"Sorry." I feel terrible. "The traffic on Washington Street was stopped dead. The bus couldn't get through." I'm surprised that she's calling me out on this. I hadn't expected her to last a week in here, let alone get stern with me. "Sorry," I say again, warming to her. "I'll leave even earlier in the future."

"Good," she says, and turns to the boys. "Everyone stand in front of your own drawing. Anyone who knows that he wants to start with red, yellow, or blue, raise your hand."

The boys shuffle for position, and two of the guards step closer.

"No physical contact," Kimberly orders.

Last week, after the boys finished their drawings, we projected all the images on the wall, and the boys traced them in charcoal. I worked with them to fit the images together to make an appealing whole, backing off when they resisted, trying to let them work it out. Kimberly had to step in a couple of times, and Manuel, who didn't have a completed drawing, got kicked out for swearing at Christian. After the boys went back to their cells, I stayed to outline their figures in black permanent marker and wash the charcoal away. They did a damn good job.

Ten are here today. Nine with drawings to paint and Manuel, whom I'm surprised to see. He stands to the side of the mural, arms crossed, looking tough. It's clear from his shifting gaze that he needs a task.

I pull Kimberly aside. "Manuel's going to have to work with somebody," I say. "Who should, or shouldn't, it be?" There are lots of factions at Beverly Arms, mostly based on which gang the boys are in on the outside—or aspiring to be a member of. The wrong pairing can create a high-tension situation.

"He's not from the area," Kimberly says. "Doesn't hang with anyone. He's had training as a fighter, an uncle who's a heavyweight or something. After he put a youth twice his size in the hospital, everyone stays out of his way."

"Anyone he gets along with?"

Kimberly grins. "I'd say he's an equal-opportunity hater. But don't put him with Christian or Johan."

I look at the nine boys lined up in front of the mural. All but Xavier have their hands up. I had Al send the bulk of the paints and brushes a few weeks ago so that the materials would clear contraband screening before we needed them. But because I sent the cans of silver later, they had to go through a separate testing. The guard, Rodney, one of the few nice ones, couldn't promise me that the screening would be finished by today, but he said he'd try to push it through.

I smile when I see the cans of silver on the table. Thanks, Rodney. I turn and give Xavier, who's watching me solemnly— these kids are always expecting to get screwed—a thumbs up. He grins and starts fooling around with Reggie.

"Xavier and Reggie," Kimberly calls. "Shut it down."

"How many blues?" I ask, as Kimberly hands the cans out to the boys. "Yellows? Reds?" I give Xavier two cans of silver paint. "You've got a lot of Buds there."

He doesn't answer, just ducks his head shyly.

There are three sizes of brushes—all with square, rather than pointed ends—but I only hand out the smallest, instructing the kids first to outline the inside of the permanent marker before starting on the larger spaces. Within minutes, the room is silent. The concentration is palpable.

I walk over to Xavier. "Is it okay if Manuel helps you with all your cans? You could be at this for months without him."

Xavier shrugs without turning from his painting.

I hand Manuel a brush. He takes it but doesn't move. Xavier, who's already completed outlining three cans, points to the cans farthest away from the ones he's working on. I turn to Kimberly, and she nods her approval.

Kimberly and I walk up and down the line, helping where it's needed: handing out other paint, different brushes, offering suggestions. The guards watch the boys closely.

I mix up a couple of cans of purple, orange, and green and open up a white. This is going amazingly well. I'd been discouraged from doing a group project, told it would be a set-up for hostility, but so far so good. Not that I'm complacent. I've been coming to Beverly long enough to know that it takes only a second for things to blow.

Which is exactly what happens. Suddenly, Manuel punches Xavier in the stomach. Xavier, a foot taller than Manuel, stumbles backward, hits the wall, and crumples to the ground. With lightning speed, two guards have each boy's arms twisted behind his back, his hands cuffed. The third grabs Reggie as he starts to come to Xavier's rescue and does the same.

"Everyone up against the wall with your hands up," Kimberly orders, pulling out her walkie-talkie. "Now!" The other boys turn and face the wall, hands raised.

"Fuck you," Manuel screams at Xavier, as he's being pulled across the room by the guard. "You don't know what the fuck you're talking about."

"They're my cans, asshole," Xavier retorts, "and you're fucking them up. You're going the wrong way."

I watch as Manuel, Xavier, and Reggie are removed from the dayroom. Two new guards race into the room. Kimberly motions that she's got it under control. They look dubious and post themselves on opposite ends of the line.

"Okay," Kimberly says. "Starting at the front of the line. Christian. Close your paint cans and put them on the table. Brushes, too. In that tray Ms. Roth has there. Then go stand on the other side of the room, hands up. Johan, you're next. Then Sean."

The boys do as she says. When they're all on the other side of the room, the guards march them out single file. Everyone stares straight ahead. No one says anything.

I drop into a chair and run my fingers through my hair.

Kimberly sits down next to me. "You okay?"

"I've seen it before."

"It's so close to the surface."

"Do you know why Manuel hit him? Were they arguing?"

"I just heard Xavier tell him that he wanted him to paint in the other direction so that it would match his own cans."

I walk over to Xavier's cans and squat down to look. "Was he angry?"

"You know Xavier, he's usually pretty low confrontation."

I think about asking her why Xavier's in here, then remind myself that I don't want to know. "So Manuel just belted him?"

"He's got some anger issues."

"You think?" I compare Xavier's cans to Manuel's. Both boys did a pretty good job of outlining, and although the inside of Xavier's cans are a bit neater than Manuel's, there isn't all that much difference. Then I look closer and see that Xavier's brushstrokes go from right to left, and Manuel's from left to right.

"Is one of the boys left-handed?" I ask Kimberly.

She thinks. "You know, now that you mention it, I'm pretty sure Manuel is. Yeah, yeah, he is. He was bragging that being left-handed made him a better boxer. Why? Does it make a difference?"

I don't answer. I just stare at the beer cans.

WHEN I GET home, I print every close-up photograph I have and cut them wherever there's a discernible brushstroke. I take *Bath* from the easel and lay her on the floor, move the little photo pieces around her surface, looking for matches. I find a few, some better than others. I move them around some more. When I'm satisfied, I lean back on my haunches and survey my work.

Almost everywhere, the paint's too smooth to make any determination, but there are a few places, mostly in or around Françoise, where a difference can be seen. In each of the MFA Degas photos, all the brushstrokes go right to left. But in *Bath,* a number of them go left to right.

I lean closer to make sure I'm seeing what I think I'm seeing. There is no doubt, and a low whistle escapes my lips. I knew it the first minute Markel unwrapped the painting. Knew it, but refused to believe it. My gut was right. This *Bath* is not Degas' *Bath.* It was painted by someone else. A left-handed someone else.

From the pen of

ISABELLA STEWART GARDNER

July 1, 1886
Paris, France

My dearest Amelia,

Only six more weeks and we shall be together again! I cannot wait
to see my very own grown-up married girl! You must indulge me in
my sentimentality, as you are as dear to me as any daughter could be.
In fact, as far as I am concerned, you *are* my daughter, even if I am not
old enough to have actually given birth to you.

But you have been very naughty to have purchased so many
furnishings without me. I shall be bringing a few items from our
travels that I hope will find happy homes in your apartments. I'm
glad to hear that Sumner allows you full reign over the household. I
only wish your uncle would do the same as he is always fretting that I
spend too much money.

And please, please, please, do not pay any attention to "Town
Topics" unless it is to laugh at their overblown prose. I am not sorry
that men desire my company nor that I enjoy the company of the

most talented of them. And I have seen none of their wives "scolding and stomping their feet" when the men pay me attention. Far from it, Maud Elliott and Julia Ward Howe are just as pleased to attend my soirees and dinners as are their "giddy and wayward husbands"!

And the piece about my secret rendezvous with Frank Crawford, well, he is almost young enough to be my son! But I shall not be the one to spoil such a good story with the truth. Do not distress yourself over the words of this silly rag, especially not on my behalf. I say if people like to believe such things, please don't deny them their pleasure.

You ask if I have had any further adventures with Mr. Edgar Degas, and indeed I have. I told you in my last letter that he had invited me to his studio. Well, my dear, I went to that wonderfully bohemian Montmartre, to 21 rue Pigalle (where he both works and lives) to be exact, and it was indeed an experience.

Edgar is such a complex and interesting man. Everything about him is a contradiction. His pictures are selling well and his name is everywhere, yet his apartment is so small that he must use his studio for his dressing room! His face is rather homely, but his posture and his clothes are so fine that one hardly takes notice. His eyes are dark and hooded, but in them one can see the wondrous and tortured soul of a true artist. And when he throws back his head and laughs (the gentleman is quite the card), he is most attractive.

He is the most meticulous of painters, and yet his studio is a jumble of confusion. Aside from his clothes strewn hither and yon and the usual artists' paraphernalia, the floor is loaded with the most unusual things: printing presses, bathtubs, cellos, wax figurines, and even a broken-down piano. He claims he is unable to discard any object as he never knows what might be useful to him. Another contradiction is that although he remains a bachelor at fifty years of age, he is quite a flirt! I was charmed.

Edgar is in the last stages of preparation for an exhibition this Fall with the Misters Bracquemond, Forain, Monet, Gauguin, Pissarro, and Rouart, artists for whom I have little appreciation. And I am sorry to say, my dear Amelia, that their influence is apparent. The drawing in Edgar's latest work is impeccable, his asymmetrical composition beyond perfection. And such bold and unusual viewpoints of female nudes engaged in their toilette. From above even! But I cannot say the same for his actual painting. For, to my great disappointment, he is working in pastels and appears to be leaning toward that horrid Impressionist style that makes me want to put on a pair of glasses.

Although I had taken him to task for turning his back on oil at Henry's table just a fortnight ago, I could not refrain from again expressing my feelings. I asked if he couldn't see what masterpieces the paintings would be if he had painted them in the style of the Old Masters, in his own style of only a decade ago.

He told me he had far too much work to do to wait weeks between each glazing layer, that this was the business of a young man with an inheritance, not an old one without. When I protested, his eyes twinkled and he asked which did I think was an untruth: that he was an old man or that he had no money? Although I was vexed that he would make a joke over such an issue, it was difficult to remain serious when he refused to be. And so we laughed.

He then hustled me out of the studio to the Café Guerbois, where there was so much gay conversation that we were unable to finish our discussion. I, however, shall continue to pursue my efforts to discourage him in this folly in the future.

Your Uncle Jack and I leave Paris tomorrow for Venice. And although I am, as always, thrilled to be headed to my most beloved city, I yearn for home, for the cool breezes of Green Hill, and for your company. My warm remembrance to your dear brothers.

I am your loving,
Aunt Belle

Fifteen

I'm not sure how long I've been squatting here, but my quadriceps are crying for mercy. *Bath* lies on the floor, cut-up photos sprawled on the canvas. Gingerly, I stand, stretch, then lift the painting, ignoring the triangles and squares of brushstrokes that float to the floor. Once it's back on the easel, I drop into the chair in front of it.

Now that I've admitted the truth to myself, I see evidence of forgery everywhere. The brushstrokes aren't as refined as Degas' always are, and there's a tentativeness to them. Depth doesn't flow from the focal point of the painting out to the edges and then beyond; it feels narrow, constricted.

And Françoise, how could I have been so blind? Too stiff, with an aura of self-consciousness, as if she's aware of being watched, rather than caught in an unobserved moment. Even the signature is off. There's too much space between the "a" and "s".

I'm astonished I was able to fool myself for as long as I did. That I, a self-proclaimed Degas expert, could be so taken in. I felt the truth the first moment I set eyes on the painting, yet I convinced myself otherwise. And I'm not alone. If my assumption that this is the painting that hung at the Gardner is true—and what else could it be?—then the art historians, the critics, and the public were equally gullible. This is why there are so many successful forgers, plagiarizers, con men.

Although the Repro instructors were tasked with teaching us how to make an effective copy, almost all shared a fascination with actual forgery. One quoted Theodore Rousseau, an expert from the Met, as saying, "We can only talk about the bad forgeries, the ones that have been detected. The good ones are still hanging on museum walls." The instructor backed this up with a *New York Times* estimate that 40 percent of all the artworks presented for sale in any given year are forgeries. I assumed this was completely overblown. I don't now.

Poor *Bath*. She's a fake, but I'm a fool.

I have to tell Markel. I grab my cell and hit his number. Then I cancel the call. Maybe he already knows. Maybe that's why his explanation sounded too convenient: He wasn't telling me the truth. I toss the phone from one hand to the other. Could he be testing me, giving me a fake to see if I can tell the difference? But that would be a lot of effort for little purpose. Or maybe he's the one who's being tested. Or set up. In that case, I owe him the truth.

I hit his number again, and when he answers, I say, "We need to talk ovens." The cautious route seems best.

He chuckles. "You make it sound so exciting."

"Are you free to get together sometime soon? I'd like to get moving on this."

"How about in half an hour?" he says. "Say six? The Oak Room?"

I hesitate. Even though I made the call, I need more time to think this through.

"Or I could do it early next week," he offers. "I'm off to New York tomorrow."

"No, no, tonight's cool," I tell him. "I'll see you there at six."

The Oak Room is in the Fairmont Copley Plaza, a grand hotel that resembles a Renaissance palace. It should be tacky with its soaring marble columns, painted ceilings, and overdone gold filigree, but somehow it isn't. Although I've been in the hotel's lobby, I've never been to the Oak Room—it's a little rich for my pocketbook—but I've heard they serve the best lemondrop martinis in the city.

There's not much hanging in my closet that's appropriate for the Oak Room, but I do have a longish blue skirt I bought for an anniversary dinner with Isaac. I put it on. It's a bit big, but it'll do. I throw on a little white T-shirt to dress it down and sex it up.

I leave my studio and head north on Dartmouth Street. It's only six or seven blocks to Copley Square, but whenever I make this trip, I'm always struck by how these blocks span the urban socioeconomic spectrum. I walk by a row of warehouses with graffiti-laden loading docks abutting housing projects. Then past the old Cathedral church with its lopsided swing set sitting amid the amber sparkle of broken beer bottles.

What if I tell Markel about *Bath* and he cancels everything, including my show? What if he wants the money back? I finger my new cell phone and think about that red couch I saw marked down 70 percent in the furniture store across from my studio. I think about Xavier's silver paint and the five thousand dollars I've already spent. But it's not the money. I'd do this for free if it meant my paintings would hang in Markel G. And that the Gardner would get its masterpiece back. Although, now it's not so clear that this painting is a masterpiece.

The church blends into a chunk of rundown tenements, their high stoops filled with teenagers drinking and eyeing other teenagers drinking on other stoops. There are clusters of mothers too young to be mothers keeping watch—or not—over their children. The lovers groping at each other. The elderly in their short-legged beach chairs nodding off in the heat.

When I cross Washington Street, I officially exit edgy, up-and-coming SOWA and enter an almost-there district where the rents are double mine but only a fraction of what they'll be a few blocks up. In my neighborhood, there are one or two nice restaurants or stores per block, on Washington it's probably five or six, and when I come to Tremont, just about everything from steaks to manicures is overpriced. And yet, here there are still bits of sour-smelling garbage tucked into corners and more stoop-sitters defying the state's open-container law.

As I head north, the townhouses get nicer, with painted shutters and tiny, perfect gardens; the sidewalks get cleaner, and half the cars parked on the street are those small, black BMWs. By the time I hit the blocks closest to Copley Square, there are no stoop-sitters and no litter. Ah, the Back Bay.

"To our *Bath*." Markel raises his glass to mine.

He looks directly, guilelessly, at me. He's tan, fit, and seemingly quite pleased with himself. It strikes me that in all the years he was Isaac's dealer, I never noticed how attractive he was. In the past, every time I was with him, I was also with Isaac, and now I find myself wondering if he's involved with anyone. I know he's been divorced for quite a few years, which is good, but after Isaac, I strongly question my ability to judge a man's trustworthiness.

I watch him carefully for clues that will signal what I should tell him about the forgery. Except I have no idea what these clues might be. "She is a marvel." I touch my glass to his and take a sip.

We're sitting in a couple of overstuffed armchairs, pressed close together and tucked into the raised far corner of the Oak Room.

The air is redolent with the subtle smell of fine food. A piano plays softly in the opposite corner, and the acoustics hush everyone's words. It's almost as private as my studio, but much more luxuriant.

"So you're enjoying spending time with her?"

"And looking forward to getting down to painting. I've been researching the process, and if we've got to pass atomic absorption or mass spectrometry testing, I think the full glaze, bake, and varnish is the only way to go. And now with this new digital wavelet decomposition . . ." I hold my hands up. "There's really not much choice."

Markel rubs his chin. "If we assume there'll be that kind of scrutiny."

"Won't there?"

"Depends on the sophistication of the buyer."

"Even if there's only low-level testing, it'll be pretty easy to determine that the paint isn't completely dry. Seems to me we've got to bake it."

"Bake?"

"It sounds weird, but it works. You add a special chemical in the medium, then bake the canvas between layers. The combination of the two dries the paint the same way a couple hundred years would."

He ponders his drink. "Obviously," he says, thinking out loud, "the buyer isn't going to be a museum or an ethical collector. And in most of the developing world, where I'm pretty sure our buyer will come from, there isn't access to the same level of technology or to the top experts we have here . . . On the other hand, someone willing to purchase it, knowing its origin, could be savvy enough and paranoid enough to want to check it out thoroughly."

I see my opening. "Is that what you did?"

His face closes up, and he sits back in his chair. "Of course," he says, looking over my shoulder.

"All the tests?"

"So how much time will the oven save?" he asks.

"Months. Many of them. Is there a deadline?"

"No," he says. "Not really. Although, obviously, the sooner the better."

"You're the boss." I shrug. Does it really matter how I forge a forgery?

"So, what would you need?"

"The painting's three-foot-eleven by four-foot-ten. The oven in my kitchen is sixteen by eighteen inches, so that's not going to work."

"A kiln?"

"We don't need that kind of heat. I'm thinking a commercial oven. Like something used in a bakery. Wide enough to get the painting in and out, with digital temperature control and a digital timer." I pause. "Has there ever been any discussion that this *After the Bath* was painted by anyone other than Degas?"

He straightens up in his chair. "None that I know of." His look is hard and penetrating. "What's this all about?"

"I just want to know if anyone's going to come into this thinking it might be a fake right off the bat. About how we want to go about this. How much coverage we need."

"I'll check into the oven."

"Great. Thanks," I say. "But what if it actually was—"

Markel nods at my martini. "Drink up."

I do as he instructs. It's clear this discussion is over. "Whoever told me these were the best lemondrops in Boston wasn't kidding."

"Your friend, Crystal Mack."

"What?"

He laughs at my confusion. "I mean, Crystal's got to be the one who told you about the martinis. She loves them."

"Yeah, right." Not my favorite topic of conversation.

"You must be very proud of her."

I shrug. "She's not really a friend, more of an acquaintance."

"Oh." Markel's eyes crinkle, and I can tell he doesn't like her either.

"She's gotten a bit puffed up."

"And now the Danforth purchase is going to add another fifty pounds?"

"You've got that right," I agree. "We're hoping she's so impressed with herself that she'll shun lowly Harrison Avenue and hang exclusively up here in Back Bay."

Markel holds up both hands. "Please, anything but that."

"Hey, it was the Markel G *Local Artists at Work* show that pulled her out of SOWA. You've got only yourself to blame."

"The Danforth was because of the *ArtWorld* contest."

"It's never just a contest." I try to keep up my bantering tone.

"You entered." It's not a question.

"Yup. Sure did." I take another sip of my drink.

"You know one of the judges was from the Whitney, don't you? And that it had to be a unanimous decision?" He sighs. "The Whitney's always had its thing about Isaac."

There's no denying this shit still hurts.

"It's not your stuff," Markel says. "Your work is remarkable. Far superior to hers."

This doesn't make me feel any better.

"Isaac's been gone three years now," Markel says. "Grudges die down in time. Memories fade."

"I hadn't noticed."

"Few people are as stuffy as the Whitney."

I raise my glass and force a bright smile. "Let's hope so."

"I don't know exactly what went on with *4D* and MoMA," he says, "although I've always had my suspicions. Even at the time."

I blink. Is he telling me he believes I painted *4D*?

"But my opinion isn't what matters, and now's not the time to get into it." Markel takes my free hand and presses it between both of his. "The important thing here is that your show's going to make everyone forget what happened to Isaac Cullion."

I'm both comforted by his hands encircling mine—a kinship, past and present, a level of understanding—and keenly aware of his sexuality. "What if people boycott the show because of my name?"

"I don't want to sound as 'puffed up' as Crystal," Markel says. "But it'll be difficult for people to boycott a show at Markel G."

Sixteen

Last week, I estimated I had ten more hours on the Pissarro for Repro, but somehow I've managed to stretch it into three days. And I'm still not finished. I try to focus on the painting in front of me instead of the Meissonier nagging me from the back corner. I need to strip the canvas and get on with creating *Bath II*. But I keep finding distractions that I must attend to first.

There's research to complete on Degas' paints and brushes, how he mixed his pigments and mediums, issues to resolve about the best aging techniques—even though it's going to be a while before I need most of this information. Then there's laundry and visiting that red couch one more time before I make a final decision. There's e-mail to read, bills to pay, and of course, the fake Pissarro to finish.

And there are other things to consider. Like my decision not to tell Markel about *Bath*'s origins. Despite his arguments to the contrary, it's clear that my days as a pariah are far from over and that my only chance of getting out from under this art McCarthyism is a successful show at Markel G. It really pisses me off, the spiteful way I was treated, and the thought of a full payback is hard to resist. It occurs to me that if Markel loves my work as much as he claims, wouldn't he do my show even if I told him what I know? I dab a bit of chrome yellow on the edge of a flower. I'm pretty sure he would, but I'm too much of a coward to take the chance.

I step back, compare my result to the oversized Pissarro print taped to the wall and add one more dab. I reach my brush forward again, then stop before it touches the canvas. I'm at the point where I often start overthinking—and overpainting. A dangerous prospect that, at worst, can destroy a painting or, at least, create weeks of extra work. I lower the brush. I give the fake Pissarro a hard look, then drop the brush into a can of turpentine. A final coat of varnish after the paint is dry and it will be done.

Bath, covered with a sheet, sits on the other side of the studio. I hate that she isn't real, but I dig out the acetone, rectified petroleum, and packages of cotton wool I bought at Al's. I place the Meissonier on my worktable next to the solvent and restrainer and grab a couple of cloths. If everything goes well—if the canvas is in good shape, if the paint's easily removed and the old sizing isn't too yellow—I could be done in a few days. But if the situation is reversed, or if there are additional problems, I could be looking at weeks of stripping. After going through it in Ellen Bonanno's class, I know stripping will be my least favorite part of the whole process.

If I were doing this for Repro, my first step would be to buy a new canvas and size it myself with some flake-white mixed with oil so the canvas will be ready to grab the paint. But to paint a forgery that can pass expert inspection, I need period canvas, stretchers, and sizing. Carbon dating can't be fooled, so a high-quality forgery has to be painted on a canvas made at the same time as the original. And the sizing has to be kept intact because it retains the old fissures, the foundation the new paint will rest on. All Meissonier's varnish and paint layers have to be scraped away until the old sizing is revealed. Once the canvas is stripped of these layers, I can start building my own painting over the nineteenth-century canvas and sizing.

A traditional oil painting is a series of layers: sizing, underpainting, glazing—in which up to thirty translucent coats of paint are applied—and varnishing. The purpose of this is to control the refraction of light through the painting. Stripping is one of those paradoxical tasks that is both exacting and boring, requiring intense concentration dosed with high levels of tedium. Plus, my back's going to be killing me within a few hours.

I take a deep breath and bend to my task, a solvent-soaked cloth in one hand and a restrainer-soaked one in the other. I start on the lower right-hand corner, pressing the solvent to the canvas, wiping carefully to remove the paint, watching for any sign of white, which means I've hit the sizing. Damn. My left hand swoops down with the restrainer, arresting the solvent before it can dissolve the sizing. It's a finely tuned skill to use just the right amount of solvent, which eats away the paint, but not too much, which can liquefy the sizing or even worse, the bare canvas. I labor on, pressing and wiping, and often, all too often, restraining.

Hours later, cotton pieces lie around my bare feet like a paint-stained pond. My head pounds from the fumes, and my backbone feels as if it's going to break in a dozen places. But a solid patch of the painting is gone, exchanged for an unbroken sea of sizing—slightly yellowed, but nothing a bit of hydrogen peroxide won't take care of—full of tiny peaks and valleys that will produce a spider-webbing of craquelure in the final painting.

THE CANVAS IS completely stripped down to the sizing in three days, and I'm hunched over and moving around the studio like an old lady. I think about going to see Rik's massage guy,

New Age Bob, he calls him, but decide it's not worth the money. I dig my fingers into a spot under my left shoulder blade and press down hard. Not much relief. What I wouldn't do for one of Isaac's backrubs.

The two canvases sit on easels side by side. I've cleaned the Meissonier canvas with hydrogen peroxide and the sizing glows pearly white. This is important—more than important, it's imperative. As oil paint ages, it gains translucency, allowing more light from the sizing to refract through it, giving the painting its depth and luminosity. Degas was a master at this, so the proper base is vital if anyone's going to believe he painted it.

Charcoal in hand, I begin my task: sketching *Bath* on the new canvas. It's the same process I use for Repro, and in a few hours, the drawing is done. I make a mixture of raw umber and turpentine and, using a very fine brush, go over the charcoal lines. I do some online research on Degas' use of mediums while I wait for the paint to dry. When it does, I brush off the charcoal. Before me stands stage one of *Bath II,* a drawing in line and wash.

Which is good because Markel is on his way over to check out my progress and take a look at the new stove. The stove is a beauty: all stainless steel with digital wizardry and a door more than big enough to accommodate the canvas. I can't imagine what Han van Meegeren would think of such a wonder.

When Markel arrives, he heads straight for the stove. He's dressed down today—or dressed down for Markel—in a casual but perfectly fitted pair of khakis and a silvery-green shirt that plays up his eyes and well-muscled shoulders. "One big mother oven," he says.

"Yeah. They delivered it yesterday. It's going to be great. Perfect. Thanks."

"And when you're finished, you can go into the cupcake business."

He pulls open the oven door. "You could easily bake a hundred at a time in this thing. Two hundred."

"I'm hoping the art business is going to work out."

He glances over at my window paintings still hanging on the wall. "It will." He turns to the two canvases and points at *Bath II*. "This Meissonier's sizing?"

I'm surprised that he would even ask this question, but it adds credence to his claim that he hasn't done this before. "Of course."

"The drawing looks great. Really good." He takes a step closer. "No underpainting yet?"

"Next step."

Markel glances at the couch.

"Oh," I say. "Sorry. Want to sit down?"

He takes a seat. "I see you've been shopping."

"I couldn't help it." I run my hand along the soft red fabric. "It was 70 percent off."

Markel tilts his head and looks at me with something between humor and compassion. "Don't have to rationalize it to me."

I wonder why I never noticed what a nice man he is. I guess I was too intimidated by the prestige of Markel G and his power as dealer-to-the-stars to see him as an actual person. I was younger then, too—and much more naive.

I sit down next to him. "I think I'm rationalizing it to myself."

"That's not necessary either."

"Oh, you know, ill-gotten gains and all that." I wave my hand airily to indicate that I don't really mean it.

Markel isn't fooled by my posturing. "There's no crime in copying a painting."

"It's a crime to be in possession of a stolen Degas."

"What if it weren't a stolen Degas? What if it were only a copy? Would that make you feel better?"

I sit up straight. "It's a copy?"

He leans toward me. "Look, Claire, if anything happens, which it won't, my plan is to say I told you it was a copy. That's why I gave you the $8,000 check. In case someone follows the money, your deposit is substantiation that you accepted and then carried out a standard reproduction. We'll both claim I told you my painting was a copy and that it never occurred to you it was the Gardner painting. No one will be able to prove otherwise."

I scan his face. "Is that what you're telling me? That the painting isn't a Degas?"

"If that's what it takes to get you to relax."

"Is it true?"

Markel rests his hand on my thigh for a brief moment. "You know as well as I do that she's as real as they come."

Seventeen

THREE YEARS EARLIER

The first week after Isaac left, I spent almost all my time feeling sorry for myself: crying, whining to friends, eating little, sleeping much. The following week, I flung myself into a frenzy of work, creating some of the most maudlin paintings ever made. I threw them all out. It was a month before I finally emerged from what I guessed from my undergraduate psych classes was a "situation-specific manic-depressive episode." Not truly nuts, just momentarily so. When I returned to myself, my grief and self-pity edged into fury.

Isaac and *4D* were still everywhere. Hardly a day went by without a piece in the "Names and Faces" section of the *Boston Globe* about Isaac eating at some fashionable restaurant with some Red Sox player or celebrity chef. And everything from the *New York Times* to the *South End News* contained articles about him or his work. It made me want to throw up.

Much attention was given to my hourglasses, to "Cullion's remarkable exploration of time on every conceivable level, including the inspired juxtaposition of traditional and contemporary painting styles." The critics waxed ecstatic about his "brilliant marriage of theme, image, and meaning within the paint itself" and his ability to "mesh the abstract and representational" into a conceptual whole greater than its parts.

"Artist of the Hour," *ArtWorld* claimed in its Spring catalog issue, and the *Wall Street Journal* did an editorial on the effect of curated museum shows on the price of a rising artist's work. Of course, Isaac was their case in point. It seems that his earlier paintings were being snatched up for between ten and twenty times what he'd received before the MoMA show.

He never mentioned my name. Never called. Never e-mailed. Not even when I left multiple messages asking him to talk to Karen Sinsheimer about returning my phone calls. Which is how I found myself riding the Chinatown Bus—twenty dollars round trip—into Manhattan. I was on my way to MoMA to see *4D*, my *4D*, and to give Karen another copy of the slides she'd claimed she wanted to see. Her assistant kept telling me they never arrived.

Although I'd been to the museum multiple times since the new addition, it's always a bit of shock to enter the building. After all those years of the tighter, more confined space, the wide open lobby with its soaring atrium and view of the sculpture garden took a moment to process. But I was on a mission and didn't dawdle.

The temporary exhibits are usually on the top floor of the Rockefeller Building, and that's where I headed. But as I wandered through the spacious, sky-lit galleries, I didn't see any sign of *Survey of Recent Painting and Sculpture*. I'd assumed the show would still be up, and I was simultaneously crushed and relieved. Were these really the circumstances under which I wanted to view a painting of mine hanging in the Museum of Modern Art?

Apparently so, for I went back to the lobby and got in line at the information desk. It was highly unlikely that a piece so recently acquired would already be hanging as part of the permanent collection, but still, I waited my turn.

"I know this is a long shot," I said to the woman behind the desk, "but is there any chance that a new acquisition is on public display? It was just bought a couple of months ago. Isaac—"

"Ah, yes, you must mean *4D*," she interrupted with a knowing smile. "Our new Cullion."

Our new Cullion. Like our new Picasso. Our new Rembrandt.

"Contemporary Collection. Second floor, Rockefeller," she said. "Next?"

I stumbled up the stairs. When I made it to the top, the light from the atrium windows filled all the space around me, seared into my eyes, and for a moment, all I could see was white. Disoriented, I turned toward the bookstore rather than the galleries. I gripped the top handrail, took a deep breath, and forced myself to walk slowly in the right direction.

It took me a while to find it, but when I did, it nearly brought me to my knees. There it was. Between Chris Ofili's *Prince amongst Thieves* collage and Felix Gonzalez-Torres's *Untitled (Perfect Lovers)* clocks. *4D.* A painting by Claire Roth, hanging with an Ofili and a Gonzalez-Torres. In one of the greatest contemporary museums in the world.

And although the little white card on the wall attributed the work to someone else, I knew, and *4D* knew, that she was mine.

OF COURSE, IT wasn't enough. Not nearly enough. Especially after Karen Sinsheimer's assistant—who was about my age and much, much better dressed and coiffed—wouldn't let me see her boss and informed me that although I was free to leave my slides, Ms. Sinsheimer was extremely busy and there was no guarantee she would have time to look at them.

When I explained that Ms. Sinsheimer had asked to see my work, the assistant held my gaze for a moment longer than was comfortable, then, without a word, lifted them out of my hand with her perfectly manicured fingers. I can only imagine what she did with them after I left the office.

On the way back to Boston, the bus blew a tire, and we had to wait on the side of the Mass Pike for three hours before they could find another bus to pick us up. By the time I got home, I was enraged. So enraged, I called Isaac from a phone booth so he couldn't screen my call.

When he answered the phone, I said, "I just saw *4D*. Nice spot between Ofili and Gonzalez-Torres."

His voice was a low growl. "What do you want?"

"Just calling to check in. Compliment you on your latest success. A former student connecting with her old prof. A former student who painted your current masterpiece."

"Don't be ridiculous, Claire. You and I both know she's mine."

"I don't think that's what either of us knows."

"Sure, you got *4D* started, and I've thanked you for that many times. In front of both Karen and Markel, if I remember correctly. But it was my idea, my series, my style. You didn't even know how to throw your body behind your brush. I had to show you how to do that. I had to show you! You didn't know how."

For a moment, I was speechless. "Who painted it?" I asked softly. "I did."

I couldn't believe he was actually saying this to me. "You ungrateful fucker . . ."

"What do you want, Claire?"

"I want you to tell them it's mine," I said before I realized that this was exactly what I wanted. What I'd wanted all along.

"Are you out of your mind?"

"Perhaps."

"Well, I'm not going to do it." The phone clicked dead in my hand.

Eighteen

Strong light floods the studio, which is a good sign for the first day of painting. I've played with the position of the two easels to make sure the light hits each at exactly the same angle. I've ground the underpaint—flake white, raw umber, and turpentine mixed with a touch of sienna to warm it up—to my exacting and secret recipe. A red sable brush, ridiculously expensive, but the only kind of soft brush Degas ever used, stands at the ready. I immerse the brush in the small bowl of underpaint, close my eyes, and visualize the final painting, which in this case is almost effortless since the original, so to speak, is right in front of me. I begin.

Underpainting is fast and straightforward. The perfect first step for a long project. It's a monochrome wash painted between the initial drawing and the first application of polychrome color, a thin coat covering the entire canvas that sets the tonal aspect of the painting. To make it even easier, the umber and turpentine in the mixture cause it to dry quickly so there's no need to bake it.

As I work, my thoughts turn, as they do so often lately, to the origin of the forged *Bath*. If it was painted in the late nineteenth century, which I'm almost positive it was, then Belle Gardner and Edgar Degas become potential actors in the scheme. There are many possibilities. Degas sold her a forgery. Belle had it copied after she bought it. In transit between Degas and Belle, someone else forged it without their knowledge. Belle and Degas executed the forgery together.

The in-transit option is the only one that seems remotely plausible. I was assuming that Belle purchased the painting directly from Degas, but she could just as easily have bought it from a previous owner. And who knows how many people handled it when it was shipped from Paris to Boston. There were lots of opportunities.

When I finish the underpainting, which needs a few hours to dry, I'm restless, nerved up, closed in despite the fifteen-foot ceilings and floor-to-ceiling windows. I go out for a walk, which usually works, but my head swirls with images of Belle and Degas, their possible relationship, motives, and victimizations. I wave to the optician around the corner, the boutique owner down the street, and chat with the man selling flowers on the sidewalk, but I don't feel comfortable outside the studio.

I need to be up there, smelling the paints, talking to the canvas, cracking my knuckles, priming myself. When I go back, I can't do any of those things, I can only pace. I force myself to sit down, but my hands won't stay still, so I go over to the computer and Google Edgar Degas and Isabella Stewart Gardner.

I get over fifty thousand hits, most of which are about the 1990 heist or Degas' paintings and prints in the Gardner Museum's collection. I try an advanced search, deleting all entries with the words *museum, robbery,* and *theft.* This finds over seventy-five thousand. I double-check and see that I've forgotten the second quotation mark after Isabella Stewart Gardner and therefore have results for every page on the Web that includes Degas and anyone named Isabella, Stewart, or Gardner.

I put in the quotation mark, and a single entry returns. It's in

Russian and appears to be some kind of biographical listing. I delete it from the search and try again. "Your search did not match any documents. Make sure all words are spelled correctly."

I know Degas lived from 1834 to 1917, mostly in Paris, where he was an active participant in the art scene of the day. Wikipedia tells me Belle lived from 1840 to 1924 and that between 1867 and 1906 she made at least ten trips to Europe, mostly to Paris and Venice. As these trips were primarily in pursuit of the 2,500 artworks that now fill her museum, it seems highly likely she and Degas crossed paths.

I have a couple dozen books on Degas and examine the indexes of all that have indexes. No mention of Belle. I go to Amazon and check out books about each of them, but the synopses and reviews are too vague, and I'm not about to spend hundreds of dollars on the books.

I go back to Google and read a little more about Belle and see that Rik's right, she was quite a character. I'm taken by her courage and mischievousness, purposely provoking Puritanical Boston with revealing Parisian dresses and literary and musical soirees at her home, often attended only by men. The lions and Red Sox headgear are also noted. Evidently, she was loved by the young artists she collected and disdained by the old guard, adored by the men and reviled by the women. Scandalous rumors of affairs with Frank Crawford, a much younger novelist, and the older John Singer Sargent were in constant circulation. No mention of Edgar Degas.

"I THOUGHT YOUR book was going to focus on Degas' European connections," Rik says the next day.

We're in his cramped office on the fourth floor of the museum. His feet are up on the desk, and I'm perched on its edge. The first three floors of the Gardner hold exhibition space, and the fourth is used for administrative offices. In Belle's day, this was where she lived. It doesn't look much like a home now.

"Belle made so many trips to Europe during Degas' heyday and spent so much time with artists and dealers," I explain, "that I figured there might be something in their relationship worth writing about."

Rik drops his feet to the floor and turns his chair to his computer. "She did own a number of his works. Unfortunately, most were stolen during the heist." Rik looks off beyond my shoulder. "There was a rumor just last week that some of the art was stashed in a house in Maine."

"And?"

"Came to nothing." He shrugs. "Just like everything else that has to do with the heist."

"So Belle and Degas?" I prompt.

He taps a few keys and frowns. "Did you realize that five of the thirteen stolen artworks were Degas'?"

I hadn't known there were so many. "Wonder if there's an angle in that for me."

"*Three Mounted Jockeys,* black ink on paper. *La Sortie du Pelage,* pencil and watercolor on paper. *Cortege aux Environs de Florence,* pencil and wash on paper." His fingers fly over the keys. "*Program for an Artistic Soiree,* charcoal on paper. And, of course, *After the Bath.*"

The last thing I want him to think I'm interested in is *After the Bath.* "Does it say anything about Berenson or maybe another dealer? I'm really more concerned with those kind of relationships."

"Berenson was pretty much her man." Rik rotates in his chair. "You seen Markel lately?"

"Markel?"

Rik smirks. "You know, Markel G, the guy who came to your studio a few weeks ago?"

"What's Markel got to do with this?"

"Nothing. Sorry. Mind jump. Talking about dealers. I saw him going into your building the other day and meant to ask you if something was up."

I shrug as nonchalantly as I can. "I doubt he was there to see me."

"Does he have clients in the building?"

I pretend to be seriously considering this. "Not that I know of. But Roberta Paul and Beth Weinhaus both have studios on the second floor. Maybe he was on a studio visit. Beth's been doing some fabulous multimedia with old-fashioned corsets."

Rik wrinkles his nose. "Since when are you into that conceptual crap? Or Markel for that matter?"

"Maybe Roberta, then," I say.

Rik turns back to the computer. "Just hoping it was you, Claire Bear."

IT'S A BEAUTIFUL afternoon, or at least beautiful to those who like it on the steamy side, which I do, so I decide to walk home from the Gardner. I turn at the MFA and head down Huntington Avenue. It's odd how little Rik and I were able to find on any relationship between Degas and Belle. There were hundreds of pages on his works and the robbery and plenty of reviews and critiques of both Degas and *Bath* but nothing about Belle and Degas ever meeting. When I asked about Belle's personal letters, Rik told me she burned all her correspondence before she died and demanded that those she wrote to do the same. Unfortunately, almost all complied.

"It makes you wonder what she was hiding," I said.

"With Belle," Rik replied, "it could be just about anything."

This surprising dearth of information deepens my curiosity. And Rik's. He promised to do more research through the museum and continue his investigation when he gets to Paris. Which is all good. I need to put my energy into finishing *Bath II* and getting it the hell out of my studio. I've got a lot of windows to paint.

With this in mind, I head to Al's. The underpainting should be almost dry, and I need more paints and brushes for the next phase. *Bath II* must be made only from materials that were obtainable in the nineteenth century. Fortunately, Degas' taste in brushes is well known, and he worked in the late 1800s, when paint became available in premixed tubes. Before this, artists ground their own pigments using only natural compounds such as raw umber, terre verte, and arsenic trisulfide. Still, every ingredient must be pure and devoid of any chemical discovered after the 1880s. I'm also fortunate to have Al, who's painstakingly careful about what she buys and from whom she buys it.

My cell rings. "Hey," Rik says, "I've got something for you. Don't know how I could have forgotten about her. She's such a complete pain in the ass. Sandra Stoneham. Belle's only living relative. And she's not even a real blood relative." He sniffs. "Granddaughter of Jack Gardner's niece. Lives in Brookline."

"You think she might know something about Belle and Degas?"

"If there's anything to be known, she's the one who'll know it."

"Would she talk to me?"

"If you suck up to her and ooze all over about Belle, I'm guessing she'll give you whatever she's got. Just don't tell her you have anything to do with the museum. Or, better yet, bad mouth the museum, and she'll fall at your feet."

From the pen of

ISABELLA STEWART GARDNER

September 1, 1890
Paris, France

My dearest Amelia,

I haven't heard from you since we were at my Palazzo Barbaro, my heart of hearts. I pray that all is well at home. Ah, Venice. It would take a true literary genius to describe the effect that city has on my soul! And now we are in Paris, which is at its best in September, full of warm, rosy light. Although I hated to leave Italy, I am not unhappy with the change of scene.

It is just a few years since I last walked the wide boulevards of Paris, and I cannot believe that in that time you have metamorphosed from a blushing young bride into a mother! My congratulations to you and Sumner and to all the family as well. Indeed, I must be very old to be a great-aunt. A title not at all attuned with my own view of myself!

How is my dear baby Jackie? It touches my heart every day when I think of him, and I thank you every day for naming him Jack in honor of my own dear departed little boy. Clutch his plump body to your breast and press your nose into the creases of his sweet-smelling neck, for there is nothing greater in this world than to hold your own babe, warm and breathing, in your arms.

I am so sorry for not being a better correspondent, but this trip has been a whirlwind, filled with grand purchases and even grander disappointments. The prices for artwork are terrible! The trouble is I cannot have all the pictures I desire and must pick and choose so some money will remain to expand my collection on our next trip. Your Uncle Jack is always reining me in with accusations that I shall break us. But you know about eating and having the cake. And I want all the cake!

But now to your questions about Mr. Edgar Degas. As you know, my dear Amelia, you are my closest female relation and truly my dearest friend as well. Being of young age and a progressive attitude not found among the ladies of Boston, you are the only one in whom I can confide.

And even had you not asked, confide I must, as it is impossible to keep this delicious tale to myself! I trust that this, and all future discussion of said subject, shall be kept in the strictest of confidence.

Where to begin? I will simplify, but shall stay as true as I am able to the actual discourse so you can fully appreciate what transpired. Again, Edgar invited us to his studio, but your uncle could not come as he had a meeting at his bank. I admit to you, I dressed with great care and arrived at the appointed hour in a blue tulle dress that was appropriate for the occasion, although perhaps the neckline was a bit more revealing than those Boston ladies might prefer for afternoon.

Edgar poured us each a glass of the most wonderful wine, recently procured on a tour of Burgundy. He then launched into a number of humorous tales of his trip, including a very funny one about drinking too much of this very wine at a vineyard in Aignay-le-Duc. We laughed gaily, and he brought out a picture he crafted from his Burgundy sketches. It was lovely to behold, but sadly, painted in pastels using the Impressionist style. He knew quite well that I would disapprove, and I daresay that was his intent.

He then directed my attention to a new painting he had added to the bathers' series he was working on at my last visit, *Woman Leaving Her Bath*. To my horror, the paint appeared to have been applied with a palette knife, and the images were virtually out of focus. I knew then that he was indeed trying to get a rise out of me, and I pretended to take no offense by complimenting him on his use of such vivid colors.

He thanked me, but his eyes twinkled in that way I now recognize as the predecessor to an Edgar prank. "I have a proposition for you, my dear Mrs. Gardner," he said. "One I think you will find extremely interesting, if perhaps to some extent indiscreet."

Assuming any proposition from Edgar must involve a picture, I didn't want to appear too eager and clung to my light manner. "If you are going to offer me an indiscreet proposition, sir, don't you think you should call me Isabella?"

He exploded into his hearty laugh. "Right you are, Isabella." Then he paused. "Do they ever call you Belle?"

"Some," I replied. "Those who are particularly close."

His eyes found mine, and for a moment I felt as if all the air in the room had retreated. "May I be considered to be part of that group?" he asked.

I could barely contain myself and quickly agreed. "Now what is your proposal?"

"It's simple. I will paint an oil painting using the multilayered technique you so admire, if you agree to be my model."

Well, Amelia, I cannot tell you how my heart leapt. A portrait of me by Edgar Degas in the classical style! Could I wish for anything more? And perhaps he would be willing to sell it to me at a lowered cost. "Do you really mean it?" I cried.

"I wish you to model nude," he said, as if it were the most natural thing in the world. "To add to my bather series. It will confound everyone that I've returned to the style of my youth. The critics will drive themselves mad trying to ascertain why. But it will be our secret, Belle. Just yours and mine."

"But, sir, you are mad. I am far too old for such a thing."

"Is that the only reason?" he asked with a sly smile.

I was so overwhelmed by his proposition that I did not understand the meaning of his words or his smile, so I continued, "I am not a young woman, and even then, I was never a beauty, so this is completely out of the question."

Now he laughed uproariously, and it finally dawned on me that I had not mentioned the impropriety of his suggestion. I began to gather my things, feverish heat climbing my face. "And your proposal is most indecorous."

"Oh, my dear Belle," Edgar said when he finally caught his breath, "with your grace and fine figure, your extraordinary complexion and those lovely shoulders and arms, you radiate a beauty that defies age."

I wrapped my shawl tightly over the scoop neckline of my dress. "I could never, sir."

"It won't be as you imagine, I promise you that. There is no shame. I am offering you a job that is actually quite boring and tedious."

"I don't need a job," I declared, as I moved toward the door. "I am a married woman."

Again, the mischievous eyes. "Then not a job. The painting will be my gift to you for doing me this great honor."

A gift. I stood motionless, facing the door as my thoughts whirled. Edgar Degas was offering to make me a gift of one of his paintings. A gem for my collection, perhaps the crown, at no cost. Or at a cost that, between you and me, I would be both willing and honored to pay. The scandal would be delicious but, alas, your poor dear uncle would die of shame.

"It is impossible," I said, and closed the door behind me.

Please kiss baby Jackie a hundred times for me and give my best to your Sumner. We shall be together soon and will be able to talk to our hearts' delight. I so look forward to a big bustling family Christmas at Green Hill with a new precious baby to spoil.

I am your loving,
Aunt Belle

Twenty

I called Sandra Stoneham and told her I was working on a book proposal about Isabella Stewart Gardner's personal relationships with artists of her day, a switch that seemed best given the whole stolen-masterpiece-in-my-studio thing. She was curious but insisted she wouldn't be able to tell me anything useful as the museum controlled everything about her aunt. When I complained that the Gardner had been less than helpful in my pursuit, she immediately invited me over. "Oh, those people are so difficult," she grumbled. "Everything has to be done *their* way."

I pick up some hydrangeas—I'm thinking older ladies like hydrangeas, though I'm not sure why—at Copley Station, and I contemplate the lush blue orbs as the summer's late dusk wraps itself around the trolley windows.

The directions are excellent, and I find the house easily, although the final leg is quite steep. She explained on the phone that the estate had belonged to her great-grandfather, Sumner T. Prescott, but in 2000, she sold the whole "kit and caboodle" to a developer, who carved her a "lovely apartment" out of the first floor, broke the rest of the house into condominiums and, built two dozen free-standing "cottages" on the property—if you can call these McMansions cottages. I see a swimming pool and tennis courts as I climb the front steps.

I figure Mrs. Stoneham has to be somewhere between eighty and ninety, but when she opens the door, I see I'm wrong. This handsome woman wearing a tennis outfit and sporting a full head of stylish hair can't be any more than seventy. If that.

"Please excuse me," she says, as she grabs her tennis bag and leads me into a vast soaring space with twelve-foot ceilings and dozens of tall windows, which is the living room, kitchen, and dining room. "My game ran late, and I didn't have a chance to change."

"It's fine, Mrs. Stoneham. Not a problem, though I'd be happy to wait if you want to change. I really appreciate your taking the time to talk to me."

"No, let's talk. And it's Sandra, please." She points to a chair in the living room. "I was married for almost sixty years and still think of Mrs. Stoneham as my mother-in-law. That's what she made me call her."

"Sandra then," I say as I sit. Guess that makes her older than seventy.

Her artwork also surprises me: mostly high-quality cubist lithographs by Picasso, Le Fauconnier, and Gris mixed with work by abstract expressionists such as Pollock, Rothko, and de Kooning. I squint at the Gris. It appears to be an original. There are a number of mixed-media pieces and some extraordinary metal and ceramic sculptures. Everything is unexpectedly contemporary: the kitchen with its granite breakfast bar and high-end appliances, the art, the furniture, Sandra herself. It's clear I need to reevaluate my conception of eighty. Although her eyes did light up at the sight of the hydrangeas.

Sandra presses a glass to the water dispenser in the refrigerator. "Can I get you something? Water? Tea? Soda?"

When I tell her water is fine, she hands me the glass she just filled and gets another for herself. She downs her water, refills it, and sits across from me.

"You've got some fabulous pieces here," I say. "That Gris is awesome."

Her eyes twinkle. "But not what you'd expect from an old lady?"

"No, no. I wasn't thinking that. I, uh, I'm just a bit awed by the collection."

She laughs, and I question Rik's description of her as a pain in the ass. "I have some traditional works also." She sighs. "Although nothing from my Aunt Belle. Every piece she ever owned is in the museum."

"She was your great-aunt?"

"Actually, great-great. My grandmother, Amelia Prescott, was her niece. Her favorite niece, I might add. My mother, Fanny, was Grandma's only surviving child, and I'm the only one left, Belle Gardner's only living relative." Sandra purses her lips. "Something you might think the Isabella Stewart Gardner Museum would appreciate. But no, they have no interest in maintaining Aunt Belle's legacy, of upholding her preeminent place in history. It's all about their artist-in-residence program and lectures by people who know nothing about my aunt or her work. Not to mention those people trying to dig up dirt. All of this about her having affairs or being friends with homosexuals. What does it matter? What matters is what she accomplished. Her museum. Her collection."

I fear I've come to the pain-in-the-ass Sandra and search for a topic that will reestablish her good mood. "So, is this your contemporary art area? Do you have your older paintings in other rooms?"

Her stern expression disappears. "Yes, yes, that's exactly right. Because this area has been renovated and modernized, I thought that would be appropriate. In the more formal areas of the apartment, I have my more traditional pieces. We collectors are a fanatical bunch, even down to the type of interior design that's appropriate for our artworks. And that's just the beginning of it. Once a piece of art crawls into your heart, you'll never let it go." She stands. "Come, let me show you a wonderful nineteenth-century painting of my grandmother."

I follow her back toward the entryway. Directly across from the front door is a portrait of a beautiful young woman whose skin glows in a way that only the most talented painters are able to achieve. I must have missed it in my surprise at Sandra's youthful appearance.

"This is Grandma Amelia. Lovely, Isn't she?"

I lean closer and try to make out the signature. "Rudell? Never heard of him."

"Rendell," Sandra corrects. "Virgil Rendell. Not very well known."

"He's good," I say. "Really good. And yes, your grandmother was quite a beauty." But it's more than Amelia's beauty that makes the painting so powerful. It's the light in her eyes, the warmth Rendell managed to capture, her inner happiness flowing outward, passing through time to touch the present.

"She looks so happy," I say. "So innocent."

"That's because it was painted before she married my grand-father."

I turn toward the other side of the apartment, which retains the house's original moldings and wainscot. "So this is the traditional art side?" I point to a pair of handsome mahogany sliding doors held together with a fancy brass key, closing off what must have been the original parlor. "Can I see?"

"I'd be happy to show them all to you when I have more time."

Sandra looks at her watch and leads me to the living room. She takes her seat and I take mine. "So, let's talk about your book."

"As I said on the phone, I'm working on a book proposal on Isabella Gardner's relationships with various artists, but I'm having trouble finding enough information. Your aunt was so significant to the art movement of that time," I say, taking Rik's advice to gush about Belle, "I can only imagine there must be many other artists she influenced who I don't know about."

"I'm sure that's correct," she says and smiles. "You're an academic?"

"I recently received a Master of Fine Arts from the museum school, but I've always been fascinated by Belle Gardner, so I thought I'd give this a try. Can't count on art alone to pay the rent."

"Do you know Ben Zimmern?"

"Yes, of course," I say with pseudoenthusiasm. "But my area was studio painting so I didn't take any classes with him."

"I'm on the MFA board, and Ben and I have worked together on a number of sculpture-related projects."

"Are you also on the Gardner board?" I ask, hoping to move her away from a discussion of any other museum school faculty she might know. Boston is a deceptively small town.

Sandra frowns. "I was until I wasn't anymore. Again, it's their contemporary concerns I can't abide. And now with the horrid new addition. A larger café. A bigger bookstore. Glass walkway. Ha! It was her home, her legacy, for pity's sake. Aunt Belle is surely doing somersaults in her grave."

There's no good response to any of this, so I switch back to the book. "I'm looking for—"

"What's your medium?" she interrupts.

"Oil."

"When did you get your degree?"

I hesitate, her intensity making me a bit uncomfortable. "Three years ago."

"Ah. Then you must have been a student of Isaac Cullion's." She shakes her head. "So, so sad. Such a young man. And such promise."

Caught off guard, I hesitate a nanosecond too long. "Yes. Yes I was. Great talent."

She studies me for a long moment. "I thought your name sounded familiar."

I lower my gaze. What spectacularly bad luck.

Sandra leans over and pats my knee. "You won't get any grief from me, Claire. I have friends at MoMA and know that things aren't as straightforward as many believe."

"You do?" My eyes meet hers, and I see that she does. "Thank you."

She brushes this off. "So what can I tell you about Aunt Belle's famous friends?"

I pull a notebook and pen from my backpack. "I know she hung out with lots of well-known people who weren't artists, like Henry James and Julia Ward Howe, but I thought it would be interesting just to focus on the artists." I look through the pages. "I've got lots of information on her relationships with Whistler, Sargent, and Ralph Curtis, but I need a few more, and I'm coming up short."

Sandra beams at me. "Well, she was such an amazing patron of the arts. As you say, all arts, music, literature, architecture. A muse to many, but she did have her favorites." She taps her finger on the arm of her chair. "Let's see, artists, artists . . . There was Joseph Smith, Ralph Adams Cram, Martin Mower, and oh, yes, of course, Dennis Miller Bunker."

I scribble down the names, smiling up at her, taking in her every word. "How about artists who were better known?" I ask. "I'd like to gear the book to both scholarly and popular audiences. Manet? Cassatt? Pissarro?"

Sandra shakes her head. "Aunt Belle wasn't fond of the Impressionists. She probably didn't have much to do with any of them."

"She owned a number of Degas' pieces."

"If you note, there isn't a single work by Edgar Degas in her museum that would be considered part of his Impressionist period. Almost everything she bought of his was created far earlier than any of her European visits. Even *After the Bath,* which was a later work, was painted in his traditional, pre-Impressionist style."

"Now that you mention it," I say, with admiration in my voice, "that's really true, isn't it? You know, it might be an interesting angle. Her friendships in terms of her personal feelings about the style of the artists' work." I begin to scribble again. "It would be just great for my book if it turned out that she and Degas were friends. And it's possible, isn't it? They moved in the same circles, had the same interests . . ."

"I can't say I've ever heard or read anything about her knowing him," she says. "And, unfortunately for you, I've been told more than once that I know more about Belle Gardner than anyone else in the world. Including her biographers and those who work at the museum, I might add."

I struggle to keep the disappointment from my face.

"I'm sorry." Sandra leans toward me. "I see this book means a lot to you."

I shrug. "Just trying something new."

"So you're not painting?"

"Ah, no. I'm . . . I still paint."

She raises an eyebrow.

"I'm actually working on some new pieces for a show this winter."

"Well, that's wonderful, Claire." Sandra seems genuinely pleased. "Good for you. Where's it going to be?"

"Markel G."

The lines in her forehead deepen. "Aiden Markel is including your work in one of his shows?"

I nod.

"Well, well," Sandra says, collecting herself. "Well, that's good to hear. No point in harboring old grudges. No point at all." She eyes me shrewdly. "But then isn't this an odd time for you to be researching a book?"

"Keeping my options open. A show's just a show."

She nods her approval and stands. The interview is over.

I shove my notebook in my backpack and stand also. She has no information, and I have many paintings to paint. "Thanks for seeing me. I really appreciate your time."

"Again, I'm sorry I couldn't have been more help." Sandra says. "There are some boxes of old family memorabilia in storage I can check through for you. The museum took everything Aunt Belle owned that was in the building at the time of her death, but maybe there's something my grandmother managed to keep out of their greedy hands."

"Thanks, that would be great," I say, as I walk out the door, but I'm thinking that it's time to let this go of this whole Belle-Degas thing and get to work.

I've been holed up in my studio for almost a week now, talking to no one, working in stretches of up to fourteen hours, subsisting on take-out Thai and orange juice. I haven't been to Jake's, Al's, or even the convenience store. Rik, Markel, and my mother have called, but I blew them all off with promises of seeing them "soon." This is easier than it may seem. An artist feverishly at work to the exclusion of life's mundane routines is a romantic notion people love to embrace. "I'm in a frenzy of work," I say, and they're gone.

The truth is, it's not romantic at all. It's tough and exhausting, yet satisfying. I'm making good progress, thanks to my research and classes, Han van Meegeren, and Markel's top-of-the-line oven. Without these, this project would take up to two years and even then, the final product probably wouldn't pass muster.

Van Meegeren, who worked in the first half of the twentieth century, is considered the most ingenious art forger of his time, maybe of all time. A Dutch painter who felt his own work to be grossly misjudged by the critics, he devised a plan to make fools of his detractors as well as establish his own genius: He would produce such high-quality forgeries that the critics who denigrated his paintings would declare his fakes priceless masterpieces by the likes of de Hooch, ter Borch, and Vermeer. Which, after six years of experimentation, is exactly what happened.

To this end, Han invented the processes of stripping an old painting down to its sizing and painting the new one over it to maintain the craquelure, of using phenol formaldehyde as an additive to harden the paint, of baking each layer to desiccate the paint so it's as dry as it would be after centuries, of further aging the painting with a final wash of India ink and tinted varnish.

But the most intriguing part of the van Meegeren story is how his success as a forger got him arrested as a war criminal. During the German occupation of the Netherlands, Han—he was also an art dealer—sold one of his Vermeer forgeries, *Christ with the Adulteress,* to a German banker, who then sold it to Hermann Goering, number two in Hitler's command. When the painting was discovered hidden in an Austrian salt mine after the war, it was traced back to Han. On the assumption that he had sold a Dutch national treasure to the enemy during wartime, van Meegeren was charged as a Nazi collaborator and thrown into jail.

Han was then faced with a choice: Confess to forging the painting or spend the rest of his life in prison. After a week in solitary confinement, he told his jailers that the painting was not a masterpiece by Vermeer, just a forgery by van Meegeren. But, to both his dismay and gratification, no one believed him. So, under the vigilant eyes of reporters and court-appointed witnesses, he repainted the forgery while a prisoner at the Headquarters of Military Command. Both of his works were "authenticated" as forgeries, and the war crime charges were dropped.

Brush, palette, phenol formaldehyde, canvas. Brush, palette, phenol formaldehyde, canvas. It's a new rhythm for me, but after a few layers, I'm getting the hang of it. Which is good, as I plan to complete this first phase tomorrow, and I have two or three more glazings to go.

In this initial stage, I've been confined to a limited palette, to creating a base of layers in medium tones, no greens, yellows, or reds, from which the rest of the piece will grow. In order to build depth and luminosity in the rich, subtle ways of Degas, I have to work outward from the middle color range to the darkest darks and lightest lights.

This is because light travels through the transparent layers of glaze, bounces off the canvas, and reflects back at the viewer, whose eyes mix the layers of translucent pigment to "see" the final colors in a brilliant intensity not possible using any other method. This is also why the layers have to be so thin and so many. And why each must be devoid of surface moisture—wet-on-dry—before the next can be applied. To do anything else would muddy the tones.

I approach the gleaming stainless-steel behemoth that crouches in the southeast corner of the studio and set it to preheat. As it takes up to seventy-five years for the liquids in oil paint to completely dry, a contemporary forgery can easily be detected through the alcohol test I used on both *Bath* and the Meissonier. But van Meegeren's recipe of phenol formaldehyde as an additive baked for ninety-five minutes at 248 degrees absorbs the remaining fluids so thoroughly that the paint is as dry and hard as if Degas himself had applied it in 1897.

When the oven's preheated, I slide the canvas dead center on a rack sitting dead center, set the automatic timer, and close the door. The baking must be closely monitored, as lots of things can go wrong: blistering paint, melting paint, singed canvas, fire. Despite my earlier decision to drop the Belle-Degas issue, I grab a few books on Degas, click on the oven light, and settle into a chair in front of the glass window to watch, read, and wait.

THE ONE COMMITMENT I've been keeping throughout my voluntary incarceration is juvy. If I don't show up, the boys spend that time in their cells, and I don't want to be the cause of any additional confinement. Plus, today the boys are applying the final coat of varnish to the mural and then, if Kimberly can pull it off, we're having a small celebration. It won't be much—the kids aren't supposed to be having fun—but she figured she could scare up some cookies or brownies and maybe a bottle or two of apple juice. It's amazing how happy and childlike these hardened criminals become at the prospect of a treat.

The mural came out really well, even better than I expected, and the boys are justly proud of their work, joking and horsing around as much as they're able under the steely stares of the guards. Undeterred by the small brushes they're forced to use—the larger the brush, the more easily it can be used as a weapon—each boy stands in front of the space I've allotted him, seemingly happy to be varnishing. Kimberly brought in a couple of boxes of Munchkins from Dunkin' Donuts, and the boys keep stealing glances at the bright pink cartons.

Even Manuel and Xavier aren't sending daggers at each other, although I made sure to put them at opposite ends of the mural. The spiky smell of the varnish permeates the room, and I wonder if it reminds the boys of glue or some other drug, and that's why they're all so congenial.

I kneel and inspect X's silver cans.

"Yo, Ms. Roth," Reggie calls. "Tell this fuc—, this guy here," he points to Xavier, "that my needles are way better than his fuc—, than his stupid beer cans. Best in the whole mural. Mine. No contest. So why don't you stop hanging with that loser and come help someone with real talent."

Xavier and Reggie are buds. Rumor has it they're in the same gang, so I say, "Hang on there, Michelangelo. You're next."

Michelangelo he's not. His work is so bad it questions my assumption about all the boys having art inside them. But Reggie's defense mechanism is humor—or what he considers humor—which is a rare commodity here among the rage and hopelessness. I'm more than glad to have him around.

"But you gotta admit mine are way better than his," Reggie persists.

"I'm not going there." I hold my hands up, palms flat, and bring an affected tone to my voice. "But I must say, Mr. Martinez, that the juxtaposition of that needle to the vial of white powder makes an extremely powerful artistic statement. Meaty. Meaty and true."

Reggie laughs loudly, but Xavier just looks perplexed.

"Don't worry, X," I tell him. "You've got great juxtaposition, too."

He smiles shyly. "Thanks for the silver."

"Anytime," I say, pleased. These boys find it difficult to express gratitude, they view it as weakness, and I'm proud to have broken down even this small barrier.

Kimberly catches my eye and winks.

I step behind Christian, whose basketball player and pizza maker really are the best in the mural. Not to mention, much more appropriate yearned-for objects than needles and beer cans. "These really are great," I tell him. "Did you ever do any drawing or painting before?"

He shrugs and keeps varnishing.

"I mean it, Christian. You're really good." The boys aren't much better at taking compliments than they are at gratitude. "You've got a natural talent for this."

His brush doesn't slow and he doesn't look at me, but it's clear from the stiffness of his shoulders that he's listening, and I think I can detect the tweak of a smile at the corner of his mouth.

"Maybe next project we can work more closely together, see what you can do when—"

I catch a movement out of the corner of my eye and stop speaking. By the time I turn, both Xavier and Reggie are face down on the floor, hands cuffed behind their backs, a guard with a knee on each. A third guard holds a vial of white powder in his hand. Kimberly's already yelling into her walkie-talkie.

"Hands up!" the fourth guard orders the remaining boys. "To the wall. Hands above your heads. Legs spread. Now!"

"Where'd the stuff come from?" Xavier's guard growls, yanking the handcuffs and jerking him to his feet. Xavier struggles to get his balance and glares at the guard. He says nothing.

Reggie's guard does the same. "You tell us where you got this or you're both gonna be at Walpole into the next century." He wrenches the handcuffs, and Reggie cries out in pain. "You ain't seen nothin', kid. Nothin' like what you'll be seeing if you don't tell us who you copped from."

"In or out, shithead?" Xavier's guard demands. "Who is he?"

I back up, but not before I see a look of mutual panic and fear pass between the boys. If I were a betting person, I'd bet that whomever they got it from is scarier than the guards, scarier than years at Walpole. Stupid, stupid, stupid kids.

"Her," Reggie says loudly, jutting his elbow at me. "She brought it in. Does every week."

"Me?" I demand. "You're saying I bring you drugs?" I look at Xavier.

Xavier turns to his guard. "Yeah. Every week."

I stare at him in disbelief.

Two more guards barge into the room. Reggie's guard says something to the older one, and the new guards march toward me, stone-faced and menacing.

Kimberly steps in front of me. "Ms. Roth's a volunteer who's been coming here for years. This is a misunderstanding, a false accusation, and needs to be treated that way until proven otherwise."

I can't believe this. Until proven otherwise? I turn to Kimberly. "You can't possibly think—"

"Please go with the guards, Ms. Roth," Kimberly says, as if she's speaking to someone she just met. "I'm sure that this will all be cleared up quickly."

When I reach for my purse, she says, "Leave it. Someone will get it back to you after it's been searched."

Twenty-one

THREE YEARS EARLIER

At dawn, one day after a photograph of Isaac sitting in the bar of the Intercontinental with an extremely hot and scantily dressed woman described as an "unidentified art student" appeared in the *Globe*—so much for going back to Martha—I once again boarded the Chinatown Bus and headed to MoMA. That photo was the proverbial straw. Karen Sinsheimer was going to hear the truth. Enough was enough.

Based on my last experience with Karen's assistant, sentinel would be a better descriptor, I didn't bother going to her office. Instead, I planted myself in front of the elevator and stairwell on her floor. Fortunately, both were off the same lobby, and even more fortunately, there was a bench. I settled myself in with the book I'd brought as a prop and waited.

As my watch edged toward one-thirty, I started to get nervous. I'd called yesterday, claiming to be Isaac's assistant, explaining that he was coming into New York today and wanted to make a date with Karen for lunch. Later, I'd called back and canceled, patting myself on the back for the clever way I'd made sure Karen would be in. But apparently, not clever enough. She was probably sick or on some unexpected museum business off-site. Damn.

Just then, Karen strode around the corner. She didn't notice me, didn't even glance around, just punched the elevator button with the purposefulness of a woman without any time to lose.

I jumped up. "Karen!" I cried like someone who'd spotted a long, lost friend.

She turned with a smile ready at the corners of her lips, but when she saw me she frowned. It was clear she had no idea who I was.

I stuck my hand out. "Claire Roth," I said. "We met at Isaac Cullion's studio. The day you accepted *4D* for your survey show."

She shook my hand cordially. "Of course. Claire. It's nice to see you again. How have you been?"

"I need to talk to you. Somewhere private."

"I'm sorry that I haven't had time to review your work. I promise I'll—"

"It's not about my work, it's about Isaac's." I shook my head. "No. That's not true. I take it back. It is about my work."

"I don't understand."

"And that's why we have to talk."

Karen's brow furrowed. "Is something wrong? Is Isaac okay?"

"He's fine, but I'm not sure he will be after this."

Karen watched the elevator doors open and then close. She sighed. "We can go to my office. But I warn you, I don't have much time and even less patience for artists' stunts."

"This is no stunt," I said, as I followed her clicking heels down the corridor.

When we were seated in her office, I met her gaze straight on. "Isaac Cullion didn't paint *4D*."

"Of course he painted *4D*. You must be mistaken."

"Unfortunately not."

"I know his work. I've seen many of his previous pieces."

"And *4D* isn't his," I insisted calmly.

Her eyes focused over my shoulder, most likely visualizing Isaac's paintings. "Then who painted it?"

"I did."

Her eyes snapped back to mine. "But that makes no sense. Why would you paint it?"

"He was blocked. The painting was due in a few weeks, and I wanted to help him get it started so he wouldn't lose the opportunity." When Karen said nothing, I continued, "He couldn't get himself to work. He was too depressed, too down on himself. So I kept painting. We didn't mean for it to happen. He was there with me the whole time. In his studio. Giving me tips."

"Tips?"

"How to put my whole body behind the brush. How to scrape wet-on-wet. My style is more classic wet-on-dry. That kind of thing."

"And he signed it?"

"It was the day before the deadline," I said. "There really wasn't anything else for him to do."

"Why didn't you say anything at the time?"

I opened my hands to her. "I was in love with him."

Her eyes narrowed. "And you're not now?"

"No."

"I assume you've got proof?"

"The realistic and abstract hourglasses are painted in my style. Isaac only works wet-on-wet."

"I'm sure a man of Isaac's talent is more than capable of painting wet-on-dry if he wanted to."

"Then ask him."

"You want me to call Isaac Cullion and ask him if he painted *4D*? Just like that?"

I nodded, and we stared at each other for a long moment. I knew Isaac would come clean if she asked him directly. It was a matter of truth and fairness, and despite his recent behavior, his love and respect for me.

Karen broke the contact first. "Okay. Let's do it."

I leaned back. Exhausted, but relieved. I'd done what had to be done. I watched Karen pick up the phone and press a speed-dial button. MoMA's got him on speed-dial. For a moment, I felt a stab of sympathy for Isaac. It was a long way to fall.

"Isaac. Karen Sinsheimer. Glad I caught you." She listened, then said, "I'm going to put you on speaker phone. Your friend Claire Roth is here." She pressed another button.

Isaac's voice boomed into the room. "In New York?"

"Yeah. In my office. She's claiming that she painted *4D,* not you, and said I should call you to verify her story."

No sound came from Isaac's end, but in the silence I could hear him wrestling with his conscience, struggling with anger at my audacity, sadness over what he was going to lose, relief that the lying was finally going to end.

A look of concern passed over Karen's face. "Isaac?"

"Saac," I said. "Tell her the truth. It'll be better for everyone if you do. Especially you."

More silence.

"Isaac," Karen demanded. "Are you saying it's true?"

Isaac heaved a huge sigh. "Karen," he said softly, "please don't make any trouble for Claire. Don't hold this against her. She's a hurt kid, lost and angry. Talented, very talented, but—"

"That's a load of crap, and you know it," I interrupted. "Tell her the truth. You no more painted *4D* than you painted the Mona Lisa. It's over, Isaac. Over."

"I'm sorry Claire brought you into this, Karen," Isaac continued in the same soft, even tone. "It's personal, never should have involved you. I decided to work on my marriage, and she's been having a tough time with it. Jealousy. You know how it is. Do me a favor, just let her go home and forget this ever happened."

"Forget it ever happened?" I jumped up and yelled into the speaker. "That's just what you'd like to do. But you can't and neither can I!"

Karen waved me back into the chair. "I'll call you later," she said to Isaac. "Let me handle this from here."

I sat down, devastated. I'd tossed the dice and lost the gamble. Isaac was a lying bastard, and I was an idiot. An idiot who had just destroyed her fledgling career.

When Karen hung up the phone, she turned to me with a confused, almost sad, expression on her face.

"He's lying," I said, without much enthusiasm. Karen was clearly going to believe Isaac-the-Great over a lowly graduate student.

When she didn't correct me, I sat up in my seat.

"The hourglasses . . ." she mumbled to herself.

I didn't move, didn't breathe.

Finally, she asked, "Ever hear of Han van Meegeren?"

"Who?" I had no idea who Han van Meegeren was or what she was talking about.

"Never mind," she said. "It doesn't matter. The thing is, I'm going to give you the benefit of the doubt here. Let you prove yourself."

"Prove myself?"

"I want you to paint another *4D*."

Twenty-two

The two guards lead me from the dayroom, each with a hand clenched around an elbow. I look back at Kimberly, and she mouths the words, "Stay calm."

Which isn't easy, as I'm being physically escorted by two armed guards through a maze of corridors and locked doors to who-knows-where. I keep asking them what's going to happen, where they're taking me, do I need a lawyer. But I get no answers.

"You can't put me in a cell," I declare with authority. "I'm innocent, innocent until proven guilty. And I'm not guilty. Not close to guilty. Those kids are just trying to save their own asses."

Silence except for the sound of our shoes on the tile floor.

"I have an appointment," I say, as if this is going to make them let me go. Markel's coming over to check my progress on *Bath II*. "A business meeting I can't miss. Very important. And I can't go in a cell. I'm kind of claustrophobic. I could get sick or, or . . ."

The younger of the two finally takes pity on me. "We're not putting you in a cell."

Instead, I'm led into a dimly lit, narrow room with a desk and two chairs. It must be for lawyer visits. Or interrogations. I look for a two-way mirror, but there isn't one. The only window is in the door, and it's crisscrossed with wire mesh. The empty walls are the usual rotting-vegetable green. I look at the guards, hoping they aren't going to leave me in here by myself.

"Someone will be in to talk to you soon," the younger guard says. They quickly exit, closing the door with a snap behind them.

I immediately try the handle; it's locked. I look through the meshed window; all I can see is the cinder-block wall across the corridor. Was it only minutes ago that I was overseeing the mural with the boys?

The room smells like cheap cologne mingled with stale sweat, and the odor is making me nauseous. Underpaid lawyers. Scared, stupid boys. And now me. Locked in. The air is overheated, and the walls are tight. I begin to sweat.

I pace. There's no reason to freak out. Reggie and Xavier are clearly lying, and the authorities will pick up on that in a second. Eight steps across. Four down. This is just standard operating procedure. It's a drug bust, after all. This has nothing to do with me or any presumption about my guilt. Just procedure, that's all. SOP.

Eight steps across. Four down. They had to separate me from the boys. Take precautions. Search my purse to make sure there really aren't any drugs. A chill runs through me. Are they going to search me? The phrase "body cavity" flashes through my brain in neon letters.

No. I can't go there. Can't let this get the better of me. I glance up at the weak bulb above my head, and the ceiling appears to shrink, to press down on me. Think of something else.

Markel will be at the studio by five. He's curious about the whole baking process, and I promised him a demonstration. That means I have to do some painting in order to have something to bake. I have to get out of here. What will he think if I'm not there? That I've double-crossed him?

Can't go there either. Eight steps across. Four down. Pace and count. Someone will be here any minute.

But it's almost an hour before there's a knock at the door. By that time, I'm really sweaty, actually on the verge of throwing up. And despite the overly warm room, I'm very cold. I hug myself as I watch the door open, hold my breath.

When I see that it's Kimberly and that she's holding my purse and smiling, I surprise myself and burst into tears.

As I RIDE the bus home, I'm mortified by my over-reaction to the situation. Kimberly explained that it was immediately obvious to everyone that Reggie and Xavier were lying, that I was never a real suspect. Obvious to everyone but me. There will be an inquiry, and I probably won't be able to come back to Beverly Arms until it's over, but it's just the system, the way it has to be done. She said to think of it as the process necessary to clear my name. I wondered why it was necessary to officially clear the name of an innocent person, but I didn't ask.

And she was perfect, offering me tissues and telling me how sorry she was, that she would have responded in exactly the same way under similar circumstances. But still. I'm thirty-one years old, and there I was, blubbering like a baby over what turned out to be nothing. Something I should have recognized as nothing right from the beginning.

When I get home, I stumble into the shower. I have less than two hours before Markel shows up. The shower cleans the sweat and the odor of fear from my skin, but it does nothing to wash away the residual emotions smoldering inside my body. Once I start painting though, the feelings disappear. I'm well beyond the middle-range colors, and it's easy to slip into the zone as I work with the breadth of oranges that dominate the bottom right-hand side of the painting and then weave their understated way throughout the entire image, pulling it together from bottom-right to top-left as green pulls from top-right to bottom-left.

The more I work on *Bath II,* the more sure I am that the forgery Markel brought to me was copied directly from an original Degas. Except for Françoise and the space around her, the scope of the colors, the subtlety of the shadows, the juxtapositions of tone and light have to be based on the work of the master. I don't believe any forger could have created this without a model from which to work. At its most essential heart, this is an Edgar Degas creation. Which, if I'm right, means there might be an original somewhere. Degas was famous at the time it was painted, and it's unlikely an object of such value would have been destroyed. But you never know.

By the time Markel arrives, the canvas has been in the oven for almost an hour, and I'm experimenting with greens for the next layer. He wipes paint from my cheek with his thumb and gives me a hug. "A little too orangey for your coloring," he says. "Might want to add a touch more red."

I'm not displeased at his familiarity. We've never hugged before, and he feels bigger than I expected, more solid. And he smells good, like summer. I hug him back, lengthening the embrace a moment or so longer than might be considered proper between colleagues.

I pull away. "Don't come by tomorrow." I gesture to the palette I've been experimenting on. "I look even worse in green."

He turns to the oven. "Is it cooking?"

"Got about another fifteen minutes before the first test."

He sits down in my chair and stares into the oven. "It's such a weird image. A baking canvas."

"Almost seems normal to me now."

The light is on inside the oven, and he leans in closer. "You're already into the rich tones?" he asks. "How did you get so far so fast?"

"Thanks to your trusty oven."

"Can we take it out?"

I cluck my tongue. "No, little Aiden, I'm sorry, Santa isn't coming until morning."

"Patience isn't my strong suit." He wanders over to the table where my paints, brushes, and mediums are scattered in a messy jumble only I can understand. He sniffs. "You got a dead animal in here?"

"Shit. I sure as hell hope not." I go to the kitchen area, squat to check the base of the cabinets. I open the door under the sink and warily stick my head in. "But it's not unheard of."

"No. I mean it smells like formaldehyde. Like a science lab or something."

Relieved, I stand. "Phenol formaldehyde. Another van Meegeren invention. Like I told you, a kind of a medium, but not directly mixed in. It hardens the paint and helps it dry."

Markel frowns. "But if Degas didn't use it, won't they be able to tell?"

"The baking breaks it down and completely disperses it. The paint's hard, but the chemicals are gone."

"And you wondered why I chose you?"

"Anyone with time to do the research and the ability to copy can do this." The juvy boys aren't the only ones uncomfortable with compliments.

When the timer chimes, I grab two potholders, squat, and open the door. I carefully inch the canvas toward me, giving it small pushes through the rack on the underside of the painting. Then I lift it and place it on the top of the stove.

Markel says nothing as I dampen a piece of cotton wool with

alcohol and wave it an inch or so above the area on which the newly applied orange is the thickest. The paint remains unchanged. No softening, no desaponification. I press the alcohol swab to a dab of paint I purposely leaked over the edge of the canvas, holding the contact while I count slowly to ten. When I remove the cotton wool, it's completely white. I lightly press a finger to the paint. Hard as a rock.

"Done," I say, lifting the canvas to the easel.

Markel's eyes swing from my forgery to his original, then back again. "It's phenomenal, Claire," he says in a low whisper. "Absolutely phenomenal."

"Now for the varnish." I twist the top off a can of varnish and pour a bit into a small bowl. When the smell hits my nose, I'm back in juvy, sweaty and scared. I quickly pick up my brush and start talking about van Meegeren. "So he figured out that if you applied a coat of varnish while the paint was still warm from baking, the cracks from the original sizing would come out as each layer cooled."

"Clever man."

"I had a rudimentary understanding of the whole craquelure thing, but I never knew any of the details before I took those Repro certification classes and started doing research for this project. Never even heard of van Meegeren. We didn't learn about him in art school. Hardly anybody seems to be aware of his contribution."

"I'm guessing academics aren't all that keen on beefing up the reputation of a forger," Markel says dryly.

"And even though you can't see it right now because the paint's still hot," I continue, "in another couple of hours, a tiny tracery of miniature hills and valleys will rise magically until they're written on the surface."

"Both artist and poet." He's beaming at me like a proud papa.

But the softness of his eyes has nothing to do with fatherhood and everything to do with sexual attraction. He takes a step toward me. "Claire?" he says, and I know exactly what he's asking.

I want him, I have for a while. It's been a tough day, and I'd like nothing better than to crawl into his arms, have him obliterate all my fears and replace them with pleasure. But I've made too many bad choices before him, and now there are too many secrets between us. I shake my head.

He blinks, steps back. "Okay. That's cool. Has nothing to do with the rest of the project. Or anything else."

The longing on his face mirrors what I feel. "Maybe later," I say, wishing for sooner. "Maybe after this is all over . . ."

"Probably smart," he says, in a flat voice that reveals that he doesn't think it's smart at all.

Twenty-three

I t's September, and as the cool breezes come off the water and the sunlight becomes more angular, I'm seized by that back-to-school exhilaration where anything is possible and no one knows what the new year may hold. I told Repro I needed to work on my own projects for a few months. Beverly Arms "granted" me a leave of absence pending further investigation. Rik's in Paris, and I let it be known at Jake's that I'm deep into a creative burst. Markel's stopped by a couple of times, but the visits have been short and slightly awkward. When he leaves, I wish he were still here.

But I see the end. I can feel it, taste it. In a Herculean effort that puts my labors of the past weeks to shame, I sprint toward the finish line. There's nothing to stop me except the time required to paint and bake. And if I do say so myself, *Bath II* is looking good.

There's a marvelous interaction between the phenol formalde-hyde and the baking that renders the colors with the depth and brightness of a finely cut jewel. They sparkle under the light, almost shimmer. Although I'm going to have to tone this down at the end with a wash of India ink to mimic the effects of time, it occurs to me that no such thing will be necessary on my windows.

When I accepted Markel's offer, I thought I'd be learning at the feet of a master painter; instead, my most powerful lessons have come from a master forger. Markel has already agreed to let me keep the oven until the opening. As my excitement grows at the thought of working on my own paintings, I push myself even more.

I've taken to sleeping in multiple, short stretches during both night and day, upsetting my natural circadian rhythms and further cutting myself off from the cadence of the world. I do two, maybe three, glaze-and-bake cycles, then tumble onto my mattress for a few hours of rest. When I get up, I eat some cold pad Thai, drink a glass of orange juice, and get back to work. I often feel as if I'm observing myself from afar, from outside, while, in seeming contradiction, I remain in the zone for longer periods of time than I ever believed possible.

The downside is the dreams, recurring ones. Of Isaac, of Belle and Edgar Degas, of Markel. Usually I'm being held hostage by Isaac, pursuing Belle and Degas, being pursued by Markel. But sometimes it's the other way around or all mixed together. A couple of times, Xavier's been there, too. And in more than a few, Markel and I are making love. When I wake up, the dreams seem boringly predictable, but when I'm inside them, they are terrifyingly—or orgasmically—real.

I push myself harder and harder, paint faster and faster, hoping that by finishing the painting, I'll also be finishing off my demons. That I'll be able to climb out of this vortex and into my actual life.

Then, one day it's done. With the sweep of the brush, I sign Degas' name, making sure to leave the somewhat too large space between the "a" and the "s." Adrenaline surges through my body as I step back and admire my handiwork.

I do an overall comparison between the two paintings. Except for the brilliance of the color in *Bath II,* they appear virtually identical. I come closer and inspect them inch by inch, stroke by stroke. Excellent. I check for the tiny spot of green I put on the back of the top-right corner of *Bath II* to make sure I'm always able to tell the difference, then carefully go over the painting. I close my eyes, open them, take it in. Do it again.

I open the closet door so the full-length mirror is facing out and position the two paintings so I can see both reflections simultaneously. I turn one upside down, then the other, lay them sideways on the couch.

My stomach twists. There's something wrong with *Bath II*. Something Degas would never do. I try to find what I'm reacting to, sliding my eyes back and forth over the painting until something clicks. The shadows off to Françoise's left don't have enough depth. I turn back to *Bath,* study Françoise, compare her to mine. She and her shadows are identical in both paintings. *Bath II* may not be a Degas, but I've created an accurate forgery of the forgery.

There's only one more thing left to do. I apply a thin layer of varnish over the entire canvas. When it's dry and the craquelure has risen to the surface, I lay the painting flat on my work table, grab a wide brush and a bottle of India ink. Then I hesitate. I know I need to do this. Have to do this. But I balk at the idea of restraining the vivid tones I worked so hard to create.

I force myself to put brush to canvas. Force myself to cover the entire image with the blue-black ink. Force myself to watch the canvas turn completely dark, obscuring every line and every bit of color. When the ink's dry, I wipe it away with a soapy rag, then carefully remove the new varnish with a mixture of alcohol and turpentine.

Again, I'm awed by Han's genius. The last bits of ink have adhered themselves to the ridges of craquelure, creating a network of fine lines that duplicate those of the original forgery. I cover the canvas with a final coat of varnish, tinted with a touch of brown to mirror aging, and the faux masterpiece is complete.

MARKEL STANDS IN front of the two paintings, his eyes roving from one to the other and then back again. He doesn't say a word, and his face is inscrutable. For a moment, I'm back in Isaac's studio waiting for Karen and Markel's verdict on *4D*. The nauseating anticipation is the same, as is the relief when he turns to me with a huge smile.

"Bravo." He claps his hands in appreciation, and I see that he wants to hug me.

I step away and pull a bottle of champagne from the refrigerator. "You brought over the one that we drank to cement this project, so it's my turn to provide the one to celebrate its conclusion."

Markel is so riveted by the paintings that he doesn't notice the awkwardness in my voice. "I don't know what to say. I honestly don't." He turns to me, and his eyes are warm with admiration. "Which one is which?"

I grab a couple of glasses and walk back to him. "Guess."

He steps in closer, inspects each carefully, then walks around and inspects the backs. "Would've thought I'd know it anywhere."

"A good sign."

He returns to the front and looks some more. "But I can't tell. I really can't tell."

"Oh, go for it."

He stabs at the painting on the right. "This one."

I laugh, and he swivels his arm to the left one. "This one."

I hesitate, toying with him.

"Claire . . ."

"Should've stuck with your original bet."

"You've done phenomenal work here." He takes the champagne

bottle from me and pops it open. "To you," he says, raising the bottle and allowing the foam to cascade down its side. "The most amazing woman ever."

I hold the glasses out and watch the rims as he pours, avoiding his eyes. Half of me wants to throw myself into his arms, while the other half is all too aware of the lie I've told—or, at least, the lie I've allowed him to believe. And I've no idea how truthful he's been with me. It's difficult to own, given the pounding of my heart and the dampness between my legs, but I'm not sure I can trust him. Although I've never been particularly astute about relationships, as my rock-strewn romantic history attests, I'm astute enough to know this is not a good basis for one.

We sit on the couch, touch glasses, and toast our success. I snuggle myself into a corner cross-legged and smile, hoping not to look like I'm trying to avoid contact. "So what's the next step?"

"Authentication."

I take a sip of the champagne; it bubbles nervously down my throat. "You really think it'll pass?"

"What are you the most worried about?"

An interesting question. "I think we're relatively safe on all the standard measures. But the newer tests like atomic absorption or mass spectrometry might be able to pick up something I didn't control for. It's like you said, it's all going to depend on the sophistication of the buyer."

"My plan is to use the same authenticator I did for the original."

"Is that the best idea?"

"You look concerned," Markel says.

"Not really. Or not any more than I'd be about any expert going over it. But what are you going to tell him? How are you going to explain why you need to test it again?"

Markel finishes off his champagne and pours both of us another glass. "I'll just tell him I've got some concerns. That I want him to go over it one more time."

"And he'll buy that?"

"Why not? In a situation like this, anyone might want to double-check."

"Right. Sure. I guess." I run my fingers through my hair. "Sorry, it's been a long haul. I'm pretty wrung out. Exhausted actually. I can't even remember what we were just talking about."

He puts his glass on the table and stands, smiling indulgently down at me. "Of course you are." He holds out his hands to help me up. "What you need is sleep, not a lot of talk."

I let him pull me to a stand. We look at each other for a long quivering moment, then he puts his arm around my shoulder and turns me toward the door. I slip my arm around his waist.

When we reach the door, he drops his arm and lifts my chin with a finger. "Is it okay if I come by tomorrow afternoon so we can pack them both up? I'd like to get your version to the authenticator and the original into safe storage as soon as possible. And I'll bring you your money."

I nod, thrilled. And not about the money, although that's nice, too. It's about having them gone. About regaining my studio, about coming out from under the shadow. A fall cleaning to make room for my own work to thrive.

WITH THE TWO forgeries gone, the studio feels open, alive, truthful. And I feel that way, too. I have both my home and myself back. Not to mention another $17,000, which hopefully will be followed by the last installment of $16,000 when *Bath II* is authenticated. If it's authenticated. What will Markel do if I don't pass the test? Will he give up his Gardner idea and tell the owner he can't find a buyer? Will he take back the money he paid me?

Cancel my show? The truth is, I've no idea what he might do. I try to push these thoughts away. Just as I try to push away the memories of painting *Bath II*.

I don't always succeed. At times, the past months come rushing back at me in flashes I can't control. Bits and pieces interspersed with the continuing nightmares of chasing and being chased. Sometimes it seems as if none of it ever happened, and other times it's as if there's an indelible stain that will never go away. If I catch myself washing my hands twenty times a day, I'll know I've gone over the edge.

But there are gifts from my walk on the dark side: the oven and phenol formaldehyde. I've always been proud of my window series, viewing it as my best work, as the culmination of everything I've learned thus far. But adding in the phenol formaldehyde to achieve these otherworldly jeweled tones is raising my hopes.

A dangerous thing, hope, as I know all too well, but also a powerful motivator. Where my drive to finish *Bath II* was frenzied and hallucinogenic, preliminary work on my windows is surprisingly soothing. Like scuba diving off a coral reef. A slow-motion immersion into the exotically foreign, compelling, and breathtaking, heightened by the hint of peril.

And van Meegeren's gift isn't only the colors, it's the time that baking will buy me. I need twenty paintings for my show, all realistic and all highly glazed with layer upon layer of diaphanous paint. I look at the dozen window paintings still hanging from Markel's first visit. My original plan was to use six or seven in the show, but now that I've seen the range of color I can produce à la Han, I'm afraid they'll pale in comparison to my new work. But they're good, they're why Markel offered me the show, and unless I'm willing to wait until spring, they're in. So, thirteen new paintings.

I have enough preliminary drawings for at least thirty, although there are a number of new ideas, like one I've already named *Pink Medium,* I want to include. I'll make the canvases and apply the sizing and underpainting assembly-line style, which will cut down on time. I glance around the studio. It'll be tight to work on thirteen canvases at once, but there should be just enough space to pull it off. I'll sketch out each of the new paintings in advance, then move quickly from one canvas to the next to render the underdrawings. And when I start in on the actual painting, I'll have my oven to move things along. A daunting project. An incredible opportunity.

Twenty-four

I walk up the granite steps of Markel's house with trepidation. I probably shouldn't be here. Nonetheless, I am, standing before a nineteenth-century mansion facing the broad, tree-lined mall that sets Commonwealth Avenue apart from—and above—all the other tony streets of Back Bay. Plus, I'm on the Arlington/Berkeley block, which is set apart from and above all the other tony blocks of Comm Ave. There's never been any gentrification in this part of Boston because it's never fallen out of favor with the gentry.

Markel called early in the week and invited me to dinner. "Did you know I can cook?" he asked, when I answered the phone.

"You do?"

"Probably better than you."

"That would mean you can make something other than mac and cheese."

"Is that what you'd like for your surprise dinner?"

"Surprise?"

"Yup. Two actually."

"Can you tell me more?"

"Nope."

"Well then, if you're going to all the trouble of cooking," I told him, "I'll take something a bit more gourmet than mac and cheese."

"Done," he said. "Does seven o'clock Saturday night work for you?"

I hesitate. "Sure. I guess."

"See you Saturday." Then he was gone.

I didn't really have a chance to say no. Yet, I probably wouldn't have said it anyway. I'm a fool for surprises. Has the painting been authenticated? Is it something about my show? Is he going to poison me with his soufflé because now he's got the finished painting? A lesser woman would run. But not me. I want to see his artwork.

I press the doorbell next to his name, and when it buzzes, I step into a wainscoted, marble anteroom separating street and house. I push through a pair of etched-glass doors into a soaring, elegant space. In the late 1800s, well-dressed gentlemen and their ladies would have been received here. It's quite likely Belle Gardner was, at some time or another, one of them.

A wide mahogany staircase dominates the foyer, turning two times before it meets the second-floor landing. I hesitate, not sure where to go, when Markel comes down the stairs.

"Welcome," he calls. "We're up here." The lighting emphasizes his high cheekbones and square chin. He looks relaxed, boyish, comfortable in his own skin, pleased to see me. It's a tough package to resist.

I walk up the stairs toward him, curtsy, and hold out my hand. "Charmed, sir."

He takes it, turns it over, and kisses my palm. "Handsome lady."

When we enter the apartment, I don't know what to look at first: the exquisitely preserved architectural elements, the eclectic furnishings, or the artworks sprinkled liberally, but flawlessly, about. He shows me around. John Baldessari's spider, Tony Feher's sculpture of four jars with red tops, Sharon Core's photograph of a coconut cake. There's one from Zeng Fanzhi's *Mask Series* and my favorite David Park, *Four Nudes*, a Koons, a Cottingham, a Warhol, a Lichtenstein, and, of course, a Cullion.

"Amazing," I keep murmuring. "Wow. Great." I don't know what else to say. His collection rivals that of a small museum. Then he shows me his "Impressionist nook": a Manet, a Cézanne and a tiny, perfect Matisse.

"No Degas?" I ask.

"An unfortunate hole in my collection." He waves his hand to encompass all the works. "This is the advantage of owning a gallery. I get to buy what I love. At a much lower price than I would charge."

His portion of the house is three stories. The living room, dining room, and kitchen form the first floor, with seventeen-foot ceilings, three fireplaces, original crown moldings and medallions. The second floor is a huge master suite with a separate office, clean and masculine, but not overly so. Everything is updated, yet it all fits perfectly within its nineteenth-century frame. We climb to the third floor, which has three bedrooms, one perfectly appointed guest room and two others for his children.

"Children?"

"Robin's six and Scott's four. They mostly live with their mother in Weston, but I get to see them a lot."

"Oh" is all I can manage. I knew he'd married fairly young and had been divorced for a few years, but how could I not have known about the children? Why hadn't Isaac ever mentioned it? Why hadn't Markel?

We head back downstairs, and I catch artwork I missed on the way up: a Louise Bourgeois statue in a niche in the stairway, a William Kentridge drawing, a Calder mobile. He takes my hand

and leads me back into the living room. We sit on the couch, in front of a low table on which a bottle of champagne chills.

"Seems like we've been drinking a lot of champagne." I'm in such awe of his art collection I can barely get the words out.

He pours two glasses and hands me one. "We've had a lot to celebrate." A dramatic pause. "And now we have even more."

I hold my breath.

"Your *Bath II* has been authenticated. As far as anyone's going to be concerned, she's the real thing."

A flood of relief washes over me. "Wow." I knock back the glass of champagne, hold out the empty for a refill. "I can't believe it." But, of course, I know all too well that experts can be fooled.

"Were you that worried?"

"Of course I was that worried. I told you I was."

"I'd have been shocked if it turned out any other way."

"Then you're made of sterner stuff than I am."

He pulls an envelope from a drawer in the coffee table and hands it to me. "There's a bonus included."

"Thanks." I quickly put the envelope in my purse. It feels thicker than the others.

"That's not the real surprise," he says.

"It's not?" If *Bath II*'s been authenticated, could it be about my show?

"Well, I guess it's actually a presurprise, or the first part of one because we have to wait for the second part."

This doesn't sound like it's about my show. "You made macaroni and cheese for dinner?"

He bursts out laughing. "How'd you know?"

"You did?"

"With three kinds of mushrooms and tomatoes and herbs from my garden. Is that gourmet enough for you?"

I try to hide my disappointment. Although I like food as much as the next person, it would never fall into the surprise category for me. "Thank you. It sounds delicious."

He offers me a tray of black olives. The tray is long and narrow and looks as if it was made specifically for olives. I've never seen such a thing. I pop one into my mouth. It's perfect: sharp and dark, salty and oily. "Did you grow these, too?"

"There's something else," he says.

I eat another olive and wait.

"I sold it."

I almost swallow the olive pit. "*Bath II?*"

"I've worked with this collector before. I set up a number of levels between us, put out a feeler. He grabbed."

"He thinks it's the original? The one stolen from the museum?"

Markel touches his champagne flute to mine. "What else would he think?"

I struggle to keep my breathing normal. I've no idea why I'm reacting like this. What did I think was going to happen? Selling the painting as the original was always the plan.

"Hits you kind of weird when it finally happens, doesn't it?" he says.

Again, he's reading my thoughts. There's no denying the power of this experiential intimacy, especially when it's ours alone. A chill runs up my backbone. "You're sure he won't know it came from you? That he can't trace it back?"

"Too many people between us. And each one only knows the one who contacted him and the one he contacted," Markel says with certainty, but I note that he didn't directly answer my questions.

"What's he going to do with it?"

"He's a collector, Claire, a nutty bunch. But this guy's nuttier than most, a complete fanatic. Totally blinded to anything but what art he can own, what he can possess. That's why I went to him first with the Degas."

"But if he can't sell it or show it to anyone, if it's not a status symbol, and if he's not going to use it on the black market, what's in it for him?"

Markel leans back into the couch and sips his champagne. "It's the rush of knowing you have it, that it's yours and no one else but you can ever see it." His eyes roam to his Warhol, the Lichtenstein. "It's like an addiction. No, it *is* an addiction, one serious collectors can't and probably don't want to control. We're not talking regular people here."

I remember Sandra Stoneham saying something similar and how I felt when I looked at the empty frame in the Short Gallery. How thrilled I was to be the only one who knew where the missing painting was, how proud I was that Degas' *After the Bath* was in my studio, for me to touch and look at whenever the urge struck. No one but me. Suddenly, none of us are regular people.

"But what about his authentication?" I ask. "What if it goes to someone who figures out it's not real?"

"He's from India, but he's doing it here."

"But you said that's why foreign buyers, Third World, are better. That they don't have access to high-level experts or all the new equipment."

He puts his arm around me and pulls me toward him. I let him, too overwhelmed to resist. "That's normally so," he says, playing with a piece of hair that's dropped to my forehead. "But in this case, because of the painting's notoriety, his choice of authenticators is limited."

"So he's going to have to use the same guy you did?"

"Nowhere else to go."

"And then what'll happen?"

"After he's got the all clear from the authenticator, we agreed that he'd take the canvas off the stretchers and get it out of the country by either flying or sailing with it on his person."

"But what about security? They check everything now."

"Paintings don't set off metal detectors."

"If he did get caught, could it get back—"

Markel leans down and kisses me. A sweet, wet, warm kiss that goes on and on and works its way down between my legs and then back up and out to every nerve ending in my body. I've never had an orgasm from just a kiss before, but this feels as if that's exactly what's going to happen.

Markel pulls away and asks, "You said maybe when the project was over?"

"Where did you ever learn to kiss like that?"

"Is that a yes?"

Now that the kiss is over, some semblance of intelligence returns and my questions reemerge. I run my fingers through my hair and sit up. "How come you never told me about your kids?"

"Does it matter?"

"No. Not at all. Not in and of itself. It's just that it seems like something you might have mentioned."

"Do you know how many brothers and sisters I have? If my parents are alive? Where I grew up?" He shrugs. "I don't know any of those things about you either. We just never got that personal before."

"Can't argue with that," I say, but even after three years, Isaac's betrayal is still raw. I separate myself from him and stand. "Now where's that gourmet mac and cheese you were bragging about? I'm famished."

He stands, too, kisses the end of my nose. "We've got some

business to discuss over dinner, and I need your opinion on something."

The dinner is delicious, adding another check in his plus column. And he's a wonderful host, attentive without being overly solicitous, charming and self-deprecating. We laugh a lot, drink a bottle of wine, talk about my show.

"I'm planning on thirteen new paintings," I tell him.

"Sounds good," he says. "What's your estimate?"

"I was figuring a painting a week, thirteen weeks, which puts us in early January."

"It's either December or March," he says. "January and February are booked but I just got a cancellation for December. Think you could do it by then? Would be a great slot."

"Early or late?"

"Middle of the month."

"When would you have to know?"

"I need at least two months up front for promotion."

Could I pull off December? Two months ahead would be the middle of October. Which means I'd have to commit a month from now. Tight. Very tight.

"You could do fewer," he offers.

Fewer won't work. That would leave him room to have a second, albeit much smaller, show at the same time as mine. I want the whole gallery.

"Give me a month," I say. "I'll bust my butt and see how many I can finish. That'll give me a better measure. If I can do it for December, let's go with that. If not, we'll have to hold off till March."

"That works fine for me as far as Markel G goes. I've got a number of artists who'd take the slot in a nanosecond."

"But?" I ask, my stomach sliding to my feet.

"I can't say I like it personally."

At first I'm confused, lost in my ambition, then I understand. He's talking about us, about wanting more of my time for himself. "Ah, yeah. Yeah. There's always that."

"Is there a that?" he asks.

But I don't know how to answer. I need more time to think, yet I don't want to blow this. I can see there's some real potential here. I like him. "Yes," I finally say. "Just maybe not tonight."

He grins, and his whole body relaxes. "How about you cook me dinner tomorrow night?"

"If I do, there won't be a 'that.' We'll probably end up dead from food poisoning." I change the subject before he has a chance to respond. "Didn't you say you wanted my advice on something?"

He sobers. "It's about the original. About getting it back to the Gardner."

"Where is it now?" I ask cautiously.

"Locked up where no one but I can get to it. In a highly secured vault."

I know he's trying to protect me, or so he's said, but his evasiveness makes me uneasy. So many secrets.

"It doesn't matter where," he continues. "I just want to think through all the options."

I decide to give him the benefit of the doubt. "Obviously, you can't just go there and hand it over to them, so it has to be left somewhere."

"Somewhere where it's safe, protected," he says. "Not outside. Somewhere that can't be connected to me."

"Not in Boston."

"But not too far away. The less transporting the better."

"When do you plan on doing it?"

"After your forgery's out of the country."

"And the sellers have their money. And you've gotten your fee." So much for the benefit of the doubt.

"Yes. When I've gotten my fee." He gets up and clears the dessert plates from the table. His movements are brisk as he puts the dirty dishes on the pass-through counter.

"I'm sorry. I shouldn't have said that. I've no right to judge you. I'm far from blameless in all this." I watch his earnest face, his purposeful movements, and I want to believe that he's doing all of this to get the painting back to its rightful owner. "For me it was pretty straightforward. But for you?" I look at the art on the wall beside him: a Calder and a Koons.

"Even I have to work for a living, Claire. Things aren't always the way they look."

"But your art? A Warhol, a Calder, a Matisse?"

He sits in the chair beside me. "Remember what I was saying about art collectors? How they can be fanatical? Irrational at times? Well, I'm one."

"You're going to keep *Bath* for yourself?"

"No, no," he says. "Of course not. What I'm trying to explain is how I feel about my art. For those of us with no artistic talent, collecting is our means of self-expression. A way of discovering beauty, of making it, in a way. A collection that's something greater than ourselves." He shakes his head. "Not for sale. None of them."

"You haven't ever sold anything?"

"I keep adding, almost never subtract. It's like I said, an addiction. 'I'm Aiden Markel, and I'm an art collector.'" His smile is sheepish. "Maybe not as crazy as the guy who bought *Bath II,* but crazy enough."

"But what about this house?" I ask, unwilling to let him charm his way out of answering my questions. "The gallery?"

"Both mortgaged. Don't assume just because a person has lots of expensive things that he's not in debt." He takes my hands. "Yes, I'll get my fee, which will be substantial. But that's secondary. The whole point is to get *After the Bath* back on the wall of the Short Gallery. Is it illegal? Yes, I'll admit that. Will it be worth it? Obviously, I think the answer's yes."

I stare at my hands in his. It all makes sense, but I can't bear the thought of, once again, being played the fool.

He pulls me to my feet, and we walk silently to the front door, his arm loose around my shoulders. "I'm still open for tomorrow," he says. "We can always order out for pizza." Then he leans down and kisses me.

Again, I'm lost in the velvety sweetness of him. Of his lips, his chest, his body pressed against mine. I pulse toward him, and he pulses toward me. I tear myself away. I need to think, think, work it through. I give him a hug and rush down the stairs into the crisp autumn night.

On the sidewalk, I pause to catch my breath and look up at his front windows. He's standing in the bay, watching me, a wistful smile on his face. He places his palm to the window with a gesture so full of longing that something inside me breaks.

I press the doorbell again, and when I get the answering beep, I rush up the stairs even faster than I came down.

Twenty-five

THREE YEARS EARLIER

The first time I arrived in New York to paint the second *4D,* I went up to Karen's office. There, she introduced me to Beatrice Cormier, a bejeweled older woman with sharp, ice-blue eyes.

"Beatrice is a major collector," Karen explained. "She has multiple degrees in art history and knows more about painting than most art professors." She handed Beatrice a key. "She's going to observe you as you work."

For a moment, I was put off. I don't like being watched while I paint. But then I realized, of course, MoMA had to ensure that the work was actually mine.

"The supplies you requested are already in the studio." Karen pointed to the cardboard tube I had under my arm. "Are those your paintings I asked for?"

I was reluctant to hand them to her, but did. She wanted them for comparison purposes, to match to *4D,* which was to my advantage, but somehow it made me feel smarmy, like I was the guilty party.

"I'll get these back to you as soon as we're finished with them," she said, and turned to her computer in dismissal. "Beatrice will take you there now."

Beatrice's driver took us to a building in an up-and-coming-but-not-yet-arrived section of Brooklyn that reminded me of SOWA. Artists are always the first to find these places, pioneers who get the area started and then get pushed out when gentrification jacks up the rents.

We took the elevator to a small studio whose owner was out of the country. I didn't recognize his work—it had to be a man's—and had no idea whose space I was appropriating. Which, I supposed, was Karen's plan. This whole arrangement was very hush-hush. No one was to know about it until my claim had been validated. Or invalidated. And maybe not even then.

A large, empty canvas, the same size as *4D,* was set up on an easel facing south so the north light would hit it. My supplies lay on a paint-streaked table next to it. I checked the paints and the brushes, turpentine, mediums.

"Do you have what you need?" Beatrice asked.

"Looks good," I said. "But isn't it going to be awfully boring for you?"

"We need to establish a timetable so I can fit this into my schedule," was her answer.

"I only have one class. On Tuesdays. I'm almost done with my class work, focusing on my final capstone project. I'm hoping to get my degree at the end of next semester."

"Yes . . . ?" She was polite but left no doubt that she had little interest in the details of my life.

"So I guess anytime on either side of that is fine with me?"

Beatrice tapped out a series of commands on her phone. "It

would be best to complete this as soon as possible. How long would you presume it's going to take you?"

It hadn't taken me that long to paint *4D,* which had amazed me at the time. Wet-on-wet was much faster than wet-on-dry. Still, there was no guarantee this would come as quickly. Isaac wasn't the only painter to succumb to artists' block under pressure. "Three, four days?"

Unfortunately, Beatrice was a very busy woman and wasn't available for many sessions of two days in a row. But we managed to arrange a series of times when we could both meet at the studio. She explained that I was to have no more contact with Karen, that she, Beatrice, had the key, and she would be responsible for letting me in and locking me out.

And so it went. I came into the city three times and stayed for two days each. It took more sessions than I estimated because Beatrice never had a full day free. I painted when she was available, slept at the Y. She was easy to have around, reading or quietly talking on her cell phone, but ever vigilant. I'd have guessed they paid her handsomely for this tedious duty, but it was clear she was way too rich to be persuaded by money. I never did find out why she did it.

The whole process was actually quite pleasant as long as I didn't spend too much time thinking about what was behind it. I was out of Boston, away from the pressure of classes and the one-upmanship that's the hallmark of highly ranked MFA programs. And Beatrice turned out to be an excellent companion: both watchful and respectful, saying little, but clearly communicating that she was impressed with my work. Karen had told me I didn't have to make a copy of *4D,* just to paint something similar, another piece in the series. Which is what I did.

When I finished, Beatrice locked the painting in the studio and told me someone would be in touch. She thanked me for my graciousness, and I for hers. She smiled warmly at me for the first time since the project began and patted me on the shoulder. "Way to go, girl," she said, and winked. Then she got into her waiting car and was driven away.

It was six long weeks before I heard the official verdict.

Twenty-six

I buy a queen-size mattress, box spring, footboard, and headboard. I haven't had anything this official to sleep in since I was a little girl snuggled into my faux–French Provincial twin bed. For the first time in my life, I actually have money—the $5,000 bonus was a nice addition to my ill-gotten nest egg—and it just didn't seem fair to ask Aiden to deal with a mattress on the floor.

The dark cloud has passed. No more nightmares of being smothered or chased or locked up. No Isaac, no Belle, and no Degas. And lots of Aiden.

Although the shortening angle of the fall sun and the decreasing hours of daylight usually make me cranky, this year, despite all evidence to the contrary, the world is so much brighter than it was during the summer. As I'd hoped, completing *Bath II* banished my demons.

I'm working furiously on my windows, at almost the same pace as *Bath II,* but this time I have thirteen paintings to contend with and must pace myself. If limiting painting time to no more than fourteen hours a day can be considered pacing. Obviously, there's no time to trek to Back Bay, so if Aiden and I want to be together, it's got to be at my place. He claims he doesn't mind coming down to the studio, that he likes both the walk and the smell of turpentine. But I think it's sex he's after. And I've got no problem with that.

The man makes love even better than he kisses, and he can do things with his tongue that turn me inside out. I've had a number of short flings and one-night stands since Isaac, but it's been over three years since I've had sex on anything close to a regular basis. And, man oh man, is it addictive. In some ways it's fortunate that I'm working against a tough deadline; otherwise we'd never leave the new bed.

"I've got to get back to work," I say, as we loll around in postcoital bliss. Actually it's the second postcoital bliss of the afternoon, and I'm falling farther behind by the moment.

"I think March would be a wonderful time for your show." Aiden's tongue follows the contours of my ear. "Lots of time between paintings for a little fun," he says. "Spring and renewal. It's so appropriate."

A shiver runs through me. For a moment I consider the possibility, even though I know there's no way I can wait that long. I leap off the bed before he can convince me to stay. "You're my dealer. You're supposed to want what's best for my career."

"I'm also your lover." Aiden sits up and puts his hands behind his head, watches me as I get dressed. "So I have to consider what's best for your body."

"And don't think I don't appreciate it." I step into my work jeans, which are so stiff with paint they practically stand by themselves. "But you know what happens to girls who are all play and no work."

"They're not dull?" he asks.

"They're not successful."

Aiden throws his arms up in mock despair. "Mankind! Beware

the overly ambitious woman. She'll leave you cold and alone, your balls blue."

I stick my tongue out at him. "Beware the overly melodramatic man."

He picks up the remote from the floor and aims it at the small television perched on a pile of old cookbooks I never use. "Just want to check the market close," he says. "Then I'll head back to the gallery."

I've no interest in the market, having never owned a single stock, so I pick up my brush and inspect my current piece. It's the *Pink Medium* I've been thinking about for months, and it's coming out better than I expected. I'm thrilled at the radiance the phenol formaldehyde and oven have given to the many tones of pink. Greedily, I reach for my palette.

"Shit!" Aiden yells. "Claire. Shit. Shit!"

I whirl around.

"It's *After the Bath*. Our *Bath*." He jumps out of bed and stands, naked, in front of the television. "I think."

I suddenly understand what the term "heart in your throat" means; it feels as if every major organ in my body has squeezed itself behind my larynx. Still clutching my brush, I join him.

"Assumed to be one of the unrecovered paintings stolen from the Isabella Stewart Gardner Museum in the brazen 1990 Boston robbery that has stymied the world's most renowned investigators," intones the CNN newscaster.

And there it is, filling the screen. If that isn't my *Bath II*, then someone did a hell of a forgery. Although it's impossible to see the details on my tiny screen, structurally, the painting appears to be an exact replica of the one Aiden has in storage. My brush clamors to the floor. I take his hand.

"The painting was discovered last week during a security screening in San Francisco aboard a ship destined for New Delhi, India," the newscaster continues. "If it proves to be Edgar Degas' *After the Bath*, it will be the first object recovered from the 1990 heist in which priceless masterpieces by the likes of Vermeer, Rembrandt, Manet, and Degas were stolen. The painting is currently en route to Boston for authentication. There is no word on any arrests made in the case, but the FBI has announced a full investigation. We will have updates for you as soon as we receive them."

Aiden and I stare at each other, neither able to speak, the glazed shock in our eyes saying it all.

"I thought you said he was going to carry it with him?" I finally say.

Aiden pulls his pants on. "We don't know that he didn't. All they said was that it was caught during security screening. And we don't even know if it's my buyer."

After the Bath. A ship. Leaving from San Francisco. Going to India. Who else could it be?

"It's important we sit tight," he says. "Don't panic. Don't talk to anyone. I'll try to get some more information. Be back as soon as I can."

"Where are you going?" I ask, as he grabs his jacket.

Aiden looks at me and blinks, almost as if he's surprised to see me. Then his eyes soften, and he wraps me in his arms. "It'll be okay. I promise. I won't let anything happen to you. Or me."

I let him hug me, wanting to believe what he's saying, but all too aware that these promises aren't his to make. Or to keep.

WHILE I WAIT for Aiden to return, I try to work, but for the moment, my powers of concentration abandon me. Afraid I'm going to make some fatal error that will put me even farther behind or burn down the entire building, I force myself to stop. I keep the television on, but it's just a repetition of the same information. Even the shot of the painting is the same. I do some Internet surfing, but the only thing I learn is that the TSA discovered the painting almost a week ago and didn't authorize the release of the information until today. Which means they probably know a lot more than they're telling.

I put on an extra pair of socks and a sweatshirt, but I can't get warm. I add a down vest and wool gloves with the top of the fingers cut off. But my bones seem to be emanating cold from their marrow. I want to jack up the heat, but the forced hot air has erratic effects on paint that isn't completely dry. So I walk in circles, hoping movement will help.

It's dark when Aiden returns. I throw myself into his arms, seeking both warmth and protection. As he's just come in from the cool night air and doesn't have any magical defensive powers, I'm disappointed on all counts.

He sits on the couch and presses a finger to the bridge of his nose. "They arrested Patel."

"Who?"

"Ashok Patel. The buyer."

"So it's my painting?"

He looks at me as if I've lost my mind.

"Right, right," I say, as I run through the implications. "You said you've worked with him before. So he knows you. Your name, what you look like."

"Yes and no."

"Which?"

"He knows me as the owner of Markel G. Been a client for years. But he's got no idea I was involved in this sale. As I told you before, I went through a number of middlemen."

"So they know who you are."

"It's a levels thing, again. I'm covered, and because I've never done anything like this before, it's unlikely I'll come up on anyone's radar screen."

This doesn't sound as convincing as Aiden is trying to make it appear, but there are more pressing issues at the moment. "How'd they find him?"

"I don't know for sure, but my brokers gave him explicit instructions to take the canvas off the frame and carry it with him. I assumed he'd do what he was told."

"But he didn't."

Aiden slides over and puts his arm around me. "Patel doesn't know where the painting came from, who he was dealing with or, obviously, that it isn't real. Even if he wanted to, he wouldn't be able to tie it to me."

"The FBI or the TSA or whoever, they could get things out of him. Work up through your layers."

"That stuff's a lot less effective than it looks on TV."

"But they're going to be all over the whole Gardner theft thing again. Where the paintings are, who's got them. They could connect it to you from that end. "

"I'm saved by both my own ignorance and others' ignorance of me." He cups my chin. "The important thing is that no one can connect any of this to you. I'm the only one who knows you're involved, and," he kisses me lightly, "my lips are sealed."

"But what about you?"

"I brought you a high-quality copy and paid you eight-thousand dollars to make a copy from it. That's all you know. And don't worry about me. I'm a big boy. I can take care of myself."

"Is it really that simple?"

He flashes a quick grin. "I sure as hell hope so."

The grin throws me off balance, and I again find myself thinking about how little I know about him.

"Guess the good news is that I don't have to worry about how to get the original back to the Gardner anymore," he says. "Or at least not for a while."

I bite my lower lip. Of course, there is no original, or at least no original he can give back. Aiden, too, knows little about me. "What if they figure out it's a forgery?" I ask. "Or, maybe worse, what if they don't?"

Aiden takes my hands. "Claire, you're going to make yourself, and me, crazy with all these questions. There's no point in getting ahead of ourselves. Let's take one thing at a time. As my grandmother used to say, 'Assume the best until you know the worst.'"

"Right," I tell him, although I know I'm incapable of that kind of control. "Whatever Grandma Markel says."

Aiden slaps his thighs and stands. "Want to order out for pizza?"

When the pizza arrives, neither of us eats much. We play with our slices and pretend to be engrossed in reruns of *Seinfeld* and *Taxi*. We even laugh now and then.

"Are we whistling a happy tune?" I ask Aiden after a particularly boisterous bout of amusement.

He shrugs. "If it works . . ."

We turn in early, and for the first night since Aiden made me macaroni and cheese, we don't make love.

Twenty-seven

A bove the fold, on the front page of the *Boston Globe,* is a photograph taken from the Gardner Museum archives of *After the Bath,* the one that had hung in the Short Gallery for almost a hundred years, the one stolen in the heist. Only Aiden and I know that this isn't the painting recovered on a dock in San Francisco. Only I know it wasn't painted by Edgar Degas.

STOLEN GARDNER MASTERPIECE FOUND? asks the large-font headline. It's the lead story on almost every news site on the Internet. The *Today* show, too.

Aiden and I comb every source we can find, reading snippets out loud to each other. But the bottom line is that nothing additional has been released since yesterday's announcement. No mention of Patel or an arrest. The authorities are keeping whatever they know very close.

"Do you think they're doing that thing where they withhold evidence that only the killer could know?" I ask Aiden.

Aiden rolls his eyes. "Claire, there is no killer. And there very well could be no evidence. Which is probably why they aren't sharing it."

"You know what I mean."

He stands and massages my neck, another thing he's really good at. "Unfortunately, I know exactly what you mean."

I lean back into his expert hands and groan. I'm in my paint clothes, and *Pink Medium* has been cooking for over an hour. I drop my head forward so he can get at the sore muscles above my shoulder blades.

"Are you scared?" I ask.

His fingers keep working, but he doesn't answer.

His silence jolts me, and I turn to look at him. "Could we go to jail?"

"Don't be a child, Claire," he snaps.

I take a step away from him. He's never raised his voice to me before.

"Sorry," he says, drawing me back. "Sorry. As you might have guessed, I'm a little stressed."

My eyes scour his.

He sighs. "Anything's possible, and this is not an insignificant crime. But no, I don't think we'll go to jail. Or at least you won't."

I hold onto him. I don't think I could bear to lose another man due to a situation for which I'm partially to blame.

"Don't worry so much," he says. "I'm checking into a number of options. Things to keep us safe."

While this is hopeful, there's evasiveness in his voice that makes me uneasy. "What kinds of things?"

Aiden gently untangles himself. "I have to get going," he says. "Should be at the gallery most of the day. I'll call you if I learn anything."

When he leaves, I go right back to work. The zone is the only safe place for me now.

TWO DAYS LATER, it's confirmed that a man named Ashok Patel, an Indian national from Bangalore, has been arrested for transportation of stolen goods. It's also reported that the canvas was on its stretchers, not rolled up as Patel had been instructed. Nor was he carrying it with him. Instead, it was concealed inside a large container of blue jeans destined for a New Delhi department store.

Over the next few days, there's talk of extraditing Patel to Massachusetts, about charging him in the heist, about sightings of the other stolen paintings all over India. But a week after the arrest, there's no additional hard news on Patel or the authentication of *Bath II,* just speculation by television anchors who don't have a clue what they're talking about. If it weren't for my windows, I'd be a madwoman by now.

Taking refuge in painting has worked double duty: Not only am I ahead of schedule but also I'm either too engrossed or too exhausted to obsess about Patel. Only part of this is due to my current workaholism; the other piece is the sheer number of hours I've put into this window project over the past two years. I've made hundreds of drawings and taken thousands of photographs, so my difficulty wasn't what to paint but which ideas to choose.

I've made all thirteen canvases, applied the sizing, sketched all the underdrawings, and covered them with a coat of underpaint. *Pink Medium* should be finished today and *Tremont* tonight. I'll start polychrome painting on *Corridor* and *Bay* tomorrow. Aiden is very impressed with the quality of the work. I'm pretty pleased myself.

I check the calendar. I'm working at almost twice the speed I estimated, finishing two paintings in a little over a week instead of just one. At this rate, with ten weeks and eleven paintings to go,

I should be on pace to stage a December show. With a couple of weeks to spare. I recalculate to make sure. The numbers stay the same. I can do this.

I've felt this conclusion coming for the past few days, but now I'm ready to make it a decision. Instead of calling Aiden to tell him the news, I take a long shower and spend more time drying my hair than usual. I put on a touch of makeup, something I haven't done in ages, and my lace underwear. Unfortunately, my closet is pretty sparse, but as the weather's unseasonably warm, a sexy tank top and the cute little jacket I bought at Filene's Basement years ago will work just fine.

When I get to Markel G, I stand inside the door and watch Aiden at his desk at the rear of the gallery. The current show is about line, and it's very impressive, particularly curatorially. There are anthropomorphic sculptures created by thin lines of thread. Drawings of what at first appear to be sheets of graph paper but are in actuality a delicate webbing in ink. A twenty-foot spiral created by miles of wire. White circles upon circles upon circles etched into a black canvas. And most impressive, a single-line drawing, maybe twenty-five feet long and covering two walls, depicting life in a Kenyan village. A very smart show.

Aiden's unaware of me, speaking into the phone with a warm smile. No one would ever guess that he's worried about anything greater than the installation of his next show. It strikes me that if Aiden's that calm, then I should be, too.

When he sees me, a wide grin stretches across his face. He hangs up and comes toward me but checks himself before giving me a hug. I'm nervous that if our relationship is known, people will think that's how I got the show—which I suppose is better than how I actually got it.

Although Aiden thought it was silly, he's humored me and

agreed to be discreet in public. "You look fabulous. An occasion I don't know about?"

I bat my eyelashes from an appropriate distance. "Just a visit to my dealer to discuss my upcoming December show."

"You're sure?"

"Sure."

We decide on the second week of the month, with the show to stay up through the new year.

"It's good timing," Aiden assures me. "Really good. We'll have the opening on the sixth, well before Christmas, and the show will hang through the holiday season when the street's always full. You'd be surprised how much business gets done the week after Christmas."

I listen to all this, watch the owner of Markel G put my name in his calendar, glance at the walls, and mentally replace the artwork with my own, but it's not real. It's not happening to me, Claire Roth, the pariah of the Boston art world. The Great Pretender. It can't be. Or can it? Unaware that I'm not listening, that I'm pretty much incapable of doing so, Aiden talks on about placement and promotion, wooing curators and collectors, price points.

"Oh," I cry as a pulse of happiness surges from the center of my being. I actually clasp my hands together with a clap of pure joy. It *is* happening to me.

Aiden bursts out laughing and introduces me to his two assistants, Chantal and Kristi, who together must have at least twenty piercings and less than a yard of fabric below their waists. Very high boots, though.

He tells them about my December show and goes to my website. Chantal and Kristi ooh and ah over the paintings while Aiden gushes to them about the unique combination of classical techniques and contemporary subject matter. For a moment, I feel left out of the conversation, an outsider looking in. An interloper. I have to remind myself that I'm not. Right now, right this very moment, the dream I never believed would come true is happening. My entire body buzzes with the improbability of it all.

Two middle-aged women wearing high-style haircuts and designer jeans come through the door, and Kristi immediately goes to greet them. I show Chantal the early windows I plan to include in the show and tell her a bit about the new ones. She seems sincerely excited. I try to act cool and unimpressed, as if I do this every day, but I can tell from the heat in my face and the wild waving of my hands that I'm not doing a very good job.

When Chantal is called away by another customer, Aiden says, "So how do you want to celebrate?"

I put a forefinger to the corner of my mouth. "I heard there's a place just a block or so from here that has the most wonderful etchings . . ."

When we get to Aiden's, we head straight to his bedroom. But I'm so excited, I can't settle down. I babble on about *Pink Medium*, whether to include *Tower* in the show or paint another new one now that I've got some extra time, where I should buy an outfit for the opening. I'm completely unable to focus. But Aiden's sexual prowess and patience finally win me over. In the end, my orgasm is so wide and rolling and intense that I gasp, "Best ever," as I hold him inside me, pushing him to go even deeper.

His laugh is a growl, and he does what I want.

Afterward, satiated and sweaty, we lay curled like nested question marks, Aiden's heart beating into my back.

I FINISH *TREMONT* that evening and spend the next day working on the medium-range tones in *Corridor* and *Bay*. Three layers painted and baked on each, which meets the pace I need to keep. I think about doing another round through the oven but decide to call it quits. Aiden will be starting his promotion in a couple of weeks, and I have to tell the crew at Jake's what's going on before they hear about the show from someone else.

I waltz into Jake's as if I'd been doing it every night. It's been well over a month. The longest time I've been away since I started hanging here after Isaac.

Maureen sees me first. "Look who's risen from the dead," she says. "Or is it the canvas?"

Mike, Small, and Danielle are on me in a flash.

"Are you okay?"

"How's the painting going?"

"Where have you been? We missed you."

"Are you too cool for us now that you're on a creative tear?"

"I missed you all, too," I say, and mean every word of it. "But I'm probably not going to be able to come around much for the next six weeks either."

Small grabs my hands. "Something's happening? Something good with your career?"

My throat closes up, and my eyes fill with tears. I can't speak.

Small steps closer. "It's not good?"

I shake my head.

"Oh, honey," she says. "Whatever it is, we're here for you."

I try to blink back the tears, but one rolls down my face. They all look at me with a mixture of concern and compassion in their eyes. I swipe at the tear. "No, no," I finally manage. "It's good."

They all visibly relax, and Maureen pushes a Sam toward me. "Drink up," she says.

I quaff down half the bottle. "You're not going to believe this." I look around at their expectant faces, but I can't form the words.

Danielle crosses her arms over her chest. "If Rik were around he'd say, 'I'm getting old here.'"

Might as well get it over with. "I'm going to have a show at Markel G."

For a moment, there's dead silence, then the bar erupts.

"That's fabulous."

"Unbelievable."

"Markel G. What a coup."

"How'd you do it?"

Mike grasps my shoulder. "Well deserved. Well deserved."

"I already comped Claire a beer," Maureen grumbles. "And now it looks like I'm going to have to comp a whole round."

Everyone cheers. When the bottles are opened, Small raises hers and says, "To the success of one of our own."

We all raise ours, drink, and return the bottles to the bar with loud clunks. "Amen," says the chorus.

Twenty-eight

THREE YEARS EARLIER

Six weeks is a long time. It's long enough to develop headaches, insomnia, digestive issues, fear of success, fear of failure, fear of fear itself, and a host of other psychological problems. I managed to acquire every one, and a few others, while I waited for the verdict from Karen Sinsheimer. Self-diagnosed, of course. By the time she called, I was a complete wreck.

"I'm sorry," Karen said, after introducing herself.

I bit my lip. "About what?"

"The committee has determined that $4D$ is the work of Isaac Cullion."

Twenty-nine

"You fooled the best of the best," Aiden says. It's after closing, and we're in the understated comfort of the small alcove of Markel G in which deals are done.

"I mean, it's one thing for your authenticator to believe it's real, but this . . . It was well executed and all . . . I'm not taking anything away, but still," I stammer.

He'd just told me the authenticators hired by the Gardner had pronounced *Bath II* an original Degas, the very *After the Bath* stolen from the museum during the 1990 heist. After *4D,* I suppose I shouldn't be so surprised. But I am.

I shake my head to clear it. "One of my Repro teachers once said that only the bad forgeries have been discovered because the good ones are hanging on museum walls."

Aiden chuckles. "Guess you're in good company."

Of course, this isn't my first time. "So does this lessen our exposure?"

Aiden turns toward the main room of the gallery. "Do you want to hang the paintings in a linear loop around the open gallery? Each alone in its own space? Or maybe we should bring in the transportable walls so people can feel visually and emotionally surrounded?"

But, for once, I'm not interested in discussing my show. "Does this make it better or worse for us?"

He sighs. "I'm not going to lie to you. They're going to be all over Patel. Looking for evidence. Clues to where the other paintings might be. Trying to make a deal for information." He pauses. "Have you ever been fingerprinted?"

I shake my head no.

"Good."

"You?"

He, too, shakes his head. "It's okay, Claire. The odds are in our favor. Chances are we're going to be fine."

I don't say anything, but I'm thinking that denial is a beautiful thing. Until it isn't.

THE PUBLIC IMAGINATION is captured, and their desire for information on *After the Bath,* the heist, Edgar Degas, and all things Gardner is insatiable. The media is, of course, more than happy to fill the void.

I was just a kid when the robbery occurred, and despite growing up outside Boston and going to school here, I knew few of the details. I, of course, knew that in the middle of the night, two men dressed as police officers handcuffed and bound two inexperienced guards and stole thirteen works, including Rembrandt's *Storm on the Sea of Galilee,* Vermeer's *The Concert,* and, of course, Degas' *After the Bath.* That until now, and despite thousands of hours of police work and a $5 million reward, none of the artworks have been found.

In the last few days I've learned that one of the guards was stoned, that an experienced guard had called in sick at the last moment, that the thieves drove up in a rusted-out hatchback, spent only about an hour in the museum, and then loaded their loot into the back of the car and drove away.

I've also learned that the museum had no insurance, that the guards were really night watchmen, more concerned with protecting the building from fire and leaky pipes than theft. That when one of the thieves told a guard if he didn't give them any problems he wouldn't be hurt, the guard replied, "Don't worry, they don't pay me enough to get hurt." That was probably the stoned one.

Suspects include everyone from the Boston mafia to the Irish Republican Army, internationally known art thieves, local thugs, crooked cops, ex-museum employees, and even the Catholic Church. All of them, even those in prison, on the lam, or in their graves, are back, dead center. Unfortunately for Aiden and me, so are a host of new leads. The journalist, cop, or FBI agent who cracks this case is looking at long-term fame and fortune. It's exhilarating stuff. And it scares the shit out of me.

I sit in front of the oven watching *Doors* bake even though I'm supposed to be painting the midranges of *Old North*. I force myself to stand and walk over to *Old North*. I pick up a brush and my palette, but my eyes stray over to the bed, and I think about taking a nap.

After acknowledging that the authentication puts us in more danger, Aiden returned to reminding me to assume the best until we know the worst. But now my sleeping-to-the-top concerns are superseded by the notion that if we appear romantically entwined we'll be perceived as entwined in everything else. I make up excuses to avoid being in public together, even to being seen going in and out of each other's apartments. Explanations are easy because of my impending deadline, but Aiden's taking notice.

"I understand how busy you are, the pressure you're under," he says when he calls that evening to say good night. "I know more than anyone, but you can't stay cooped up in your studio. It's not good for you. Or for your career. Think of it as your job: You need to make contacts, get out there and network. The opening's in just over a month. The press releases are going out tomorrow. You need to start promoting the show, the new work."

"I thought that was your job."

"It's yours, too. There's a fundraiser at the Mandarin Oriental Hotel this weekend, which will be your perfect entrée. It's a day after the press release and—"

"I don't want to start with something that major. All those people who know my history will never—"

"It's not an official art bash. It's a Halloween party for the national gay marriage initiative, so it'll be a good mix. A good place to start."

"Costumes?"

He laughs. "It would be a shame to cover your beautiful face, but yes, Claire, everyone will be in costume."

This is a plus.

"This melodrama about us not being seen together is a bunch of crap," he continues. "And anyway, we've got a business reason to be there: dealer and artist."

"Can't we wait until after the opening?"

Silence on the other end.

"All right, all right," I finally say. "I'll go. Fine."

"And between now and then, get yourself out and into the air, away from all that paint and turpentine. Not to mention the formaldehyde."

"Formaldehyde's a preservative. It's keeping me young."

"I doubt that," he says dryly.

"You used to think I was funny."

"You used to be."

FINDING A DECENT costume on the day before Halloween is no easy task. Of course, the drugstores are packed with plastic Spidermans, Cinderellas, and Harry Potters, but I'm guessing none of these are appropriate for a $500-a-plate fundraiser. There's no costume store in walking distance, and after a visit to a couple of vintage clothing shops, I come up empty. So I rush back to CVS for a poufy white wig and a heavily feathered Mardi Gras mask on a stick, then buy a slinky, secondhand dress on my way home.

As I walk up to the Mandarin Oriental Hotel in my sort-of new dress, wig and mask in hand, I wonder why I didn't get something like the robot or dinosaur. Some assembly was required, but the result would have been a box over my head. If no one recognizes me, no one can snub me. And why didn't I let Aiden pick me up as he'd offered? It seemed noble to refuse at the time, as he lives only a few blocks from the hotel and I live about twenty, but now the idea of walking in alone is far from appealing. I check the bag to assure myself the mask is inside.

I've never been to the Mandarin before, and I'm blown away by the lobby. It's full of subtle but powerful Asian influences: silk wall coverings over Jerusalem limestone, exquisite furniture of inlaid wood, lacquered bamboo, glass, and mother-of-pearl. And the artwork. Incredible. Two colorful, hand-painted lithographs by Frank Stella frame the entrance, and a Terry Rose triptych hangs over the front desk. On my right is an unusual David Hockney, *Deux,* in which he used muted colors to create Picasso-like figures. To my left, over the fireplace, is David Mann's *The Given,* a commanding, almost three-dimensional, black-and-red abstraction that brings to mind the Big Bang.

I spend more time than I should admiring the art, then stop in the bathroom to put on my Halloween accessories. As planned, I'm an hour late. Once I'm coiffed and masked, I wend my way through the hotel in search of the ballroom. This place could double as a museum: ten Terry Winters's shadowgraph images, framed with bamboo-textured mats, rise two-by-two up a tall stairwell; Judith Brust's *Life Line #3* hangs on the second-floor landing.

I hear the party before I see it and pause to collect myself. My palms are damp, and I'm afraid the hand holding the mask will shake. I remind myself that I've done more difficult things before, for instance, telling Karen Sinsheimer that I painted *4D*. Although this probably isn't a good choice as it wasn't one of my wiser decisions. Still, I raise the mask and step into the ballroom.

It's a wild scene. Sexy cops and naughty nurses. Pirates and cavemen and Greek goddesses. Homer Simpson, Harry Potter, Indiana Jones, Tiger Lily, Shrek, and the Joker. Nefertiti and Cleopatra. Of course, given the cause, Cleopatra is a man and Indiana Jones a woman. Other cross-dressers are decked out in full Miss America regalia, and a good percentage of the men are buff, oiled, and underclothed. A lot of the women are, too. I'd bet my show that not a single costume comes from a drugstore.

The cocktail hour appears to be shifting into dinner, and I look around for Aiden. He's coming as Professor Henry Higgins, and his tux should be easy to find amid all these revealing costumes. But before I can find him, George Kelly, my museum school drawing professor, sidles up to me. He's dressed in an army uniform that's at least a couple sizes too small, perhaps his own from many years earlier.

"Claire Roth," George exclaims. "Don't you look fabulous. I heard about your show at Markel G, and I couldn't be happier for you."

I lower my mask, stunned.

Right behind him is a 1920s-era gangster, aka Sandra Stoneham's friend Professor Zimmern, director of the Sculpture Department. He takes my hand. "We are so proud of you, Claire. Nothing better than one of our own coming into her own."

I never took sculpture and knew Zimmern only by sight, and George was one of the first to take a stand against me when the news of *4D* broke. I remind myself that I'm here to network and accept their congratulations with the appropriate self-deprecation.

Professor Henry Higgins comes toward us with his slicked-back hair and high-collared tux; there's even a faint resemblance to Rex Harrison. Aiden takes my hand, kisses it. "And don't you look fetching tonight, my dear," he says in a proper English accent.

I introduce the three professors to each other. George and Zimmern flutter a bit of suck-up, then back off.

"Hope to see you at Claire's opening," Aiden calls after them.

George snaps an awkward salute. "Wouldn't miss it."

"See," Aiden says, as he leads me to our table. "You're a natural at promotion."

"They came up to me, congratulated me."

"They won't be the only ones."

And Aiden's right. It's as if this very evening, in this very ballroom, I've burst from the cocoon I entered as the abhorred into a world where I'm now the adored. It's quite disconcerting, and at first I don't know how to handle it, but halfway through dinner, I've become confident and loquacious. The Great Pretender is banished. And no one appears to be aware that Aiden and I are anything other than colleagues. By the time the seven-layer, chocolate-and-white-mousse cake is served, I'm having more fun than I've had in years.

Two hands cover my eyes. "Guess who?"

I recognize the voice immediately, jump up from the table, and throw my arms around Rik, who's dressed as a French artist, beret and all. "I thought you were in Paris for another week," I cry, and give him a kiss.

"Just got in an hour ago. Rushed right over." He glances at Aiden. "Didn't expect to see you here though . . ." The question hangs in the air.

"Did I get the dates wrong?" I ask quickly. "Were you due home today?"

"When all this stuff started breaking at the Gardner," he explains, "I worked my tight little buns off so I wouldn't miss any more of the drama than I already had." He gives me a big kiss on the lips. *"After the Bath,* Bear, can you believe it?"

Aiden stands and sticks his hand out to Rik. "Aiden Markel," he says. "You must be the famous Rik."

Rik looks from Aiden to me, and his eyes widen. "Not very famous, I'm afraid."

"Famous to Claire," Aiden says. "Pull up a chair and join us."

When Rik sets his chair down behind us, we both push outward, apart, so he can get closer to the table. "And the Gardner plot thickens," Rik says.

"What thickens?" I demand at the same time that Aiden asks calmly, "How so?"

Again Rik looks from me to Aiden and then back to me. Others may have been fooled, but he doesn't miss a thing.

The food I just ate feels like a block of cement in my stomach. "Have you got some inside info?" I wink at him. "Do tell."

Rik leans in. "It hasn't been released to the press yet, but according to the grapevine, this guy Patel is going to plead not guilty to the charges and agree to be extradited to Boston for trial."

I don't immediately know whether this is good or bad news for us. It takes all my effort not to look at Aiden.

"Is that bizarre?" Aiden asks, his voice as unruffled as if he were discussing the quality of the seven-layer cake. "Isn't that the way it usually goes?"

"That's not the bizarre part," Rik says.

I try to look casual, interested, but not overly so.

"It's the reason for the not guilty plea. According to Patel's lawyers, he never thought the painting was the real thing, never even wanted the real thing. Patel claims that as far as he knew, he was buying a copy through an online company that does high-quality reproductions of nineteenth-century European masterpieces." Rik grins at me. "Wouldn't it be a kick if he claimed it was from Repro and that he'd been told that you, the renowned Degas expert, was the one who painted it?"

THE NEXT MORNING, everything Rik told us is confirmed by the media. Which makes me very nervous. A possible trial. A possible deal with prosecutors. A possible betrayal in the levels between Patel and Aiden. A possible connection to Repro. I hastily switch to thinking about the happier parts of the party last night. The acceptance, the congratulations, the promises of support. Only Crystal Mack was less than gracious.

"Is it true?" she demanded.

"Is what true?"

"Don't be coy, Claire. How'd you do it?"

"Well, first I primed the canvas, did the underpainting, and used charcoal to draw the—"

"Is that all?" Crystal sneered in an obvious reference to Aiden.

"Of course not," I said, my voice thick with honey. "I mixed my medium with the pigments and applied layer after layer—"

She flipped her hand at me. "Got it."

"I'll make sure you get an invitation to the opening," I called to her retreating back.

"I think I'm busy that night," she said, before disappearing into the crowd.

Everyone else seemed truly glad to welcome me back from exile. Which means they will come: the critics, the collectors, the curators. If the paintings are as good as Aiden thinks, I could be on my way.

I check on *Charlie's,* which is baking in the oven, and return to applying the bright oranges of the final layers of *Nighttime T. Nighttime T* is going to be one of my favorites, if not my favorite of the series. The faces that stare blankly through the windows of the moving train, lost in the omnipresent nighttime of the tunnel, have a Hopper-esque quality. But because of the luminosity of the paint and the authenticity baking brings to their skin tones, they appear almost three-dimensional, a shade more real than real.

I'm glad when the oven timer goes off. This means not only that *Charlie's* is ready for the final coat of varnish but also that it's time to go to Beverly Arms. My leave of absence has been suspended, and I'm allowed back into juvy, no longer a criminal in their eyes. As much as I feel my deadline pressing, I need to be out of the studio, away from my paintings, away from myself. These kids are in far worse shape than I am, and it'll be nice to think about someone else's problems. I leave myself plenty of time so that I won't be late.

The moment I enter the facility and see the rotting-vegetable walls and wire-mesh windows though, my heart begins to pound. I slowly approach the metal detector.

"Name," the guard barks, looking from my photo to my face, although he knows exactly who I am.

I ball my hands into fists. "Claire." My nose fills with the odor of cheap cologne and stale sweat. I'm back in that tiny room in the bowels of this building. Locked up and confined. "Uh, uh, Claire, Claire Roth."

He looks at me closely, warily. "Purpose of visit?"

The room's overheated, small, and claustrophobic. I'm lightheaded, unsteady. I reach out and clasp the edge of his desk. His face blurs.

"Purpose of visit," he demands, his voice edged with annoyance.

I try to speak, but nothing comes out. Patel snitched. It's over. Aiden and I will be locked up forever.

"Is something wrong, Ms. Roth?" he asks suspiciously.

I visualize the boys sitting in their cells, bored, angry, frustrated, swearing at me, at Kimberly, too. Giving her a hard time. She's already got one of the toughest jobs ever, and all she needs is a wimpy, useless volunteer to make it even more difficult. "Nothing, sir," I say. "I'm fine.

When I pull open the door of GE 107, Kimberly jumps up. There's no one else in the room.

"I've been calling you for almost an hour," she says.

I pat the outside pocket of my backpack. It's flat. I left the damn phone at home again. "Where's everyone?"

"I'm really sorry, Claire. That's what I was calling about. It just came down from on high: no more art classes."

"No art classes?"

"I'm really sorry to have dragged you down here for nothing."

"You mean like ever?"

" 'Until further notice' is how they put it," she says.

"But the boys?"

Kimberly shakes her head.

"Is this because of what happened?"

"Could be. Or the budget." She shrugs. "I just get the orders, not the whys."

"But I don't cost anything." I drop into a chair. "Xavier?"

Kimberly sits down next to me. "Not good."

I think about how surprised Xavier was when I came through with the silver paint, how clear it was that he wasn't accustomed to getting what he asked for. The shy nod and the brief skim of eye contact: his only way to say thank you without losing face. "Prison?"

"Last I heard, both Xavier and Reggie were headed for Walpole."

"But they're too young." Walpole is a maximum-security prison.

"Like they say: Don't do the crime if you can't do the time."

June 17, 1895
Paris, France

My dearest Amelia,

Thanksissimo for your cable. It has put me in such good spirits. I only wish all the more I was with you. A baby girl! Is there anything more divine? And I do so love the name you have chosen: Frances Isabella. I am both proud and touched by your kindness. I also agree that "Fanny" is indeed a more fitting name for a baby, and I will refer to her as thus in my thoughts. You must write immediately with all the details of her tiny self. And, of course, of you and your men. What does my Jackie think of his new little sister? Not much, I suppose. I trust your convalescence goes well.

While Paris is at its most exquisite and the marble buildings glow under the summer sun, this has been a most frustrating trip thus far. I thought the prices were outrageous the last time we were on the continent, but now, oh, my dear, they are beyond, beyond, beyond. It is a very bad time here. Even the dealers, Bernard Berenson among them, are distressed. Although I venture they are not all that distressed with their percentages, only with the limited sales.

Your uncle claims that my father's money is almost gone and that I must go on a budget or we shall be drowning in a sea of debt. I find it difficult to imagine that the Stewart money is gone or that the Gardner money is not sufficient to cover my little flings.

Remember I told you many years ago that Edgar Degas invited us to sit in his private box on opening day at Longchamps? Your uncle and I have never been available before, but last month we were! Edgar has a villa up there. Clearly a man's home, no woman's touch anywhere, and despite all the servants, the food was far from first rate and the decorating left much to be desired. Edgar claims he hates the countryside, but you would never know it from his demeanor, and we had a grand time.

We stayed for three days, and the house was full of "The Talent," so we talked horse from dawn to dusk. Your Uncle Jack and I were so excited when we finally took off for Longchamps with our belt and jockeys all up.

It was a marvelous day, although quite warm, and I was happy for the wide-brimmed white hat Charles Frederick Worth made for me this season. I think this hat would be fetching on you and shall bring it home for you to try on. Henry and John Sargent joined us in the box, as did a host of others. Such festivities! Such smart people! Such a fine open air horse show! It was indeed a delightful afternoon.

But now to the part that you must keep in utmost confidence. I'm sure you remember our discussion this past winter at Green Hill about Edgar and the reiteration of his proposal in his letter

this past March. And, yes, this is more of the same. After we returned
to the villa, Edgar invited us to his studio in town to see a new oil
he's working on to be called either *At the Races in the Countryside* or
Afternoon at the Races, set in Longchamps. Of course, I had to go.

Although Edgar has been nothing but a proper gentleman in all
the time we've spent together this season, I was still a bit leery when
your Uncle Jack could not accompany me. But I thought that if Edgar
had once offered to make me a present of a nude oil painting, perhaps
I could convince him to do a clothed one instead.

When I arrived, he first showed me his painting in progress, and
it was quite a delight. Edgar has a way of capturing a moment, private
yet universally shared, like no other artist I know. In this one, a
mother and nursemaid sit in a carriage, utterly entranced by the little
one in the maid's lap. A proud papa stands by, his head also tilted
toward the babe. It is just enchanting, heartfelt, and the composition
is most unusual; more than half the canvas is taken up with sky, and
the horses and carriage are trotting right off the lower right side of the
painting! There is no doubt this is a great work.

Again, I shall try to be as exact in my rendering of the events as
is possible. The maid brought in tea and we sat. Edgar poured and
offered me a lemon tart, which was luscious. Clearly, his help in town
is far better than his servants in the country.

"So have you thought about my proposition?" he asked, as soon as I
took my first sip of tea.

I am not a young woman and not easily embarrassed, but, as the
last time, I felt heat rush to my face. "As I told you before, sir, that is
impossible."

"Oh," he said, with a twinkle in his eye. "I thought perhaps, when you came without Mr. Gardner, that you'd had a change of heart."

"Indeed not." I tried to be brisk, emphatic, to show I would brook no argument. But somehow I did not sound that way to Mr. Degas.

He stood. "I have a gift for you."

I must tell you, Amelia, my heart began to pound so. A gift? A picture? Had he made a painting for me after all? I clasped my hands together as he went over to one of his messy corners, squatted, and began to rummage through his things. He returned with a gaily wrapped box, far too narrow to hold a picture.

I rearranged my face so as not to appear ungrateful, and indeed I was curious. "What is it you have there?"

"See for yourself."

My hands flew at the ribbons, and soon the top fell away to expose layers and layers of tissue paper. I threw back sheet after sheet, now quite excited, until a long piece of material was revealed. It looked like some kind of elegant drapery. I must have appeared perplexed, for Edgar laughed and lifted it from the box.

"It's a gown," he said, holding it up. And indeed it was a gown, pale blue and diaphanous, Grecian in form, of the finest spun silk, so light it almost floated in the air.

I wanted so badly to touch it, to feel it against my skin. But, of course, this, too, was impossible. "I cannot accept—"

He leaned over, put his finger to my lips, and lay the dress across my shoulder. It smelled of lavender and fell to my feet with a whisper. I couldn't help but run my fingers over the silk, pressing it to my breast. "Oh," I said. It was one of the most beautiful things I'd ever seen.

Edgar stood watching me, a half smile on his face, but his eyes were focused far away, and I knew he was imagining how it would look on me, how he would paint the flowing folds.

"I, I don't understand."

"It's our compromise," Edgar said.

I stared at him blankly.

He took the gown from me, and I was sorry to let it go. He held it away from his body so I could see it lit from behind, and suddenly I understood. For although the gown wasn't transparent, it wasn't completely opaque either.

"Will you, Belle?"

I didn't move. The gown shimmered in the light, translucent, all the colors of the rainbow sparkling within its folds.

"For me?" Edgar pressed.

I stood, almost as if I were under a spell, and held out my arms. He placed the gown in my hands and motioned for me to step behind a screen I hadn't noticed before. Still trancelike, I did as he asked. As I was changing, he put on music, but although it was a thoroughly familiar piece, I cannot tell you what it was. Now, as I attempt to re-create the events for you, the whole thing feels like a lovely dream of which I can only grab onto snippets as the details fly away into the day.

When I emerged, he resettled the silk that formed the single shoulder, and the gown fell about my hips in the most delicious way. I don't think I have ever felt so beautiful, which as we all know, I am not. He had me lie on the sofa, arching my body this way and that, tilting my head and then turning it so he could only see a sliver of profile. All this time, the softness of the silk caressed every inch of my body and aroused such a tingle that I felt it deep inside the core of me.

It was difficult to hold the poses he required, but when I complained, he didn't acknowledge it. His charcoal flew across his sketchbook and his eyes were focused on every detail of me, without, I suspect, seeing "me" at all.

Finally, he allowed me to stretch. This felt so loose and warm and wonderful that I began to form poses of my own without even knowing I was doing so. Edgar continued to draw and later praised me as "a natural."

I shall tell you here that it was pure and chaste from beginning to end. An artist and his model, rather than a man and a woman. Although, I must confess, I'm not sure I've ever felt as much of a woman as I did that afternoon.

So my darling, Amelia, I must end here and dress for dinner. It will only be two months, eight short weeks, until we are together again. I cannot tell you how I long for the moment I am finally able to hold my sweet Fanny and smile into her beautiful, tiny face (you see, I already know she is beautiful!) as well as rest my weary eyes on you and Jackie and your handsome Sumner. We shall also be able to talk in womanly confidence and share things I dare not put to paper.

I am your loving,
Aunt Belle

Thirty-one

The next day, Rik texts me to meet him for a drink anywhere but Jake's. We agree to go to Clery's, where our privacy will be guaranteed by the enthusiastic throngs of on-the-make, young professionals creating way more noise than necessary to prove to each other that they're having fun.

It's an unseasonably warm night, and when I arrive I see that Rik has snagged us a couple of chairs near a half-wall open to the street; still, it's impossibly loud. He's already ordered two beers, which sit on the tiny table. I squeeze as close to him as I can and scream into his ear. "Good thing it's just us. Three people couldn't have a conversation in here."

"Why didn't you tell me about Markel G at the fundraiser? I didn't hear about it until after you left," he yells back. "I want to hear every last delicious detail."

"There wasn't time," I shout, and explain my turn of luck.

His face is suffused with pleasure as he takes it in. "Oh, Bear," he roars, and grabs me into a hug. "This is the best news ever!" When he pulls away, his eyes are damp.

I look down at the table and blink back my own tears.

"Long time coming," he says, patting my arm. "It's your party. Cry if you want to."

I wipe my eyes with a napkin and laugh.

"And Markel?" he yells in my ear.

I swear him to secrecy and admit to the affair. "Nobody knows."

He crosses his arm and searches my face. "This all started at that first studio visit that you said nothing happened at?"

"Not really." I take a gulp of beer. "But I guess, thinking back, that's when it first came up."

"And is that when Markel's best attribute first came up, too?"

I punch his arm. "Stop it. You're the—"

"You're blushing!" he screams. "You naughty, naughty girl."

"No, no," I say, flustered. "Not then. It wasn't until much—"

Rik bursts out laughing and holds up his hands. "No explanations needed."

"That part didn't begin until after he offered the show."

Rik grins.

"I didn't have sex with him to get Markel G," I insist. But I did forge for him.

He sobers. "You into him?"

I nod.

"He to you?"

"Think so."

Rik whistles. "Well, good for you." He raises his beer mug. "About fucking time."

I touch my mug to his.

"Jesus," Rik says. "I go away for a few weeks and the whole world changes."

"Let's hear about your trip."

We finish our beers and order another round as he describes

traveling around Paris, talking with curators, archivists, librarians, art historians, and museum directors.

"Can I go with you next time?"

"All you need is to come up with the airfare and—" He stops and his eyes widen. "You're going to be able to travel. Do anything you want. Shit, girl, after your show you're going to be rich. And famous."

I hold up my hands. "Rich is fine, but I can do without the famous."

He studies my face, then reaches over and takes my hand. "Being famous as a great pretender is very different from being famous as a great painter."

I look down at my chipped fingernails. What about being famous as a great painter because you're a great pretender?

"Claire, look at me," he orders.

I raise my eyes.

"This time, you'll be known as an accomplished artist. Appreciated for what you created with your talent. With Isaac, it was about his celebrity, something created by the media for their own ends. An image, a name, nothing that had anything to do with you."

"You're the best," I say, and mean it.

"Well, it's good you think that as I've got nada for you from Paris."

"Nothing on Belle and Degas?"

"A complete zero."

"Does that make any sense to you?"

"They traveled in the same world. Knew the same people. Even had close friends in common. She bought a number of his works . . . No, not really."

I shrug. "Different times. No instant communication. Two ships."

"Remember I told you that, before she died, Belle burned all her letters and asked her friends and family to do the same? Maybe that's where all the secrets are."

"Don't rebels usually like their exploits known?"

"Belle never fit into any mold."

"I talked to Sandra Stoneham."

"Was she any help?"

"Not much," I say. "And I don't think she's awful at all. She was really nice, showed me her artwork. Although she didn't seem particularly pleased with your museum."

"To say the least," Rik grumbles, then brightens. "Guess what I have for you?"

"A present from Paris?"

"No. I mean, yes, I bought you a present in Paris, but this is better." He pauses to build the suspense. "I nabbed an extra ticket to the reinstallation, and it's yours."

"Reinstallation?" I repeat, stalling for time.

"*After the Bath*. It's going to be *the* event of the season. Aside from your opening, of course. The museum's going all out. The Boston Pops, the international press, literary lights, artists, a caterer to the stars . . . Very la-di-da."

"Aiden's going. He tried to get another ticket but couldn't." I'd been half relieved, unsure if I was ready to stand in front of yet another of my paintings hanging in a great museum but attributed to someone else.

"Do we have to call him Aiden now?" Rik asks, with a pseudo-frown.

I punch his arm again.

"It's the Saturday night of Thanksgiving weekend," he says.

"That's only two weeks before my show."

"It's just one evening, Claire."

"I'll be wreckage."

"Perfect time to mix with influential art lovers," he cajoles. "Couldn't ask for a better PR op."

"You sound like Aiden."

"Not taking no. After the ceremony there's going to be a mega-elegant black-tie dinner." He grins. "You'll need a stunning new dress to hobnob with the rich and famous. And if you're too wasted from working, Aiden and I will be your front men and broadcast the news of your imminent opening."

I remind myself that this time won't be like MoMA. This painting isn't mine like *4D* was. It's Degas'. He composed it, painted it. Sort of.

"It'll be great fun . . ."

"Okay," I say. "Let's do it. Thanks." This time Aiden will be there to help me if there are any tough moments, to stand beside me so I'm not the only one who knows the truth.

Rik leans in very close. "It's possible by then we'll know more of the story."

"What story?"

"Hello? Claire? *After the Bath,* the painting we've been talking about for the last ten minutes?"

"Sorry."

Rik heaves a great sigh. "By the reinstallation, we should have more information about what really happened to it. Maybe even some of the other paintings."

I suck in my breath.

"Rumor has it that Patel is considering an FBI offer of immunity."

"He's going to rat?" I gasp.

Rik laughs. "Well, I wouldn't put it quite like that, but yeah, and who knows how much he knows?"

AIDEN IS UNMOVED by my news. "Patel's got nothing to give the FBI."

"That's not what Rik said."

"Rik's getting his information second- and thirdhand."

"His sources have been pretty right-on so far."

"Not this time."

I called Aiden as soon as I left Clery's and went right to his house, although I should have gone home to my windows. We're in his kitchen, and he's making grilled cheese and tomato sandwiches, which I'm thinking are going to be about as close to my two-American-cheese-singles-on-white-bread as his macaroni and cheese was to my Kraft special.

He slides his creation onto my plate: multiple cheeses with cherry tomatoes and fresh basil oozing out of slabs of homemade, multigrain bread. It looks and smells brilliant. He puts knives and forks on the table as the sandwiches are way too thick and gooey to eat with our hands. I push mine around with the fork. My stomach is squeezed shut.

He sits down across from me and takes a bite of his. "If you don't eat, you're never going to have the stamina to finish those windows."

"Patel can't be an idiot," I say. "He's got to know how it's going to be for him."

"Got himself caught. Can't be all that bright."

"Even worse."

"Tell me what you think of the basil." Aiden points his knife at my sandwich. "It's a new variety. Not sure I like it." He takes another bite. "A little too bitter."

"We've got to have a plan."

"Okay," he says amicably. "Let's plan."

"You're the one who knows about this stuff."

He stands. "Want wine?"

"Beer."

He opens a Sam and hands it to me, pours himself some wine from an open bottle of Cabernet, sits down, and resumes eating his sandwich.

"What do I do if you get arrested?"

"Chantal and Kristi will handle the show."

"I'm not talking about the show, and you know it. How can you be so laid-back about this?"

He puts down his sandwich and looks at me with a patient expression. "Just tell them you don't know anything about it," he says, with annoying calm. "Artists aren't responsible for their dealers' actions."

"How long do you think it's going to take them to figure out that I'm a professional Degas forger?"

"We discussed this before. I brought you a high-quality copy and paid you to paint a high-quality copy from it, which I told you I was going to sell as a reproduction." He raises his knife and fork triumphantly. "Even better, our story matches Patel's exactly."

"But you didn't bring me a high-quality copy, did you?" I watch him closely.

"No one can prove what you believed," he says. "Or what I told you."

I notice he didn't answer my question.

"I'm not going to get arrested." He takes my hand. "I promise."

I just look at him.

He lets go and leans back in his chair. "Claire, I know you're under a lot of pressure with the show and all—"

"It's not about the show. It's about you. Going to prison."

"This isn't helping."

"And ignoring it is?"

"Freaking out's no better."

"It's better than digging your head in the sand." I want to shake him out of his complacency. Shake him until he acknowledges the danger.

"Even if Patel tried to turn evidence, he has no idea I'm involved. He's only got a flunky to give them. And that guy knows even less than he does. It'll prove worthless to the FBI. There's no deal to be made." Aiden's tone is assured, his equanimity perhaps a bit too sound. I'm thinking he knows something I don't. Or he believes he knows something I don't.

I drop my head to my hands. He's lying to me. I'm lying to him. Our fates are inextricably entwined. And being together doubles our vulnerability.

"I don't know," I whisper, staring through my fingers at the un-eaten sandwich swimming in its own juices. The cheese has hardened, and oil glistens darkly where bread meets plate.

The frown lines in Aiden's face deepen as I raise my eyes to meet his. "Don't know what?" he asks.

I look back down at the soggy sandwich. A split basil leaf protrudes from the slabs of toast like the tongue of a snake.

Thirty-two

After Karen Sinsheimer said good-bye and hung up, I continued to stare at the phone in my hand. The tendons holding my knees in place turned to mush, and I slid to the floor. It was as if I'd been told a friend died unexpectedly. Half of my mind raced ahead, taking in the message and its meaning, while the other half remained frozen in denial. Although I'd been worried for weeks about this exact outcome, I clearly hadn't believed it would happen.

For how could it? I'd painted *4D,* I'd painted the second one, and I'd given Karen three of my paintings for comparison. The museum had access to many of Isaac's paintings, and they must have evaluated them against mine. How could the experts have gotten it so wrong? Didn't they have all those fancy high-tech techniques? Didn't they have PhDs and decades of experience? My eyes flew around the studio, searching for something, anything, to throw.

This was bullshit. An injustice had been done. To me, certainly, but also to Isaac, and not to get too hyperbolic, to all artists and art lovers. What does it mean when a top museum acknowledges the wrong artist of one of its own paintings? What does it say about all museums and all the great works of art? Isaac had to appreciate this, had to know how wrong it was. He was, after all, an artist before all else.

I e-mailed, texted, and called him, leaving message after message to contact me, that it was important. No response. I changed tacks and went for the guilt. "How can you do this to all the people who love and appreciate your work?" "How does it feel to have one of my paintings as part of your legacy?" No response. "How can you look at yourself in the mirror?" He changed his e-mail address and cell number.

"Way to go, girl," Beatrice Cormier had said, surprising me with both her youthful cliché and her intimation that she believed I'd painted *4D*. Of course, she'd never said anything of the sort, but Karen had told me that Beatrice was an art historian and a major collector, and I wondered what she thought of all this.

I reached her at the John and Beatrice Cormier Foundation, and she took my call immediately. "Claire," she said. "I've been thinking about you."

My hand holding the phone shook. "Because of what happened?"

A long pause. "And because of what didn't."

"Did you agree with the decision?"

Another long pause. "Can we meet somewhere?"

"I can come to New York any day but Tuesday."

The next Monday, we sat at a back table in a crowded deli on a side street in the Lower East Side. An odd choice, I thought, when she'd suggested it. But not so odd if she didn't want us to be seen together.

"I can't tell you anything definitive," Beatrice said, after we'd both ordered matzo-ball soup and a salad. "I wasn't a voting member of the committee. I was just there to give my report."

I waited.

"I told them that you'd painted the second painting, that I'd watched your every brushstroke, and although it wasn't my job to say, I added that after spending that much time with you, and more than a few hours with *4D,* it was my opinion that you were responsible for both."

"Thank you," I whispered. "But no one agreed with you?"

She looked at me with both compassion and sadness. "I wasn't there, but I heard later that there were others."

"But, but then, how . . . ?"

"The decision didn't have to be unanimous."

I poked at a matzo ball with my spoon. "I've tried to reach Isaac, to get him to come clean, but he won't."

"And MoMA probably won't either."

"What does that mean?"

"Isaac isn't the only one with a reputation at stake," Beatrice said. "Or a lot of money."

I put down my spoon. "So they did this to protect their own asses?" I was immediately sorry for speaking so crudely, but Beatrice didn't seem to notice, or if she did, to care.

"Did you ever hear of cognitive dissonance?" she asked.

"No."

"Basically, it's a theory that people subconsciously reinterpret their motives and actions in a way that makes them feel better about themselves afterward. And then they start to believe that the basis of the reinterpretation is also true."

Sounded just like Isaac.

"So," I said slowly, "you're telling me that even though they know I painted *4D,* they've convinced themselves that they don't believe it because it's in the best interests of the museum?"

"Some of them, maybe."

"Then I'll just have to force them to see the truth. To tell the truth. I'll go to the higher-ups in the museum. The media."

Beatrice placed her papery hand over mine. "I don't think you want to do that. You've got a great talent, a great future ahead of you. Now's not the time to look back. Leave it be, Claire. Move on."

So I went home and tried to do what she advised.

Thirty-three

I scuttle into my building like a cockroach running from light. I never should have gone to Aiden's. I should have come straight home from Clery's, back to my windows, away from my fears and Aiden's pat answers. I think about the Faustian bargain Aiden mentioned the first time we discussed the forgery. He quickly reconsidered and decided the better analogy was to pawns on a chessboard. But he should have stuck with his original assessment. A deal with the devil is exactly right.

Now that I'm inside, out of view of the millions of people who couldn't care less about the absence or presence of my soul, I feel somewhat better. I make myself a pot of coffee and put *Bay Village* and *Apple* on the easels. The drawings look at me patiently, reminding me of Aiden's tranquil expression, of his unruffled practicality in the face of Patel's potential betrayal. I pick up my palette and a brush. I hate it when these suspicions rear their nasty little heads, yet I'm afraid to ignore them. I can't allow my feelings for Aiden to cloud my common sense.

I mix a few batches of middle-range tones and begin painting. If I'm losing my soul for this show, I'd damn well better get the work done on time. It feels good to work. In a few hours, *Bay Village* is in the oven, and I'm mixing up some pale blues for the reflections.

When the oven chimes, I pull *Bay Village* out and replace it with *Apple*. I'm exhausted, more than ready for my first nap of the night, but I can't sleep until *Apple's* finished baking. So I brew up another, stronger, pot of coffee and pour myself a bowl of cold cereal. As I eat, I check the Internet for news on Patel. There isn't any, but this does little to allay my fears. If Patel knows more than Aiden believes, it could easily lead to Aiden's arrest. And while it may not be against the law to copy a painting, conspiracy to commit a crime—knowing my copy was to be sold as an original—could lead to my own. As could possession of stolen property. And then there's the whole stolen masterpiece thing.

I chew at a cuticle. If I found the original painting, could that help us? I scan the studio as if the clues are hidden here. My eyes light on Degas' sketchbooks, and it occurs to me that maybe I could work backward. Maybe finding the forger might lead me to the original.

It's a long shot, I know, but the desperate can't be choosy. I begin scribbling on a piece of paper. Everything I've learned points to the conclusion that the *Bath* Aiden brought me, the first forgery, was installed at the Gardner Museum when it opened in 1903. Assuming Degas painted his original *After the Bath* in 1897, then *Bath* was created sometime in those six intervening years. Given the difficulty of travel in those days, it must have been painted by someone living in either Paris or Boston. Ergo, my forger lived in France or the United States and, figuring that he painted between the ages of twenty and eighty, he was born between 1820 and 1880.

I Google "forgery between 1880 and 1903," but it's not cut that finely, and the best I can do is "known art forgers." There are roughly fifty on the list, all men. Who knows, perhaps I'm the first female to join their illustrious ranks. Great. I've always wanted to be a gender-busting role model.

Laboriously, I exclude the artists one by one. Most don't fit my timeframe: Giovanni Bastianini died in 1868, while Tony Tetro and my buddy Han were all born too late. Many of those who remain don't fit geographically: William Blundell lived in Australia, Zhang Daqian in China, and Elmyr de Hory in Hungary. Others specialized in sculpture or medieval miniatures. At the end, I'm left with four possibilities and a couple of revelatory tales that might reflect on my own.

The first story is about Alceo Dossena, an Italian stonemason and struggling artist who copied classical Greek and Roman sculptures, which, unbeknownst to him, his agent sold as originals to collectors and museums, including Boston's MFA. When, according to Dossena, he stumbled on some of his work in museum collections of ancient art, he realized his agent had been reaping far more than the $200 he'd paid Dossena. He sued his agent, claiming that he hadn't known his work was being sold fraudulently. He won at trial and received thousands of dollars in restitution. This appears to be a good omen for me, but I'm unsettled by the fact that when he had a one-man show at the Met following his acquittal, it was a complete failure.

Then there's David Stein, a French painter who created pastiches of his favorite masters and made millions of dollars selling fake Chagalls, Klees, Mirós, and Picassos. When one of his forgeries was discovered in a New York gallery, he was arrested. But his prosecution proved difficult: Art dealers refused to cooperate because they feared publicity questioning their expertise, and collectors wouldn't give up Stein's paintings, claiming they filled important holes in their collections. Unfortunately for Stein, and for me, he was found guilty anyway and sent to prison for art forgery and grand larceny.

Ambition, talent, antiestablishment vengeance, greed, and hubris run rampant through all fifty stories, and I see myself everywhere. Plus, they all share the same outcome: the ultimate exposure of the forger as the charlatan he is.

"WHY ARE YOU doing this to yourself?" Aiden says when I tell him about the forgers. He showed up around nine to make sure I was all right after I left his condo right after dinner last night.

"Curiosity?" I offer.

"Masochism."

"The forgers, they all had the same baggage. Most with the same motivations as me."

He throws his hands in the air. "All medical students want to help people."

"Almost every one wanted revenge of some sort. Usually on the art world. For not appreciating their work."

Aiden's eyes soften. "You've got true talent, Claire." He waves at the completed window paintings lined up against the wall. "And your grievance comes from a very different—" He squats in front of *Nighttime T,* stares at it, then turns back to me. "This is great. Very compelling. The depth of the color . . ." He reaches a finger toward the canvas, then stops himself. "Maybe your best. I'm thinking front window. Major frame."

"You're just trying to make me feel better."

"Don't give me that crap." He comes back to sit with me on the couch. "I can tell by the expression on your face that you think it's good, too."

"Is larceny the same as theft?"

"You didn't steal anything."

"I possessed stolen property."

"You don't anymore. And you had no idea it was stolen when you did."

It strikes me how easily Aiden appears to believe his own lies. "But, what if—"

"You know where this is going to get us, don't you? All the ruminating? The Internet scavenging? Driving yourself crazy with what-ifs? This is how people get caught. They do something stupid, put themselves in the wrong place, look nervous, and wham. Someone gets suspicious, and it's over."

"Like the—"

"You've got to promise me you're going to quit this," he says. "You've got to focus on your painting, on your show. And get your emotions in check."

I know he's right, so I promise him I will. But, of course, he doesn't have the complete picture, so to speak. And although part of me would love to share the secret, I find his ease with his own lies and his composure in the face of real jeopardy too troubling to take that step.

When he leaves, I go back online to search for more information on my four possibilities. I have three Frenchmen and an American: Yves Chaudron, Jean-Pierre Schecroun, Émile Schuffenecker, and Virgil Rendell. All painting and forging in the times and places of Degas and Belle.

During the late nineteenth and early twentieth centuries, Yves Chaudron, a struggling painter, lived in the Montmartre district of Paris, as did Degas. Chaudron gained fame as the forger of the *Mona Lisa* stolen by his partner, Vincenzo Peruggia. There's still speculation over whether the *Mona Lisa* now hanging in the Louvre is the original or one of many high-quality Chaudron forgeries Peruggia sold to foreign collectors. Now I know where Ely Sakhai, the New York City double-dealer, got the idea.

It turns out that Jean-Pierre Schecroun was born in 1940 rather than 1861—Wikipedia isn't the most reliable source—but Émile Schuffenecker is a strong second possibility. He was a close friend of Gauguin and van Gogh, who were also friends of Degas', and he was suspected, although never convicted, of forging Impressionist masters, particularly Cézanne. He claimed he wasn't forging, that he was exposing the idiocy of those who refused to acknowledge the brilliance of his own paintings.

Virgil Rendell fits the same mold. He turned to forgery when his work was disregarded by the prestigious dealers of the day and committed suicide in 1928 after getting caught trying to sell a fake Sargent. I pause. The name sounds familiar, but I can't place it. Then I remember. Rendell painted the portrait of Sandra Stoneham's grandmother Amelia Prescott. Amelia was Belle Gardner's niece, her favorite niece, as Sandra was quick to point out.

I close my eyes and recall *Amelia*. I see Rendell's exquisite technique, how Amelia's skin glowed, how her happiness pulsed from the canvas. It's a powerful painting, full of emotion and character, created by an artist of great talent, in the classical style of the masters. My eyes fly open. An artist who, in all likelihood, was a personal acquaintance of Belle Gardner's.

From the pen of

ISABELLA STEWART GARDNER

January 1897
Paris, France

My dearest Amelia,

I am your very cranky aunt today and probably should not be
writing when I'm in such a fret. But there has been so much noise and
tumult in our apartments this past month, that now that I am alone, I
must take advantage. The weather has been wretched, cold and windy
and even a bit of snow, so we are all cooped up inside. I am so much
driven by people talking, talking, talking and asking question after
question, that I am almost pleased to be on my sick bed.

Please do not worry. I have only a head cold. But a most miserable
one. My throat is very bad, and I can scarcely hold up my head,
but there is no fever. The doctor has threatened to send me off to
the countryside if my breathing does not improve. Of course, the
countryside is out of the question as I have a number of purchases to
complete before we leave in less than a month.

As you well know, it has been a long trip: England, France, the Netherlands, Germany, at Palazzo Barbaro for the summer, then back here to Paris. But I've had a number of successes that make it all worthwhile! I have purchased Botticelli's *Tragedy of Lucretia,* Peter Paul Rubens's *Portrait of Thomas Howard, Second Earl of Arundel,* and my very favorite of the year, a little Madonna, barely one-foot square, that is now before me on a chair.

The Madonna and Child in a Rose Arbor is the work of Martin Schongauer, a German and a contemporary of Holbein and Dürer, but to my mind, a far better painter. The present frame is ghastly, far too bold and garish for my little babe, and I shall order a new one as soon as I am out of bed. Best of all, she is small enough to smuggle inside my suitcase and avoid those nefarious taxmen and their horrid duties. Now that your Uncle Jack has agreed to my museum, I am in full cry.

Your uncle still complains about all the money we are spending, but I daresay he is anticipating the excitement of the planning and building to come. It is quite intoxicating, and I am anxious to return home to begin work with the architects. And, of course, to see you and my two favorite children, dear Jackie and adorable Fanny. Sweet Fanny already had such a vocabulary when I left seven months ago, I can only imagine the paragraphs she must be speaking now!

Last night we dined with Henry James and Edgar Degas. When we told them of our plans for the new museum, they were both taken with the idea, and we talked long into the evening about whose work should be purchased. When Edgar said he would be proud to be considered, I told him that Mr. Gardner and I would be thrilled if we three could agree on a price, and the man had the audacity to say

I had already heard his price! Fortunately, neither Henry nor your uncle was listening carefully.

When Uncle Jack said he must work at the bank's offices for the rest of the week, Edgar invited me to his studio on Wednesday. After his comment, I am a bit nervous, but nothing will keep me away. As you are always so interested in these adventures, I will continue this letter when I return from Montmartre.

Wednesday evening

I have returned. As always, my Edgar stories are told to you in the strictest confidence. Out of respect for your uncle, I ask you to burn this letter after you have read it. It would be most unfortunate if it fell into the wrong hands.

As soon as I arrived in the studio, as I expected, Edgar offered to paint a picture for my museum if I would model nude for him. He did not seem surprised at my refusal and asked if I would put on my silken robe. To this I agreed. I have learned that once you have done a risky thing, it is quite easy to do it again.

And it was as luscious as the last time! He had a fire going, and, if anything, it was even more sensuous than in the heat of summer. Of course, it was difficult work holding a pose, but when he released me and allowed me to stretch in any way I liked, I can only say, I have never felt so playful, so much myself. I closed my eyes, and it was as if I were dancing with a gossamer angel.

But instead of continuing his sketching, as he did the last time, Edgar knelt and touched the single strap of my gown. "Please, Belle," he whispered. "Allow me to take this from you. Allow me to see you as you truly are."

I was lying on the sofa, and when I opened my eyes, I looked directly into his. They were so deep and pleading, so without guile, that before I realized what I was doing, I raised my arms, and he pulled the slippery silk from my skin. Oh, Amelia, I can't describe to you the bliss, the joy, the gay abandon. I was unrestrained, reckless, and more open to the experience of being alive than ever before. It was as if I were a newborn babe.

"You'll never show the sketches to anyone?" I murmured, as he positioned my arm, my leg, unpinned my hair. His touch was dry, courteous, respectful.

He smiled and picked up his sketchbook. "You are a beautiful creature."

"Most certainly not," I said, but I must confess to you, I was no longer sure.

And it only grew more so. When, once again, Edgar released me from my pose, and I was allowed to assume positions of my own choice, a great warmth and tingling began within my body. This grew and grew until it burst from the very core of me and flowed outward to my every extremity. I gasped with the power of it, the joy of it.

I had the thought that I was breaking from the chrysalis that has imprisoned me all these years. That I was, for the very first time, unbound, able to truly connect to the physical world. To connect to myself. And, of course, to connect to Edgar.

I know this is something no proper woman would ever do, particularly not a Stewart or a Gardner. And I am well aware that the gossip and rumors that have swirled around me since I arrived in Massachusetts would be nothing compared to what would take place if this ever became known. But I tell you now, no matter what consequence there might be, I shall never be sorry. Mum's the word.

I am your loving,
Aunt Belle

Thirty-five

A iden has been doing heavy publicity for the show; he's received requests for the video portfolio from as far away as
Mumbai and Paris. As the show grows closer and more certain, in
true imposter-syndrome fashion, I find myself worrying whether
I'm good enough for this kind of stage, if the critics will wonder
what Markel G could have been thinking. After being unappreciated for so many years, now I'm fretting that I'm reaching for
something I'm not. As my friend Jan used to say in graduate school,
"No insecurity too obscure."

The only news on Patel is that he was arraigned, pled not guilty,
and is being held at the Nashua Street Jail. Not even a whisper of
a possible deal with the FBI. I'm feeling a bit safer, although my
excitement about a possible Virgil Rendell/Belle Gardner connection has been put on hold. When I called Sandra, she was rushing
to catch a plane to Athens for a ten-day cruise, but she did encour-
age me to contact her when she returned. Which I will definitely
take her up on.

It's a beautiful day, the last kiss of fall, so I decide to trek down
to Newbury Street to shop for the dress Rik's been hounding me to
buy for the reinstallation. I wander in and out of the high-end (who

wants to pay $10,000 for an "elegant evening jacket"?), the midrange (who wants to pay $1,000 for a dress the size of a blouse?), and into my old standby, the vintage, where everything is shoved on too many racks and there's barely room to stand. I don't try anything on.

Instead, I go to Markel G. Aiden's alone in the gallery, so I give him a hug.

"You smell wonderful," he says, nuzzling my neck. "Not a whiff of phenol formaldehyde." Then he lifts his head and pulls a frown. "Why aren't you working?" He points to his watch. "Time's a wasting."

I wrinkle my nose. "I'm on my way. On my way. Just wanted to let you know I'm pretty sure I'll have them all done in a week."

"Only pretty sure?"

"Okay, okay, I'm sure. Positive."

He beams. "I knew you'd make it."

"But you're relieved anyway?" I tease.

"Templeton's started in on the first batch. I haven't seen anything yet, and he said he'll need another full week to frame what he's got and another to finish up the last ones." Templeton is Aiden's framer. We were originally going to go with all the paintings unframed, but Aiden changed his mind a few weeks ago. This cut my deadline down by a couple of weeks. And increased Aiden's costs tremendously.

I hug myself. "We're really almost there."

"And then you'll have plenty of time to do some of that publicity you've been pretending doesn't exist."

"Hey, I'm doing those radio shows in a couple of days."

"Reluctantly." He looks at me critically. "You need some new clothes."

I laugh. "Clothes for radio interviews?"

But he's serious. "Don't kid yourself, Claire. In this world, your appearance makes a huge difference. And it's not all radio." He rummages through a drawer and pulls out an envelope. "I was going to give this to you when you were completely finished, but you're close enough. A present."

I take the envelope, shake it, turn it over, then face it up again.

"For a job well done."

"What is it?"

"Open it."

When I do, I've no idea what I'm looking at. A receipt of some sort. For Canyon Ranch. Three days and two nights. And a ticket for a car service. I look at him, confused. "For me?"

"When you're done, I want you to get out of here for a few days. Pamper yourself. Rest, relax. It's only going to get hairier from here on—"

"What about all the promotion you've been pushing me to do?"

"It's not even three days. You can do it all when you get back."

"I can't take this from you. This place costs like five hundred dollars a day."

"Let me worry about that."

"No, no. I'm not doing it. Can't. Won't."

Aiden takes my hands in his. "Okay, you can pay me back after the show. When you're dripping in money."

"But what about the show? We've got to hang it. I want to be there for every step of the installation. And then—"

"We won't be doing the installation until well after you get back. Templeton won't have the framing done until then."

"But, I—"

"If you don't go, I'll cancel the show."

"You will not."

He shrugs. "Probably not, but that gives you an inkling of how important I think this is for you."

"Because I'm losing it?"

"Nothing a beautiful spa and a bunch of massages won't cure."

The truth is, I've always wanted to go to Canyon Ranch. Fantasized about it even. Nothing I ever thought possible, but up there on the pipe-dream list. Delusions of indulgence. I lean over and kiss him. "You're a very sweet man, you know."

"Not at all," he says. "I have a lot invested in you. I'm looking out for my own ass."

IN LESS THAN a week, I'm finished. Done. It's three o'clock in the morning. I walk to my spot at the windows, rub my lower back, and scan the deserted street. The weather's nasty. A wintery mix of rain, sleet, and hail, with a bit of snow thrown in to warn of what's to come. Late November isn't Boston's best moment.

I'm relieved, proud, euphoric. I'm exhausted, headachy, and filled with an overwhelming sense of loss. All twenty paintings behind me. All twenty paintings marching forward on their own. I've created them, labored over them, made them who they are, but what happens next is up to them, not me. I wonder if this is how a mother feels when she sends her child off to college.

I flop down on the couch, stretch my legs out, and put a pillow under my head. I hook my hands around the back of my neck and visualize the opening. I close my eyes, and I'm there. Except it's a larger version of Markel G, with taller ceilings, wider windows. There are at least fifty paintings hanging on the walls. They can't be all mine. But next to each painting is a little card that reads, "Claire Roth." I must have done more than I thought.

I'm surrounded by a kaleidoscope of color: in my paintings and in the room. Both women and men are dressed in jewel tones, luscious and rich, deeply burnished, almost edible. But I'm in the most delicious of them all. A one-shouldered silk gown of the most magical amethyst, sparkling and fluid, falling to my feet, whispering with every step I take.

As I flow through the room accepting congratulations, I become aware that each color has its own fragrance, not necessarily what you'd associate with the hue—mine smells like a forest in the morning, rather than lavender—but just as breathtaking in their own way as the colors are. Because, of course, now I realize the colors come from my oven, that that's the only way they could have happened: fashioned and shaped, baked, and then left to cool. The paintings have transformed themselves into a third dimension and created a new sense all their own: a combination of sight, smell, and taste, larger and more powerful for being one.

I open my eyes, and early sunlight streaks the ceiling. I close them again and fall into a deep, untroubled sleep.

At nine o'clock, the telephone wakes me. "So?" Aiden asks.

I rub my cheeks, a bit disoriented, and struggle up from the couch. I'm still in my grubby paint clothes, and my mouth feels like dry pigment has been poured into it. "Hey."

"Should I send Chantal over with the truck?"

My eyes rest on the finished paintings, and I take them all in in one greedy gulp. "Yup."

"All done?"

"All done."

"Never doubted it," he says.

I go over and check the coffee pot. Empty. "So why'd you ask?"

He chuckles. "When are you leaving?"

I run the cold water and start scooping coffee beans. "I have to confirm with the car service, but sometime late afternoon."

"Have time to stop by the gallery to say good-bye? Kristi's off and Chantal's running errands all day, so I can't leave."

I look around the messy studio. Although I'm far from neat, I'm particular about my art materials, and I can't leave them like this for three days. Nor, given the mice, can I leave the kitchen in its current state. "I'll call you later, but probably not," I tell him. "This place is disgusting—and so am I."

Cleaning takes longer than I anticipate. It's been quite a while since I wielded a sponge, and the combination of strong coffee and my need for closure drive me into uncharacteristic tidiness. When I call Aiden at one to tell him I can't make it, the gallery phone goes to answer mode, as does his cell. I text a message promising to be in touch as soon as I get back and thanking him again for Canyon Ranch.

I've never had a professional massage before but have no trouble imagining the feel of strong fingers pressing into my tight shoulder muscles, releasing the tension and breaking up those nasty chemicals Small is always telling me I've got to get rid of. Yoga classes, good food, and lots of sleep. Heaven.

When I finally finish and Chantal's come for the paintings, I shower, change, and pack. The car's picking me up at four, which should get me there about seven. In plenty of time for dinner, the woman at the ranch assured me. When I get a call from the service a bit before four telling me they're running about fifteen minutes late, I switch on CNN and relax into the couch until the sound of the newscaster mentioning Markel G brings me upright. Could they be talking about my show on CNN? My heart pounds. Has Aiden's promotion actually reached that far?

It takes me a few moments to understand what's happening. They're not talking about my show. They just mentioned the gallery because Aiden owns it. Because it's where he was arrested. Because it's where the film clip they're showing takes place. Of Aiden being led onto Newbury Street. In handcuffs.

Thirty-six

A month or so after my meeting with Beatrice Cormier, rumors began circulating that some woman had gone to MoMA claiming Isaac Cullion hadn't painted *4D,* that she was the artist who created it. At first, it was just whispers that were easily scoffed away. But soon, notices began appearing on art blogs and in gossip columns reporting that the museum, which had determined *4D* was Cullion's work, was wrong: The claim was legitimate.

After disclosure that Isaac had been having an affair with "a much younger graduate student," it didn't take long for people to conclude that the "she" in both stories had to be me. Isaac, of course, denied everything, as did MoMA. Initially, I did, too. I still hadn't recovered from the shock of the museum's original decision, and I didn't know what to do.

But plenty of other people did. I was stared at, whispered about, and often strangers, not to mention friends, asked me intrusive questions. Some were quite cruel.

"So did you do it because he broke up with you?" Like it's your business.

"How much less do you think *4D* is worth now?" Like I know.

"Do you still love him?" Like this is appropriate.

"Why would you try to destroy such a talented man?" Like that was my intention.

Although I was dubbed "The Great Pretender" by the tabloids and it was generally assumed I was seeking some kind of wrong-headed publicity for myself, the possibility that my claim was legitimate also sparked interest. Editorials appeared about museum experts who saw what they wanted to see and collectors who were willing to pay hundreds of thousands of dollars for a name. Journalists and pundits speculated on the rights and wrongs of the situation. And to whom they belonged.

"Where does art's value lie?" an editorial in *ArtWorld* demanded. "If it was painted by a graduate student, is *4D* still a masterpiece?"

These were good questions, questions I kept asking myself. And although almost all of the arguments concluded that the value lay within the painting itself, that brands and celebrated names were nothing but "the glaze of our ego-driven consumer society," one only had to look at the meteoric rise in the value of Isaac's paintings after *4D* to know the truth.

I WAS IN such a deep sleep that it took me a while to understand that the phone was ringing. The clock radio said it was 3:24 a.m. I fumbled for the phone.

"Murderer!" a woman's voice screamed.

"Huh?"

"You killed him. You killed him. If it weren't for you he'd still be alive!" Then she burst into huge, heaving sobs.

I shook my head to clear it. "I think you've got the wrong number."

More sobbing, deeper now, more painful.

"Listen, ma'am," I said, "I'm really sorry, but I didn't kill anyone, so you've really got to hang up and dial again. Or, better yet, get someone to help you. Are you alone? Is there someone I can call for you?"

"You and your goddamned ego," she managed to spit between sobs. "If you hadn't, if you hadn't gone there, claiming, claiming, if you'd let things be, then he, then he . . ."

I snapped straight up in bed. "Who is this?"

A wail. A keening that froze the marrow of my bones.

"Martha?" I asked, hoping against hope I was wrong, but knowing I wasn't. Isaac's wife.

A long intake of breath, a sob, a hiccup. "He's gone, Claire."

"Isaac?" I whispered.

The sobbing began again.

"No," I said, but it came out as a moan. "No, no, please no."

"He shot himself." Martha's voice was suddenly hard and clear. "But it wasn't suicide. Not even close. And you're going to have to live with the fact that you're responsible for ending his life for the rest of your own."

"Ending his life," I repeated, sickened by her words. "No, no. I . . . I didn't do that. I'd never do anything—"

"You can deny it all you want, but that doesn't change the facts," she spat, and hung up.

I dropped the receiver on the bed. I was numb, freezing cold, shivering as if I were running a high fever. I wrapped myself in a blanket, tried to pace the studio, but my knees wouldn't hold me up. I collapsed on the floor, curled into a fetal position, rocked. And rocked. Isaac was dead. His great talent along with him. If only I hadn't, if only I hadn't, if only I hadn't . . . But, of course, I had.

THE FUNERAL, HELD at Trinity Church in Copley Square, was a mob scene. News vans and reporters swarmed the plaza in front of the church, onlookers ogled. Rik came with me, and it was a good thing. When Martha Cullion turned her back in response to my condolences, he was there to catch me. When no professor from the museum school would meet my eye, he was there to hold my hand. And when I found I couldn't bear the sight of Isaac's casket, Rik took me home.

Martha told the press she blamed me for Isaac's death. That my "preposterous claim" was an attempt to punish him for going back to her. Intellectually, I knew I hadn't caused his death, but there was a great distance between my head and my heart, and guilt filled my gut.

I ignored the media calls for a statement. Although my friends begged me to tell my side of the story, I felt too responsible to defend myself. I wasn't sleeping or eating, I wasn't working, and I wasn't leaving my studio. Rik tried to convince me to pack up my canvases and paints and move into his parents' barn in Connecticut to finish my capstone project. I didn't want to go anywhere—I'd become addicted to soap operas and daytime talk shows—but my overwhelming desire to put the whole museum school experience behind me finally got me to the barn.

When I returned to Boston with the first two completed works though, none of my professors was impressed. "Derivative," Maya Myers, the chair of my committee, declared, and I noticed George Kelly and Dan Martin share a smirk.

"Derivative of what?" I asked.

"Go back and sit with them, Claire," Maya said. "Review your early expressionists. I'm sure you'll see what we mean."

Expressionists? I stared at my paintings. Marc Chagall? Edvard Munch? Distortion of reality for emotional effect? Not even close.

These were portraits of homeless people, one a man and the other two women, both highly representational. They were emotional, yes, that was the point. But there was no bending of reality, just reality staring you in the face.

I looked at George and Dan, waiting for someone to contradict her.

"I agree with Maya," Dan said.

"Me, too," said George.

I gathered the paintings and marched over to Rik's apartment. I set them against the wall behind his kitchen table. "Would you call these expressionistic?"

He scrutinized them. "Well . . . they do create emotion. Strong angst. So I suppose, in that way, they're expressionistesque."

"Through distortion?"

"Couldn't say that."

"Are they derivative?"

"Of whom?"

"That's what Myers claims. She and her two monkeys."

Now Rik scrutinized me. "And you're thinking this is because of Isaac?"

"What else?"

"Maybe she's testing you, pushing you to new creative heights."

"Except that she loved the idea when I first presented it. Told me to get right to work after she saw the initial sketches."

"You've got to let this go, Bear. Not everything that happens to you is about Isaac."

Yet everything else seemed to be about Isaac. Despite hurricanes and blistering heat, international unrest and a presidential election, the media wouldn't let the story go, quoting Isaac's friends and colleagues about his great talent and all that the world had lost. I finally gave the *Globe* an interview, explaining how everything happened, how *4D* was mine, and that I'd gone to MoMA to set the record straight. But it seemed that no one, except my family and a few friends, was willing to believe me. Martha's story had much more appeal.

So when I finally emerged from the barn, reworked "non-expressionist" paintings and a newly minted MFA in hand, I wasn't surprised to step into a world that pretended not to see the Great Pretender. But when the freeze flowed into the responses I received to the slides I submitted to galleries and competitions, to the lack of responses I received to my résumé, I realized that Rik was wrong. Everything was about Isaac. And in contradiction to conventional wisdom, I was fast discovering that there was, indeed, such a thing as bad publicity.

Thirty-seven

The Nashua Street Jail looks more like a high-end hotel or classy office building than a house of correction. Facing an open expanse of the Charles River, its angled windows and imposing entrance façade rival most courthouses. But inside, the disrespect of the defiant guards mingling with the odor of sweat, Lysol, and hopelessness is all too reminiscent of Beverly Arms.

While the whole rigmarole at juvy is demoralizing, Nashua Street brings this to a new level. And not just because Beverly is a juvenile facility and Nashua maximum security. It's that now I'm a visitor rather than a teacher, supplicant rather than volunteer. Still, being white, English-speaking, neither hostile nor whimpering, and more-or-less appropriately dressed works in my favor.

The guards turn away a boy wearing oversized jogging pants, a girl in a shirt deemed too tight, and a man with only a photocopy of his birth certificate for identification. An elderly woman, who tries to explain in halting English that she spent over two hours getting here, is told she can't see her grandson because he's already had three visitors this week. Begging, tears, offers of favors, and children crying for Daddy make no difference here. Yelling and swearing, not to mention punching the wall, do even less.

By the time I'm questioned, searched, scanned, stamped, and ordered into a room the size of a bathroom stall, I don't know whether to be relieved or distressed. The tiny room is overheated and claustrophobic. A small metal stool is attached to the wall, and I sit, facing an empty glass panel with a circle of small holes at the bottom.

A similar metal stool and a closed door face me from the other side. My nose fills with the stench of dirty socks, and acid bile burns up into my throat. But I'm aching for Aiden. The thought of him locked up in here crushes my ribs. I haven't been able to speak to him since his arrest.

Apparently, Patel knew more than Aiden thought or the FBI was better at working its way through the levels that Aiden believed would protect him. According to the paper, he's charged with sale of stolen goods, transportation of stolen goods, and conspiracy to commit fraud. The FBI spokeswoman said that charges of grand theft are pending.

I focus on the murmur of voices on either side of me, although I can't make out what anyone's saying. Guards shout names and numbers. I listen for his name, close my eyes, try to breathe normally. It feels as if I've been waiting for hours, but I've no idea how long it's actually been. The clock on the wall reads 6:15, and the hands haven't moved since I entered. My watch is in the locker room. Only wedding bands and medical-alert jewelry allowed inside.

Finally, the door across from me opens, and Aiden walks in. At first glance, he doesn't look all that bad: dressed in a too-large faded jumpsuit, a bit rumpled, yet clean-shaven and standing tall. But when he sits down across from me, I see his face is deathly pale. Lines etch his bloodshot eyes, and blue-black smudges circle beneath them.

I try to smile. "Hi," I say, and it comes out high and reedy.

He leans down to the holes, "You've got to go, babe. Now."

I press my hand to the glass. "How are you? Have they told you anything? When are you getting out of—"

"I mean it," he says. "Out of town. Away. And don't come here again. It's too dangerous."

"Aiden, I want you to know that you can count on me. That we're in this together. As soon as you get out we can start to fight—"

"I'm not getting out. They've told me that much. Flight risk." His mouth squeezes into a grimace. "The Gardner heist."

"But these things can change, right? What does your lawyer say? Are they filing motions or whatever they do? I can check with another lawyer for you if you want."

"You've got to stay out of it. You haven't done anything wrong, and you've got to keep it that way. The less contact you have with me and this mess the better."

"But if I haven't done anything wrong, I'm not in any danger, so I'm going to do whatever I can to get you freed as soon as possible."

"You're not listening to me: I'm not getting out. No chance of bail."

"But—"

He holds up his hands as if this will stop my words. "But nothing. They think—"

"What happened?" I demand. His right forefinger is in a metal brace wrapped in adhesive tape.

"Nothing." He lowers his hand.

"It doesn't look like nothing."

"Please, Claire. Believe me, some things are better off left alone."

"Somebody hurt you," I say.

"It's nothing," he repeats.

"Tell me."

"I warned you." He hesitates, sighs, and says, "I never got a chance to pay the sellers."

"What sellers? What pay?" But as soon as the questions are out of my mouth, I know the answers. "Patel's money? The men who gave you *Bath*?"

"They want it now."

"But what does your finger have to do with that?"

"It's a threat."

"What kind of threat?"

The circles under his eyes appear to grow even darker. "It's what's going to happen to my finger if I don't get them their money."

"They're going to break it?"

"It's already broken."

"I don't understand."

He raises his right forefinger and makes a slashing motion at the finger's base with his left hand. "They're going to cut it off."

My stomach rolls, and for a moment I think I might be sick. "That's insane," I protest. "No one would do that."

He just looks at me, his eyes steely, his jaws clamped together.

"But you're in jail. How could anyone get to you to, to . . . ?"

"The same way they got this to me." He shows me his finger again.

"Where's the money?" I cry. "Tell me and I'll bring it to them."

"No."

"I'm not a child you need to protect. It's you who needs help and I want to give it. Are you actually saying you're willing to lose your, your . . ." I can't say the word.

"It's already gone."

I look at his two hands resting on the small ledge and my

cramped cubicle starts to spin. "What are you talking about?" My voice rises with each word.

"Claire," he says sharply. "Don't do this."

My eyes fill with tears. "I'm just so scared for you."

His face softens. "If you promise to leave right after I finish and not freak out, I'll explain."

I close my eyes and take a deep breath, not sure I actually want to hear the explanation. "Okay."

"The only way to get into the gallery's vault is with the print of my right forefinger."

It takes a moment for this register, and when it does, I'm certain I'm going to be sick. I choke back the bile rising in my throat.

"You promised," Aiden says. "No freak out. Now go."

"But, but," I stutter, not wanting to leave him alone with this. "What about your rich friends? Clients? Someone you could go to for a loan?"

"Already tried," he says. "I'm kind of persona non grata at the moment."

"Your paintings? You could sell—"

He shakes his head, and I understand that he'd rather lose a finger than part with any of his artwork. "Then bail," I say. "If you could get out, even for a day, an hour, then, then . . ." My mind grasps around for any solution, but all I find are blank spaces.

"Please," he says, with such sadness that I feel it inside of me. "Go."

Then I realize what I can do: I'll find the original painting. It would prove Aiden's *Bath* was a forgery. And then, at least for a short time, none of the charges against him would apply: no transportation or sale of anything stolen, no fraud, no initial connection to the heist. His lawyer could get him out on bail then. Even a short time will be long enough to save his finger.

"Aiden, Aiden." My voice fractures. "I'm so sorry, really sorry. I never told you this before, I should have but I didn't, but the painting you brought me isn't what you thought it was. I knew—"

"To your mother's, a friend's, wherever," he interrupts, too concerned for my safety to hear me. "I can't have you go down for this, too." He presses his left hand flat to the window that separates us, just as he did the first night we made love. "I love you."

A full sob escapes my lips. "I love you, too," I manage to whisper, and as I say it, I know it's true.

"Kristi and Chantal can handle the details of your show."

"It's not about the show. You know that. It's you. In here. It's about what they might do—"

"My beautiful Claire." Aiden stands and opens his door, turns back and gives me a crooked smile. "Don't you know I'm going to need all the money from the sale of your fabulous paintings for my defense fund?"

WHEN SANDRA STONEHAM ushers me into her apartment, I take a moment in the entryway to examine *Amelia*. There's no doubt Virgil Rendell had the technical skills to pull off a high-quality forgery of Degas' *After the Bath,* but why would he? Could he have stolen the original and replaced it with his own? Could he have blackmailed Belle, forcing her to turn over the real one and replacing it with a forgery? Could the original have been lost or destroyed and Belle hired him to paint a replacement? But the whys and hows are inconsequential in light of Aiden's current situation.

"Did your aunt know Virgil Rendell?" I ask, as I try to determine the direction of his brushstrokes.

She furrows her brow. "I thought you were looking for famous painters?"

"I am. Yes, I am, but this Rendell is quite good. I guess, I'm just kind of more curious, seeing the painting here, than actually considering him for my book."

Sandra looks at me strangely. "Not that I know of."

I throw a pointed glance at the closed mahogany doors leading to the parlor, hoping she'll give me a peek at her more traditional artwork. But if she notices my curiosity, she chooses to ignore it and motions me to follow her down the opposite hallway.

"I found a few boxes in the attic," she says, when we reach the living room, "I've only just started going through them, but I've been having a great time. I found all sorts of lovely things I forgot were there. I've decided that, while I still have my faculties, I'm going to do a thorough catalog of each and every one." She points to items scattered on the coffee table: a pillbox with a tiny ballerina carved on its broken lid, a porcelain doll, a handful of old coins, a sheaf of photos, yellowed newspaper clippings. "These are important pieces of history."

"Seems like a worthwhile project," I say, although at first glance, I don't see anything that looks important to history. Or to me.

"But, unfortunately," she continues, "I haven't found a single item of Aunt Belle's." She purses her lips. "The museum has a stranglehold on everything that belonged to her. Every painting, every art object, even her clothes and the few letters that remain."

"Because of the conditions of her will?" I ask.

"Because of the museum's *interpretation* of the conditions of her will," Sandra corrects.

"So unfair to the family," I sympathize.

I'm rewarded by a smile. "As the kids say, 'You got that right.'"

I look from the coffee table to the half-dozen cartons on the floor. I'm not at all sure what I'm looking for, but I'm sure it isn't a broken pillbox.

"I haven't gone through all of them, but it seems to be mostly paper. Documents and mementos and such. As I told you on the phone, it all appears to be mainly from the twentieth century. Mostly my mother's. The women in our family have always been the savers, the legacy keepers. Something a family, rather than an institution, should do."

"You got that right." I grin at her. "Early twentieth century could work."

"As you know, Aunt Belle lived until 1924, so, with any luck, maybe you'll stumble on something I missed," Sandra says, but her tone implies she doubts that very much. "Well, they're all yours. I'll be on the other side of the apartment paying bills, so just give a yell if you need me."

As she walks into the back of the apartment, I sit on the floor and reach for the first box. I lift up a stack of newspaper clippings. But as my fingers close around them, they fracture like thin sheets of crystal and fall back into the box, unreadable slivers of dust and yellow paper.

Since Aiden's arrest, I haven't had more than an hour of un-interrupted sleep; the visual of his broken finger won't leave my mind. I push the newspaper slivers to the bottom, so I can see what else is inside. I've got only a couple of hours before I have to be at Markel G. All my paintings have been framed and delivered, and Kristi needs me to inspect them before they can be hung. An object in motion.

I dig into the box. Love letters written during World War I, photos of children presumably long dead, crushed flowers, yel-lowed report cards filled with perfectly rounded script, menus from restaurants popular in the 1930s. A delicate mantilla, moth-and perhaps mouse-eaten, that, when it was white and proud, must have been its owner's prize possession. I press my fingers to the

graying, threadbare material, taking some comfort in the small-
ness, the unimportance, of an individual existence.

I scoot over to the next box. This one's filled with baby clothes
and more unyielding dolls that don't look like they could have been
much fun to play with. One has a painted face reminiscent of the
Wicked Witch of the West. Right away, the third box looks more
promising. Everything in it appears to be older. House accounts
from 1894 through 1898, a photo of a family, horribly trussed in
nineteenth-century garb, each one more stiff and repressed looking
than the next. But no Belle.

Then I find a notebook with the initials "VR" in the top right-
hand corner. It's full of difficult-to-read hen scratching, some
dated, some not. A journal. The first semilegible date is either 1884
or 1885 and the last one seems to be 1889. I quickly skim the pages,
hoping to find a name. It's obvious that the author is a young man
madly in love with a girl named Amelia, who's sitting for a portrait
he's painting. It has to belong to Virgil Rendell. My heart begins to
pound. The timing fits, as does the writer being a painter. But why
would his journal be in the Gardner family attic?

I stop turning pages when I see a mention of Belle, or Mrs. Jack,
as he refers to her. And as far as I can make out, none of what's
written about her is flattering.

"Mrs. Jack is the most bull-headed woman I have ever known."

"Amelia won't stand for it and neither will I."

"She's her aunt, not her mother."

"Just because she's rich and knows all the right people, that
doesn't mean we have to fall to our knees and do as she commands."

There's a lot more scribbling; clearly, this was not meant to be
read by anyone but the writer. Yet, every page or so, a readable
sentence stands out. "Sumner Prescott is a prig and Amelia will

never agree to marry him." And toward the end: "Belle Gardner is such a hypocrite, pretending to be the renegade of Boston society, while harboring her belief in the superiority of her own 'class' to the detriment of her niece's happiness. I shall never again step foot in Green Hill or her horrid, overfurnished Beacon Street house. Nor will I have anything to do with Mrs. Jack ever again."

So much for my theory that Belle hired him to paint the forgery. I glance down at my watch. It's already past three. Kristi has begun limiting the gallery's hours to avoid the press, and she was adamant that I check the paintings today. I hesitate, then put Virgil's journal back in the box and call out to Sandra that I have to get going.

"I haven't finished going through this box yet," I tell her when she comes in. "But I'm late for a meeting downtown . . ." I let the sentence dangle, hoping she'll offer to let me take it with me.

"I'll be home tomorrow afternoon cooking for Thanksgiving," she says. "If you'd like to come by then and finish up, it's fine with me."

I take her up on her offer and speed to the Green Line. As I wait in the cold for the trolley, I run Rendell's words through my head. *Nor will I have anything to do with Mrs. Jack ever again.*

Obviously, Amelia did marry Prescott instead of Rendell, presumably due to the influence of her rich and powerful aunt, who felt Virgil's family lineage wasn't good enough for her niece. It would give the story a Shakespearian twist if Rendell had decided to exact revenge. What better way to destroy Isabella Stewart Gardner than to steal one of her most valuable paintings and replace it with a forgery?

From the pen of

ISABELLA STEWART GARDNER

January, 1898
Paris, France

My dearest Amelia,

As soon as you open this letter, take it to a private place and read it only when you are sure you are truly alone. Then, when you have finished, you must burn it and ensure the ashes are also destroyed. This might sound a bit hysterical, but when you read on, you will understand. I should not be putting these thoughts onto paper, but I must talk of it with someone, and I desperately need your guidance in this matter.

I have gotten myself into a most extraordinary pickle. Oh Amelia, I have been so very foolish! Remember how, last summer at Green Hill, we discussed my meetings with Mr. Edgar Degas at his studio, and I said I would do everything all over again? Well, I was wrong. So very wrong. If only I could take it all back!

Just before we left for London last October, I received a cable from Edgar telling me he had heard we would be abroad this winter.

He said that I must come to visit as he had a surprise for me. I did
a bit of rearranging of our itinerary and managed to get us to Paris
for Christmas. On arrival, I immediately left a card at Edgar's
apartments.

The next afternoon, he turned up unannounced at our hotel. Your
Uncle Jack was at the Free Masons with, coincidentally, none other
than your father-in-law, whom I assume you are aware is in Paris for
the holidays. He is such a fine man, and I am deeply gratified that you
and your children are Prescotts. I shudder to think where another
choice might have brought you. But I digress.

Edgar's carriage was parked outside the hotel, and he whisked me
away to his studio. "What do you suppose this surprise might be, my
dear Mrs. Gardner?" he asked, as we rode along the wide boulevards.

Of course, I was hoping it was a picture, but I didn't want to be
disappointed or insult him if this was not the case. "Another gown?"

Edgar chuckled and told the driver to go faster. "Perhaps it is," he
told me. "I fear you might have guessed." But his eyes twinkled in
such a way that I knew I had not.

I cannot tell you how excited I was. I knew it had to be a painting
for my new museum, but I did not know the style in which he had
painted it or whether it would be a gift or require payment. I am sure
you can guess my hopes on both of these matters.

When we entered his studio, a large canvas sat on an easel in the
center of the room. It was covered with a sheet. I pressed my hand to
my breast to control the beating of my heart. I tell you, Amelia, I was
afraid it would leap from my chest, so hard was it pounding. Edgar
watched me, his face alight with pleasure.

"Show me," I begged, like a child on Christmas morning. "Please."

"Settle yourself, my dear girl," he said, pointing to the sofa. "Shall I call the maid to bring tea?"

"No," I said, not caring that I was being unpardonably rude. "I want to see my—your—picture."

He laughed outright. "If only you were a man with that spirit. Just think of the things you could accomplish!"

I crossed my arms and glared at him. "I shall remind you, sir, that I am in the process of accomplishing many things. Most of which I see no man doing at all."

"You are exactly right, my dear Belle," he said. "I apologize to you and *toutes les femmes.*"

He bowed in my direction, then pulled the sheet from the canvas with a flourish.

At first, all I could take in was the brilliance of his colors. Blue, green, and coral burst into the room as if they were alive. The depth of the values, the saturation of the paint! The brushwork! It is a tour de force! The man is a genius, and I applauded myself for convincing him to return to his early classical style.

"My fifth and last *After the Bath,*" he said proudly. "Do you like it?"

I blinked and focused on the composition. It is a depiction of three nudes toweling themselves dry, not an unusual subject for Edgar. But this is so much superior to his recent work, translucent layers of vibrant color set on top of one another, expressing the inexpressible with a luminosity that can only be the finger of God. I wanted to touch it so badly that I had to clench my fists to keep my arms by my sides.

"Well?" he demanded.

I tore my eyes from the painting and looked at him. "Like it?" I
breathed. "It is your masterpiece."

"So you will accept it? As a gift for your new museum?"

And although this is what I had hoped for, prayed for, I was
momentarily speechless.

Edgar's face clouded with concern. Did he really believe I might
say no?

"Of course!" I cried. "Of course, I accept it. I'll cherish it. It shall
hang in one of the most prominent places in the museum."

"Only one of the most prominent?" he teased.

"The most prominent! Absolutely," I promised.

He beamed. "Then champagne rather than tea? To toast your new
acquisition?"

We settled into the sofa, and his maid brought champagne and
the loveliest little cakes. I was delirious with joy and grew so tipsy on
the champagne that I barely looked at my new picture. Edgar and I
sipped and chatted gaily of my plans for Fenway Court and the gossip
of Paris.

Only after we finished the bottle did I take a closer look at the
painting. And, oh, Amelia, it appears that I only saw what I wanted
to see, not what was there in front of my own eyes the entire time. It
pains me to tell you this, but one of the nudes is me!

There is no doubt, and everyone will know. Do you remember
how your Uncle Jack reacted to John Sargent's picture of me with the
heart-shaped décolletage? He was so angered by how "revealing" it
was that he banished it from public viewing until after his death. And
I was completely clothed!

What shall I do? Edgar made it expressly for my museum, and I cannot insult him by not displaying such a gift. And yet, it cannot be displayed! Nor can I turn it down. This *After the Bath* is his true masterpiece, and he gave it to me! It is mine and must remain mine. And to receive such an item at no cost! I shall never give it up. Never.

So, my dear Amelia, you now see why this letter must be burned. Please do so immediately and send a cable with your thoughts as quickly as you can. I am desperate for your counsel. We must devise a plan.

I am your despairing and foolish,
Aunt Belle

Thirty-nine

Three stacks of bubble-wrapped canvases sit on a worktable in the overcrowded back room at Markel G. All twenty of my paintings. Fresh from the framer. Although we can't start the installation until two days before the show, as the current show will be up until then, Kristi likes her ducklings lined up ahead of time.

I touch the bubble wrap and remember the afternoon Aiden and I unpacked *Bath*. It's so wrong for him not to be here. A deep sadness sits in the center of my chest. My vibrant colors strain through the semiopaque bubbles the same way Degas' did, but the thrill of that day is conspicuously missing. It's painful being here without Aiden, moving ahead with the show as if nothing's wrong. And as if things might not get far worse.

Chantal's out front with a customer, of which there have been many since the arrest, and Kristi's coming back to help me unwrap the paintings as soon as she's off the phone. We pretend that Aiden's at a meeting or getting lunch, gone for only a moment. We avoid mentioning his name.

Under normal circumstances, I might have already unwrapped the paintings, leaned them up against the wall, carried a few to the front to see how they might fit. Instead, I sit in a wobbly chair with one arm thinking about Virgil Rendell blackmailing Belle. If I'm right, then his family might have the original *After the Bath,* which they may or may not know is a real Degas. If he's got a family.

My phone rings. "How you doing, Bear?" Rik asks.

"I'm fine," I say, but my words come out a little raggedy.

"I'm here for you. You know that, don't you?"

My throat closes up and, for a moment, I can't speak. "I know that," I finally whisper. Would he be there for me if he understood the part I'd played in Aiden's debacle?

There's a hollow emptiness on the line, then Rik asks with false cheerfulness, "Have you bought a dress yet?"

I know he's trying to be kind, to distract me, but this is the last thing I want to talk about. "I took a cruise down Newbury Street the other day."

"And?"

"I didn't see much."

"Did you try anything on?"

I dread the reinstallation without Aiden. A hole at my side. "There's still time."

"Like four days. Not including Thanksgiving."

"I'll go when I leave here."

"If you want to wait until about eight, I'll go with you."

I don't want him to come with me. He'll just be going on about the rich and famous guests, the celebrity-chef food, Yo-Yo Ma on the cello, the Dutch tulips. Just as the media's been doing all week. There's never a mention of the reinstallation without a mention of Aiden, and I'm thinking about him enough as it is. And about how stupid we've both been.

"No thanks," I say. "I'm at Markel G now, so I might as well do it while I'm down here."

"Have you seen Aiden?"

I lower my voice. "We'll talk later."

Rik hesitates. "How about a hot haircut to go with the new dress?" he asks in another misguided effort to lift my spirits. "You never got to go to Canyon Ranch, so how about I treat you to a new do at Salon Arnaud? If you want some PR attention for your show, there's nothing like a great haircut to make you stand out."

My eyes fill with tears, an event that's become increasingly common. It's only an art show. As Isaac once said: *We're not curing cancer here.* "Please. Rik. I've got a lot on my mind, and—"

Kristi comes in, and I jump at the excuse. "Got to go," I tell Rik. "Got a meeting."

"The limo will be at your place around seven on Saturday," Rik says, and I click off.

Kristi grabs two pairs of scissors, slides one across the table to me, and says, "Let's see what Templeton's magic has done for these puppies."

And, indeed, I almost can't believe that these extraordinary paintings are mine; like a good haircut, framing makes all the difference. For a moment, my troubles vanish, and pure joy overpowers me. I created this. And this. And this. My babies standing proud, bursting with life and beauty, graduating into the world, their future unknown but full of promise.

I'M ON THE floor in Sandra's living room with the last of the boxes. I've been at it for almost an hour with no luck. Nothing more about Belle or Amelia in Rendell's journal, nothing else belonging to him. But I've found a few photos of Sandra as a girl. She's one of those rare women who have improved with age.

Last night, I scoured the Internet for information on Rendell, but aside from what I'd already found, there wasn't much. Nothing on whether he was married or had any children, nothing on a painting career other than that of a forger who committed suicide. I know the chance of finding anything belonging to him is beyond remote, but remote is all Aiden and I have.

"Anything?" Sandra calls from the other side of the island, where she's chopping vegetables for Thanksgiving soup.

I shake my head. "I figure I need solid information on at least five artists to write the book proposal, and I've only got three, maybe four. I was really counting on finding another one here."

Sandra's smile is warm with understanding. "Who are your others?" she asks.

"Like I said the other day, Whistler, Singer Sargent, and Ralph Curtis. I've found some information on Dennis Miller Bunker and your aunt, but not nearly enough. And nothing much on her personal relationships with Smith, Cram, or Martin Mower."

"Maybe you can pad the proposal with marketing materials," Sandra suggests. "If it looks like it'll sell, the publisher will probably be satisfied with an annotated table of contents and three strong chapters."

"Spoken like a woman who's written a book proposal."

"When you get to be my age," Sandra says, "you've done just about everything at least once."

I pull the last carton to me. Every item, folder, stack of ribbon-tied letters is from the 1930s and 1940s. In the beginning, I was more curious about each box's contents, but now I couldn't care less about pressed flowers from the courtship of some unknown girl who's probably been married to the old fart for fifty-plus years by now. I pull each item out of the box and toss it on the carpet, then feel guilty that Sandra might think I'm not being respectful of her family's history, and lay them down more carefully. But Sandra's so engrossed in chopping vegetables, she doesn't appear to be aware of me.

And then I see something that looks like a sketchbook. I remind myself that, so far, everything in this box is after Rendell's time, that there's no reason to expect something else of his to turn up among Sandra's memorabilia. But still. I pull the book out, wipe the dust from the cover; a small "VR" is written on the top corner, just like the journal I found before. I press it between my hands, glance up at Sandra, who's dicing onions with Julia Child–like energy, and open it.

The first quarter of the book is filled with landscapes, the next dozen or so pages contain sketches for a portrait of an older woman and four younger ones, most likely her daughters. Then there are nudes. The earliest ones are finely drawn, voluptuous and beautiful. But as I turn the pages, the bodies become more sturdy and coarse-looking.

The book falls open to two compositional sketches facing each other on opposite pages. Sweat scratches at my hairline as a full-body flush races to my face. I blink, sure that desperation, coupled with wishful thinking, is driving my vision. I blink again. It's still there.

In the drawing on the right-hand page, Simone and a hefty Françoise are seated on either side of a standing Jacqueline, just as they are in Aiden's *After the Bath* and my *Bath II*. But on the facing page, a delicate Not-Françoise stands next to Jacqueline with a hunched Simone at Jacqueline's feet, just as they are in Degas' sketchbook. My mind goes blank, and the room seems to slide away.

AS IF WAKING from a dream, I hear the sizzle of onions hitting hot oil, inhale the sharp, sweet odor, but can't quite find my bearings. I look at the open sketchbook on my lap, dumbfounded, muddled, not sure what to do next. *Thunk-thunk* goes Sandra's knife. More sizzle. Celery perhaps. I slowly put the scattered items back in the box but hold onto the sketchbook. Although the two drawings appear to confirm my theory that there was an original *After the Bath* and that Virgil Rendell painted the forgery that Aiden brought to me, I can't be certain until I compare them with Degas' compositional sketches.

My brain struggles for a way to take Rendell's book with me. Clearly, Sandra would never know if I dropped it into my backpack, and the idea has some appeal. But despite my adventures on the wild side and my omissions to Aiden, I can't do it. I stand and say in a tremulous voice, "Just as you thought, nothing in here."

"Oh, Claire." Sandra keeps chopping, but she looks at me sadly. "I'm sorry."

"It's okay. That's the way it goes with historical research. Maybe this whole book proposal thing isn't the greatest idea."

She perks up. "If the Markel G show is a success, the last thing you'll be thinking about is writing a book." Then she frowns. "Such a shame. Such a handsome young man. Will any of this affect your show?"

"Everything's moving forward as planned. He's got some very talented assistants who are doing a remarkable job. Believe it or not, since all this happened, traffic at the gallery has doubled, maybe tripled. Sales, too." I try to sound upbeat, but I don't fool Sandra.

Her eyes fill with sympathy. "Take it from an old woman, if this doesn't work out, something else will. Life is like that."

I hold up Rendell's book. "There are some interesting sketches in here," I say. "No name or anything, but they're quite nice."

She throws some fresh oregano in the soup, tastes it, throws in some more.

"Would you mind if I took it with me? Just for a day or two. I'd like to study the drawings more closely."

She squints at the sketchbook. "I don't know . . ."

"I'll take good care of it, I promise," I plead, hoping her compassion will translate into consent.

She hesitates, then shrugs. "Sure. I guess. Maybe it'll take the edge off your disappointment."

"Great. Thanks." I put the book in my backpack and leave before she can change her mind.

As I ride the T to Copley Square, I don't open my backpack, just hold it tightly to my chest. I want to wait until I get to the studio, until I have Degas' compositional sketches in front of me. The sketches of Not-Françoise. Of her altered position in the painting's arrangement, of her altered body. I stare out the trolley window at the snarled traffic on Huntington Avenue and try not to think about what I may, or may not, have here. Whether it might help Aiden.

When I get home, I scramble through my book piles for *Edgar Degas: Sketches and Drawings, 1875–1900* and quickly locate the drawings I want. Then I open to Rendell's two sketches. I place the books side-by-side on the floor and raise my eyes to the ceiling. I don't know how I'll bear it if I've only invented the similarities.

I lower my gaze to Degas' compositional sketches. They are almost identical to the left-hand page of Rendell's book: Jacqueline, Simone, and Not-Françoise. Not-Françoise, who is small, refined, and tiny waisted. Not-Françoise who is standing rather than sitting, shifting the composition from *Bath*'s symmetry to Degas' preferred asymmetrical balance.

I look again. And again. There appears to be no doubt.

I'm holding my own personal Rosetta Stone. Aiden's, too. I hope.

Forty

I told you not to come back here," Aiden says, but he can't suppress
a slim smile.

I dare to look at his hands and see he still has ten fingers, although the one is still splinted. "How long do you have?"

He follows my eyes, and his smile disappears. "A week, maybe two,"
he says, his voice flat and toneless. "That's why you have to leave."

A week. "There's something I have to tell you." I'm sitting in
a different bathroom-stall-sized room. I know because there's a
22A instead of a 35A on the door; other than that, the overheated
stuffiness, the broken clock, and the claustrophobic closeness of
the walls are exactly the same.

"It's good, possibly great," I say. "I've found proof that the painting you brought to my studio was a forgery."

"No, it wasn't," he says. "I know where it came from. It was
authenticated."

"So was *Bath II.*"

His jaw tightens. "It's impossible."

"Degas' compositional sketches for *After the Bath* don't match
the painting you brought me."

"So what? How many of your finished paintings match your initial drawings? Artists change their minds. Art's changed by the process of making it. You know that."

I choose my words carefully. "I have sketches by a known forger. One set that match Degas' compositional drawings and another that match the finished painting."

"What forger?"

"Virgil Rendell."

"Never heard of him."

"He knew Isabella Gardner. Was apparently on the outside of her circle. It appears they had a falling—"

"Claire, don't lose it on me here."

"I'm thinking Rendell either stole the original painting or blackmailed Belle or pulled some kind of sleazy revenge act, which forced her into hanging his forgery as her Degas. If that's the case, then his family most likely has it. So if I can find it, it'll prove your painting was a copy, and the one they caught Patel with was a copy of a copy. Just like he claims."

"The painting I brought you was not a copy of anything." Aiden grips the edge of the shelf; his knuckles are white. "It hung in the Gardner for almost a hundred years."

I keep my voice measured. "If I can find the real one, it'll prove your *Bath* was a forgery."

"Which it isn't."

I continue as if he hasn't spoken. "And if that's true, then the charges are moot. If the painting they got from Patel is a confirmed forgery and they assume the thieves stole a real Degas, then there's no transportation or sale of stolen goods. There's no fraud. No connection to the heist. And your lawyer—"

He takes a deep breath, and I see he's trying to calm himself.

"Even if all of this were true, which it's not, if the painting was the one stolen in the robbery, none of this changes anything."

"Aiden, you're not listening to me. It doesn't have to be true. It just has to be a legal possibility. An argument your lawyer can use to get you out on bail. At least for a little while."

We both look at his right hand, which he places on his lap. "Why are you so sure it's not a Degas? That there's another painting?" he asks.

I see that he's finally listening. "I knew pretty much from the beginning that it was a forgery."

"You knew and didn't tell me? Why would you keep such a thing to—"

"We've got to focus on finding the painting. I'll explain everything later. Please just believe me. And now that I have the sketches—"

"This is crazy. Insane. We don't know the damn painting exists. Or if there ever was one. And even if it does exist, we've got no idea where it is."

Despite Aiden's catalog of difficulties, I notice his shift to the plural. He's warming to the idea. "I've got some leads," I say. "About Rendell. His life, his family. His relationship with Belle and her niece."

"This isn't worth the effort."

"What have we got to lose?" I stand and press my palm to the glass. "Lots to gain."

He matches all five fingers of his right hand to mine. Desperation meets desperation.

AFTER I LEAVE the jail, I grab a cab and call Rik to see if he can meet me for a drink when he gets out of work.

"Can't," he says. "I'm up to my ears in reinstallation. Maybe I can make it to Jake's around nine. Or ten."

"How about I bring over some coffee? I have a quick work question to ask you. I'll only stay a few minutes."

"Double cappuccino grande with skim milk. Two sugars."

I have the cab drop me at a Starbucks around the corner from the Gardner, pick up Rik's coffee, and walk to the museum. When I arrive, trucks are parked everywhere: caterers, construction companies, electricians, plumbers—even closet designers. Workers, some punching high-tech handhelds and others carrying bales of wire or planks of wood or stacks of nested chairs, are walking into, out of, and around the building. I text Rik, and he comes down to get me.

He motions me into the entryway and leans against the tall ticket counter. "This is nuts. They had no business trying to do all this so soon," he grumbles. "This big a spectacle needs years, not months, to put together."

I offer him the coffee. "But you love it."

"Can't deny that." Rik stirs sugar into his coffee and takes a long sip. "I'm flat out here. What kind of work question you got for me?"

"Ever hear of a forger named Virgil Rendell?"

A horde of electricians pounds through the narrow entryway, and we press ourselves to a wall to let them through.

"Name sounds kind of familiar," Rik says. "Who is he?"

"Was. Late-nineteenth-century painter. He was in love with Belle's niece, Amelia. Did an amazing portrait of her that I saw at Sandra Stoneham's. Anyway, seems like he had some kind of a big falling out with Belle. I think over her forcing Amelia to marry someone else."

"And you're telling me this because . . . ?"

"His painting style is very similar to Degas, and I was thinking that they must have worked together at some time." I have to stop as two huge speakers are wheeled in. "I was hoping you might be able to get me some information on him."

"You're working on your book now? Don't you have enough on your plate?"

"I'm not painting anything. I'm antsy about the show and need some distraction. And with everything that's going on with Aiden and all . . ."

"How's he doing?"

"Not well."

"Sorry, Bear." Rik touches my cheek. "When this is all over, we'll be able to spend some time."

"I just need something else to think about."

"Excuse me, sir, miss," a man in a power suit with a power voice says. "We need to secure this area. Do you have identification?" Rik flips his ID card, but when I start to burrow in my backpack, the man stops me. "Sorry, miss, only museum employees and cleared contractors allowed in the building."

"I'm really sorry," Rik says, as he follows me outside, "but I don't have time to help you with this now. Maybe after the reinstallation. This place is crazy. And so am I." He squints at me. "I think maybe you're a little crazy, too."

We have to step off the sidewalk to allow four burly men with matching headsets jutting from their ears to pass by.

"These security guys are the worst," Rik grumbles. "They're crawling all over the building and getting in everyone's way. Checking out every closet and cabinet. Worried about the riff-raff who are coming to the reinstallation. Like you and me. I heard they found places to wire no one even knew existed." He gives me a quick kiss and strides into the museum.

Disappointed, although I suppose not surprised, I watch him

disappear. Even though it's dark and the temperature is hovering in the midforties, I walk past the trolley stop and set out across the bustling Northeastern campus, where students are bailing out for Thanksgiving break in droves.

I hesitate in front of the Ruggles T station, which is on the campus, and think about taking the Orange Line. It'll be faster, warmer, easier, but I need the energy burn. I pass by the station entrance and climb the stairs to the parking garage, which doubles as a walkway to Columbus Avenue. I dodge the screeching cars, so intent on vacation escape, and cross over to the South End.

A week. Maybe two, Aiden said. I walk down Mass Ave, alongside the belching busses and deafening trucks, searching for options. If Rendell's a dead end, at least for the moment, maybe I should look at it from Belle's side. If my theory about the blackmail is true, then maybe part of the deal was that Belle was forced to hide the original.

Checking out every closet and cabinet, Rik had said. *Heard they found places to wire no one even knew existed.* And Sandra Stoneham had complained that everything Belle ever owned was in the museum.

WHEN I GET home, I call Rik. "I know, I know, you're busy and I shouldn't be bothering you, but I really need this one thing. I'll owe your forever. Whatever you want. For the rest of your life."

Rik's sigh is long and theatrical. "What is it?"

"You know how my undergraduate degree is in art and architecture?"

"Claire. Please."

"Anyway, the bottom line is that I'm thinking of doing a new series on the architecture of museums."

"Paintings of museums? Doesn't sound like you."

"I'm not talking about the usual aspects of museums, but how their little-known spaces and corners portray them. The details the architect inserted that most people never notice that set the structure apart, give it its unique meaning and personality." It's not a half bad idea. "You know, the whole seen and unseen, but with a new subject. Buildings instead of people, but not just any buildings, buildings where people come to see."

"What about the Degas book?"

"Oh, that, too. I'd do both."

"Claire, I'm getting a little worried about you."

"I'm fine. I'm fine. Really. But I was wondering if you have access to the original—or obviously, copies of the original—blueprints for the museum. Because what museum is more architecturally interesting than the Gardner? What museum has more personality?"

Exasperated, he agrees to e-mail me the blueprints in exchange for the promise that he won't see or hear from me until the reinstallation.

The e-mail doesn't arrive until two days later. I've barely managed to refrain from calling him to ask him where it is. The time shows he sent it at 3:42 a.m.

Sorry there are so many attachments, but apparently Belle kept changing the specs, which necessitated new drawings and blueprints. Some dated. Some not. Hard to tell which ones were the last. Guess she drove the architect and masons crazy. No surprise there. Reminds me of you. xooox

I click on the first attachment. Each drawing is more difficult to read than the last. Almost all are poorly scanned. Many are drawn with so many flourishes that they're illegible. And some, scrawled in pencil, are just vague blurs. I print them all out, upping the contrast on the printer, which helps a little, but not much. It's a good thing I spent all those hours at BU sprawled over a drafting table. No way an untrained eye would be able to get anything from these.

I use my magnifying glass and study the first page. It's a drawing of the courtyard but appears to be more concerned with the decorative than the architectural. There are sketches of the lion stylobates, the mosaic, and various columns in the margins. I put the magnifier down and stare out the window. A hiding place that's out of the way. Large enough to hold a three-foot-eleven by four-foot-ten painting, but small enough to be overlooked. Perhaps even disguised as something else.

I raise the magnifying glass and resume my search. Two hours later, I've found nothing but a pounding headache. I stand, stretch, take a couple of Tylenol. I think about going to Jake's. I haven't been there in forever. But, of course, I can't. Too much talk of Aiden. Too much talk of my show. Too many of Danielle's mindlessly insensitive comments.

I stare at the piling schedule for Fenway Court. Like the Back Bay and South End, the Fenway is mostly landfill, and it looks like the museum sits on piles driven ninety feet through the fill to the bedrock below. An amazing architectural accomplishment. Although the construction process probably wasn't all that different from that for the Venetian palazzo Belle used as the basis for her own palace. Except in Venice, the piles would have gone through water.

Ninety feet of landfill. Beneath the museum. Could there be a more perfect place for a secret chamber? I flip through the pages, looking for basement drawings. When I find them, I follow every line with my finger. Nothing.

Then I notice a small plan in the corner of the blueprint. "Sub-basement" is written under a drawing of a space a fraction of the size of the basement. Against the east wall of the sub-basement is a narrow space, fronted by a door almost as large as the interior. Big enough to hold a large canvas; isolated enough to hide a secret.

Forty-one

It feels as if it's been raining forever. I stand at the window in my new dress and trendy haircut, watching the soaking-wet street for Rik and the Gardner limousine. There's got to be some reasonable art-related or research-related explanation I can come up with to gain access to Belle's secret room. I'd love to ask Rik, but that might put him in a difficult position at work. Maybe something will come to me at the museum.

A long, white limo slides sensuously up to my building. A uniformed driver steps out with an umbrella so that I won't get wet. As I slowly make my way down the stairs in my too-high high heels, I flash back to that afternoon at MoMA, standing in front of *4D,* reading the little white card with Isaac's name on it. But this time will be different. No one is making a fool of me. And Degas' name attributed to my painting is, I suppose, an accomplishment of sorts.

"Love the hair!" Rik cries, as soon as I stick my head in the limo. It's cut in a mass of newly highlighted layers, curly and full, spiky bangs. "Let me see the dress," he demands.

I slip into the long seat across from him and open my coat to reveal the lapis-blue dress I found in a vintage shop this morning; its shredded hem hits my thighs in places and my calves in others.

It came with an "enchanting evening jacket" of lapis, purple, and deep red, is bigger than a blouse, and cost fifty bucks. "Looks better when I'm standing up."

"Looks damn good when you're sitting down." An older man next to Rik eyes my legs.

I close my coat.

Rik pours me a glass of champagne and introduces me to the others in the car. Without specifically mentioning the venue, he tells them about my upcoming show, and I try to be as charming as Aiden would want me to be. But my lack of enthusiasm undermines me. I stare out the window as we glide silently through the sodden streets, thinking about Aiden in a prison jumpsuit when he should be in a tux.

At the museum, there's a line of limos in front of us surrounded by reporters and photographers holding umbrellas along with their microphones and cameras. A red carpet leads from the street to the entrance, and as each guest alights, the media throngs forward. Rik wasn't kidding. The Gardner is maxing out.

I spent considerable time studying the blueprints during the afternoon, and once inside, I look around to locate myself within the configuration of the museum. The sub-basement is down two flights straight ahead to the left; the door to the basement is half-way down the building to the right.

We filter into the North, East, and West Cloisters, whose Venetian archways frame the courtyard. The enclosed garden is in full fragrant flower, so green and lush after the dreary gray outside that it almost hurts to look at. Champagne is passed by tuxedoed waiters, and a string quartet plays in the corner. It's gorgeous, but it's clear there are far too many people to view a single painting in a tiny room. The stairway that leads to the Short Gallery is roped off, and guests in the West Cloister are already queuing up behind it.

"How's this going to work with all these people?" I ask Rik.

He points to a covered painting sitting on a pedestal in the middle of the courtyard. I try to conceal a gasp. She's no more than a few yards from me, and I didn't notice. Or maybe I didn't want to.

Rik checks his watch. "The director's going to unveil *After the Bath* in a couple of minutes, say a few words, then carry it upstairs to the Short Gallery."

"And we follow her like the Pied Piper?"

"No. We wait." He frowns at me. "After the painting's hung—we don't get to be there because the room's so small—we'll all go upstairs in staggered groups to see the old girl back where she belongs. There'll be a videotape of the actual hanging at dinner."

I bite my lip. I'm going to have to pretend I haven't seen her in twenty years.

"You don't look very excited. I thought *After the Bath* was one of your favorites. Degas your idol. That you'd be thrilled—" His frown deepens. "Oh, shut up, Rik," he admonishes himself. "You're an idiot. Forgive me, Bear, I wasn't thinking. Aiden. Of course. He was supposed—"

"No, no, it's okay. I am thrilled to be here." I take a few deep cleansing breaths.

Rik throws an arm around my shoulder. "I'm so sorry you have to go through this. Bad timing."

"I'm good," I assure him, and look around for something to distract us. But before I do, the lights flash on and off, the quartet stops playing, and the room quiets.

Alana Ward, the museum director, walks along one of the courtyard pathways where no mere mortal is normally allowed. Although she's wearing a nicely cut cocktail dress, her jacket is buttoned too high and her shoes are too low. Interesting that a woman who has dedicated her life to art is so uninterested in her own appearance. But according to Rik, she's doing a bang-up job for the museum and fights for what she believes in—which he says doesn't always lead to a stress-free working environment.

Alana stands next to the painting. "I just want to thank you all for coming tonight to celebrate this glorious moment in the life of the Isabella Stewart Gardner Museum."

Loud applause and a few whistles, which is surprising for this crowd. But Alana looks happy enough to whistle herself. After a few minutes of the predictable sentiments about the return of the long-lost scion and how pleased Belle would be, Alana pauses dramatically. The museum goes totally silent.

My heart begins to pound, and I'm guessing many hearts are racing all around me, but for a very different reason.

"This is it," Rik whispers unnecessarily. His eyes are wide with excitement.

"You haven't seen it yet?" I ask, surprised.

He clasps his hands. "Hardly anyone has."

With a whoosh, Alana pulls away the velvet covering.

A loud gasp fills the chamber, followed by rollicking applause and more wolf whistles. I keep my eyes on the floor.

Rik presses a hand to his chest. "Oh," he says, his long eyelashes spiked by his tears.

Alana dabs her eyes with a tissue, and I notice that I'm one of the few dry-eyed in the crowd. Everyone believes Belle's masterpiece has been returned to her, and they're deeply touched at the sight of a well-loved lost work of art.

A guttural growl that sounds like "no" escapes my lips.

"Claire!" Rik grabs me, and I sag into him. "What the—"

"I'm fine. I'm fine," I say quickly, pushing myself away from him. "It's, it's just the painting. It's so, so mind-blowing. I drew it, copied it, as a girl . . ."

"Guess it *is* one of your favorite paintings." Rik points to a granite bench. "Let's go sit down. I'll get you some water."

I struggle to regain my composure but find it difficult to stand with the room spinning around me. "Really. Not necessary."

But he won't take no for an answer. When he leaves me on the bench and goes in search of water, I turn so I'm facing away from the painting. Fortunately, the water does revive me a bit. "I don't know, pal," I tell Rik. "I'm thinking maybe you should get yourself another date."

"You sick?"

"Not really. Just a little dizzy, kind of nauseous."

He presses the inside of his wrist to my forehead. "No fever," he says, then gives me a long look. "When was the last time you had a full night's sleep?"

"It's been a while, but—"

"You probably haven't eaten much today, either." He gives me an aggrieved parental scowl. "And how many glasses of champagne?"

I smile sheepishly. "I still think it'd be better if I just took a cab home."

He jumps up. "I'm not going to let you miss the reinstallation of your favorite painting. Stay here and drink that water. I'm going to find Alana and get her to put us in the first group. That way you won't have to wait in line as long."

"Really," I call after him. "You don't need to." But he's not listening.

I think about slipping out and grabbing a cab before Rik comes back. I'll call him and apologize when I get home. It's believable. I already said I wasn't feeling well. But before I can put my plan into action, he's standing in front of me.

"You're looking better already." Rik holds out his hands to help me up. "Let's go, Ms. Roth, we're on."

I allow him to pull me through the crowd.

"Truth is," he says, "this is a great excuse to get in there first. It's going to take hours for everyone to file by. So thanks for getting sick." He rubs his hands together.

Halfway to the second floor, the line stops. I look behind us; people stretch all the way back to the Spanish Cloister. Above the ground floor, each level of the museum is essentially a circle surrounding the courtyard. Open arches provide views of the gardens from almost everywhere as well as views into the opposite galleries; the stairs are on the west side and each gallery flows into the next until you reach the stairs again. From where we're standing, hemmed in by the crowd, there's no going down, only up.

Rik checks out the throng in front of us. "I'm guessing half an hour."

This gives me either thirty minutes to calm myself or thirty minutes to freak myself out. "There are worse places to be stuck in line," I say, going for the former. "At least there's plenty to look at."

Rik gives me a hug. "Feeling better, I see."

I stare out over the bubbling crowd in their jewels and fine attire, so pleased with themselves and the great moment they've come to experience. A wave of loneliness and isolation washes over me, and again I wish Aiden was standing beside me. I turn my attention to the art. Unfortunately, Italian High Renaissance has never been one of my favorites. Nor is the ornate furniture that fills the gallery. There's a beautiful Pesellino, *The Triumphs of Love, Chastity, and Death,* but as I study it, all I can see is evil stalking good. A Bellini, *A Seated Scribe,* is superb, but the Turk is so earnest, so decent, that just looking at him makes me feel guilty. Almost all the other paintings in the room are religious, pious, and righteous. Woe be to the sinner . . .

"So what's Belle thinking?" I ask.

Rik chuckles. "Since when do you believe in an afterlife?"

"Must be all the religion in here."

"I guess it's hard not to imagine her looking down on her museum, in constant contact to make sure everything's being done exactly the way she wants. But to tell you the truth, I think she'd still be so mad about the heist that the return of one painting would only make her fume more about the absence of the others."

Especially when she knows the prodigal painting is a forgery. I take Rik's hand as we cross into the Raphael Room. "Only one more gallery to go."

The Raphael Room is bigger and brighter than the Italian Room, which is a relief. Although, it, too, is filled with religious art. Even Raphael's brilliant *Portrait of Count Tommaso Inghirami* portrays him in the red robes of the church. And although Inghirami is looking upward—evidently Raphael's camouflage for a wandering eye—I feel the count is looking down on me with contempt. As are the many Madonnas and Child, the archangel Gabriel, and the dove representing the Holy Spirit in *Annunciation*.

As we make our way across the Raphael Room and closer to *Bath II,* I look to my favorite painting in this gallery, Botticelli's *Tragedy of Lucretia,* for distraction, thinking it's safe as it's based on a pre-Christian legend. But I've forgotten that the story is of a virtuous wife who's raped under the threat of death. In the aftermath, Lucretia is so appalled and guilt-ridden over what she perceives as her immoral behavior that she stabs herself to death rather than live with her depravity.

The Short Gallery is actually a narrow, high-ceilinged corridor linking the galleries on the north side of the courtyard with those on the east and south, rather than an actual room in and of itself. We cross the threshold into the small, overheated space. The odor of expensive perfume tinged with genteel sweat is cloying. As are the waxing and waning murmurs of admiration that swirl around me like seasickness. I can't look.

Rik grabs my shoulders. "Oh, Claire, look at her. Just look at her. Have you ever seen anything as stunning?"

My eyes light on the painting. "Oh," I cry, but not in praise. I don't know what else to say. This isn't mine. I didn't do this. The experts weren't fooled. And after all my whining and carrying on, I don't know what to feel.

"Speechless . . ." Rik says.

It's the real original, an authentic Degas. The dense layers of vibrant color. The pulsating greens, blues, and corals. The women's skin so pale and luminescent. Françoise, with her reddish hair and sharp nose. Jacqueline, tall and beautiful. Simone, introverted and fine-featured. But how did it get here? I elbow closer.

I immediately realize I'm wrong. I just haven't seen *Bath II* in a frame before, only as a canvas. At first glance—hung in the spot I remember from my childhood, bordered in the familiar, heavy gold leaf—I didn't recognize her. But Françoise is still not Degas', and the craquelure on the bottom left corner, which I worried was too deep, is definitely mine. Although I can't see it, I know there's a tiny spot of green on the back.

This painting will hang here forever—my painting, a double pretender, a forgery of a forgery—while Degas' real masterpiece gathers mold in the sub-basement and Aiden loses his finger. I turn to Rik. "We need to talk. Right now."

Forty-two

I don't think I've ever had a conversation with Rik in which I speak for so long and he doesn't interrupt. We're in his office, the door closed tight, the noise from the party muted but discernable: Beethoven, laughter, clinking cutlery. The space is cramped, damp, and cold, my chair hard and uncomfortable. Rik's elbows rest on his desk, his hands over his mouth, nose resting on his forefingers, eyes focused on me. When I run out of words, he continues to stare as if I'm still talking.

"Well?" The relief I felt at unburdening turns into doubt in his heavy silence. "Say something."

He shakes his head as if emerging from a swim in the ocean. "For real?"

"All too."

He crosses his arms over his chest. "What if I said I didn't believe you?"

"I probably wouldn't believe me either."

"But it's true?"

I nod.

"All of it?"

"I probably left a few things out."

"I don't even know how to begin processing this," he says, then pauses. "So this means Markel knows where the other paintings are."

"He was the broker for just this single painting. He didn't have anything to do with the original robbery. And probably the people he got it from didn't either."

"And you're sure because . . . ?"

"He's in danger." I twist my hands together. "From the sellers. Physical danger."

"But he's in jail," Rik argues.

"They've got a long reach."

Rik stands up, looks surprised that there's nowhere for him to go, sits down again. "And you're positive the one downstairs is the one you painted?"

"I recognize the craquelure."

"I don't believe this."

I smile wryly. "Full circle."

He stares off into the distance, focuses back on me. "And you decided you had to tell me about this right now because . . . ?"

"I need to get into the sub-basement. To see if it's possible. If it's there, the Gardner's got an authentic Degas to hang, which could easily be his finest work ever. And the world has a new masterpiece."

He squints his eyes as if this will help him understand.

"But even more," I plead, "if we find the original, it should be enough to get Aiden out on bail," I swallow hard, "long enough to save his finger."

"His finger?"

I steel myself, then look Rik straight in the eye. "They need the print of his right forefinger to get into the gallery's vault. Where the money is."

"Oh," Rik cries, stricken. "No. Oh, Claire . . . No."

I close my eyes and nod.

"But, but what if the painting isn't down there?" he asks.

"Then I'll have to try a different angle."

"And what if it is there? How are you going to explain how you knew about it?" His face is awash with worry. "What if they decide you were involved in the heist and arrest you?"

"Rik, think about it. What can they arrest me for? Copying a copy? This is what I do for a living."

He does think about it. "I didn't even know there was a sub-basement." His words are slow and thoughtful. "Let alone how to get into it."

"Like I said, it's on the blueprints." I see the first crack and dig into it. "Can't be that hard."

He opens a desk drawer, closes it, opens it again, closes it. "You really think an original Degas could be down there?"

"It could be," I say. "And wouldn't it be quite the coup if we found it?"

A fleeting smile crosses his face. "It sure would." He pulls the blueprints up on his computer, finds the basement, and outlines the contours of the sub-basement with his finger.

I clasp my hands together and wait.

"I don't know, Claire," he finally says. "Scrounging around in the bowels of the museum without permission—if security will even let us in there."

"Aren't you pretty tight with some of the guards?"

"Yeah . . ." His fingers fly over the keyboard. "There are papers here that indicate Belle brought a Degas oil painting back from Paris with her in 1898, and," he says as he scrolls, *After the Bath* is listed in the Certificate of Incorporation of the Collection in 1900, so that must be the same one."

I say nothing as the click of computer keys fills the room, and Rik confirms what I already know.

"It was also featured in the invitation Belle sent out in 1903 for the gala opening of Fenway Court—and it hasn't been moved since. Until it was stolen." Rik pushes back in his chair. "Sorry, Bear, but Belle would never have been fooled into buying a forgery. Nor would Bernard Berenson."

"But my theory is that Belle *did* bring a real Degas home," I argue. "Then, after she got the original to Boston, either Virgil Rendell blackmailed her into hanging his as the original—in which case it might be downstairs. Or he stole it and kept it for himself—in which case his family might have it. All I know is that Degas' and Rendell's sketchbooks prove there were two paintings."

"It just doesn't seem like enough . . ."

"Enough for what?" I demand. "To get a pretender out of the Short Gallery? To find an original Degas? To save Aiden?"

"Claire . . ."

"It's okay, Rik." I stand. "Really. I'm sorry I got you involved, but I'm getting pretty desperate here."

"Where are you going?" His voice swells with concern.

"To tell Alana. What else can I do? Someone's got to go down and look."

He jumps up and grabs my shoulders. "No, you can't do that. She'll freak. Not yet. At least not until we know for sure it's there."

"Aiden doesn't have a lot of time. I can't—"

"Meet me here first thing in the morning," he says.

I wrap my arms around him. "Thank you," I whisper.

He kisses the top of my head. "Now let's go back to the party and act like we're having a good time."

I STAND IN the front of the Gardner, watching Rik, umbrella in hand, cross the street. It's as cold and raw as yesterday, with a freezing drizzle to increase the misery. I'm sweating inside my raincoat.

"Ready?" he asks, as he ushers me through the employee entrance.

"Ready to find it. Scared not to."

"That about sums it up." We walk to the cloakroom, our wet shoes squeaking on the stone floor. Rik grabs a flashlight from behind the desk, waves it, and shouts, "Onward!"

I laugh, but it comes out as a snort.

We take the elevator to the basement, which is as far down as it goes. Rik explains that there's only a little storage down here, that the basement primarily houses mechanical equipment: electrical, heat, AC—and the new security system installed after the heist. Despite this, it's poorly lit, shadowy, and I'm glad Rik thought to bring the flashlight. The air has that dank, underground mustiness.

I hear the scurrying of little feet and hope they're the very little feet of mice, not the much larger little feet of rats. I take a step closer to Rik. The walls are exposed brick, uneven and haphazard, obviously original, and although the floor is poured concrete, it, too, is uneven, and laced with cracks large enough to trip over. Rik shines the flashlight on the area directly in front of us as we walk.

I check the blueprints. "Over there," I say, pointing to the south wall. There was no indication of an entrance to the sub-basement from this level on the plans, which initially made me nervous, and now makes me very nervous. But then I see that there actually is something there.

We kneel at the edge of an opening more or less five-foot square. Rik shines his flashlight into the larger space beneath. The floor is dirt, and instead of brick, rough-hewn boulders form three of the walls. It looks like an afterthought. A poorly and quickly constructed afterthought. A rickety ladder leads down into it.

"Can you see anything?" I ask Rik. "Do you see a door?"

"Can't tell from here."

I swing myself onto the ladder. "Keep the flashlight on me, and then, when I get down, throw it to me, and I'll shine it on you."

I scramble down and drop to the floor. Rik quickly follows. It's dark and, even with the flashlight, it takes us a moment to orient ourselves. The space is smaller than it appeared from the blueprints, maybe twenty-by-thirty with a ceiling of less than six feet. But it's hard to get a real read because it's filled with junk. Ostensibly, a century of it, dusty and piled high, stuffed into almost every available space: furniture, file cabinets, ledgers, books.

We both sneeze and turn toward the place where the doors fronting the narrow chamber should be. Rik raises the flashlight. But even with all the debris, it's immediately apparent there are no doors. The light falls on a solid wall of concrete.

"Damn," Rik says.

I'm almost knocked over by the depth of disappointment that floods me. I kneel down and inspect the edge of the wall where it meets the uneven boulders. There are lots of gaps. When I find an especially large one, Rik points the flashlight into the space beyond the wall.

I twist until I can see in without blocking the light. There, maybe a foot or two beyond the concrete, is a set of double doors. "They're there!" I cry, not quite believing what I'm seeing.

"What?" Rik presses his eye to another hole in the concrete. "What's there?"

My hands are trembling as I take the flashlight and allow him to look in.

"Holy shit." He turns, looks at me, then turns quickly back to the hole. "You're right. You're right. The doors. They've got to be hiding—"

Suddenly, there's a burst of light from above. I look up, but I'm blinded by the brightness.

"Hey!" a gruff voice bounces off the walls. "Stop where you are!"

I freeze, raise my hands.

"It's Richard Gramont," Rik calls out. "I'm one of the assistant curators." He turns to me. "You can put your hands down now."

"No!" commands the voice. "Keep them up. Both of you."

"It's just the museum guards," Rik whispers to me, and pulls his ID card away from his chest. "I work here. It's cool."

"I don't care where the fuck you work. Boston Police. Now climb up that ladder nice and slowlike—and keep your hands where I can see them. Ladies first."

Forty-three

One policeman has a grip on my upper arm, one has Rik in a similar hold, and the third, the voice, watches us suspiciously. Three Boston cops, signaled by the beefed-up silent alarm installed for the party last night.

"Call Alana Ward," Rik says. "She's the director, probably in her office upstairs right now, she'll vouch for us."

"What the fuck do you think you're doing down here?"

"This is my friend, Claire Roth," Rik explains. "She's researching a book about Isabella Stewart Gardner and her circle of artists. I was told there were materials down here that might help her. So we came down to check it out." He's one quick-thinking man.

The cop is far less impressed than I am. "Researching a book this early Sunday morning?" But he calls Alana, who tells him to bring us to her office.

As the cops lead us across the basement and up to the main floor, Rik gives me a look that clearly says, "Don't say a word."

We head for the stairs to the second floor, and I take in the majesty of the courtyard in its stillness, the flukes of the Gardner that often annoy me, yet make it so exceptional, matchless actually. At the second-floor landing, I look through the open arches into the

Early Italian Room, the Raphael Room. There's no view from here of the Short Gallery, but I can visualize *Bath II* hanging there, feel her, like a ghost floating in the air. A shiver runs through me. Degas' *After the Bath* should be on that wall. Not some imitation of an imitation.

The first cop opens the roped-off stairwell to the fourth floor, lets us through, closes it behind him, and leads us to Alana Ward's office. She comes out from behind her desk, and says, "I'll take it from here, officers."

The cops don't move.

"Really," she adds. "I'd like to talk to them alone."

"We'll be right outside the door if you need us, ma'am."

When the cops leave, she orders us to sit in the two chairs in front of her desk and glares at Rik. "What the hell's going on?"

"I'm sorry, Alana," Rik says. "It's really no big deal. Claire's a friend of mine from the museum school, and she's working on a book about Belle and her personal relationships with a number of artists. We were just looking for materials that might help her."

"At eight o'clock on a Sunday morning?"

"You're here," Rik says, with a wry smile.

"In the basement?"

"There's a room down there that's full of stuff. Lots of files and books. I didn't think there would be any—"

"You aren't authorized," she snaps, and turns to me. "What artists?"

"Well, the obvious, of course. Whistler, Singer Sargent, and Ralph Curtis. But I'm also interested in some of the more obscure artists she befriended, like Smith, Cram, or Martin Mower, Virgil Rendell."

Rik looks at me in surprise, and Alana watches him closely. "This is a serious violation, Rik," she says. "You can't—"

"It's not his fault."

"It most certainly is," she snaps.

"He didn't want to take me down there," I say. "But I talked him—"

"She may have asked me if I could help her find materials," Rik interrupts, "but I suggested we look in the basement."

"Why would you do such a thing?" Alana demands. "And why would you sneak around like that?"

"We weren't sneaking. Or at least I didn't think of it as sneaking. It just seemed, like, you know, like a natural thing to do."

As I listen to Rik struggle to come up with an answer, the pros and cons of my next step flash through my mind like they claim your life does right before you die. Although less than thrilled with this analogy, I say, "I told him an original Degas may be hidden down there."

"What?"

"Claire," Rik says. "You don't—"

"The *After the Bath* you hung last night is a forgery," I tell Alana. "I think the real one, the one Edgar Degas painted, may be in the basement."

"That's absurd," Alana says with disdain. "It was authenticated by a team of international specialists. Certified as Degas' work by some of the most respected experts in the field."

"I know," I say. "But they're wrong."

"And just how do you know this?"

I swallow hard. "Because I painted it."

Alana looks at Rik.

"I know it sounds weird," he says, shifting in his seat. "But Claire works for Reproductions.com. She's a certified Degas copyist, and—"

"A certified Degas copyist?" Alana explodes. "What the hell is that? Are you telling me I'm supposed to believe some 'certified Degas copyist' over our experts? That I'm supposed to buy that she painted that masterpiece?"

Before Rik can answer, I interject, "There's a long history of art experts seeing what they want to see. What they expect to see."

Alana furrows her brow. "Claire Roth . . . Claire Roth . . ." She snaps her fingers. "Cullion. The Great Pretender. Is this another one of your publicity stunts?" Before I can answer, she stands. "I've heard enough. The police can take it from here."

"No!" Rik jumps up. "Please, Alana, just hear her out. Maybe, just maybe, she's on to something you need to know."

She glares at him, then at me, then sits. "You've got five minutes."

I tell her about my job, my expertise in Degas. "So I get a call one afternoon from Aiden Markel. We'd met, but I hadn't spoken to him in years. He said he had a Repro-like job for me if I was interested. I'm just a consultant for Repro, no noncompete or anything, so I said sure."

Alana waits. Rik studies his hands.

"He told me the gallery had a client in India," I continue. "Some guy who had seen a high-quality reproduction of *After the Bath* owned by a friend of Aiden's. The man wanted one that was equally as good."

"Why didn't he just have whoever painted the first one do another?" Alana asks. A legitimate question.

"The painter died," I say quickly, wishing Aiden and I had spent more time on this story, hoping I'll be able to think fast enough to fill in the holes.

Alana is stone-faced.

I clear my throat. "So Aiden said he'd heard I was the best, the only one who might be good enough to please his client, and he wanted to hire me to do the reproduction. He said he'd bring me his friend's painting to use as a model."

"There's nothing illegal or unethical about copying a painting," Rik says. "It's done—"

"I'm speaking to Ms. Roth," Alana barks. "I'll hear from you later."

Rik rubs his forehead with the palm of his hand, but he doesn't say anything more.

"So," I continue, "the next day, he showed up with two canvases. One was a late nineteenth-century painting by Ernest Meissonier. And the other was what he claimed was 'the best copy ever produced' of Degas' last *After the Bath*."

"Was it?" Alana asks.

"It was very good—but it was a copy."

"How can you be so sure?"

"I reproduce paintings for a living."

"So the Meissonier was for you to strip so you could use the canvas for your forgery? And because you're a 'certified copyist' you knew how to do this?"

"I've worked for Repro for years, taken classes, done a lot of research. I relied on known techniques." I look at Rik, whose eyes are wide. "Used my notes, my experience, how-to forgery manuals."

Alana's lips are taut. "Are you telling me you created the *After the Bath* that's hanging downstairs by following instructions in a paint-by-numbers book?"

"I guess that's kind of true," I admit. "Plus an oversized oven and a bit of phenol formaldehyde."

Alana's eyes narrow. "Is this some kind of joke?"

"I wish."

"Let me get this straight," she says. "Aiden Markel contacts you out of the blue, and you think the whole thing is on the up-and-up? You never wonder? Never question his motives?"

"It was Aiden Markel of Markel G," Rik begins. "Who wouldn't—"

Alana silences him with a fierce look.

"I just figured the client was really rich," I say. "And after I studied the painting, I knew it was a copy, so why would I suspect anything?"

"You're saying it wasn't until the reinstallation that you realized what was going on?" Alana asks.

I look her straight in the eye. "I'm still not sure what's going on."

"Wait here," Alana orders, then turns to Rik. "You come with me."

A HALF AN hour later, Alana walks back in, followed by a wide-shouldered man in a sport jacket and tie. Although his head is too small for his body, which might make him look a bit comical, the hard expression on his face overrides this effect.

I stand, my stomach clamping down on itself. A cop if I ever saw one. High-ranking.

"Agent Lyons, FBI," Alana says to me, then turns to the agent. "This is Claire Roth."

"Hi." I hold out my hand. Even worse than a cop.

The agent shakes it with his surprisingly soft one, but his face remains chiseled in steel. He doesn't say anything, just nods curtly.

Alana sits at her desk, and Lyons takes Rik's chair. "Explain to Agent Lyons what you explained to me," she orders.

After I do, Lyons asks, his voice thick with incredulity, "And you believed Mr. Markel when he told you the painting he brought you was a copy? It never occurred to you it might be the one stolen in the robbery?"

"I could tell right away it wasn't a real Degas, so, no, it never occurred to me to question it."

"Do you think that was naive?"

I hesitate. "No. I'm still certain it wasn't painted by Degas, and I know Aiden was certain of that, also."

"How can you be so sure what he believed?"

"That's what he told me, and the man knows his business. Plus, he's Aiden Markel."

"We see how far that got him." The agent scribbles in his notebook, frowns, scribbles again.

I eye him warily. "I, ah, I think I should get a lawyer."

Lyons and Alana share a glance. "Why?" he asks, looking perplexed. "You're just reporting a possible incident, aren't you? We've no idea if there's been any law-breaking here. Or that you're involved in any kind of criminal activity."

When I don't respond, the agent's body language shifts into nice-guy mode: elbows on knees, torso toward me, smile on face. "So," he says, "Ms. Roth, you believe Isabella Stewart Gardner was blackmailed by this . . ." he checks his notes, "this Virgil Rendell. Into hanging *his* painting instead of Degas'? And then she hid the real one?"

"That's one theory. It could have happened for many other reasons. The important thing here is that the painting hung last night is the copy I was hired to paint. The copy of Aiden Markel's copy."

"How can you be so sure?"

"I recognize the craquelure."

He looks at Alana and raises an eyebrow.

"It's how paint cracks over time." She glowers at me. "A way of determining the age of a painting."

"I know what it means," Lyons says, and I sense that he may be more open-minded than he seems.

"As I told you before, this isn't the first time Ms. Roth has made this kind of claim," Alana says. "Her credibility is more than a little suspect."

"Ah, Cullion's *4D*." He smiles at me. "But weren't there some questions? Didn't you have support from a number of people at MoMA?"

"Yes there were. A lot actually." I'm well aware they're playing good-cop-bad-cop, but the less said about *4D* the better. "I know the painting downstairs is mine because I was worried about a particular dark area along the bottom. That I didn't wipe enough of the ink off before I sealed it. It felt overdone to me. And when I saw it last night, I knew it was."

"Are you certain of this?" Lyons asks.

"I put a green dot on the back right-hand corner of the painting. On the stretcher. Check and you'll see it."

"That doesn't mean a thing," Alana argues. "A random spot of paint could have come from anywhere. She could have seen it last night—or know about it because she was involved in the heist."

"That's ridicu—"

The agent leans in toward me. "Fair enough, but I still don't understand how you know this Virgil Rendell forged the painting."

"I don't *know* for sure, but he is an established forger, and I saw his sketchbook. There are drawings in it of both the original and the forgery."

"Now I'm really confused."

"I have a book of Degas' drawings containing preliminary compositional sketches for *After the Bath*. One set of Rendell's drawings matches Degas' preliminaries, and the other matches the painting that was in the Gardner."

"Couldn't Rendell have seen these same sketches? Been playing around with them?" Lyons asks.

"It's unlikely. Although they were contemporaries, Degas was in Europe and Rendell in Boston, and I highly doubt they ever met. My theory is that Rendell saw the original when Belle brought it back here but before it was hung in the museum. Then, for whatever reason, when he forged it, he changed it."

"How do you know what the original looks like?"

"It looks like Degas' preliminary sketches."

"And the one downstairs doesn't?"

"No. Like I said before, one of the women is different, the configuration is different, and if you look at it closely, it doesn't look like a Degas."

"Preliminary sketches are never the same as the finished painting," Alana snaps. "It's a Degas. And I've looked very closely. As have a number of expert authenticators. People with training and credentials. Not some random certification by some Internet art copying company."

"So," Lyons says to me, "you knew it was a forgery when no one else did?"

"I just happened to have the right combination of background and skills to detect it. But mostly, I think I was the first one to really look."

"Meaning?"

"Well, if we go with the idea that Isabella Gardner hung Rendell's forgery, even under duress, then the painting would never have been officially authenticated. Everyone would have assumed it was a Degas and never questioned it. And because her will says nothing can be moved, the painting never went out on loan, where the duplicity might have been caught."

"Could this have happened?" Lyons asks Alana.

"It's absurd."

"But possible?"

Alana crosses her arms over her chest. "Pretty much anything is."

He turns back to me. "But wouldn't Degas have known it wasn't his painting? Wouldn't he have visited the museum? Or seen a photo of it?"

"Degas came to this country only once," I explain. "To New Orleans, and it was way before the museum opened. Communication wasn't the way it is now, nor was travel. No phones, no planes. So, no, in all likelihood, he never saw it after he sold it to Belle."

The agent sets his face in an overly thoughtful expression. "So, no one but you, three years out of graduate school, ever *really* *looked* at a painting that hung in a major museum for almost a hundred years? No one but you ever figured out it wasn't a Degas. Impressive. Very impressive."

I just stare at him.

"Remind me how you did this," he asks, again with disingenuous respect. "What were the clues?"

I explain again about the brushstrokes, the colors, the compositional sketches, the symmetry, the secret room in the basement. "It just all started to add up. And when I recognized my painting at the reinstallation last night, well . . ." I shrug.

Lyons whistles. "Excellent detective work, Ms. Roth. Ever consider a career at the FBI?"

Alana laughs.

Although I feel like planting my fist in both of their faces, I say, "I didn't have to come forward with this information. I could've kept quiet, and everyone would have gone happily on their way. I did this to find out the truth and hopefully return a great masterpiece to the Gardner. I don't appreciate being treated like some idiot child."

"You didn't 'come forward,'" Alana reminds me. "You were caught trespassing by the Boston police."

Lyons studies me closely, then says, "If I understand you correctly, then the Rendell forgery is the one that was stolen in the heist, and that's the one Mr. Markel brought to you."

"No, no, that's not what I said." I give him a hostile look so he'll understand I'm on to his tricks and won't be that easily tripped up. "The one Aiden brought me was a copy, a copy of Rendell's forgery. Or, or it could have been a copy of someone else's copy, I guess. I don't really know. How could I know?"

"That's the question, isn't it?" Alana points out.

"Do you happen to have these famous sketchbooks with you?" Lyons asks.

"They're in my studio," I say, furious with myself for falling into his trap.

"And you also tracked these down with your highly tuned detective skills?"

My first reaction is to tell him to go fuck himself, but instead, I say, "Yes, as a matter of fact, Agent Lyons, that's exactly what I did."

I'm rewarded by a quick flash of amusement in his eyes before he asks Alana, "You've got the blueprints, right?"

She glares at me before turning to her computer and starting to type.

"Perhaps, when you pull it up," Lyons says, "Ms. Roth here can point out her secret room to us."

I stand and move around to the side of Alana's computer.

"You said the basement?" Alana asks without looking at me.

"Sub-basement."

"Didn't even know there was one," she mutters, as she searches for the right page. "Here," she says and pushes back her chair. "Show us."

"We found a concrete wall that isn't on the blueprints," I explain, as I outline the drawing with my finger. "Just about here.

Right in front of these double doors. Which are there, behind the wall."

"And that's where you think Degas' painting is?" Lyons asks.

"If it's not there," I say, "it's somewhere. And we need to find it."

"This is ridiculous," Alana barks. "We don't need to find anything. Degas' *After the Bath* is hanging downstairs in the Short Gallery."

Lyons says they'd like to excuse themselves. Alana tells me to take a seat at her assistant's desk right outside the office, which I do.

When they close Alana's door, I stand and press my ear to the wall, but their voices are too low to understand. In a few minutes, they come out, and Alana orders me not to move. I think of Aiden, forced to sit in a cell, at the mercy of someone else's relentless commands.

To distract myself, I look at the sepia-toned photographs hanging on the wall. There's a photo of Belle, wearing a horrible black hat and climbing a ladder during the construction of Fenway Court. A wiry little thing, quite homely without her jewels and fancy dresses, and clearly displeased with what she's seeing. How did this woman have all those men at her feet? Amass so much power? Everything about Belle Gardner is either improbable or contradictory, and I can only hope I'm on the right track.

"Is the oven still in your studio?" Alana demands, as she walks up to me, Agent Lyons at her heels.

I blink at what seems like a non sequitur, then understand: They found the green dot. "Yeah, I have the oven."

"And despite what happened with MoMA, you still want to claim the painting downstairs is yours?" Lyons asks.

"That one was mine, and this one is, too."

"Not exactly what MoMA concluded," Alana mutters.

"Look, Agent Lyons, Ms. Ward, I may not be sure about a lot of things right now, but I know my own work. I'm sorry to disappoint you. The museum. Everyone. To create this huge hassle. But I thought that in the end, you'd prefer the truth."

"This is the plan," Alana says. "Three of us will be at your studio at eight o'clock tomorrow morning. I'll bring an old canvas and you'll go through your whole process for us."

"That's fine. No problem. I can—"

"I'm not asking your permission, Ms. Roth."

I look down at my hands.

"I'm going to have to fly a number of experts to Boston to begin the second authentication," Alana continues, "and order special chemicals and equipment so the process can be done quickly and onsite. This will be expensive and time-consuming. And if, I'm thinking when, we discover this is all a hoax, you'll be liable for all costs and damages. Including loss of revenue due to our inability to display *After the Bath*."

"It's not a—"

"And if it turns out the painting *is* a forgery," Agent Lyons interrupts, "and that you're the one who forged it, my colleagues from the agency and I will want to sit down with you. In what you might call a more official capacity."

Forty-four

As promised, Alana shows up at eight a.m. with two academic types: an older man and a young woman who looks as if she's still in high school. Both wear glasses and pull laptops from their briefcases: his cracked and beat-up, hers pristine and expensive. His name is Mr. Jones, and she's Ms. Smith. When I smile at this, they just stare at me. Looks to be a fun time.

Not that I'm so jolly this morning either. Yesterday, after I left the Gardner, I went directly to Nashua Street to update Aiden and make sure he was okay. But they wouldn't let me in. Said he'd already had his allotment of visitors for the day. Later, Kristi texted me: "Markel said 2 tell u 1 week left."

Needless to say, I spent a long sleepless night pacing, beating up on myself, and talking to Rik on the phone. I told him about Aiden's deadline, and he told me that Alana was furious at him but that he didn't think his job was in jeopardy. Some good news. The rest was bad. Alana is on a mission to prove me wrong, to destroy my career and my life, to get me arrested. And if that doesn't work out, I have Agent Lyons to contend with.

Now, Alana hands me a one-foot square canvas; it's an oil painting of a waterfall, a bad painting of a waterfall. "Work from this," she says, her voice crisp and no-nonsense. "Paint one of the *After the Bath* nudes. Go through the process you claim you used to produce your so-called forgery and—"

"Copy." I know I have to stay calm, but the parallels to repainting *4D* have me on edge. I remind myself that the situation is reversed this time around: Then my object was to be recognized as the painter, now it's to be recognized as the forger. Not surprisingly, this doesn't make me feel any better.

Nor do the much higher stakes. I try to cheer myself by noting that the stakes aren't as high as they were for Han van Meegeren. He'd had to repaint his fake Vermeer to prove he didn't sell a national treasure to the Nazis, thus avoiding a death sentence. This doesn't make me feel any better either.

"Explain to us everything you're doing," she orders. "Even if you think we already know it."

I nod. "Can I get anyone coffee? Tea?"

"This isn't a social visit, Ms. Roth," Alana reminds me. "The sooner you start, the sooner we'll be finished." I've got no problem with that.

I go through the now second-nature motions, explaining as I proceed. Smith and Jones are mostly quiet, except for a few respectful questions, but Alana can't contain her irritation. She shrugs derisively at my comments, rolls her eyes, mutters under her breath. I do my best to ignore her, but her every response, her every movement, reminds me how much she holds in her hands.

It's growing dark by the time I've gone through three rounds, and Alana says, "Let's call it a day." No one objects. She turns to me. "I'm going to take this painting with me to make sure it isn't altered in our absence. We'll be back with it first thing tomorrow morning."

"Sure," I say, too exhausted to take offense at her not-so-veiled aspersion on my character.

"And," Alana adds, "I'll need Degas' and Rendell's sketchbooks. Agent Lyons and I want to examine them."

Although the sketchbooks corroborate my hypothesis, I'm reluctant to part with them. Alana takes the books from my hands. "Thank you," she says, in an overly polite tone that indicates she's not thankful at all. Of course she isn't. Nor should she be.

They return the next morning with the painting and their phones and computers. Last night, Rik told me that he got news on the hush-hush from his buddy who's a security guard, who has a buddy, another security guard, who went into the sub-basement with Alana and Lyons. Although Alana was completely against it, Lyons plans to bring ultrasound equipment in to determine if anything is behind the concrete wall. The guard thought he heard Alana mutter, "Fucking bitch."

Alana, Jones, Smith, and I take our places. I paint and bake. They watch. It's a lot less interesting today as I'm not doing anything they haven't seen before. I have nothing to explain, and they have no questions. After two more rounds, the painting is actually starting to look pretty good. Even with only five layers, the colors are growing deep and luminescent; Jacqueline's arm holding the towel glows. I stare at her, think about my own work, my windows. Kristi texted yesterday to remind me we're going to start hanging my show on Thursday. It almost seems trivial.

"Are there other steps you do at the end to make it look old?" Alana demands.

"It has to be inked."

"Can it be done now?"

"Sure," I say, more than glad to comply. "We just need the craquelure to show through the last layer of varnish. Then it'll be good to go."

"Do it," she says.

I glance up and notice the dark circles under her eyes, the wrinkles I hadn't seen before, and feel a stab of sympathy. Also a stab of guilt. I've been nothing but a complete pain in the ass to this woman who only wanted to enjoy her museum's moment of glory. Driven by my own hubris to right a wrong that may be better left unaddressed. But it's a bit late for these regrets now. Especially when I know that there's more pain to come.

When the craquelure has risen, the India ink applied and dried, I begin cleaning the ink off with a soapy rag. They watch, transfixed, as I wipe away the top layer of varnish, which leaves a hairthin web of fine lines on the painting. I then add a touch of brown paint to the original varnish, explaining that the tint mirrors aging, and cover the canvas with it. When I'm done I hold the canvas up for their inspection.

Alana gasps.

First thing the next morning, I call Kristi at Markel G. "I'm back."

"Great," she says, but I hear annoyance in her voice.

"I'm really sorry about screwing this up. You think it'll be possible to reschedule any of the interviews?" A half-dozen interviews had to be canceled because I was painting for the Gardner. I told Kristi it was a family emergency, age-old excuse yet always reliable, and guaranteed to keep questions to a minimum.

"Some. I hope."

Although I never wanted to play the publicity game, the distraction is now welcome. I don't have anything to do while I wait for the Gardner but look for Virgil Rendell's family. And that's not going well. "What did I miss?"

"Arts reporters for the *Globe,* the *Phoenix,* and *Boston Magazine,*" she says testily. "*Newbury Street Gallerie. Metro.*"

"Do you have the names and numbers? I'll call them and set up new ones."

"They don't like dealing directly with the talent. I'll see if I can get any of them to come by the gallery when you're here doing the installation. Today you've got radio interviews all day. You've got the list I e-mailed you?"

"Sure." I haven't had much time for e-mail of late. "It's all under control."

"Are you free in the evenings?"

"Whatever you need."

"Good. These things mean more than you might think." She hesitates. "So is the emergency taken care of? Everything okay?"

"Pretty much," I assure her. "But you know how family drama is. Never really over."

Kristi laughs, which must mean she sort of forgives me. "Oh, don't I," she says with meaning.

As soon as I hang up, I check my e-mail and scan down the seemingly endless messages. There are at least ten from Markel G, and I quickly open them one by one. When I find the radio interview list, I groan. Four interviews. The first one in an hour. I race for the shower.

When my hair's dry, I mentally thank Aiden for making me buy an interview outfit, climb into it, and head for the door. My cell rings, and I press it to my ear as I run down the stairs.

"They've got some ultrasound or sonic or sonar thing in the basement," Rik says.

"Do you think this means I convinced Alana? Or that maybe the authenticators decided *Bath II* is a forgery? The equipment's got to be expensive."

He hesitates. "I don't think so . . ."

"What do you know?" I don't like the sound of this.

"Nothing," he says quickly. "Haven't a clue. Really, I'm pretty much out of the loop. All I can say is that I hope to hell it's down there."

"Me, too," I say, as I wave down a cab.

"What're you doing now?"

"Four radio interviews in the next seven hours."

"Keep your phone on vibrate. I'll call as soon as there's anything to tell."

"You're a prince."

"And here I thought I was a queen," he says, laughing, then clicks off.

I do better at the interviews than I expect. I'm thinking it's because I'm distracted, waiting for the phone to buzz, worrying about what's happening at the Gardner, about what's happening to Aiden, rather than worrying about what I'm saying. Plus, my concerns about interviewers trying to trip me up about *4D* or Aiden are unfounded. Almost all the questions are banal or benign: No one mentions *4D*, and only one makes a passing reference to Aiden's "troubles."

As I ride the Red Line home from Cambridge, I check my phone for the umpteenth time. It's two minutes later than when I last looked, but nothing else has changed: Rik still hasn't called, and somehow this feels ominous.

I hang onto an overhead strap, pressed on all sides by strangers' bodies, suffocated in their heat and unpleasant odors. My only consolation is that there's no way I can fall down. The train is packed and overheated, everyone stuffed into their winter coats, grumpy to be forced to suffer this final indignity after a long work day. Me included.

As the train slithers out of the sooty darkness and over the Longfellow Bridge, the city springs to life, fully formed. Shiny glass towers flood the sky with their interior illumination; the exterior of the State House dome glows yellowy gold. Pedestrians in brightly colored coats flood the sidewalks, and the cars looping down Storrow Drive wink between bare trees. Even with everything on the verge of falling apart, the sight, the pulse, the energy of the city send a jolt of joy through my body.

Maybe Rik hasn't called because they're breaking through the wall right now. Maybe they've already opened the room, found the painting. Maybe Aiden will be freed, his fingers intact. And not just on bail, but for good. Maybe it will all happen in time for my show. Maybe the show will be a stunning success, and Aiden and I will celebrate with a very expensive trip to Paris. Maybe I'm out of my fucking mind.

RIK DOESN'T CALL until close to nine, and by then I've given up on Rendell's family for the night—even the Mormon website doesn't have anything—and fallen asleep on the couch. I grope for the phone.

"I got nothing for you, Bear," he says. "The FBI wouldn't let any of the Gardner guards down there with them."

"No one has any idea what's happening?"

"The ones who know ain't talking. But I'm sure there'll be some leaks by tomorrow. I'll let you know as soon as I catch wind of one. Not to worry."

I flop onto my bed and stare at the black, uncurtained windows in search of solace, but all I see is my own muddled reflection.

After another night with little sleep, I'm pleased to see the white, watery light of a December morning pressing at the edges of the panes. Unfortunately, it's way too early to go to Markel G, so I roam around the studio drinking too many cups of coffee. I try but can't focus on the news, e-mail, the Rendell search, or a *Seinfeld* rerun. I can't paint. I can't call anyone. Aiden's absence aches.

When I finally climb the stairs to Markel G, I see that the previous show has been taken down; the walls are empty, blank vessels waiting to be refilled. Although the door's unlocked, for all intents and purposes, the gallery will be closed today and tomorrow so we can replenish it with my windows.

Both Chantal and Kristi are already there, leaning paintings against the walls. The two women are wearing more comfortable but still outrageous versions of their usual attire. Kristi is in downscale UGGs, but she's attached an oversized, costume brooch to the top of the left one and is wearing a pair of bright yellow short shorts and matching tights. Chantal's in a more upscale pair of UGG-like boots paired with diamond-patterned red fishnet stockings and a hugely asymmetrical, off-the-shoulder, wool, poncho-like, dresslike thing. I'm in paint-splattered overalls. But, of course, I'm the talent.

They greet me warmly, and, once all the paintings are lined up, we stand in the middle of the gallery space and examine them.

"We're all in agreement that *Nighttime T* goes in the bay, yes?" Kristi asks.

I'm thrown back to the first time Aiden saw the painting. How taken he was with it, how he declared that it belonged in the front window. I also remember how sweet he was that afternoon, how handsome. I think about his warm arms surrounding me at night. I want him out of there. I want him here.

I assume Kristi and Chantal do, too, but the unspoken pretend-Aiden's-down-the-block accord still holds, so instead of mentioning that this was Aiden's first reaction, all I say is, "That's good with me."

"Me, too," Chantal agrees.

"One down." Kristi picks up the painting and leans it against the half wall facing the sidewalk.

We turn back to the other nineteen, and I surprise myself by asking, "Can we hang it now?"

They look at me with bemused expressions.

"I mean, *Nighttime T.* Like, I don't know, I think I'd just like to see it there," I say, embarrassed. "You know, to see how it looks. Maybe it's not the right choice."

Although they're at least five years younger than I am, they smile at me as one would at an eager child. "Sure," Kristi says, grabbing a hammer and stepladder. "Good idea."

When we finish hanging *Nighttime T* in the front bay, I stare at it, stunned. Kristi walks over to the door to see how it hits an entering visitor. Chantal goes to the corner closest to the bay to check out the view from there.

I go outside to see it from the sidewalk, wrapping my arms around myself, cold and hot at the same time. The truth is, *Nighttime T* looks even better at this distance. I did this, and people are going to recognize that I have a body of work of my own. I won't be known as the woman who pretended to paint *4D* or even, if all goes well, the one who copied Degas' final *After the Bath.* I'll be Claire Roth, myself, artist, painter in her own right.

Chantal comes down the steps and hands me my coat, which I gratefully put on. She studies the painting. "It's haunting," she says. "So striking." She gives me a hug. "I know this isn't the way you wanted it to be, Claire," she adds, breaking the accord, "but the work stands on its own. And it's wonderful work. You should be very proud. Markel would be. He is."

Tears run down my cheeks, and I brush them away with the sleeve of my coat. "Sorry," I say. "I'm just so happy. And so sad." It seems as if I'm crying at least twice a day.

"Come on, crybaby," Chantal throws an arm over my shoulder. "No wimping out. We girls got a whole show to hang."

For the next couple of hours, the three of us are completely immersed in our collective vision of the show. We organize clusters of paintings. Move them around on the floor. Hang them. Remove them. Rearrange. Some higher than others? Same height all around? Organize by subject or theme or color? Shift the lighting. Shift the paintings. Climb ladders and crouch on the floor. Stand at a distance. Close up. It's physically, emotionally, and intellectually draining. For the first time in a long time, I don't think of anything else.

When my cell rings, I put it to my ear, unaware that I'm doing it.

"News is both good and bad," Rik says. "Ultrasound found a room just like the one in the blueprints. And it looks like there might be something inside it."

"But?"

"But because the space's so small and full of junk, there's no way to get big equipment down there, so it's going to take a while to get the wall down."

"What's a while?" I demand.

"It's unclear. Could be days. Could be weeks."

Of course, Aiden doesn't have that kind of time.

Forty-five

Although it's barely three when I leave the gallery, the shadows are deep, and the first significant snowfall of the winter appears to be upon us. They're forecasting up to six inches, which this early in December doesn't bode well for the rest of the season. My ski parka is stuffed somewhere in the back of my closet, but I've been in denial and have refused to look for it. As tiny pieces of icy snow lacerate my cheeks, I'm thinking it might be time to face up to the reality of winter. But maybe it'll be warmer tomorrow and I won't have to.

Despite the weather, I pause before I turn the corner from East Berkeley to Harrison. Although it isn't clear what spurred the activity in the sub-basement, between Alana's gasp and the ultra-sound equipment, it's more than possible that Agent Lyons's "official capacity" visit is in the offing. I pray to the god I know isn't listening that it's not, steel myself, and step onto Harrison Avenue. Lyons is nowhere to be seen, but a Boston police cruiser is parked in front of my building. Maybe god is listening. And she's got a sense of humor.

I walk slowly down the block, my heart booming in my ears. It feels as if my stomach is literally in my throat, and I try to console myself with the fact that there aren't any flashing blue lights, no one posted at the front door with a gun. When I'm a few steps away from the cruiser, two officers, a man and a woman, climb casually out. Again, no threatening stance, no weapons, no paramilitary garb. They just watch me impassively as I approach.

The woman steps forward. "Claire Roth?" she asks.

I find I can't speak, so I just nod.

"I'm Detective Farrell, Boston Police Department," she says, as if we're meeting at a cocktail party. "And this is Officer Rodriguez."

I look from one to the other, still unable to say anything, and now I find I can't even nod. It's as if my body parts aren't connected to me anymore. I have the vague feeling I'm not breathing.

The detective reaches out and touches my arm. "Let's keep this as simple as possible. With as little stress as possible."

I try to stand straighter, but I'm not sure I've moved.

"Claire Roth," Officer Rodriguez says, "of 173 Harrison Avenue, fourth floor, Boston, Massachusetts, we have a warrant for your arrest." He waves a sheaf of papers at me, then pulls out a pair of handcuffs.

I begin to tremble.

Farrell shakes her head. "Not necessary, Rod. She's not going anywhere." She turns to me. "You're not, right?"

"No," I manage to whisper, the first word I've spoken.

POLICE HEADQUARTERS IS a few miles away in a different section of the city, but I barely remember the ride over, just that Officer Rodriguez drove, Detective Farrell sat next to him, and I sat alone in the back. There were no door handles.

The detective and I are in a small cubicle, one of many lined up along one wall of the large cinder-block room. According to the sign on the door, I'm in the Processing Room. Being processed. For committing a crime. A felony.

My body's still shaking, but not nearly as much as before, and although I feel as if I can't get any air into my lungs, I appear to be breathing. I'm even able to give my name and address. Then Detective Farrell reads me my rights.

"I want to call my lawyer," I tell her immediately, having watched enough cop shows to know this is the right thing to do. "May I please call my lawyer?" I add. Being polite can only help. Of course, I've got no lawyer. The only criminal lawyer I know is my friend Mike Dannow from Jake's, the lawyer/artist. I've no idea if he's any good, but I'm the beggar here.

Farrell hands me a cell phone and leaves me alone in the cubicle, which is open to the room.

"Claire?" Mike demands, when his assistant gets him on the phone. "What's going on?"

"I've, I've been arrested," I say, keeping my voice low. "I didn't know who else to call."

"For what?"

"All kinds of things," I hesitate, not wanting to put it into words. "Forgery, conspiracy to commit fraud, and transportation and sale of, of stolen goods. I think, I think maybe a few other things. Trespassing."

"Okay," Mike says. "You need to remain calm. Take a deep breath. It's important not to lose it, to stay in control."

I try to take a breath, but it gets caught on a sob.

"What station are you at?"

"Headquarters," I manage to say. "I think they're going to lock me up. I—"

"Listen to me, Claire," he says, in a voice so crisp and professional I'm not sure I'm talking to the same man I drink with at Jake's. "First thing: Say nothing. Nothing to anyone. Just your name and address. Nothing else. No matter what they tell you, they're not being nice, they're not trying to help you, and they aren't your friends. You will not speak to anyone, that means anyone, without your lawyer. Say it."

"I, ah, I won't speak without you."

"Now say: 'On the advice of my attorney, I will not say anything unless he's present.'"

I repeat it twice before he's satisfied I have it down.

"I'll be there within the hour."

"Please come as soon as you can," I beg. But he's already gone.

Detective Farrell fills up the hour with processing: mug shots, fingerprints, a computer scan of my criminal record, confiscation of my backpack, and a body search, which thankfully doesn't involve cavities. The whole time, she peppers me with questions that I refuse to answer. Her good cop façade fades a bit more each time I speak my line. Then finally, horribly, she puts me in a cell. This can't be happening. I can't be locked up. I have to find the painting for Aiden.

It's a holding cell, she informs me, but all I care about are the bars, metal poles from floor to ceiling, separating me from the processing room, from freedom. A single, molded-plastic unit takes up most of the cell, forming the base of a cot along one wall before elbowing into a sink/toilet along another. No sharp edges. If I sit at the bottom of the cot and face the toilet, I can avoid seeing the bars. And avoid seeing what isn't there: a handle to open the door.

I remind myself that there's no crime in copying a painting, and there's no way copying a copy can be considered forgery. There's also no way I'm guilty of transporting or selling stolen goods. Mike will be able to get me out of here. He'll come and straighten the whole thing out. Then I'll go home. If it weren't for the conspiracy to commit fraud charge, I'd almost believe myself.

IT TURNS OUT that Mike's well known and well liked at police headquarters, an uncommon situation for a criminal defense attorney. And well connected at the courthouse. Within an hour, he convinced everyone who needed to be convinced that I should be released O.R.—on my own recognizance—because I have no criminal record, I have a job, I've lived in Massachusetts my whole life, and my release would pose no threat to the community.

He pulls his car out of the station's parking lot and we head to the South End. I'm so thrilled to be free, I can hardly focus on what he's saying. "Thanks," I keep repeating. "Thanks for everything. You saved my life."

"Claire, you're not listening to me. The arraignment's first thing in the morning, and we have to go through this."

I've known Mike for years, but it's clear I've never really known him. Because he's insecure about the quality of his art and because he's so short, I have to admit, I assumed he was unsure of himself in all aspects of his life. But now I see he's confident, and clearly more than competent, in his lawyer role. I suppose I should have figured this out as he lives in one of the high-end buildings around the corner from me.

"—and after the arraignment there'll be a probable cause hearing, which isn't about whether you're guilty or not guilty, but an assessment of whether the evidence is strong enough to take to the grand jury." Mike shoots me a look. "Claire," he says sharply. "I'm not going to be able to help you if you're not a willing participant."

"Probable cause hearing," I say, to prove I'm participating. "Not about guilt."

"And what's going to happen at the arraignment?"

I shrug and smile sheepishly.

"Tomorrow," he says, in an overly patient tone, "nine o'clock, Boston Municipal Court. The judge reads the charges, you plead not guilty, the judge confirms your O.R. and sets a date for probable cause."

"We should be out in less than an hour." I finally remember something he said before.

Mike laughs.

"This is bogus, right?" I ask. "It's not a crime to copy a painting, right?"

"Copying a painting isn't a crime, in and of itself. It's what you do with the copy afterward that matters. Or what you and someone else plan to do with it afterward. Knowledge. Intent."

"Aiden hired me to copy a copy. I painted it on an old canvas he gave me, based on a high-quality copy of *After the Bath* that belonged to a friend of his, that he also gave me. When I finished, he paid me and took both canvases away."

Mike lifts one hand off the wheel. "That's all I need to know for now."

"But you've got to understand that—"

"I'll decide what's important for me to understand," Mike interrupts.

This, too, I remember from cop shows. Lawyers like to presume their clients are innocent.

"I *am* innocent," I tell him. "I didn't have anything to do with what happened after the painting was gone. I had no idea what—"

"We'll talk about the details after the arraignment," Mike says, as he pulls up to my building. "I won't be making any arguments against the charges tomorrow, so we'll have a few days to go over everything after that. The probable cause hearing is where we can call the evidence into question, try to convince the judge that the prosecutor's case isn't strong enough. So that's what we'll gear up for."

"You mean there's not enough evidence?" I grasp for any good news. "That they'll drop the charges before anything even starts?"

He throws the car into park and turns to look at me. "I didn't say that." His voice is stern. "What I said is that we won't know anything until probable cause."

"Oh," I say, deflated.

"But you never know," he adds. "Every case is different, and frankly, from what I've seen so far, their evidence is weak." He holds up a hand as my face lights up. "But that doesn't mean there isn't more evidence. We just need to see how it all comes down. Give it a few days. Now go—"

"A few days?" I interrupt. "We don't have a few days."

"—get a good night's sleep and try not to worry," he continues, as if I haven't spoken. "I'll meet you at eight-thirty in the lobby of the courthouse. Outside the metal detectors."

"I don't know how to thank you." I reach over and touch his shoulder. "You're, you're, well, you're just the best."

"Boston Municipal Court. Government Center. Twenty-four New Chardon Street."

"Got it." I start to climb out of the car, then turn back. "You think the media's got wind of this already?"

"Arrests and arraignments are public information," Mike says. "Anything involving the Gardner heist is likely to get picked up."

WHEN I WAKE up in the morning, I don't turn on the television or check the Internet, as I usually do. *Arrests and arraignments are public information.* I'm just not ready to go there. I've always been the type of person who needs to know all, who would want to know if I had the bad gene, even the date of my death, if it were possible. But here I sit, in a virtual news blackout of my own making, pretending that if I don't know about it, it isn't happening.

I pour myself a cup of coffee and check to make sure my phone is charged in case Mike needs to reach me. I'm on my second cup when it rings. At barely seven o'clock, this can't be good. When I see it's Kristi, I know it isn't.

"They closed down Markel G," she says, without preamble.

I don't have to ask who "they" is.

"Claire? Are you there?"

"On, on," I croak. "On what grounds?"

"The door's padlocked. FBI. Something about misuse of funds."

I close my eyes against the pain.

"Are you okay?" She pauses. "After what, ah, after what happened yesterday?"

So it's out. Everyone knows. I'm not surprised, just horrified. "As good as can be expected."

"If there's anything I, we, can do, just let us know. Chantal and I just feel terrible. It's, well, you know, it's just not fair."

"Thanks, Kristi. I appreciate that." Tears roll down my cheeks. "I'll be in touch."

As soon as I put down the phone, it rings again. Mike. He's already at his office. "Hey," I say with all the false cheer I can muster.

"I'm coming to pick you up," he says. "I'll be in front of your place at eight."

"You don't need to do that," I say, thinking what a nice guy he is. "Thanks, but I can take the T. It's not a problem."

"It's the media. I don't want you walking in there on your own."

I take a moment to process this.

"Claire?"

"I'll be on the sidewalk."

As I dress, I remind myself that I'm not in jail, not locked up in a cell, and Aiden has at least a few more days. Mike said we should be out in an hour. I'll still have the whole day.

When I reach the sidewalk, I blink at the brightness; about four inches of snow covers the ground. It doesn't seem possible that my walk through the gray and stinging snow was only yesterday. Now the sky's a fierce, clear blue, and the sun shoots sparks of light from every surface. It's quieter, prettier, less gritty than yesterday. But it's also terrifically cold. So short a time. Such great changes. I close my eyes against the glare and pull my collar up against the wind. I think about the joy I felt at the sight of *Nighttime T* in the window of Markel G. That, too, was only yesterday.

The honk of a horn breaks my reverie. It's Mike, of course, and his face is grim.

"What do they know?" I ask, as soon as I'm inside.

He doesn't ask why I'm not up-to-date on the events, just looks at me with an expression of knowing sympathy. "Well, obviously, about your arrest and arraignment. At about the time we were down at headquarters, the Gardner announced their *After the Bath* is a forgery. And later in the evening, all the major media outlets were reporting that Markel G had been closed down by the feds."

An official forgery. More reason for the Gardner to push to find the painting. A ray of hope. But more reason for Lyons to be suspicious of me.

"Is it true?" Mike asks. "About the gallery?"

I can only nod.

"I'm sorry, Claire." He touches my knee. "Tough break."

I look down at my hands.

"And there's one more thing . . ."

I close my eyes. "What?"

"It's not major, just the judge. We got Zwerdling. In public, she's referred to as the witch. In private, as something that rhymes with it."

"Does that really matter? I thought you said the arraignment was pretty straightforward?"

"It is. As long as the prosecutor doesn't ask to revisit your O.R. status."

My stomach takes a nosedive. "They could send me back to jail?"

"Hardly ever happens," he assures me.

I search his face. I want to believe him, desperately want to believe him, but I can't be sure if he's telling me the truth or telling me the truth he thinks I need to hear.

"The main issue now is getting into the courthouse," Mike says, moving on. "It's not going to be pretty, which is why I want to be with you. We have to walk up the main stairs, but there'll be cops there to clear the way for us. Still, reporters are going to be yelling questions at us, thrusting microphones in our faces, taking pictures. Do you think you can handle that?"

"I've been through this before, remember?" I say, with much more bravado than I feel.

He takes his eyes off the road. "Not even close."

I raise my chin. "I can handle it."

He gives me a searching look, decides to let it go, and says, "One of my associates is meeting us there. Emma. Emma Yales. She'll be on one side of you, I'll be on the other. Stare straight ahead, don't make eye contact, and keep walking. Don't say a word to anyone. No one. No matter what they say to you. And no matter how pissed off you get. Okay?"

"Okay." Shit.

"Emma and I will take care of anything that might come up. But it's unlikely."

"Why are they making this into such a big deal?" I ask, hoping he'll tell me it's not. "It seems like a bit of media overkill, doesn't it?"

"December's a slow news month" is his answer. "And fortunately or unfortunately, you're a beautiful woman with a past."

Forty-six

We sit in Mike's car in the parking lot behind the courthouse with the heat blasting. We're early, waiting for Emma to show so she can protect my left flank as I walk the media gauntlet.

"So it's like I said before," Mike explains. "The arraignment's totally procedural. A preliminary step. More like setting up a doctor's appointment rather than actually being examined."

"So I don't have to take my clothes off until probable cause?" I ask.

Mike laughs. "Pretty much exactly right. Never heard it put quite like that before, but, yeah." He grins at me. "Glad your sense of humor's still intact. It's a good thing to have around."

A knock on the window.

Mike climbs from the car. "Emma," he says, smiling and shaking her hand with both of his.

I follow, and he introduces us. Emma is buff and black, with a do-not-tread-on-me aura emanating from every pore. I'm glad she's on my side.

In silence, we walk along the side of the building. When we turn the corner, I come to a complete stop. Mike and Emma each grab one of my arms and try to propel me forward. I don't budge.

"It's better to get it over with," Mike says. "Faster the better."

"We've got your back." Emma gives my arm a squeeze.

But my feet are cemented to the sidewalk. Dozens of reporters, photographers, videographers, and hangers-on line both sides of the steps, held back by yellow police tape and strategically placed cops. Vans with bold graphics and satellite dishes clutter the street. *Not even close,* Mike said when I told him I'd been through this before. He wasn't kidding.

"Take three deep breaths," Mike says. "Then we're going in."

I do as he says, and before I know it, I'm at the bottom of the stairs and climbing; Mike and Emma have their elbows out, clearly not afraid to use them. Despite the bright sunlight, camera flashes spark at the edges of my vision. A sea of voices call out.

"Where are the rest of the paintings?"

"Who's behind the heist?"

"Are the paintings safe? Have any of them been destroyed?"

"How does it feel to have painted something good enough to dupe the Gardner?"

"Does this mean you're not a pretender?"

I stumble on a step, but Mike and Emma hold on tight. "Keep moving, Claire," Mike murmurs. "Almost there."

But we're not almost there. We're barely a quarter of the way up.

"Where's the original? Does Aiden Markel have it?"

"What about Whitey Bulger? Have you spoken with him since his arrest?"

I'd laugh at this last question if I weren't so freaked out. How connected do these people think I am?

"Claire," a woman calls in a friendly voice. "What do you think they're going to find in the basement of the Gardner?"

I turn to her. "Degas' original."

She shoves a microphone at me. "Who put it there?"

Mike yanks me away before I can answer. "I told you not to say anything," he growls under his breath.

"But that's what's going to help us," I argue. "Finding the original's the way out of this mess."

"What's going to help us is for you to shut the fuck up."

I'm so dumbfounded that he's spoken to me this way that I shut the fuck up. Jake's Mike would never raise his voice, never use the *f* word, and never be rude. I stare at my feet and climb.

We finally step through the front door, and Mike points toward the metal detector on the far left. "We'll meet you on the other side," he says, as if speaking to an annoying child who's pushed him too far. Which, I suppose, is an apt description.

"Sorry," I say, as soon as we're cleared. "My bad."

But he doesn't smile and forgive me as I expect him to. Instead, he spears me with his gaze and says, "You've got to understand that we're no longer friends. Or not friends in the present circumstances. I'm the lawyer and you're the client—the defendant is how you'll be referred to in this courthouse—and it's important that you do everything, and I mean *everything,* I say. If you don't like my advice, you should think about getting a different lawyer."

"Ms. Roth," Judge Zwerdling says sternly, looking at me over tortoise-shell reading glasses. "You have been charged with four crimes against the Commonwealth. I'm going to read each one out to you, and you will respond with your plea: guilty or not guilty. Is that clear?"

I glance at the prosecutor sitting at his desk across from us, then at Mike, who's standing next to me. Mike nods.

"Forgery," she intones.

Mike told me to say just "not guilty," nothing more nothing less, to maintain eye contact, and to think about how innocent I am. I was sure I could do this, but now I look down at my shaky hands, and heat rushes to my cheeks. My mouth is so dry, I don't think I can speak. I must look like a guilty mess.

"Forgery." This time it's louder, more harsh.

"Not guilty," I say, but my voice comes out a whisper.

"Speak louder, Ms. Roth."

I clasp my hands behind my back in a losing attempt to still them. "Not guilty."

"Transportation of stolen goods."

"Not guilty." I square my shoulders and look at her.

Mike leans in. "Good. Better."

"Sale of stolen goods."

"Not guilty," I say, with more force as the charges get more and more absurd.

"Conspiracy to commit fraud."

I do everything I can to maintain eye contact, to show her I'm not afraid of the charge. "Not guilty."

Judge Zwerdling looks at me, then at the papers in front of her. She reads through some files, frowns. She turns to the prosecutor, who's shuffling files at his table.

"Mr. Oden, is there anything you want to add."

"Yes, your honor." Oden steps forward, holding a sheaf of papers in his right hand. He's clearly quite young, but his wispy hair has receded to behind his ears, and he's flabby and pale and has the look of a fish. I dislike him immediately.

"The government believes that Ms. Roth is a danger to the people of the Commonwealth and a flight risk," he says. "We make a motion to revoke O.R. status in lieu of bail to be set at $100,000."

I grab Mike's arm. "Jail? Me back?" is all I can manage to get out.

"Stay cool," he whispers, but the look he exchanges with Emma is anything but.

"But $100,000?" I hiss in his ear. "I don't have $100,000."

"On what do you base this motion, Mr. Oden?"

"Ms. Roth has admitted to painting a forgery of a priceless painting by Edgar Degas that was stolen from the Gardner Museum in 1990. It is such a good forgery that experts believe she copied it from the original Degas taken in the heist. This would put her in direct contact and collusion with the thieves, making her both a danger and a flight risk."

I can't believe I'm hearing this. My worst nightmare. The absolute worst outcome.

"May I speak, your honor?" Mike asks. When the judge grants permission, Mike says, "There is absolutely no basis to the contention that Ms. Roth had the stolen Degas in her custody. Not only is there no evidence to place it in her possession, but the thought of anyone being able to attest to this fact is absurd. The painting hasn't been seen by anyone in over twenty years."

"Do you have any proof of this claim, Mr. Oden?"

"There is also another concern, your honor. The painting that Ms. Roth does admit forging was found in the hands of Ashok Patel, a man suspected of trafficking in stolen artworks. Now, we know for a fact that that painting was in her possession and that it ended up in his. So it follows that she is also involved in criminal trafficking. It is also quite interesting that her own artwork is to be displayed at the Newbury Street gallery Markel G, owned by Aiden Markel, who, incidentally, has been arrested for selling this very same painting to Patel. The coincidences here are as large as the profits involved in such crimes, and her access to a large amount of cash is definitely a risk factor."

"Again," Mike says, "there is absolutely no evidence supporting

Ms. Roth's purported involvement with art thieves and traffickers. The logic is completely circular and erroneous. There is no evidence that Mr. Markel is guilty of the crime with which he is charged, and there is absolutely no evidence that Ms. Roth was involved with his business dealings. Should every artist represented by Markel G be locked up in jail? This is complete fantasy on the part of the—"

"I'm not as sure of that as you appear to be," Zwerdling interrupts. "She did admit to painting the forgery, and it was confiscated by the FBI soon after she claims to have finished it. There very well might be a connection there."

"Ms. Roth has never admitted to painting a forgery," Mike corrects. "She has admitted to painting a *copy* of a *copy*. There is a large difference here, and it is this difference that makes Mr. Oden's argument moot."

"Go on," the judge says.

"The only reason the painting was confiscated in the first place," Mike continues, "is because the authorities assumed it was a real Degas, a stolen masterpiece. It has now been determined not to be a masterpiece, not to have been painted by Degas, and not to have been stolen. If it had been known to be a copy painted by Claire Roth, it never would have been seized, and the men now in jail for its sale, possession, and suspected trafficking would not have been arrested. Nor would Ms. Roth."

"Even if what Mr. Dannow says was true," Oden interjects, "which it isn't, the government also contends that as this case has a very real bearing on a much more serious crime, the multimillion-dollar Gardner heist, we need to be assured that any evidence pertaining to the second case is preserved."

"I may not be a constitutional lawyer, your honor," Mike says, "but that sounds like an unconstitutional argument to me."

"Yes, Mr. Dannow," the judge agrees, "you are not a constitutional lawyer."

Emma laces her arm around the back of my waist. "I don't think it's as bad as it sounds," she whispers. Unfortunately, I'm pretty sure it is.

Zwerdling again studies the papers in front of her. "Mr. Oden, is this police report complete?"

"To date, your honor. But of course, there is more evidence to be collected."

She frowns at the report, then looks up and scowls at each of us in turn. "Is this your best case, Mr. Oden? The sum total of your current evidence?"

"At the present time, your honor."

I lean into Emma, close my eyes.

"Motion denied," the judge finally says. "Ms. Roth will remain free on her own recognizance."

Before I can react to this statement, Mike says, "Your honor, I request an oral motion to dismiss."

Judge Zwerdling raises an eyebrow. "All the charges, Mr. Dannow?"

"Yes. Now that you've heard what Mr. Oden says is his best case, I make a motion for dismissal on the basis of lack of evidence to proceed to the grand jury."

"Interesting move," Emma whispers.

"And which evidence is lacking?" Zwerdling asks.

Mike clears his throat. "According to the arrest report, there is no evidence that Ms. Roth had contact with any stolen goods, no evidence she had contact with any known criminal, no evidence that she transported these goods she didn't have, and none that she sold anyone the goods she didn't have. And yes, while she has admitted to painting the painting that was confiscated by the FBI, the last time I looked, copying a painting was not a crime. As a matter of fact, this is exactly what Ms. Roth does for a living as an employee of Reproductions.com.

"Therefore," Mike continues, "the government has no evidence of forgery or of possession, sale, or transportation of stolen goods. In addition, they have no evidence of Ms. Roth's involvement in any conspiracy to commit fraud. Frankly, your honor, there isn't even evidence that there was any fraud. Ashok Patel, Aiden Markel, and my client all tell the same story: Ms. Roth was copying a copy. Which is not against the law."

"Your honor," Mr. Oden argues, "the fact that three persons currently under arrest attest to the same lie in no way sanctions the release of one of them."

"I've heard enough," Zwerdling says. "I've never seen a more insubstantial arrest report in all my days on the bench." She taps the police report. "This is either complete police incompetence, or as I suspect, a bit of political theater."

I look to Mike and Emma. They stare straight ahead, their faces impassive.

"Where's the beef, Mr. Oden?" At his blank stare, the judge laughs. "You may be too young to catch the reference, but I'm sure you've caught the meaning."

"Your honor, I—"

"No need, Mr. Oden."

"Yes, your honor."

She turns to me. "I'm in no position to fully understand what's involved in this situation or to know how innocent or guilty you might be of these or any other charges. But I am in a position to recognize that the evidence the state has amassed is flimsy at best."

Mike takes my hand and squeezes it. Am I getting this right?

Is what appears to be happening really happening? I don't want to think it, but it looks like I might finally be getting a break.

The judge frowns at both Mike and Oden. "Mr. Oden, you better go out and collect that 'more evidence' you promised, or you're going to find yourself on your butt on the dance floor. And Mr. Dannow, you should know better than to attempt this type of fancy footwork in my courtroom."

Her frown flattens a bit when she looks at me. "I'm sorry, Ms. Roth, but an arraignment is not the appropriate venue for this decision." She slams down the gavel. "Motion denied. The defendant remains under arrest and free on her own recognizance. The probable cause hearing will take place next Monday at eight o'clock in the morning."

Forty-seven

Instead of accepting Mike's offer of a ride or taking the T, I walk home from the courthouse. I need some time and space, not to mention cold air, to process everything that's happened in the last twenty-four hours. Markel G is closed down, my show canceled. *Bath II* has been declared a forgery. I glance at my watch. It was just about this time yesterday that I stood on the sidewalk in front of the gallery ogling *Nighttime T.* Six hours after that, I was sitting in a jail cell, and now, I'm walking free. Sort of.

Talk about highs and lows. I look up at the cloudless cobalt sky, breathe in the painfully sharp air, smile at the people coming toward me. An admittedly odd occurrence in reserved Boston. The judge—Mike said she must have started taking Zoloft—was nice enough to let us leave the courthouse through a back door, duping the media, who are probably still lined up on the entrance steps. I laugh out loud at the image as I cross the wide, brick eyesore that spreads out in front of Government Center.

As I head toward Downtown Crossing, I plan my next steps. Go see Aiden, find out what he knows. Call Rik, find out what he knows. Call Sandra Stoneham, find out if she knows Virgil Rendell's middle name so I can track down his mother's family.

Somehow get into the Gardner basement to assess their progress and find out if Aiden's got a chance.

I hand a dollar to a woman crouched on the stoop of an empty storefront shaking a Dunkin' Donuts cup. I wave at a toddler who's chirping, "Hi! Hi! Hi!" from her stroller, and I scratch the head of a tail-wagging cocker spaniel straining against its leash to get closer to me. I'm no fool. Things are bad, but not as bad as they could have been, and I'll be damned if I'm not going to enjoy this admittedly minor victory. If there's one thing I've learned, it's that things can change in a nanosecond, and I don't want to regret not having savored the moment.

As if to prove my point, my phone rings. It's Agent Lyons, and he wants to come by and talk to me.

"I'm sorry," I say. "On the advice of my attorney, I will not say anything unless he is present."

"It's really not necessary." Lyons's voice is warm and friendly. "I've no reason to arrest you. Frankly, I think the Boston police, prodded by your friend Alana Ward, jumped the gun a bit. I just wanted to give you an update on the case and pick your brain about Virgil Rendell's sketchbook and the whole painting-in-the-basement thing."

I hesitate. This sounds innocent enough, but I remember how angry Mike was when I spoke to that reporter on the courthouse steps. "On the advice of my attorney, I will not say anything unless he is present."

"Ah," he says. "Lawyered up, are you?"

"I'm not an idiot."

Lyons chuckles. "No, you're not, but you are an extremely talented artist." When I don't respond, he continues. "I walked past Markel G this morning. I'm no art connoisseur, but your painting in the front window touched me. So powerful. Amazing colors."

I warm to the compliment, and to the news that *Nighttime T* is still in the bay, but I say in as cool a tone as I can, "Flattery will get you nowhere."

Again, the chuckle. "How about you give me your lawyer's name and phone number, and I'll call and set up an appointment. Would later this afternoon work for you?"

MIKE'S OFFICE IS on the thirty-fourth floor and looks out over the harbor. When I walk in and see the view, I realize Mike and I haven't discussed his fee, but it's clear there's no way I can afford him. Especially without my show. But Lyons follows on my heels, and this isn't a topic to talk about in front of an FBI agent.

After a few minutes of coffee and chatter, Mike clears his throat. "Just so we understand each other, Agent Lyons, as I told you on the phone, at Ms. Roth's arraignment this morning, the judge warned the prosecutor he didn't have enough evidence to present to the grand jury and implied there wasn't even enough evidence for an arrest."

Lyons holds up his hands. "Our interest is in finding the missing paintings and putting the people who stole them behind bars." He smiles at me. "Not to hassle a young woman trying to make a living. I'm here because I need her help, not because she's a suspect."

Mike's face is unreadable. "And how exactly can she help you?"

Lyons opens his briefcase and pulls out my copy of *Edgar Degas: Sketches and Drawings, 1875–1900* and Virgil Rendell's sketchbook. He puts them on the table between our chairs, taps the sketchbook's cover. "I just need some clarification on what the drawings in here actually show us. But first, if you like, I'll tell you where this particular piece of the investigation stands as of now."

He doesn't bother to hear if we like or not, he just continues.

"There's definitely some kind of closet or room behind the wall in the sub-basement. And the ultrasound confirms there's something inside it. But that could be anything, including hundred-year-old construction debris."

"Or a painting," I say.

"It's certainly possible, but until we're able to get in there, it's anyone's guess. And, unfortunately, because the area is so cramped, we may be at it for a considerable time."

"More than a few days?" I ask, thinking about Kristi's text: *Markel said 2 tell u 1 week left.* And that was five days ago.

"Why so long?" Mike asks.

"The wall's thick, and we've got to use hand equipment. There's load-bearing considerations, dealing with a historical building, old construction methods. And to make matters worse, the damn space is full of junk and a curator has to check out every item before it can be moved. Could be tomorrow, could be a week."

"Do you allow visitors?" I ask.

Lyons looks confused. "At the museum?"

"I promise I'll stay out of the way."

"It's a real mess. Lots of dust and too many people already."

"I'd be happy just to watch from the basement level, and if you have any questions, I'd be there to answer them for you."

The agent thinks on this. "I suppose that might be helpful."

"Tomorrow?" I ask.

Lyons looks amused as he hands me his card. "Just call before you want to come to make sure it's okay."

"Great," I say, taking the card. "Thanks. I'll do that."

"Agent Lyons," Mike says, "I'm not clear how finding this particular painting is going to help you find the stolen paintings."

"It's a lead," he says. "Could be something. Could be nothing."

Mike gives him a searing look. "Sounds like a lot of energy to expend for a minor lead."

Lyons grins. "Welcome to my world."

Again, Mike appraises the agent, again with suspicion. "May I see the sketchbook, please?" he finally asks.

Lyons hands it to him, but says to me, "We've ordered Markel's lawyers to turn over the painting he brought you to make your copy from." He watches me closely for a reaction. "It should be in our hands within the week."

"And what will that show you?" Mike asks, before I can figure out whether the fact that the FBI will soon have Virgil Rendell's painting is a plus or a minus.

"The first thing we'll do is test it for authenticity," Lyons says, then turns to me. "And that's one of the things I need your help with, Ms. Roth. I'd like to go through this step by step. Can you take me through the process you used to determine you weren't copying the original?"

I look at Mike. We discussed on the phone that I can only repeat what I've told Lyons or Alana already and that I have to use as close to the same words as possible. Mike nods at me, and I try to remember exactly what I said.

As soon as I begin to explain about Aiden bringing me a copy, Lyons interrupts. "You said before that you never thought it might be the stolen painting, but something must have crossed your mind." He taps the sketchbook on Mike's desk. "Otherwise, why would you have started your investigation into possible forgers?"

I struggle to sound offhand. "As I worked on my copy, getting into the nitty-gritty of every detail, I started to wonder why the compositional elements weren't consistent with Degas' other work.

Which led me to Degas' sketchbooks and, ultimately, to Virgil Rendell's. It didn't have anything to do with whether it was the Gardner painting or not. That was irrelevant."

"So," Lyons asks, "although the painting you had was identical in every way to the one you'd seen many times at the Gardner, it never occurred to you that it might actually be that exact one? It's hard for me to believe that with all your investigative skills that this wouldn't have at least crossed your mind."

"I want to remind you, Agent Lyons," Mike interjects smoothly, "that my client is helping you, on your request, and that she isn't obligated to answer any of your questions."

"Of course," Lyons says, in a similarly smooth voice. "And I appreciate her cooperation very much." He smiles at me again, then looks at Mike. "Can she tell me the specifics of what she did to answer her question?"

Mike nods to me.

"First, I tried to find Degas' compositional sketches for *After the Bath*." I point to the book on Mike's desk. "In there, for one, but there weren't any that looked like the painting I had."

"Which was a copy, not actually the painting."

"Yes, a copy. Right. But it was a copy based on a painting that I was starting to believe Degas didn't paint." My voice rises despite my efforts to keep calm.

"And none of the thousands, maybe millions, of people who have seen it over the years ever thought this?" Lyons points out.

"It's like I told you before: People see what they want to see. Even experts."

"But not you."

"That's enough," Mike snaps, standing up. "My client isn't accused of anything, hasn't done anything, and I won't have you badgering her. We're done here."

"So what are you saying?" I glare at Lyons. "That it *was* the real Degas? That I'm just making this up? Why would I do—"

Mike's hand clamps down hard on my shoulder.

"It just seems strange," Lyons says, "that you could make that kind of determination from a copy of a painting. No matter how good it was."

Mike presses a button on his phone. "My assistant will show you out," he says.

The agent takes both books from Mike's desk, thanks us for our time, and leaves.

When the door closes behind him, I steel myself for Mike's anger. But when I look up, he's standing at the window, gazing out at the harbor.

"What was all that about?" I ask. "Does he have something on us?"

"I don't know that he actually 'has something.'" He turns from the window. "But it sounds like he's thinking Markel never brought you a copy, that you painted your copy from the original. Ergo, the two of you know where the original is—and who Markel got it from."

Forty-eight

Rik calls at eight the next morning. "Did you see today's *Globe*?" he demands.

My heart sinks. "I avoid all news sources."

"Claire, don't be such a baby. It's good. Or at least it's ironic."

"I've never been a big fan of irony."

"Call me after you've read it."

I go downstairs to the tiny foyer, if you can call a metal-lined cubicle with a couple dozen mailboxes a foyer. There are always extra newspapers lying around on the weekend when the artists who have enough money to live elsewhere don't come into their studios. I pick up a *Globe* from the mud-caked floor, curse the messiness of winter, then scan the headlines. Iran. Afghanistan. Another killing in Dorchester. A brave little girl who beat cancer. What's Rik talking about? I flip the paper over. And there, beneath the fold, is the narrow headline: FBI BOMBARDED WITH DEMANDS TO OPEN MARKEL G FOR ROTH SHOW.

I walk up the stairs reading the article. Finish it on the couch. Read it again. It's the fulfillment of my dreams. And the manifestation of my nightmares. Evidently, the petitioners argue that when Markel G released promotional materials detailing the specific paintings and prices, the gallery entered into a legal contract to sell them, which the FBI is impeding. All the collectors interviewed claim their interest is solely in my windows, that they fell in love with my work when Aiden advertised it, that my *4D* and *After the Bath* infamy is irrelevant.

But no one's fooled. Least of all me. The last paragraph of the article points out that despite comments to the contrary, it appears that everyone wants to "own a painting by the woman who's good enough to fool the most prestigious art experts and hoodwink one, perhaps two, of the greatest museums in the world."

I call Rik back.

"They think you're fabulous," he cries, before I can say hello. "That your windows are fabulous. What—"

"They think my notoriety is fabulous."

"It's not just that. You know it's not. And they're talking as if they're acknowledging that you *did* paint *4D*. The media's never gone there—"

"I don't know anything, and I don't want to talk about it. Lyons said I could go down to the sub-basement this morning."

"Really?" Rik says. " 'Why would he do that?"

"Because I asked him. He said the equipment's already blasting through the concrete."

"When'd you talk to him?"

I hesitate. "Yesterday afternoon. In Mike's office."

"What'd he want?"

"Just to catch us up. To ask me for some help understanding Rendell's sketches."

Rik doesn't say anything, then clears his throat.

"Don't."

"Okay, okay. It's good you're thinking positive. I'll call you later."

I pick up Lyons's card from my desk. SPECIAL AGENT JONATHAN LYONS, BOSTON DIVISION, FEDERAL BUREAU OF INVESTIGATION. I think about Mike's theory that Lyons believes Aiden brought me the original and figure it's smarter not to spend time with him. Then I think about how fabulous it would be to watch as they break through the wall and open those double doors. To be a part of the historic discovery of Degas' real *After the Bath*. To know at the first moment that Aiden will be spared. I punch in Lyons's number.

THE DUST IS thick and the noise deafening. Upstairs, a guard gave me a hard hat, ear plugs, and a surgical mask before Lyons brought me down. I thought this was overkill at the time, but now I'm glad I've got all three. Floodlights are strung over the opening to the sub-basement, and two men work with what appear to be jackhammers. But instead of being driven into the floor, the hammers are aimed horizontally at the outside edges of two large holes in the wall. All of the junk that was once a jumble is now neatly laid out on the basement level.

I kneel down to take a closer look, white-gray dust blowing up into my face, my brow already damp with a century of humidity. Each hole is roughly three feet in diameter, with about three feet of solid wall between them. I can't see how deep the holes go because of all the dust, but it appears that they extend through the wall. The holes are bigger than I expect, given Lyons's estimate for reaching the chamber.

Agent Lyons motions to me, and I follow him to a corner where the noise isn't quite so jaw-breaking. "We're going to get the wall down faster than expected," he yells.

I pull out an ear plug. "What?"

"Curators got all the crap out, and we brought in some new

equipment. Smaller and about ten times as powerful. It's cutting right through." He slices his hand from side to side. "Like butter."

I only catch a few of the words, but I get the gist. This could be it.

He leans in close and yells in my ear. "We might reach the chamber today."

"Today?" I lean against a dusty pole for support. Within Aiden's window.

"We'll bring in lunch, dinner if we need to," he yells. "You want turkey or roast beef?"

Seven hours later, a gaping hole in the concrete frames a set of double doors. It's well after six, and the jackhammers and workmen are gone. Lyons and I stand in the sub-basement, watching a janitor clear the last of the debris from the bottom of the doors. Alana, who has refused to look at or speak to me all day, a woman with a video camera, and two other FBI agents watch, too. The silence is deafening.

It's been a long afternoon, and I'm sweating in the cool room, longing for this torture to end. As I'm sure everyone else is. We're all exhausted, but no one considers leaving.

The janitor hits the lock holding the doors together with a hammer. It doesn't budge. He grabs a chisel and hacks at the rust immobilizing the lock. For a moment, I'm thrown back to the afternoon Aiden and I used chisels and hammers to open his box. Pandora's box.

The janitor is at it for a long time. Alana paces in the small space and asks if he wants more help, better tools. He says he's got what he needs, that it's a one-man job. She paces some more, then asks again. Same answer.

Finally, between the chiseling and hammering, the lock breaks open. Lyons and the other agents climb through the hole; between the three of them, they manage to pull the doors apart.

There's silence as they stand before the open doorway, their shoulders and heads blocking our view.

"What?" Alana cries. "Is it there?"

I try to speak, but nothing comes out.

The men exchange a glance, then separate and move to the edges of the room.

Now it's our turn to stand in silence. Aside from some rocks and piles of dust, the chamber is empty.

Forty-nine

Last night, as we left the museum, Lyons informed me that I was now an official person of interest in the Gardner heist, claiming I attempted to divert his attention away from my guilt with a "scam" about a hidden painting. Mike confirmed this when he called to tell me that Agent Lyons "requests my presence" at his office at four o'clock this afternoon. He also reminded me of the probable cause hearing at eight Monday morning. As if I could forget.

I blew it. Failed to save Aiden. Got myself in worse trouble. And disappointed a lot of people who wanted the best for me. Not to mention the distress I brought to all the art lovers devastated by the loss, once again, of Degas' *After the Bath*. It's early, but I head out to the jail. I need to tell Aiden the bad news myself. It's the least I can do.

Aiden doesn't bother to hide his pleasure at seeing me, doesn't tell me to leave. He anxiously studies my face.

My eyes meet his, and I know that what we're about to lose is greater than either of us thought. "I'm, I'm so sorry," I manage to whisper.

He closes his eyes. "You couldn't find any connection to the forger? No leads to the original painting?"

I can only shake my head, afraid that if I speak, I'll burst into tears. He doesn't need that from me now.

"I wasn't going to give it back," he says, before I can tell him the details of my fiasco.

It's a total non sequitur. "Give what back?"

"Remember I told you about collectors? How they grow obsessive? How the desire to possess overtakes all reason?"

I flash back to Sandra Stoneham saying something similar, and for a moment, I think he's referring to her. But that doesn't make any sense either. Then I realize he's talking about himself. "*Bath*?"

"When the sellers came to me to broker the painting, I, of course, assumed it was the original. As I'm sure they did. And it was just like I told you that first day, I said no, but then started thinking about her, started pining for her, then craving her. I wanted her for my own more than anything I'd ever wanted in my life. Degas' *After the Bath*. In my own collection. The pinnacle."

"The pinnacle," I repeat, trying to get a grip on what he's saying.

"At first, I couldn't figure out how to make it happen." He looks down at his right hand, plays with the adhesive tape. "These aren't the kind of men you want to mess with."

I struggle to understand what he's telling me. "And, and that's when you decided to come to me?" I shake my head as if denying my own words. "You mean like, like Ely Sakhai? The double forgery?"

"I saw the article about Reproductions.com in the *Globe*. The one with your picture and the stuff about you being a Degas expert."

"You never liked my windows." My voice is dull with shock. After Mike's call this morning, I assumed things couldn't get any worse.

"No, no, that's not true. I just came that day to check it out. To see if it might be possible. Then when I saw the Degas you'd painted for Repro and your incredible windows, I realized I might just be able to pull it off."

"You never considered returning it to the Gardner."

He refuses to meet my eye. "I was pretty sure if I told you the truth, you wouldn't go along."

"You got that right."

"When we started seeing each other, and the work you were producing was so astonishing, I wanted to tell you the truth. But we were getting along so well, having so much fun." He clears his throat. "I was afraid of losing you, of you refusing to do the show."

"What about when I realized you weren't returning the painting to the Gardner? What were you going to do then? Shoot me?"

"Of course not," he exclaims, a hurt look on his face.

Then I understand, see it in all its brilliant ghastliness. "You were going to blackmail me . . . You figured I'd be in too deep to be able to tell anyone . . . Aiden," my voice breaks, "how could you have even thought of such a thing? After, after all we've been to—"

"I never thought we'd fall in love," he says, desperation coating his voice. "That was never part of the plan. But when we did, I thought, I hoped, I guess, that you'd forgive me. That maybe we could enjoy her together."

It's as if a corkscrew is twisting in my gut, spewing fury and pain outward to every part of me. I stare at him hopelessly.

"Claire, please don't look like—"

"So you were lying to me the whole time?"

His eyes flash with a slyness I've never seen before. "Seems like the same could be said for you."

• • •

I STUMBLE OUT of the jail, trying to grasp the implications of Aiden's admission. I can't believe it. I can't believe his crazed motivation. And I can't believe I never questioned his original story. This is a man willing to lose a finger rather than sell a painting in his collection. I knew this about him and still never guessed.

I'm a dupe, and he's a madman. We both deserve whatever we get. Perhaps we even deserve each other. But that's never going to happen. Never, never, never. I'm so furious, both at him and at myself, I can't even cry. It was all a lie. His lies. My lies. Our hubris and ambition. The insanity of the artist as equal to the insanity of the collector.

Once a piece of art crawls into your heart, you'll never let it go, Sandra Stoneham said. She couldn't be more right. It's as if she were speaking with Aiden in mind. I lean up against the prison façade and close my eyes against a powerful wave of grief.

Then my eyes spring open. Sandra didn't have Aiden in mind. She was talking about herself.

I TAKE THE T out to Brookline. When I ring Sandra's bell, she answers in her bathrobe, her hair uncombed and looking a lot thinner than usual. Clearly not expecting guests. "Claire," she cries, as she bustles me into her apartment. "What are you doing here so early? Is everything all right?"

I glance at Amelia's portrait across the entryway, and force myself not to look at the double doors leading into the parlor, although I register that, as usual, they are closed with the key in the lock. "I came to apologize," I say. "I screwed up, lied to you, had to give something of yours away."

"What on earth are you talking about?"

"I'm not writing a book on Belle, and the FBI has that sketchbook I borrowed the other day. I don't know if you'll ever get it back."

Sandra twists the belt of her bathrobe into a tighter knot. "Why are you telling me this now?"

"Because I'm probably going to be arrested this afternoon."

She studies me, but I don't see any of the anger I expect, just curiosity and sympathy. "Well," she finally says, "come on in, and I'll make us some hot tea. Maybe I can help." She heads toward the kitchen.

Part of me wants to follow her, to bury myself in her warmth and grandmotherly ways, to believe what I don't think I can believe anymore. I step up to the double doors. Reach for the key holding them together.

"What are you doing?" Sandra screams, racing back down the hallway to me. "Get away from there. Stop!"

But of course, I don't. I turn the key and push the doors apart.

My first image is of corals, blues, and greens leaping from a painting over the fireplace. I step in and raise my eyes to the canvas. In the same way I knew in my gut that Aiden's *Bath* wasn't real the first moment I saw her, I know that this one is. And, of course, I recognize it.

For, there she hangs, Degas' *After the Bath,* her light and life forever casting Rendell's forgery in shadow. And while Simone and Jacqueline are identical to Rendell's women, Françoise is not. She's standing as she was in Degas' compositional sketches, rendering the painting asymmetrical. But even more significant, not only is she Not-Françoise: She is Belle. And she is nude.

Behind me, Sandra begins to cry quietly. I look around the grand room. It's completely empty but for this single painting and a lone armchair sitting in front of it.

Epilogue

SIX MONTHS LATER

It's just as I imagined: laughter and bright swirls of color, champagne and the giddy scent of expensive perfume. Not to mention lots of air kisses. For here I stand, in Markel G, at the opening of my first one-woman show. I say first because I've been asked to do two more. One at the Royal Academy of Arts in London and the other at a Tokyo gallery whose name I can't pronounce. From pariah to darling in less than a year. A heady accomplishment, but one that gives me pause.

The place is packed and five of the paintings have red dots next to them. The reviews are fabulous, the buyers lining up, the curators fawning, and suddenly it looks as if I might really be on my way. Someone to be feted and petted and asked for favors. I'd let it all go to my head if I didn't know where it came from. The media is always commenting on how unpretentious and down-to-earth I am. I suppose that's one way to put it.

As I walk through the crush, I see faces I know, faces I don't, and faces I recognize who now recognize me. I'm pulled from every direction, photographed until I can't see anything beyond the re-flected light in my eyes.

Professor Zimmern kisses me on both cheeks. "Which is more fantastic, this show or how it all came down? Sandra Stoneham, of all people. I've known her for years. Who would have thought?" Then he grins. "But I guess you did."

Zimmern, of course, is referring to the return of Degas' *After the Bath,* which now hangs, brilliant and proud, in the Short Gallery, summoning people from around the world and increasing the Gardner's traffic threefold. The museum had planned a gala installation, not reinstallation, for Belle's birthday on April 14, but the painting wasn't hung until June.

And it wasn't because of Sandra Stoneham. That morning in the parlor, she explained to me that *After the Bath* was the only item she had of her Aunt Belle's, that she knew it was wrong to keep it, but that her mother and grandmother had ordered her to. "And I wanted it for myself," she admitted. "I sit in here all the time, taking her in, loving the fact that she's mine and nobody else's."

"Your mother and grandmother?" I asked.

"Grandmother Amelia had promised Aunt Belle she would bring the painting up from the basement and hang it in the Short Gallery after she died, but when the museum's director was so nasty and withholding, Grandmother decided to keep it instead. Our secret family legacy, which she passed to my mother, who passed it to me with the stipulation it must never go to the Gardner."

"To punish the museum or to hide Belle's nudity?"

"A bit of both," Sandra said, with a wistful smile. "But I suppose that's all over now."

Sandra gave up the painting willingly, said she was actually relieved, and the Gardner didn't press charges. It was clear from

Belle's will that *After the Bath* belonged to the museum, but neither the board of directors nor the FBI had the stomach to indict an eighty-two-year-old woman who claimed to be the last living descendent of Isabella Stewart Gardner.

Ironically, it was the will that caused the installation to be delayed. There was a legal battle over whether Degas' *After the Bath* could be hung in the museum. Belle's will specifies that nothing in the museum can be removed or changed, and Virgil Rendell's forgery was hanging there when she died. Fortunately, common sense won out, and the Gardner will be auctioning off Virgil's version to bolster the museum's endowment.

Karen Sinsheimer walks up to me. "Claire, Claire, Claire," she says. "You just can't keep yourself out of trouble, can you?"

"Guess not." I'm encouraged by her smile but still uncomfortable with our history. It's like this with so many people here tonight.

"I'm so sorry, Claire. I wanted to tell you in person how wrong I was not to take your claim about Isaac more—"

I wave her apology aside. "Not important. I'm just glad things worked out." And work out they did. After the Gardner determined that *Bath II* was my work, MoMA went back and retested *4D*. And this time, the experts got it right.

I'm suddenly surrounded by the gang from Jake's. They appear to be even more excited than I am, and they've clearly had many more drinks.

Mike throws an arm around my shoulders. "And you thought this day would never come."

"Crystal's here," Danielle hisses. "We're all ignoring her."

Maureen holds up her glass of champagne. "About time you were buying me a drink."

Small squeezes me around the waist and starts to cry.

Kristi pulls me away from Small. "Just got off the phone with the contemporary curator at the Whitney. They're in a bidding war with a collector in Bangkok for *Nighttime T.*" She practically pounds me on the back.

Rik comes toward us. He spent the afternoon with me, helping with last minute details at the gallery. Now he grabs both of my hands and gives me a deep, penetrating stare. He blinks rapidly to hold back the tears. I have to grab a tissue quickly so mine don't destroy my makeup.

"Bear," is all he can manage.

The discovery of Degas' *After the Bath* sent all the Belleophiles into an ecstatic frenzy, each offering different versions of the possible historical events. The biggest debate is between those who believe Belle and Degas were involved in a passionate love affair—there are enough rumors of her extramarital conquests to back this up, although no specific evidence of this particular dalliance—and those who maintain she not only never would have cheated on Jack but never would have posed nude. They attribute the body in the painting to Degas' imagination. And there's no denying he had plenty of that. Still, if Belle never had an affair with Degas and never posed nude, why would she have buried the painting and hired Virgil Rendell to forge it?

For it appears Rendell did forge it, but not because he stole it or was blackmailing Belle; according to Sandra, it was Belle herself who didn't want it seen. Based on a comparison between the painting Aiden turned over to the FBI, the same one he brought to my studio, and Sandra's *Amelia*, authenticators determined they were the work of same artist.

There was another Rendell mystery that troubled me: Why were his journal and sketchbook mixed in with the Prescott/Stoneham memorabilia? When I asked Sandra, she confessed yet another family secret: Virgil Rendell was her grandfather. He and Amelia had a long-running affair; Fanny, Sandra's mother, was their child. And yes, it was Belle, the matriarch, whose overconcern with class had forced the young lovers apart and compelled Amelia into an unhappy marriage.

It's ten o'clock, and the party's going full force, with more people coming in than there are leaving. The whole thing's surreal: the sales, the attention, the people popping up from odd corners of my life. Kimberly from Beverly Arms. Ms. Santo, my high school art teacher. Shelley McRae, my childhood babysitter. The optometrist from my neighborhood eyeglass store. Even Helene, a third cousin from Providence. It's so bizarre that at times it feels as if I'm not actually here. That I'm just a façade, smiling the smile, talking the talk, while my real self is off somewhere else being regular Claire.

Kristi and Chantal draw me into a corner. "The Whitney scored *Nighttime T*," Kristi cries.

Now I know for sure I'm not really Claire, that I've assumed the persona of some other artist. The Whitney.

"It's true." Chantal claps her hands together.

Kristi points to a chair, and I sit, stunned, dazed, not able to believe. She glances at her watch and says to Chantal, "Tomorrow's Sunday. I'll go down first thing in the morning and tell Markel." Then she throws me a guilty glance. "Sorry. Didn't mean to mention."

"Not necessary," I say, but the truth is, I'd just as soon not be reminded of Aiden.

He's still in jail, held without bail, awaiting a trial that probably won't start for another six months, maybe a year. I haven't seen or spoken to him since our last conversation, and that's the way I plan to keep it. Whatever my feelings may be for Aiden, complete disassociation from him is a penance I accept.

The FBI finally allowed the gallery to reopen just last month, and in a concession I almost didn't make, I accepted Kristi's offer to hold the show here. Rik said I had to, that I shouldn't allow misplaced guilt to inhibit my career. But he's wrong about the misplaced part. A woman who makes a Faustian bargain is not without responsibility.

Finding *After the Bath* also saved Aiden's finger. He was released on bail long enough to pay off the sellers. But after the painting he turned over to the FBI was determined to be Virgil Rendell's forgery, it was also determined to have been the painting stolen in the Gardner heist, and bail was revoked. Aiden's the only link the authorities have to the Gardner thieves, and even though he keeps telling them he has no idea who robbed the museum, they're hoping fear of a long prison term will jog his memory. For all I know, it just might.

Kristi drops a hand to my shoulder. I look around me, at all the people, at all the red dots. I think about the life stretching ahead of me, filled with such promise. But, just deserts, it's impossible to know if this newfound fortune is due to my talent or to my infamy in a world of instant celebrity. Whether I'm a great artist or just a great forger. And no matter what happens to me or to my work, no matter how big the commissions or how great the museums, I suppose I'll never know.

ACKNOWLEDGMENTS

In the "without whom this wouldn't have been possible" category, one person stands out: Jan Brogan, my dear friend, my colleague, my biggest fan, and my fiercest critic. Thanks are not enough. Nor are thanks enough to the other members of my writers' group, Linda Barnes and Hallie Ephron, nor to my family, Dan, Robin, Scott, and Ben. Your encouragement and belief pulled me through the rough patches.

For their professional expertise and patience with my questions, thanks are due to Jamie Elizabeth Crockett, Jane Little Forman, James Kennedy, Edwina Kluender, Kimberle Konover, Victoria Monroe, Roberta Paul, Rob Sinsheimer, and Carol Tovar. Thanks to my readers: Dan Fleishman, Scott Fleishman, Ronnie Fuchs, Gary Goshgarian, Vicki Konover, Sandra Shapiro, Alice Stone, and Robin Zimmern. Special thanks to my smart, supportive editor, Amy Gash, and very special thanks to my agent, Ann Collette, whose tireless efforts and faith in my work made it all come together.

A NOTE ON THE RESEARCH

Although *The Art Forger* is based on extensive research and interviews with painters, dealers, and curators, it is a work of fiction. All
the characters, and most of the situations and places in the current-
day story, are creatures of my imagination: There is no Markel G,
no Jake's, no Beverly Arms, no Al's Art Supply, no Reproductions
.com, and the *Boston Globe* article that opens the book never appeared in that newspaper. There is, on the other hand, an Isabella
Stewart Gardner Museum—although no sub-basement—a Museum of Fine Arts, a Museum of Modern Art, a Mandarin Oriental Hotel/Boston, the South End, and Newbury Street. I have
attempted to describe these places accurately.

The painting techniques Claire uses for both her forgery and
her own work are consistent with current practices, as are the de-
scriptions of the struggles of a young artist. The forgers and dealers
she discovers through her Internet research were/are actual people,
including John Myatt, Ely Sakhai, and Han van Meegeren, and the
specifics of their crimes, methods, inventions, and punishments
are also accurate. Virgil Rendell is a fictional character.

The details of the 1990 robbery of the Gardner Museum are
factual—it remains the largest unsolved art heist in history—with

the exception of the inclusion of Degas' fifth *After the Bath,* which neither was stolen nor exists, although it is a composite based on his other four *After the Bath* works. Three of Degas' drawings, *Program for an Artistic Soiree, La Sortie du Pesage,* and *Cortege aux Environs de Florence,* were taken that night and remain unaccounted for.

The letters Belle Gardner writes to her niece, Amelia, are an amalgam of fact and fiction. Belle was in the places cited at the dated times, pursuing paintings for her collection. Her relationships with John "Jack" Gardner, John Sargent, Henry James, James Whistler, and Bernard Berenson are based on historical fact, although the actual events she describes, dinner parties, Longchamps races, travels, illnesses, and so on, are not. She did walk two lion cubs down the streets of Boston, and she did wear a headband with the words OH YOU RED SOX to the symphony. Her only child, Jackie, did die at age two, and she did raise Jack Gardner's three nephews after the deaths of their parents, although one nephew died in childhood. But there was never an Amelia, nor, obviously, a Sandra Stoneham.

Neither Claire nor I were able to discover any mention of Isabella Stewart Gardner and Edgar Degas meeting each other, although they traveled in the same circles, in the same locations, at the same times. Therefore, the entire portion of the novel concerned with the relationship between Belle and Edgar is a fabrication, as are all the story events that result from this imagined pairing. Yet, the personalities of the two are based on historical fact and biographers' speculations, so how are we to know, 150 years later, what might or might not have occurred?

The

ART FORGER

A Note from the Author

Questions for Discussion

A Note from the Author

I'm a cowardly writer. Some writers sit down and begin a novel without knowing where it will end, trusting the process to bring their story to a satisfying conclusion. But not me. I don't have the courage to begin a book until I know there's an end—and a middle, too. I need an outline that allows me to believe my idea might be transformed into a successful novel. Some writers need a working title; I need a working plot. Which is why it takes me so damn long to get from that first glimmer of an idea to a complete manuscript.

The Art Forger was no different. The first time I encountered art collector and museum founder Isabella Stewart Gardner in 1983, I fell in love. I wanted to hang out with her, walk lions down Boston streets with her, buy famous paintings, and do all kinds of outrageous things that would scandalize the stuffed shirts around us. But, alas, she died in 1924. I dismissed the idea of a "Belle" novel because she intimidated me—see, more cowardice—but I never forgot her.

Then in 1990, she burst on the scene, or at least her namesake, Boston's Isabella Stewart Gardner Museum, did, when two men dressed as police officers bound and gagged two guards and stole thirteen pieces of art, including Rembrandt's *Storm on the Sea of*

Galilee, Vermeer's *The Concert,* and works by Degas and Manet from the collection. Now, I thought, now I might just be able to make it work.

But despite the media's having taken the theft international, suspects who ran the gamut from the Mafia to the Vatican, and the lack of any arrests, I just couldn't find my story. What could Belle possibly have to do with a heist seventy years after her death? How could I write a book about a robbery that hadn't been solved? What if it was solved before I was finished—or worse, just after I'd completed it—and the real solution was nothing like mine? Cowardly writer that I am, I put the idea back in the drawer.

Nineteen years later, the mystery of the Gardner heist still hadn't been solved, and Belle was still haunting me. I read half a dozen biographies and hundreds of letters, and I scoured the Internet. I was thinking I might do something like Irving Stone or Gore Vidal would, writers whose books I loved, and considered a fictionalized biography. But embracing the entirety of Isabella Gardner's action-packed life was too daunting—some things never change—so, once again, Belle was shelved.

Around this time I began taking a series of art courses that toured galleries and museums with a well-known artist for a guide. She opened my eyes, not just to the wonder of what we were seeing but to the complicated worlds of creating, collecting, curating, and selling works of art. I also developed a fascination with art theft and art forgery. Now, I thought, now I really might have my Belle book. So I wrote synopses, created plot charts, developed character sketches, then scratched it all and did it again. I was growing closer, but the pieces weren't all quite there; something was missing: I couldn't see the end.

One day, as I was wondering if I should just give up the whole endeavor, my missing link appeared in the form of a question:

What would any of us be willing to do to secure our ambitions? Unknown artists, famous artists, collectors, brokers, and gallery owners? Me? Belle?

So I expanded my cast of characters, including a struggling artist willing to make the ultimate Faustian bargain, and gave each one a temptation their egos couldn't resist, and then I added them to the mix of art theft, art forgery, the Gardner Museum heist, and, of course, my buddy Belle. Suddenly, just like the Cowardly Lion, who became brave when he had his medal, I became brave when I had my plot. *The Art Forger* is the result.

Questions for Discussion

1. At the novel's opening, Claire is a pariah in the art world. Has the community been unfair to her? In what ways, if any, is she responsible for her own exile? Does she share any blame for Isaac Cullion's death?

2. *The Art Forger* explores the darker side of human nature. All of the characters in the novel have a price, a line they're willing to cross to further their own ambitions. Do you think Claire does the wrong things for the right reasons? Is she a moral person or not? What about Isabella Stewart Gardener? What compromises would you make to secure what you most desire?

3. B. A. Shapiro juggles three plot lines in the novel, moving back and forth through time. Each section tells of secrets and deceit. How does each of these storylines intersect and deepen the themes of the novel?

4. This novel was inspired by an actual art heist, which included works by Manet, Rembrandt, Vermeer, and Degas. But what if Rembrandt didn't paint *Storm of Galilee*? What if an unknown

artist did instead? Would the painting be any less beautiful? Would it no longer be admired? Would it suddenly be worthless? What is it that gives an object value?

5. It is estimated that 40 percent of all artworks put up for sale in any given year are forgeries. Theodore Rousseau, an expert from the Metropolitan Museum, said, "We can only talk about the bad forgeries, the ones that have been detected. The good ones are still hanging on museum walls." Does knowing this affect the way you view great art? How can we tell the difference between what is inauthentic and what is real?

6. The novel explores the idea that we often only see what we want to see. If an expert is told a painting is a masterpiece, she sees one. If an artist desires recognition, she convinces herself that her deal with the devil is for good. How are people complicit in missing the truth?

7. Art forger Han van Meegeren, whose techniques Claire uses to create her own forgery, was a frustrated Dutch painter. An unappreciated artist struggling for recognition, his intention was to hoodwink the art dealers and critics who refused to recognize his own artistic genius. How is Claire similar to or different from Meegeren?

8. Shapiro has a PhD in sociology and has studied deviant behavior. How do you think her background informs her characters and the ethically muddy—some might say unprincipled—decisions they make? Does it make her characters more sympathetic or less?

9. Boston features prominently in *The Art Forger*. How does the author use the city as a nod to Claire's state of mind?

10. Gorgeous art can make people do incredibly ugly things, and the novel seems to suggest that it's not only for money. Why do you think that beauty and originality can have that effect on people?

11. What do the meetings between Edgar Degas and Isabella Stewart Gardner show about the relationship between a collector and an artist?

12. Claire falls hard for Aiden Markel, but she keeps secrets from him. He is also keeping secrets from her. Can a relationship survive this kind of betrayal? Do you think Aiden loves Claire? Why does Claire choose the wrong men? Do you think Aiden and Claire love art more than they love each other?

13. At the end of the novel, critics are praising Claire's work. Collectors are clamoring for the very same paintings that have hung, unsalable, in her studio for years. Why is her work suddenly more valuable? Is she successful only because she has become a celebrity?

14. Is art a commodity like any other product? What does the book suggest about the intersection of art and commerce, about talent and reputation?

15. Sometimes getting exactly what you want isn't quite what you expected. Our society loves to create celebrities and then tear them down. Can you give some examples? What happens when your dreams are realized and you can't handle it, or you don't feel you've earned it? Does Claire deserve the fame she is awarded at the end of the book?

LYNNE WAYNE

B. A. SHAPIRO has taught creative writing at Northeastern University and sociology at Tufts University. She lives in Boston. B. A. Shapiro is available for select speaking engagements. Please contact speakersbureau@workman.com.